P9-DFZ-442

"Kirk to engineering. Scotty, I'm going to need all available power for transporters."

"Transporters?!" came Montgomery Scott's reply, his Aberdonian brogue echoing in the vastness of the *Enterprise*'s engineering complex. *"In the middle of a battle? Where are you plannin' on beamin' to, sir?"*

"Not me, Scotty. I need to lock on to one of these comets and pick up as much of its mass as we can."

"Comets? Now, why in the world—" What caused him to break off was not discretion toward a superior officer so much as his sudden fascination with the technical challenges involved. *"Well, maybe if I reroute power from the AG section and tie in the subspace transceiver array . . . You weren't needin' to send a long-range message at the same time, were you, sir?"*

"Only one miracle at a time, Mister Scott. I know you're a busy man."

"Aye, now he notices," he heard Scotty muttering to himself, so caught up in the challenge that he forgot he was still on an open channel.

"Captain," Chekov asked, his Russian accent thickening under stress, "where are we beaming the cometary matter *to*?"

Kirk gave the young ensign a cocky grin. "Right in front of their ship."

3 1526 04932550 6

STAR TREK®

THE ORIGINAL SERIES

THE FACE OF THE UNKNOWN

Christopher L. Bennett

Based upon *Star Trek*
created by Gene Roddenberry

POCKET BOOKS

New York   London   Toronto   Sydney   New Delhi

The sale of this book without its cover is unauthorized. If you purchased this book without a cover, you should be aware that it was reported to the publisher as "unsold and destroyed." Neither the author nor the publisher has received payment for the sale of this "stripped book."

Pocket Books
An Imprint of Simon & Schuster, Inc.
1230 Avenue of the Americas
New York, NY 10020

This book is a work of fiction. Any references to historical events, real people, or real places are used fictitiously. Other names, characters, places, and events are products of the author's imagination, and any resemblance to actual events or places or persons, living or dead, is entirely coincidental.

™, ® and © 2017 by CBS Studios Inc. STAR TREK and related marks and logos are trademarks of CBS Studios Inc. All Rights Reserved.

This book is published by Pocket Books, an imprint of Simon & Schuster, Inc., under exclusive license from CBS Studios Inc.

All rights reserved, including the right to reproduce this book or portions thereof in any form whatsoever. For information, address Pocket Books Subsidiary Rights Department, 1230 Avenue of the Americas, New York, NY 10020.

First Pocket Books paperback edition January 2017

POCKET and colophon are registered trademarks of Simon & Schuster, Inc.

For information about special discounts for bulk purchases, please contact Simon & Schuster Special Sales at 1-866-506-1949 or business@simonandschuster.com.

The Simon & Schuster Speakers Bureau can bring authors to your live event. For more information or to book an event, contact the Simon & Schuster Speakers Bureau at 1-866-248-3049 or visit our website at www.simonspeakers.com.

Manufactured in the United States of America

10   9   8   7   6   5   4   3   2   1

ISBN 978-1-5011-3242-1
ISBN 978-1-5011-3243-8 (ebook)

To the memory of my mother and father,
who let me stay up and see
what that Star Trek *show was about*

"You know the greatest danger facing us is ourselves, an irrational fear of the unknown. But there's no such thing as the unknown, only things temporarily hidden, temporarily not understood."

—James T. Kirk

Historian's Note

The events of this story take place in mid-2269, some time after the rescue mission to Camus II ("Turnabout Intruder").

Prologue

"Get those shields back up!"

James T. Kirk clung to the arms of his command chair as weapons fire battered the *U.S.S. Enterprise*. On the bridge's main viewscreen, bursts of energetic plasma spat from the prow of a small but powerful warship as it strafed the unshielded dorsal surface of the primary hull. "Evasive, Mister Sulu! Keep our belly to them!"

"Aye, Captain," Hikaru Sulu said from his seat in front of Kirk, but the helmsman's hands were already plying his console with virtuoso skill. To Sulu's right, though, Ensign Chekov was visibly sweating as he scanned for potential evasive routes through the diffuse cometary belt the *Enterprise* had been traversing when the mysterious attacker had struck from out of nowhere. Meanwhile, at the engineering station on Kirk's left, Lieutenant Gabler tried to redirect deflector power to restore protection to the dorsal portion of the saucer section. Frank Gabler was the newest member of Montgomery Scott's engineering staff, but the dark-featured young lieutenant managed to keep the strain from reaching his voice as he called out orders to the engineering department down below.

Kirk rotated his command chair clockwise until he faced the science station. "Spock, any luck identifying the attacker?"

"Still searching for a profile match, Captain," the lanky

Vulcan responded, his angular face illuminated by the blue glow from his hooded viewer. "It does not conform to any standardized design in our memory banks."

The viewscreen switched to a ventral sensor image of the attacking battle frigate, now below and behind the *Enterprise* as Sulu flew the ship at a sharp diagonal. At the moment, the starship's underbelly was its least vulnerable portion—and it didn't bother Kirk that Sulu was more or less shoving the ship's fantail in the attacker's faces.

Still, whoever was flying the frigate had some impressive moves of their own. Somehow the foe managed to keep closing the gap, retaliating for Sulu's rude gesture by kicking the starship in the rear.

Once the noise and shaking from the impact had passed, Kirk went on: "Not everyone uses standardized ships, Mister Spock. Can you identify any of its components? Engines, weapons, sensor arrays?"

"I am attempting to do just that," the first officer replied without impatience, long fingers playing a toccata on the multicolored controls of his station. "However, with so many variables to process, it may take some time to arrive at a result."

"Sir," Sulu said, "I have an idea who they are. I wasn't sure at first, but what you said—"

Kirk turned to the helmsman. "Go on, Lieutenant."

"I think they're Betelgeusian, sir. They're a nomadic people. No home planet, no central state. So there's no uniformity to their designs." He paused to enter a rapid series of commands, veering the *Enterprise* out of the path of their latest plasma volley. "Pardon me, sir. But the way they maneuver, and the type of weapons they use . . . I've seen them before, when I was an ensign on the *Arjuna*. It was my first deep-space assignment after the Academy."

"Betelgeusians," Kirk repeated. "I thought we were on friendly terms with them."

The attacking ship begged to differ by unleashing another salvo. The deck shuddered and the viewscreen flashed even more interesting shades of red at him. *They're getting a feel for it now,* Kirk thought.

But the impact was milder than Kirk feared. Gabler gave a heavy sigh of relief. "I was just about to say: dorsal shields restored, sir."

"Good timing, Lieutenant."

"As Mister Sulu said," Spock pointed out as if the interruption had not occurred, "the Betelgeusians lack any single central authority. The designation is a misnomer; they actually hail from a main-sequence star system neighboring the supergiant Betelgeuse. They migrated off their world centuries ago, aware that it would be destroyed when Betelgeuse goes supernova sometime in the next million years."

"How proactive of them," Kirk observed. He liked these people already. What kind of wanderlust did it take to use such a remote threat as an excuse to pack up your whole civilization and move it off-planet at the earliest opportunity—even to swear off planets altogether?

"Indeed—a most logical response. However, they are also a highly aggressive, competitive people, pack hunters by nature. Thus, they tend to operate in small, highly territorial bands with no political unity among them. Relations and agreements with each band must be negotiated separately. Thus, being on friendly terms with some Betelgeusian argosies does not guarantee amiable relations with others."

"But the 'Geusians aren't warlike," Sulu protested. "They're predators, sure, but they normally channel their aggression into sports, competitions, hunting game animals, that sort of thing. They generally don't attack unless provoked. The ship we encountered on the *Arjuna* was fighting off Nausicaan pirates. We helped them with repairs afterward." His bright grin made one of its frequent appearances. "I liked them, sir."

Another plasma bolt slipped through, striking dangerously close to the port nacelle. "Something seems to have provoked them," Kirk said. "Uhura, any luck hailing them?"

"I'm trying all known Betelgeusian comm protocols and languages, sir," came the elegant East African's voice over his shoulder. "They've got to be hearing it, but they aren't answering."

"Then at least they can listen. Open a channel, Lieutenant."

"Channel open, Captain. Go ahead."

Kirk straightened in his chair. "Attention, Betelgeusian vessel. This is Captain James T. Kirk of the *U.S.S. Enterprise*, representing the United Federation of Planets. The Federation has no quarrel with the Betelgeusian people. But if you do not cease this unprovoked attack, we will be forced to retaliate. Please respond so we may discuss this peacefully."

The only response, which Uhura forwarded to the speakers, was a curt *"Earn it!"* followed by an intensification of the attack. A plasma blast hit close to the bridge, the thunder of the impact almost deafening Kirk.

"Gabler, I thought you had those shields fixed!"

"A temporary patch, sir!" the engineer replied. "It's straining the whole primary dorsal grid, and sector 47A is completely burned out."

But Sulu was dancing the ship around to keep the breach in its defenses away from the Betelgeusians' line of sight. It gave Kirk time to mull over his options. "'Earn it,' they said. What do they mean?"

"It's a game to them, sir," Sulu said, though the chase kept him too busy to say more.

Spock elaborated. "Indeed—by all accounts, the Betelgeusians are intensely competitive. If we wish them to back down, we must prove our dominance."

"By outfighting them?"

"Those are the terms of the current competition."

Kirk took that in. He had no desire to risk killing the Betelgeusian crew over what had to be a misunderstanding. But he had to do something that would be dramatic enough to win their respect.

He gazed up at one of the auxiliary screens above Spock's station, which displayed tactical tracking of the nearby icy bodies in the cometary belt. "If we've got a hole in our shields," he said slowly, "then let's use the hole in our shields. Sulu, maximum sublight. Chekov, give him the clearest straight path. I want them chasing us as fast as they can go." Among other things, he hoped to stay out of the Betelgeusians' transporter range, lest they take advantage of the hole to beam a boarding party or an armed torpedo aboard.

But he would have to act fast. His fingers on the chair arm opened a new channel. "Kirk to engineering. Scotty, I'm going to need all available power for transporters."

"*Transporters?!*" came Montgomery Scott's reply, his Aberdonian brogue echoing in the vastness of the *Enterprise*'s engineering complex. "*In the middle of a battle? Where are you plannin' on beamin' to, sir?*"

"Not me, Scotty. I need to lock on to one of these comets and pick up as much of its mass as we can."

"*Comets? Now, why in the world—*" What caused him to break off was not discretion toward a superior officer so much as his sudden fascination with the technical challenges involved. "*Well, maybe if I reroute power from the AG section and tie in the subspace transceiver array . . . You weren't needin' to send a long-range message at the same time, were you, sir?*"

"Only one miracle at a time, Mister Scott. I know you're a busy man."

"*Aye, now he notices,*" he heard Scotty muttering to himself, so caught up in the challenge that he forgot he was still on an open channel.

"Captain," Chekov asked, his Russian accent thickening under stress, "where are we beaming the cometary matter *to*?"

Kirk gave the young ensign a cocky grin. "Right in front of their ship."

The navigator's eyes widened, and then he smiled too. "I should have known, sir. Russians invented snowball fights, after all." As the ensign turned back to complete the calculations, Kirk reflected that of all the innovations Chekov claimed for the Russians, this was one of the more plausible attributions.

In moments, they were ready to begin. Kirk hit the intercom. "Scotty . . . let it snow."

What materialized in the Betelgeusians' path a few

seconds later was not an intact chunk of cometary ice and rock. Like all starships, the frigate swept the space ahead of it with a navigational deflector beam to protect it from the impact of space dust and gas—which, at the speeds Kirk was goading the Betelgeusians into attaining, would possess enough relativistic kinetic energy that even a tiny speck would hit like a tactical nuclear warhead if the beam failed to deflect it. Beaming a dissociated stream of subatomic particles into the middle of a deflector beam working at full strength was like trying to build a sand castle in front of a large fan. The chunk of cometary matter materialized—if that was the word—as a dense cloud of rock dust and water vapor. But that made little difference at these speeds; solid or vapor, its mass was the same and so was the energy of its impact. The frigate's deflector beam was able to begin scattering the mass of debris, but Chekov and Scott had placed it so close to the vessel's bow that the beam barely had time to begin dissipating it before it struck their forward shields.

Without those shields, the frigate would have been reduced to little more than a cloud of vapor and dust itself. As it was, the shields bore the brunt of the impact but were totally overwhelmed. Enough of the barrage got through that the ship appeared to erupt into flames and start tumbling. The forward portions of the ship still glowed from the heat of impact.

Spock was scanning the damaged ship with his usual efficiency. "All of their forward weapons have been neutralized. Their forward sensors and shield grids are destroyed. Serious damage to engine shield plates, intercoolers, and ram intakes."

"Casualties?"

"Inconclusive. The vessel's hull shielding makes internal scans difficult. But that same shielding has likely mitigated the crew's radiation exposure."

That came as a relief to Kirk. He was trained to fight and didn't hesitate when it was necessary, but he was happier when it could be avoided. He'd joined Starfleet to seek out new life, not snuff it out. "Sulu, intercept course. Hail them, Uhura." The communications chief nodded once she'd opened the channel.

The Betelgeusian commander's face finally appeared on the main viewer: blue-skinned, heavy-browed, pointed-eared, adorned in an elaborate helmet and a colorfully patterned uniform with an avian theme. The mouth was locked in a permanent snarl, and in place of the nose was what seemed to be a smaller, puckered, beaklike mouth. When it spoke, it was the upper mouth that moved, emitting a high, piping speech that the universal translator interpreted: *"I am Captain Chiir'hit Keer'iuv, defender of the Shining Talon Argosy. You are Captain Kirk of* Enterprise?"

Kirk stepped forward. "I am."

Keer'iuv let out a piercing crow that sounded more amused than anything, then offered a deep, elegant bow. *"You have won my submission, Captain, and my congratulations. That was a spectacular move! Inspired! Brilliant! I am privileged to be bested by such a creative tactic."*

"I'm . . . glad you enjoyed it," Kirk said, trading a nonplussed glance with Spock. "I hope we didn't damage your ship too badly. We stand ready to offer any medical assistance—"

"Gracious of you, Captain, but we can salve our own bruises. I must say, though, you are far more sporting than

*the other Federation group that attacked us. Far cleverer in
your battle tactics as well."*

Kirk frowned. "With respect, Captain Keer'iuv, we
know of no Federation attack upon any Betelgeusian argosy. Starfleet has no quarrel with your people."

*"Not Starfleet, no. Their ships were not like yours.
Smaller, no nacelles. Like clusters of geometric solids. They
attacked in a pack."*

The captain's impulse was to deny it, but he hesitated.
Keer'iuv seemed too gracious in defeat to have some
hidden agenda. And Kirk had to admit that, while the
Federation was a more unified civilization than the Betelgeusians, its member worlds were given considerable
license to go their own ways. There had been instances
of its younger or more remote members pursuing actions
that ran counter to Federation law and ethics. The Ardan-
ans' oppression of their Troglyte miners, and their torture
of political prisoners, came to mind as a recent example.
So the possibility that some other Federation member
had attacked Keer'iuv's argosy could not be dismissed.

"Spock, does that description match any class of vessel
in use on any Federation member world?"

Unsurprisingly, the first officer had already begun a
search of the computer records. A few moments later, he
looked up from the hooded viewer. "Negative. No such
vessels with sufficient range and firepower to have attacked the Shining Talon Argosy are known to exist on
any member world."

Kirk turned back to the screen. "Captain, can you tell
us anything more about these attackers? Did they speak
to you? Do you have a recording of their language, their
appearance?"

Keer'iuv straightened proudly, eagerly. *"Oh, we can do much better than that, Captain Kirk!"* He leaned forward and spoke with relish. *"We have bodies."*

———

Commander Spock was gratified to join the boarding party visiting the Shining Talon Argosy, a rare opportunity to observe the culture and technology of a species unrestricted by planetary conditions. It was a fascination he clearly shared with Hikaru Sulu, who had eagerly petitioned Captain Kirk for an opportunity to revisit the raucously competitive nomads. Kirk had not hesitated to include the helmsman along with Spock, Doctor McCoy, and Lieutenant Anne Nored, one of the newest members of the *Enterprise*'s security contingent.

In fact, Spock knew, the Betelgeusians were not averse to visiting planet surfaces for trade, exploration, or other purposes. They had laid claim to several worlds with pre-sentient animal life, using them as hunting preserves to satiate their innate predatory drives. But those drives also needed outlets closer to home, and thus large argosies like Shining Talon included their own hunting preserve ships, such as the one the *Enterprise* party now occupied. The preserve ship was a massive warp-capable craft, over three times the length of the *Enterprise*, with a cylindrical core that rotated for gravity like the old orbital habitats of the twenty-first century.

"I don't get it," McCoy said, staring uneasily at the dizzying terrain that curved up and over the group. "Don't they have artificial gravity?"

"Indeed we do," said Thuu'chi Hirr'uth, the mature Betelgeusian female who was the argosy's senior administrator, as she escorted the *Enterprise* party through the cylindrical landscape. She was slightly smaller than Captain Keer'iuv, who walked behind and beside her now, but her robes and headdress were even more ornate, in keeping with her status. While the captain's garb bore an avian theme, the administrator's robes had an intricate forest-and-stars motif. "But we prefer the centrifuge model for our preserve ships," the administrator continued, "because it lets us use the entire interior surface of the module as a hunting ground. We need our territory, Doctor. Even with the larger surface area this shape provides, the competition for ground is quite fierce."

Sulu marveled at the overhead view of the preserve ship's terrain. "Impressive terraforming," he said. "The way the streams, bluffs, and other natural barriers subdivide the landscape. I take it that's to separate each prey species from the others?"

"Indeed," Keer'iuv replied. "After all, we love a challenge. Most of the species here would gladly devour each other if they could get outside their own territories."

Lieutenant Nored surveyed the boundaries of the safe area they traversed. "I trust the barriers keeping them out of this section are reliable."

"Mostly," the Betelgeusian captain said with an amused chirp. "Well, it wouldn't be very interesting if there were *no* risk."

"Wonderful," the lieutenant said sourly, her slim fingers resting atop her phaser.

"Give them a break, Anne," Sulu said. "It's not easy being pack hunters in spaceships. Normally the young males in a pack species wander off when they're old enough—try to found their own packs, or at least earn a position of status in another."

"It is the same for us," Administrator Hirr'uth affirmed. "Our youths must leave their argosies and prove themselves worthy in another, and the competition is intense. We are a prominent argosy, and so we have many young males vying for acceptance. It is part of the reason we are in this system."

She went on to explain. This was a young, lifeless system packed with nearly a dozen small, rocky planets and large planetoids in tight orbits. Over geologic time, many of them would have near misses that could fling them out of the system, while others would collide directly. By remarkable good fortune, two of the planets were within weeks of a head-on collision. Starfleet had sent the *Enterprise* here to plant sensor probes to monitor the event. The Betelgeusians had somewhat different interests in the impending collision. For one, if the collision were forceful enough to shatter the planets, it could expose vast quantities of valuable minerals that the argosy could mine for future trade. But there was a good chance that the collision would be slow enough for the planets to coalesce into a single body of sufficient mass to become the core of a hot Jovian over the next few hundred millennia. The inhabitants of the Shining Talon Argosy had wagered heavily with one another over the outcome, and they were awaiting this impending astrophysical cataclysm as eagerly as many of the *Enterprise*'s personnel anticipated the Federation Cup each year.

Indeed, some of the younger male Betelgeusians, eager to prove themselves worthy and advance within the argosy's pecking order, had even camped out on the surfaces of the doomed planets, engaged in what humans would call a "game of chicken" to see who would be the first to break down and head for the escape shuttles. "Not to worry," said Hirr'uth. "We have ships in orbit, maintaining a constant transporter lock on both groups in case their pride overrides their sense."

"There has to be a safer way to earn status!" insisted a disbelieving McCoy.

"There are many, Doctor," Keer'iuv replied. "But so many have already been tried, and thus they have ceased to be impressive. Our young seek new ways to prove themselves that none have attempted before."

The warship captain spoke with enthusiasm, but the administrator's expression suggested that she was less sanguine about the practice. "This often goads our young to recklessness," she added, "and it is a challenge to our mature members to keep our young from killing themselves before they win their place."

"Have you considered enlisting them in Starfleet?" Sulu asked. "I can't think of a better challenge. And it's a great way to achieve noteworthy things."

McCoy looked skeptical. "Don't you think they'd be a little . . . undisciplined for Starfleet?"

"No more so than an Andorian, say."

"Indeed," Spock put in, "most Vulcans would consider humans highly undisciplined. Yet Starfleet is effective at moderating your excesses—most of the time." McCoy glowered back.

"It is an interesting proposal," Hirr'uth said. "Our youth have, on occasion, signed on to alien ships to earn achievements when there were no openings in our own argosies. But it did not occur to us that Starfleet would be open to us."

"We try to be open to everyone," Kirk said. "I'd be happy to work with you to present a proposal to Starfleet Command for an exchange program."

Keer'iuv examined Spock. "Is this why you are in Starfleet, Mister Spock? In order to win status and approval among your Vulcan kin?"

Spock was struck by the irony of his innocent question. "Indeed not. My choice to join Starfleet was made in spite of the preferences of my family and community. My people are more . . . inflexible . . . than yours. Yet I have gained considerably from my time in Starfleet."

"Yes, I see! Unable to win the status you desire among your own people, you instead pursue it within your adopted fleet. That is a wise choice under the circumstances. And it has brought you within just one tier of commanding your own starship! Yes, there is much to consider in this proposal."

Spock declined to correct Keer'iuv's misapprehension about his career goals. He did not wish to put a damper on Captain Kirk's efforts to promote cultural exchange and cooperation with the Betelgeusians, since stronger ties would surely diminish the risk of future conflicts. Moreover, the concerns that Keer'iuv had inadvertently raised in Spock were matters for private contemplation.

Starfleet was, after all, a hierarchical organization. While humans today were not quite as obsessed with status and advancement as their forebears, or as the Betelgeusians, it was still largely expected that a Starfleet officer would either continue to advance in rank or retire to create an opening for others. In particular, an executive officer with a record as notable as Spock's (for false modesty would be illogical) could surely expect to be offered a starship command before long. He had already heard intimations that such offers would be made to him upon the conclusion of his current tour aboard the *Enterprise*.

But Spock had never desired command, and recent experience had only reinforced this position. More than once in the past year, he had found himself in command of the *Enterprise* on occasions when Captain Kirk was missing or presumed dead. Those had been tense occasions during which it had proven difficult for Spock to win the acceptance and allegiance of the mostly human crew, given his inability to employ the engaged, empathetic command style used by Kirk. It had been clear that the crew had not wished him to be in command any more than he had. Spock doubted he would function any more effectively as the commander of another Starfleet vessel. There were ships with mostly nonhuman crews, of course, but most of the Federation's primary spacefaring peoples were just as emotionally volatile as humans, if not more so. (He briefly contemplated what it might be like to be assigned a vessel with a primarily Tellarite crew. It would be like attempting to command an entire ship of Leonard McCoys.)

If further advancement in rank was not an option, then, it might be that Spock had reached a dead end in his Starfleet career. Continued service might not be the optimal path for him.

Yet returning home to Vulcan did not strike him as a feasible option either. As Spock had explained to Keer'iuv, his choice to join Starfleet had not benefitted his standing among his people. His own father had all but disowned him for his choice, and though they had achieved a degree of rapprochement within the past two years, Sarek's disapproval of Starfleet remained. Moreover, his childhood fiancée, T'Pring, had been unwilling to be the wife of a Starfleet officer and had gone to rather extreme lengths to sever their engagement. As a result, Spock had little in the way of ties or prospects back home.

The place where Spock was most content was the one he currently occupied as James Kirk's science officer and friend. But as the *Enterprise* moved deeper into the fourth year of its planned five-year tour, Spock was becoming aware of the inevitable impermanence of that position . . . and the lack of a clear path to follow beyond it. The uncertainty was troubling.

Spock set these thoughts aside as the group arrived at the preserve's well-appointed and frequently busy medical facility, where the mysterious raiders' bodies were under examination. "The attackers took hold of the preserve with tractor beams," Keer'iuv narrated once they were inside. "They seemed too small to have much power, but they had no trouble holding on to a far bigger ship."

"Impressive," Spock observed. "The engines necessary to drive a vessel of this size through warp would need to be quite large and powerful."

"Indeed they are," Hirr'uth insisted. "Yet we could not break free of their grip, not before they battered down our shields and beamed their raiding parties aboard." The administrator gave an angry chirp. "We would have been happy to share our game with them, hunt together as siblings, had they requested like civilized people. But it seems they came instead to hunt *us*."

"Are you quite sure of that?" Doctor McCoy asked carefully. "Is it possible they came to, I don't know, challenge you for control of your hunting territory?"

"Doctor, my people know competition when we see it. They showed interest in hunting only the top predator in this environment: ourselves. They attacked my people quite pointedly. With the points of their teeth, in fact, and with bare hands, as well as with a variety of melee weapons—swords, knives, even clubs."

"Knives and clubs?" McCoy asked in disbelief. "When they have tractor beams and transporters?"

Nored nudged Sulu with her elbow. "Sounds like you and they have a lot in common," she whispered, making Sulu chuckle. She had only been aboard a few months, but the helmsman's interest in ancient weapons was well known, and the incident in which he had rampaged through the corridors under the influence of a psychotropic compound, believing himself to be the Comte d'Artagnan as interpreted in the fiction of Alexandre Dumas, *père*, remained a popular gossip topic among the crew to this day.

"A few carried sidearms, but most preferred a more primal attack," Hirr'uth went on. "Their savagery was almost primitive. And yet, though they fought with great strength, speed, and viciousness, they were . . . clumsy."

"Clumsy?" Kirk asked.

"Unaccustomed to the rotational gravity, perhaps?" Spock asked. On a rotating habitat of this size, the Coriolis effect could disrupt one's equilibrium until one grew accustomed to it.

"I refer more to their fighting technique," Hirr'uth clarified. "They seemed . . . inexperienced. For all that they clearly craved battle, they were not seasoned warriors." She tilted her head as far as her elaborate headdress would allow. "Perhaps they were juveniles, sent out to prove themselves and earn their place as adults, like our own young males."

Keer'iuv gave a slight crow. "If so, they proved unworthy. We slew two and drove the rest into retreat. By that time, my escort ships had closed in. We destroyed one of the enemy craft and harried the others away."

"What made you think the attackers were with the Federation?" Kirk asked.

"We retrieved computer components from the wreckage. Little data survived, but we were able to extract enough to translate the word *Federation* in a document."

"Well, that's hardly enough to go on!" McCoy countered. "Maybe it was their orders to attack us next, did you think of that?"

"Bones," Kirk said, silencing the irascible physician. "We'll see for ourselves in a moment."

"Indeed," Spock said. "But has it occurred to you that there is something familiar in the Betelgeusians' account?"

"I was thinking the same thing, Mister Spock," Sulu put in.

"Based on what?" Nored asked. "Remember, I'm still new."

"I'm not really sure," Sulu admitted. "Something about the tractor beams . . . but we've been caught in a number of powerful tractor beams."

Hirr'uth and Keer'iuv led them into the autopsy

chamber of the complex, an advanced, sterile, and mercifully small facility, suggesting they did not need to use it too often. On a pair of slabs before them, two tall, massive humanoid bodies lay covered in sheets. The heads seemed unusually large and bulbous. At Hirr'uth's nod, the coroner pulled back the sheets, revealing the creature's faces.

Kirk, Sulu, and McCoy stared at the aliens' features in stunned recognition. Spock raised both eyebrows and uttered "Fascinating," which amounted to the same thing. "This would explain the familiarity—but it raises a much greater mystery of its own."

The aliens before them were large, cadaverous humanoids, hairless and bulbous-headed with sallow greenish skin. Their gaunt, skull-like faces bore beetle brows, hawk noses, and staring, catlike eyes with deep bags beneath them. They were virtually an exact match for a face that Spock and the other veteran officers had all seen before—though it was a face that made no sense in this context.

Sulu was the first to put a name to it. "Balok!"

"Who?" Nored asked.

"That's impossible," Kirk said. "This wasn't Balok. It wasn't even alive."

Hirr'uth looked between them. "Then you have met these creatures before?"

"Not exactly," Kirk said. "Several years ago, we met a people calling themselves the First Federation. Their representative, Balok, made us think that . . . *this* . . . was what he looked like. But it wasn't real. It was just a robotic puppet, a . . . a scarecrow meant to frighten us. All part of a test of our good intentions."

"These are no puppets, Captain Kirk," the administrator replied gravely. "We have tasted their blood. They have hearts, brains, organs that our doctors have scanned and examined. Do you say that we have been attacked by some alien myth come to life?"

Kirk held Hirr'uth's fierce but bewildered eyes. "I don't know what these beings are, Administrator. But I promise you: We will find out."

One

Captain's Log, Stardate 5361.7.

Two days have now passed since our discovery of the Betelgeusians' mysterious attackers and their apparent connection to the reclusive civilization calling itself the First Federation. In the interim, we have received reports of similar attacks on a Saurian transport and an Arcturian trading post, both of which were able to repel the assaults—though not without casualties in the latter case. Whoever these beings are, they seem to be targeting races capable of putting up a fight . . . and their own skill seems to be improving. As they draw nearer to Federation space, a confrontation with Starfleet increasingly appears inevitable.

The First Federation clearly has knowledge of these beings, but our attempts to contact Lieutenant David Bailey, our unofficial ambassador to the First Federation, have proven unsuccessful. The Enterprise is proceeding toward the First Federation border in hopes of establishing direct contact with their representatives. In the meantime, the office of the Federation diplomatic commissioner has requested a full briefing on the matter.

The briefing was at 1900 hours, late by the *Enterprise*'s clocks, but that allowed Kirk to assemble all the senior officers who had been present for the first encounter with Balok: himself, Spock, McCoy, Scott, Uhura, and Sulu. They met in the largest briefing room, the one with a wall screen in addition to the smaller three-sided viewer in the table, so that Commissioner Gopal could see them all at once. Damayanti Gopal was a strong-featured woman in her mid-forties, only recently promoted to diplomatic commissioner after spending two years as assistant commissioner. Kirk had briefly known her predecessor in that post, Nancy Hedford, and had found her to be a rather prickly and undiplomatic individual, at least on the surface. So far, Gopal did not seem much different, making Kirk wonder what standards the previous commissioner had employed to select his deputies.

"I have, of course, read all the reports on the Enterprise's *initial contact with Commander Balok and the* Fesarius," Gopal said on the viewscreen. *"What concerns me is the lack of follow-up. Your Lieutenant Bailey has had three years to learn more about the First Federation, but he hasn't found the location of their homeworld or even their true name for themselves. We're forced to call them Fesarians for lack of anything better!"*

"You must understand, Commissioner," Spock replied, "that Commander Balok's people have good reason to be cautious. They are a neotenous species, retaining the size and appearance of small humanoid children well into adulthood. Many hostile cultures would be quick to take advantage of such physically fragile beings."

"Their reactions go beyond caution, Commander Spock. They embrace deception and concealment and use highly aggressive measures to defend their territory. The buoy you first encountered provided no warning, merely clung to you

and bathed your ship in lethal radiation until you were forced to destroy it."

"But we *were* able to destroy it," Spock pointed out. "With their technology, they could easily have shielded it against our phasers. The buoy was part of a test to assess our—"

"Your peaceful intentions, yes." Gopal turned to Kirk. *"I do wonder, Captain, why you thought the best way to demonstrate those was to push forward into the territory they obviously wished to fence off. You must have known that would provoke a further response."*

"I was counting on it, Commissioner," the captain replied. "We were peaceful, but we didn't yet know whether they were. Given the level of technology on display, I decided it was imperative that we learn more about what we were facing." He gave a small smile. "Consider it a chess move. You have to advance your pieces onto the board to get your opponent to reveal their strategy."

"And yet we still have more questions than answers. With the power of their technology, their effortless ability to shut down a starship's power and rifle through its memory banks, why do they feel the need for all this protective camouflage? A giant starship with only one person aboard. A threatening face and voice that turn out to be mere puppetry. This is a systematic pattern of deceit, and you had no guarantee the tricks would end once Commander Balok allowed you to board his ship and see his true face. And yet you had no problem assigning your most inexperienced bridge officer as the Federation's 'ambassador' to these people."

"Lieutenant Bailey was an eager volunteer. I felt it would give him valuable seasoning."

"*Mere hours before, you'd ordered him off the bridge when he became insubordinate and suffered a panic attack. Perhaps you were simply eager to foist him off on some other ship's captain.*"

Kirk clung to his patience. "I wanted to give him a chance to make up for that mistake. Something he was strongly motivated to do. I was that young once myself, Commissioner. I was cocky, and I made my share of mistakes." He tried to ignore Doctor McCoy, whose expression almost audibly countered, *Was?* "But I learned a great deal from assignments where I spent time living among other cultures, getting to know them. They brought me valuable perspective, showed me there was always another way of looking at any problem—and at myself." He reflected on the individuals he had befriended on those missions, leaders whose example had helped guide him in becoming a better officer and a better man—Tyree of Neural, Ren'xaan of Arkoni, King Stevvin of Shad. He had sensed a similar wisdom in Balok and had hoped the little trickster could play a similar role for David Bailey.

"*But what exactly has Bailey done with that second chance?*" Gopal challenged. "*Hit wall after wall trying to pierce the First Federation's veil of secrecy. Been stuck in an unofficial ambassadorial posting because the Fesarians unequivocally refuse to deal with a more qualified representative. Could it be that they prefer dealing with him because his inexperience makes him easy to manipulate and mislead?*"

"Excuse me, Commissioner," McCoy put in. "Maybe I got the wrong memo, but I was under the impression we were here to talk about these aliens that happen to look like Balok's mechanical scarecrow, not dissect Lieutenant Bailey's career."

"*That is exactly my concern, Doctor. Balok claimed his 'scarecrow,' as you put it, was a mythical construct.*" She checked a note on her data slate. "*The Hyde to his Jekyll, he called it. I'm not sure whether I'm more troubled by the idea that he could have assimilated the* Enterprise's *data-banks rapidly enough to be able to make that allusion, or by the implication that his people may have already known more about us than they admitted. In any case, it is now evident that Balok was lying—that these creatures are far from mythical, and that the First Federation's members are more physically intimidating than we were led to believe. Perhaps Balok is not the mature form of his species after all, or perhaps their federation includes a more aggressive race among its members.*"

Lieutenant Uhura pursed her lips in thought. "There is another possibility, Commissioner. Balok's people chose the image of these beings to frighten. To represent a deadly and implacable foe. So maybe it represents something that *they* are afraid of. Maybe they're even the reason the First Federation is so cautious with aliens."

"*Didn't the Betelgeusians' report indicate that they used the same technology as the Fesarians, though?*"

"Not the same, ma'am," Montgomery Scott replied. "I've reviewed the 'Geusians' scans of the attack and the wreckage they recovered. It's based on the same principles, for the most part, but it's a different application. Cruder in some ways, but in other ways just . . . different." He shrugged. "I'd say they and Balok's people have a history, but I cannae say what kind of history. They could be allies, sure. Or they could be enemies, spying on each other and reverse-engineering each other's technology. How do you think the current crop o' Romulan birds-of-prey ended up with warp nacelles so much like ours?"

"I concede that's possible," Commissioner Gopal spoke up, her manner making it clear that she intended to stay in control of the conversation. *"But it's all speculation until we can convince the Fesarians to cough up some real answers. We've indulged their mysterious ways for far too long, and now we might be facing a new threat on our border. Captain Kirk, when you make contact, I expect you to press for answers. No more kid gloves. Threaten to withdraw Bailey if they don't start practicing full disclosure. His Starfleet commission is still active, so you could order him to return with you."*

Kirk replied with care. "Commissioner . . . it wasn't easy to get through the First Federation's defenses the first time. I'm concerned that if we attempt strong-arm tactics, it will simply drive them into retreat—or worse. If they decide the *Enterprise* is genuinely a threat, we may not be able to handle their response."

"As you said, Captain, in chess you have to risk your pieces to expose the opponent's strategy. It's time to stop probing with pawns like Bailey and move into the middle game. Because these 'scarecrow' attacks might just be their opening gambit."

When Gopal signed off, Kirk turned to his first officer. "Spock, your assessment?"

The half-Vulcan raised an eyebrow. "Her extended metaphor was somewhat labored."

His remark broke the tension and brought a laugh to Kirk and the others—no doubt Spock's intention, though he would never admit it. McCoy played along. "Blast it,

Spock, save the literary criticism for poetry night. Do you think Gopal knows what she's talking about? Or is she just the latest blowhard commissioner in a long line?"

"She is a duly appointed Federation official, Doctor, and we are obliged to defer to her judgment on diplomatic matters."

"Bull! We're the ones on the front lines. Jim's got the full authority of a Federation ambassador when he needs it. That's how he was able to appoint Bailey as one to begin with!"

"Yet the commissioner does have a point," Spock continued. "In chess, or indeed in poker, one must be willing to provoke a response from the opponent. I believe the expression is, 'You must pay to see the other's cards.'"

"But Balok's people aren't the opponents, are they?" Sulu asked. "It just doesn't make sense that they'd be behind these attacks. Why go around operating robotic puppets of these warrior creatures if they're actually real and on their side?"

"Perhaps, Mister Sulu. But Spock's right," Kirk said. "Either way, they're hiding something from us, and we need to find out what it is. We're on friendly terms, yes, but guardedly so at best. They're very slow to trust, and they're undoubtedly keeping a great many secrets. They haven't even begun to share any of their technology with us, for one thing."

"Aye," Scott said. "And I shouldn't wonder that that's part o' the reason the commissioner's so eager to dig deeper into their secrets. I know I'd love to get my hands on the *Fesarius*'s specs."

"But you were right, too, Jim," McCoy said. "Push them too hard and we may lose what little trust we've gained. And think about the consequences to Bailey's career. Gopal's already written him off as a failure. We swoop in there and pull him out, and he's probably done in Starfleet."

"And yet," Kirk answered patiently, "there's a band of marauders out there picking fights with anyone they run across. And Balok's people know them somehow. We have to tread carefully, but we need to get answers—before these marauders get better at hitting the mark."

———

The cube spun on the viewscreen like an angular top, flashing bright colors at the *Enterprise* as it blocked the starship's path. "It's certainly . . . festive," was the judgment of Pavel Chekov, who was seeing this sight for the first time.

"They're meant to be noticed," Hikaru Sulu bantered back. "Think of it as a very aggressive stoplight."

"Lieutenant Uhura," Kirk said, "transmit the recognition code to the buoy." *And let's hope Balok was being honest when he gave it to us,* he added to himself.

As Uhura acknowledged his order and worked her console, the turbolift doors swooshed open and Doctor McCoy entered the bridge. Multicolored lights played across his face as he studied the image on the viewscreen and frowned. "Is that thing going to behave itself, or do I need to have Nurse Chapel prepare hyronalin injections?"

"No increase in baseline radiation as yet, Doctor," Spock said, not looking up from his hooded viewer. "I shall let you know if that changes, however."

Kirk glanced up at McCoy as the doctor took his

wonted spot to the left of the captain's chair. "Have you had a chance to review Bailey's reports?" he asked softly.

The doctor kept a wary eye on the twirling buoy as he replied, "I have."

"Your assessment?"

"Well, they're certainly thorough, as far as they go. I've learned a lot about the workings of the *Fesarius* and its crew. Like the fact that it *has* a crew. I remember Balok being rather insistent that he had none. Another one of his bluffs."

"To be fair, the others did retreat in their pilot vessels before the *Fesarius* confronted us," Kirk replied. "So he was technically telling the truth, at that moment."

"Yes, standard contact procedure, per Bailey's reports." Paraphrasing those reports as best he could, he adopted a singsong tone. "An orbship like the *Fesarius* is primarily a freighter and asteroid miner, large enough to support its crew for years away from home. But that size makes it valuable as an intimidating presence on the borders when necessary." He went on more normally. "But where home might be, or why they spend so much time away from it, is another matter. Bailey's reports get thinner and thinner with time—I can almost hear him getting more frustrated as he tries to find something new to say."

Kirk frowned. "Do you think he's handling it?"

"You mean, did you make a mistake giving him this responsibility?" He quirked a brow. "Honestly, Jim, I'm impressed that he didn't demand a transfer a year or two ago. It's a thankless job, but he's stuck with it and been as diligent as his hosts would permit." He threw an impatient glance at the screen. "And you know how tough it is to convince them to lower their guard," he said more loudly, as if challenging the buoy directly.

And it seemed to work. "The buoy is withdrawing," Spock announced, mere seconds before its retreat became obvious. "We are evidently cleared to proceed."

Kirk threw McCoy an impressed look, and the doctor bounced smugly on his heels. "Well. It's about time *somebody* around here started listening to me."

"What was that, Doctor?" Kirk grinned at McCoy's sour look. "Mister Sulu, ahead warp factor one."

"Aye, sir." Moments later, at Sulu's command, the ship around them hummed with power as the warp engines engaged and drove it forward. "Entering First Federation space."

"Some space," Chekov said, shaking his head. "I do not see why they make such a fuss over it. There is nothing here. Virtually no inhabited planets to speak of."

"That we know of," Sulu added. "If there's one thing we know about Balok's people, it's that they like to stay hidden."

"Habitable planets are hard to hide, Sulu. We can see the oxygen in their spectra, their warmth in infrared."

"Well, maybe they don't live on a planet. The Betelgeusians don't."

"However," Spock interposed, "while Mister Bailey has reported encounters with additional ships and outposts—even with First Federation member species besides Balok's own—their population density appears too low to sustain an entire interstellar civilization."

"What if there aren't any more?" McCoy suggested. "They say they're the First Federation—maybe they're so old that their civilization is almost extinct. Maybe there's hardly anyone left."

"You have read the reports, Doctor. Mister Bailey has not been able to learn the etymology of their name."

"So that means it's possible."

"Many things are possible, Doctor. It is thus pointless to conjecture in the absence of evidence."

"In the absence of evidence, what else *is* there to do but conjecture?"

"To be silent," Spock replied pointedly, "so that one may listen . . . and learn."

McCoy glowered. "Fine with me. You go first."

Spock made the decisive move in their latest game by doing exactly as McCoy suggested—turning wordlessly back to his station and resuming his scans. With no volley to return, and no one to blame but himself, McCoy was stymied. "If anyone wants me, I'll be in sickbay."

As the doctor left, Kirk reflected on how unusual it was for McCoy to make such an unforced error in his ongoing match of wits with Spock. Maybe McCoy was more on edge than he let on. Kirk felt a similar unease of his own. The encounter with Balok had been the first major contact with a new civilization in the course of the *Enterprise*'s current tour of exploration. Kirk and his crew had taken its positive outcome as an auspicious beginning for the mission. No doubt they had endured far worse consequences on many subsequent missions, but they would always have that early success to take pride in. But now their certainties about that mission were shaken, and it was less clear what they had really achieved. Kirk only hoped that whatever new answers they found would restore that certainty . . . rather than destroying it altogether.

The *Enterprise*'s hails to the *Fesarius* evoked only a brief reply in return, consisting of little more than a set of rendezvous coordinates in a system a day's travel from the border. As the Starfleet cruiser neared the system—a young star with a dense planetesimal disk still surrounding it—Spock's scans detected the massive orbship keeping station with a moderate-sized asteroid, an undifferentiated mass of rock, ice, and carbonaceous minerals that could be easily broken up and harvested for materials. If the *Fesarius* were in the midst of a mining operation, Kirk thought, that could explain why it had not been able to come to the *Enterprise*.

However, it soon became evident that mining was not the only thing going on. "Power readings from the *Fesarius* are fluctuating," Spock reported. "It would appear to be damaged." Indeed, as Uhura refined the magnification of the image on the main viewer, Kirk could see that for himself. The *Fesarius* was a massive sphere covered in a hexagonally tessellated grid of illuminated domes, reminding Kirk of a vast sequined Christmas ornament. Normally, the golden light from those domes pulsed on and off in a regular pattern like a heartbeat as the vessel's many power reactors cycled. Now, many of the domes were dark and most of the rest were flickering and guttering. Moreover, the spherical symmetry of the craft was broken. On one side, a large hexagonal section nearly a third of the orbship's diameter had been peeled open, exposing the vessel's innards to space. For a moment, Kirk feared the worst, until he realized that the opening was ringed by six regularly shaped triangular flaps. The orifice must have been built into the orbship's design, a vast hatch for the processing bays that filled much of its interior. The crew must have been in the process of breaking up the asteroid and tractoring its material inside the *Fesarius*. It had been the worst possible time for the orbship to come under attack.

Kirk's eye shifted from the orbship to the fighters that swarmed around the vast globular vessel—mere pulsating points of light at this resolution, but numerous and mobile. "Scans show technology similar to First Federation pilot vessels," Spock reported. "Consistent with the reports from the Betelgeusians. And more: I register numerous objects with no life signs, emitting high-intensity radiation."

"More buoys?" Sulu asked.

"But on which side?" Kirk mused.

"They do not have the size or spectrographic profile of the First Federation buoys," Spock answered. "And they appear to have the *Fesarius* in an englobement. With its interior exposed to space, the radiation levels would not be salutary for its inhabitants."

"Why aren't they closing the hatch?" Chekov asked through gritted teeth.

"There," Kirk said, pointing. "One of the doors is out of alignment."

"Correct, Captain," Spock said. "It would appear to have been struck by an asteroid fragment. I would deduce that the attackers chose to strike when the *Fesarius* was at its most vulnerable and are attempting to disable it."

"That is a pretty successful attempt," Chekov put in.

Kirk set his jaw. "Not if we can help it. Mister Sulu, take us in. Raise deflector shields, ready weapons." He hit the intercom button on his chair arm. "Kirk to engineering. Mister Scott, we're going to need maximum radiation protection from the deflectors."

"Aye, sir. I've been tweakin' them with that in mind, just in case one o' those buoys acted up."

"Not exactly a buoy, Scotty, but close enough. Keep monitoring the exposure levels. Kirk out." He switched channels. "Kirk to sickbay. Bones, you know those hyronalin injections you talked about?"

"I knew it. I've had Chapel working on them since yesterday. I'll get them ready."

"Hopefully we won't need them, but good job. Kirk out." He smiled to himself. *I have the best crew any captain could ask for.*

As the *Enterprise* closed in, a pair of the attacking ships broke off to intercept it. They soon drew near enough for Kirk to see that they were asymmetrical clusters of octahedral and icosahedral modules, connected by short struts and pulsing with a red-orange light. Just as the Betelgeusians had described, they were like angular, aggressive versions of Balok's pilot vessel. If they had anywhere near that vessel's power, Kirk knew, then they would be more than a match for the *Enterprise* despite their small size. "Uhura, hail them."

"Hailing frequencies open, sir." A moment later: "No response."

I didn't think there would be. "Evasive, Sulu. Don't let them get a tractor lock."

Sulu acknowledged the order, then fulfilled it by swinging the *Enterprise* around behind the asteroid. Many chunks of the loosely packed body had been dislodged, either by the mining operation or by the raiders' attack, and they provided effective cover against the pursuing ships' tractor beams. The angular craft fired some kind of plasma bolts at the *Enterprise*, but the energy bursts struck chunks of intervening rock and ice and blasted them into still further chaff. "Impulsive," Kirk noted. "Undisciplined. Wasting their fire without a clean shot. Maybe we can use that."

As the starship curved around to the other side of the asteroid, Spock announced, "Captain, I am now detecting a *Fesarius* pilot vessel." He altered the viewer angle to display the small craft, a cluster of pale gold spheroids of various sizes. A beam of light burst from its leading spheroid and struck at one of the raiders. At least someone was trying to defend the *Fesarius*.

"Is it Balok?" Kirk wondered. "Uhura, hail the pilot vessel."

"They're hailing us, sir."

"On screen."

The face that appeared on the viewer was not the bald, childlike visage of Balok, but a familiar human face—a young, light-complexioned man with dark blond hair, narrow eyes, and a prominent chin. "Enterprise, *this is David Bailey.*"

"Yes, Mister Bailey, this is Kirk. We read you."

"Captain, you're just in time. The attackers are trying to board the Fesarius. *The crew is trapped inside—the radiation out here is too intense for them to withstand in their pilot vessels. Only Balok was able to get away before the cubes had us completely surrounded. I'm big enough to withstand a larger dose, so I've been playing goalie out here, defending the hatch the best I can. But I'm close to my limit. And this thing's only got a mining beam, not combat-level phasers."*

"Understood, Mister Bailey." Kirk wasn't sure whether it would be more appropriate to address him as *Lieutenant* or *Ambassador*. "You get back inside—we'll take over tending your goal."

"*Negative, Captain. The* Fesarius *won't be secure or mobile until the hatch is closed. If you run interference for me, I think I can tractor the damaged leaf back into alignment and seal the hatch. This thing's a fortress when it's closed up.*"

Kirk considered it. The Bailey he remembered had been a hothead, favoring action over judgment. Was he being just as reckless now? Yet he was choosing a defensive action over an aggressive one, which was a change. And he knew the situation better than Kirk. So the captain chose to defer to his judgment. "Agreed. But as soon as your radiation tolerance reaches its limit, you're to withdraw inside. Is that understood, Lieutenant?"

Bailey didn't miss the significance of the title Kirk chose. With only a slight hitch in his voice, he replied, "*Aye, sir.*"

Sulu deftly maneuvered the *Enterprise* into position in front of the enormous, gaping hatch. Each of the large domes that dotted the *Fesarius*'s surface was big enough to hold the *Enterprise* inside it, and each leaf of the unfolded shell was covered in six of those domes, with three smaller domes at their points of intersection. Before the starship rotated to face the oncoming raiders, Kirk caught a glimpse of the gaping interior of the *Fesarius*, with a similar array of domes dotting the inner shell and a complex latticework surrounding a cluster of spherical reactors at the core. Kirk shuddered to think what would happen if the raiders managed to destroy one of those reactors. "Deflector shields to maximum extension," Kirk ordered. "Don't let anything get past us."

Of course, the downside to taking up a stationary position was that it left the *Enterprise* vulnerable to the raiders' tractor beams. But the *Fesarius* crew was not idle. Mining beams shot forth from emitters in the black, textured hull layer underneath the domes, firing through the gaps between them, and prevented the raiders from holding still long enough to get a lock on the *Enterprise*. Sulu, freed from the need to maneuver the ship, supplemented their efforts with phaser fire. The maneuverable raider ships were able to dodge the mining beams with ease, but they had less practice avoiding Sulu's keen aim, and several of them were struck. Their own plasma bolts retaliated against the *Enterprise*, rocking the ship, but the shields held.

Before long, Spock reported that the raiders were attempting another strategy. "Several attacker ships have seized fragments of asteroidal matter in their tractor beams. They are accelerating them toward the *Enterprise*."

"*That's how they jammed the hatch in the first place,*" Bailey advised from his pilot vessel. "*Those tractors pack quite a punch.*"

"Sulu, divert those chunks," Kirk ordered. "Mister Gabler, extra power to the shields."

Sulu's aim remained true. Rather than wasting energy attempting to blow apart the asteroid chunks, he struck them obliquely, vaporizing a portion and using the vapor pressure as thrust to angle the chunks off course. They struck only glancing blows against the shields and bounced away harmlessly.

"Mister Bailey has engaged his tractor beam," Spock

announced. He put the sensor feed on one of the auxiliary wall screens. While keeping an eye on the larger battle, Kirk watched as the lieutenant's pilot vessel grabbed on to the misaligned hatch with an invisible force beam. The pilot vessel trembled and flickered as it heaved at the enormous hatch. Kirk hoped Bailey's tractor beam was as potent as the one Balok had used to tow the *Enterprise* years before.

"Incoming," Sulu warned. The raiders were proving the potency of their own tractor beams, hurling asteroidal debris from multiple directions, and even Sulu and the *Fesarius* crew together could not target them all. One chunk got through and struck a ringing blow against the deflectors, and the *Enterprise* heaved mightily.

"Eighteen percent deflector shield drain, Captain," Gabler reported. "We can't take many more of those."

"We may not have to," Spock announced. "Mister Bailey's efforts appear to be efficacious."

On the auxiliary screen, the enormous flap of the *Fesarius*'s hull was moving, shifting back into alignment on its massive hinges. Before long, it appeared to click into place, whereupon all six leaves began to close inward. "*It's done,*" Bailey announced. "*Heading in now. Captain, I suggest you bring the* Enterprise *inside after me.*"

"Negative, Lieutenant. The *Fesarius* is still damaged. Once we're free to move again, we can cover your retreat."

A pause. "*Acknowledged, sir.*"

Three raider ships made a last-ditch attempt to dive toward the closing hatch. The crossfire from the *Enterprise* and the *Fesarius* forced them to veer off. After another few moments, the tips of the six hull wedges locked against one another, and one last dome unfolded from between its neighbors and locked into place over the center point. With the orbship now sealed up tightly, the raiders abruptly broke off the attack and fled, the more badly damaged ones being tractored by their fellows and towed into warp.

Bailey's image appeared on the main viewer. "*I appreciate your help, Captain,*" the lieutenant said, sounding winded. "*Since I'm the ambassador, I guess I'm entitled to thank you on behalf of the Fesarius crew. We could probably use your help with repairs, if you don't mind.*"

"We'd be glad to, Mister Bailey," Kirk said. "And in exchange, I trust your First Federation friends can tell us something about who these raiders are and what their goal is."

Bailey grimaced. "*Honestly, Captain . . . I was hoping you could get some answers out of them. All I know is that a fairy tale seems to have come to life.*"

Two

Spock was gratified to find that the crew of the *Fesarius* had modified its interior spaces with more headroom to accommodate Lieutenant Bailey. Thus, it was unnecessary for him, the captain, Doctor McCoy, or Mister Scott to crouch when passing through its doorways or corridors. There were also spaces within the orbship's interior that were quite expansive, large interior domes landscaped as park areas under simulated skies or as arenas for sporting or recreational activities. A few observation domes provided impressive views of the expansive mineral extraction and processing facilities that filled most of the *Fesarius*'s interior, along with the cluster of large, pulsating reactor spheres at the heart, the power sources for the external field emitter domes that provided the ship's propulsion and defenses. There was even a recreation room that could create tactile holographic simulations of planetary environments—though not of living beings, which was why the First Federation instead relied on robotic simulacra for that purpose. But for the most part, the Fesarians seemed more comfortable in tight, enclosed environments.

All in all, the orbship's interior was quite luxurious for a complement of ten Fesarians and one human. According to Bailey's reports, the crew spent years aboard it at a time, and thus it needed to be a home for them as well as a ship. It also had the facilities to carry large numbers of passengers and cargo. Spock noted the anomaly of this, for it implied a sizeable population for the First Federation despite the evident dearth of inhabited planets within their territory.

Upon arrival, the party was greeted by a female Fesarian, as childlike and bald-headed as Balok and dressed in similar silver robes, but with less pronounced eyebrows. She introduced herself as Linar, and her role aboard ship seemed to be similar to that of an executive officer, though with a particular specialty in administrative and organizational functions. Two other officers, males named Choda and Almis, oversaw the engineering department and the scientific and medical department, respectively. Each of the three had two junior crewmembers sharing their specialty. The organizational structure reminded Spock of the geometry of the orbship's surface domes, with each individual linked to three others, and with Balok as the center of the network, in overall charge of the entire orbship.

Linar seemed nervous and distracted when she greeted the *Enterprise* party, but she channeled her nervousness into giddy humor. "It is, yes, a pleasure to welcome you aboard our fine ship, Captain Kirk. Although I trust you have disarmed that fearsome corbomite device of yours!"

Kirk shared in her subsequent laugh, though rather less hysterically. "It's fine—I left it in my other uniform."

Linar somehow managed to laugh even harder. "Oh, Balok was right about you, Captain. He loves telling the story of your brazen corbomite bluff. To think—he was so proud of the trick he was playing on you, and then you turn around and trick him right back!" More laughter. "How did it go? An unstoppable weapon that would turn any destructive force back on any attacker? 'Death has little meaning to us!'" She cackled. "Oh, Captain, he was rolling on the deck when he heard you say that! It took him two minutes to recover his composure."

The captain smiled. "I'll be sure to tell him how the 'corbomite device' came in handy against the Romulans a couple of years ago." He paused. "Once we locate him, of course. I trust you can help us with that."

Linar grew serious quickly. "I'm afraid it won't be that easy. The attackers sent a ship after Balok when he fled, so it may take time for him to lose it, and he will maintain communications silence until then. And the *Fesarius* is in no condition to travel just yet, even with your gracious assistance. Normally we could repair the damage ourselves; we have more than enough maintenance drones aboard. But both of Choda's junior engineers were hurt in the attack, and Choda's stretched thin handling things by himself."

"Lucky thing I'm here, then," Commander Scott interposed. "If you could just show me where I can find Mister Choda, I'll be glad to get my hands dirty."

There was a slight catch in Linar's voice as she replied. "All right, Mister Scott. But . . . don't be surprised if he doesn't warm up to you right away. We're a proud people, and accepting help from outsiders is . . . still fairly new to us. Be patient."

Scott smiled. "Ma'am, I've always found that, no matter where they're from or how different they are, once you put two engineers together with a problem to solve, they're family. I'm sure we'll be fine."

"Excellently said, Mister Scott," Linar exclaimed, clapping her tiny hands together.

"And if you could show me to your medical bay," Doctor McCoy added, "I'll see what help I can provide for your injured crew."

Again, Linar hesitated slightly before agreeing. "Very well. I'll escort you both. Mister Bailey, if you could show the captain and Mister Spock to the meeting chamber . . . ?"

Once Linar had led McCoy and Scott away, Bailey led Kirk and Spock down a narrow corridor. "This is tough for Linar," he said with a hint of apology. "They're a friendly enough people, really, but they're very shy around strangers. Balok's always been the most open-minded one, and without him . . . Well, Linar's trying to fill his shoes, but it's not easy."

"I understand, Mister Bailey," Kirk replied as the ambassador led them into the curtained alcove that served as a meeting room and directed them to cushions around a low table. "My main concern right now is to learn what they know about this species that Balok used as his scarecrow."

Bailey grimaced. "Believe me, Captain, I've been trying to find out about them myself, but they just don't want to talk about it. All I've been able to get out of them is that they're some kind of bogeymen out of ancient legend, something they call the Dassik."

"Dassik," Kirk repeated. "At least we have something to call them other than *scarecrows.*"

"But they sounded pretty convinced that there were no Dassik. Laughed them off as something nobody would ever have to worry about in real life. They seemed pretty shaken when these Dassik turned up for real, but they refuse to tell me what's going on."

"Is it possible they don't know?"

"I just can't say, sir," Bailey said. "I've been trying to

get answers, believe me, Captain, but the more you push these people, the more defensive they get." He sighed sharply, clenching his fists. "It's ridiculous. They won't even tell me the name of their home planet."

"Their caution is understandable," Spock pointed out, "given their inherent vulnerability."

"That's just it, Mister Spock. It's not just Balok's people. I've met some of the other First Federation member species. They aren't all small and vulnerable. There's this one, the Bogosrin—skilled engineers, but they're built like bears with gazelle horns. And even they won't say a word about their homeworld. Three years and change, and I don't know where anyone in this federation actually lives, except the ones who live on ships and stations." He thrust himself to his feet and began to pace.

"Relax, Mister Bailey," Kirk said, keeping his tone gentle. "I knew this would be a challenging assignment when I offered it to you."

"Challenging? Sir, it's like chipping away at the Great Wall of China with a spoon."

"Mister Bailey," Kirk said, hardening his tone. "Commissioner Gopal is of the opinion that you've failed in your assignment as ambassador and should be replaced by someone better qualified to get answers. Are you saying you agree with her?"

Stunned to silence, Bailey stared at Kirk. "Do you, sir?" he finally asked.

"I'm asking you."

Bailey straightened his spine and set his jaw. "No, sir. At least I have a relationship with Balok. He tries to convince the others to open up to me, at least in small ways.

Anyone that Balok didn't know or like wouldn't even have that. They'd be starting from scratch."

Kirk gave a small smile of approval. "All right, then, Lieutenant. It seems to me that what we need to do is to find Commander Balok."

Bailey's relieved expression was short-lived. "That could be easier said than done. Like Linar said, he was fleeing pursuit last I saw him. And his people are very good at hiding."

Linar and her crew proved reticent to assist Kirk in searching for Balok, insisting that they could take care of their own. Kirk was not ready to accept that answer. On returning to the *Enterprise*, he ordered Lieutenant Uhura to send out hails to Balok's pilot vessel, in hopes of letting him know that they were seeking him. Bailey added his voice to the hailing message to reassure Balok that the *Fesarius* and its crew were essentially intact.

Some hours later, Uhura picked up a reply. "It was only a single burst transmission, a tight beam aimed directly at us," the lieutenant reported as Kirk, Spock, and Bailey clustered around her station.

"At us? Not the *Fesarius*?" the captain asked.

"That's correct, sir. They wouldn't have heard it at all. I'm amazed they have the technology to target subspace transmissions that precisely over such a distance."

"It is logical," Spock opined as he approached from his station, "that a civilization so concerned with self-concealment would master such a technique."

"Should we pass it along?" a confused Bailey asked.

Kirk considered it. If Balok had seen fit to send the message solely to the *Enterprise*, maybe there was some reason he didn't want his own crew to know about it. "That can wait, Lieutenant. For now, Uhura, what was the message?

"It was strange, sir. Only one spoken word, 'Hide,' and a set of nine numbers." She handed Kirk a data slate inscribed with the digits.

"That's it?" Bailey asked.

"Nine figures, none more than two digits," Spock said. "Coordinates, perhaps?"

"It could be," said the former navigator. "The First Federation uses an astronomical coordinate system based on Euler angles—three coordinates, each measured in a three-part system like our degrees, minutes, and seconds. It could be the course to the system where he'd be hiding."

"Unwise," Spock said, "if he was concerned with Dassik pursuit."

"Still . . ." Kirk carried the slate down to the navigation station. "Mister Chekov, run these coordinates. Is there a star system on this bearing?"

Chekov calibrated the circular astrogator display beside his seat to handle First Federation coordinates and entered the figures into the dial, then examined the result. "Negative, sir. The nearest star on that bearing is twelve hundred parsecs away in the galactic halo."

Bailey gave a bitter chuckle. "First Federation ships are fast, but not that fast."

Spock furrowed his brow. "The message was beamed to the *Enterprise*, Captain—not to the *Fesarius*. Perhaps the message was meant to have some specific meaning to us."

Bailey scoffed. "What message? One word—'hide.' What special meaning could it have?"

The answer came to Kirk in a flash. *Not "hide"*—"Hyde! Remember, Bailey? When we first met the real Balok, and he explained his deception with the Dassik puppet?"

Bailey's eyes widened. "The Hyde to his Jekyll!" He chuckled. "I remember. Balok's got a thing for alien legends and lore—his family cell generally specializes in ethnology. While we thought we were fighting for our lives, he was happily rummaging through the literature and folklore he'd scanned in the *Enterprise*'s data banks. Jekyll and Hyde resonated with him for obvious reasons. Though if he'd come across *The Wizard of Oz* first, who knows?"

"That does resolve an outstanding question," Spock pointed out, "but we should focus for now on the significance of the character of Edward Hyde in this context."

"Right. Sorry." He paused in thought. "Well, there's the obvious. Mister Hyde is the opposite of Doctor Jekyll. May I, Ensign?" At Chekov's nod, Bailey reached down and entered new figures into the astrogator. "There . . . the exact opposite vector from the one Balok gave." He studied the chart. "No . . . still nothing anywhere near First Federation space. Maybe if I enter the negative values of every number." He tried again. "Nothing!" Glancing at Spock, he took a breath and gathered himself.

Kirk stroked his chin, pondering. "That's not it. Hyde wasn't Jekyll's opposite. He was Jekyll's inner self unleashed. The darker side of his own inherent nature, brought out through . . ." Realization dawned, and he turned to Spock. "Through a transformation."

The first officer took his meaning. "You suggest a coordinate transformation."

Bailey frowned. "You mean, like polar to cylindrical? That's just two ways of expressing the same vector."

"Then perhaps some other geometrical transformation, such as translation. We have already ruled out reflection."

"We're dealing with spherical coordinates," Bailey said. "Rotation?"

"That seems the most logical option. However, we would need to know by what amount we were meant to transform each coordinate."

"Nine coordinates," Kirk muttered. "Something Balok knew we would associate with him." His eyes widened, and he laughed. "Of course! Corbomite! Nine letters!"

Spock nodded. "Would Balok be aware of the numerical values of the English alphabet?"

"Yes, sir," Bailey said. "He likes to play word games with me to help him master English."

"Then presumably we would either add or subtract the numerical values of the letters of the word *corbomite* to each of the nine figures. Three for C, fifteen for O, and so on."

Chekov tried both possibilities. Only one produced a result. "There, sir! A G9 star with a planetary system, three point four parsecs away."

"That has to be it," Bailey cried.

"Rather, it is the only valid possibility we have as yet determined," Spock corrected. "We will not know for certain until we investigate."

"With your permission, Captain," Bailey went on, "I'd like to accompany the *Enterprise*. If we find Balok, I intend to get some real answers out of him."

"You are the ambassador, Lieutenant," Kirk acknowledged. "I wouldn't have it any other way."

———

Kirk decided not to inform Linar of Balok's message before parting ways with the *Fesarius*. The orbship's crew did not particularly want their help, and it appeared that Balok did. As usual, the boyish commander's motives and goals were cryptic; but this time, at least for now, Kirk was willing to play along with his game.

It took a day and a half to reach the G9 system. They happened to approach it at a high angle to its ecliptic plane, essentially seeing the whole array of planets, asteroids, and comets face-on and allowing for a more efficient scan. "No vessels or outposts detected among the outer planets," Spock reported after a time. "Entering scanning range of inner system."

Not long thereafter, Ensign Chekov leaned forward and said, "Will you look at that!"

Kirk sat up in his chair. "Have you found something?"

"Ahh, no." Chekov blushed. "Nothing like that, sir. I was just noticing . . . the configuration of this system. Look." He called up an astrometric graphic on the main viewer. "In the third orbit . . . there are two planets. A hot Jovian—well, warm, for it is in the star's habitable zone—and a Class-K planet in the L5 position."

Kirk's eyes widened. "Now, there's something you don't see every day. Spock, how does something like that even happen?"

"It is not unprecedented," Spock said. "The Lagrangian points are regions of gravitational stability where—"

"Yes, Spock, I'm familiar with Trojan points. But this . . . not just asteroids clustering around an L5 point, but a whole planet!"

"In fact, Captain, Earth once shared its orbit with a planet called Theia in its L4 point," Chekov said. "Eventually it grew unstable and collided with Earth, and the Moon coalesced from the debris."

"I know, Ensign. That's just why this is so startling. That it's still stable after . . . Spock, how old is this system?"

"Approximately five point eight billion years, plus or minus point seven."

"Five point eight billion years," Kirk echoed, trying to absorb it. That was a good twenty-five percent older than Earth. "How does a planet stay stable in a Trojan orbit that long?"

"Jovians in this orbital range tend to form *in situ* rather than migrating, and are thus more likely to retain nearby companions. This Jovian is quite massive, so its gravity would have protected a Trojan planet against perturbation. The emergence of such a formation is improbable, but once formed, it would remain stable."

"Even so . . ." Kirk examined the readings. "That's fairly large for a K-class planet. At that distance, it should be able to hold an M-class atmosphere and oceans. Any life signs?"

"No life readings," Spock said. "Planet appears to have been Class-M once, but lost its atmosphere in an ancient bombardment. Decay of surface features suggests a bombardment date approximately . . . twelve thousand years ago."

"Natural or artificial bombardment?"

Bailey now chose to step forward. "Captain, with all due respect, may I remind you that we're here to find Balok, not conduct scientific surveys?"

"Balok sent us here for a reason, Mister Bailey," Kirk told him, his voice an exemplar of patience. "Unless or until he chooses to show himself, we can't know what clues he intends us to find." The lieutenant took his point and offered no further objection.

Within one orbit, Spock had assembled a good picture of the planet's conditions. "The surface was bombarded by a series of asteroids," he reported. "However, the craters all appear to have been created in quick succession, judging by the overlap patterns and equal degree of decay. And their distribution is consistent with a targeted planetary bombardment. The bulk of the craters center on regions where one would expect a technological civilization to place its cities, manufacturing centers, and so forth." Spock compressed his lips, then gave a stark conclusion. "This world was murdered."

It was a sobering verdict. Kirk searched for a ray of hope. "Are there any signs of habitation anywhere else in the system? Maybe they escaped to space. The Jovian is nearby—any habitable moons?"

"The moons are barren, sir. Any atmosphere and liquid water they may have once possessed has been long since stripped away by the Jovian's intense radiation belts."

"Sir," Uhura ventured, "could this be Balok's people's homeworld? It could explain why they live in space . . . and why they're so wary of strangers."

"What if the whole sector is like this?" Sulu asked. "That could explain the lack of habitable worlds."

"But that doesn't make sense," Bailey insisted. "Yes, they live on ships and stations, but I've seen people and cargo traveling to and from *somewhere* else."

"We have questions," Kirk acknowledged. "Something in this system may give the answers. The natural place to look next is the Jovian itself. Chekov, Sulu, take us there."

The helmsman chuckled. "You don't have to tell me twice, sir," Sulu said. "That's one hell of an impressive planet. What is it, twice the mass of Jupiter?"

"One point eight six times, Lieutenant," Spock said. "Though slightly smaller than Jupiter in diameter due to the greater compression of its core."

In moments, Sulu was flying the *Enterprise* on a chord across the orbital path shared by the Trojan planet and the Jovian—or, looked at another way, one leg of the equilateral triangle they formed with the system's sun. But they had only made it two-thirds of the way when the red alert klaxon sounded.

"Warp incursions, sir!" Sulu announced. "Two—no, three vessels closing at high speed on an intercept course! They're Dassik, sir!"

"Shields up! Arm all weapons!"

"Aye, sir," the helmsman said with grim determination beneath his outer calm.

Spock soon placed a magnified image on the viewer. These Dassik ships were significantly larger than the fighters that had attacked the *Fesarius*. Their individual polyhedral modules appeared the same size, but there were far more of them clustered together in uneven clumps, like the products of a small child's building-block set. Yet Kirk knew better than to underestimate their power.

"Uhura, hail them," Kirk said.

"Channel open, sir."

Kirk rose from his command chair. "Attention, Dassik vessels. This is Captain James T. Kirk of the *United Starship Enterprise*, representing the United Federation of Planets. We have no hostile intentions toward your people."

"They're responding, Captain," Uhura reported.

"On screen."

The face that appeared on the viewer was familiar— gaunt, sallow, skull-like, with a fearsome snarl. Yet this time, there was no simulated atmospheric distortion to conceal the artificiality of an animatronic scarecrow. This Dassik was clearly alive and mobile, striding belligerently toward the imager pickup. Kirk could see that its apparently male body was lanky, powerful, and covered in leather and metal armor. *"You know our name,"* the alien said, his voice a rough basso even deeper than that of Balok's scarecrow.

I thought that might get their attention. "Yes, but very little else. We would like to learn more. Ours is a peaceful mission of exploration—"

"Lies! You fought alongside the betrayers against our ships. You share their name. One of you was in their crew— he stands beside you now."

Bailey stepped forward, his gaze seeking Kirk's leave. When the captain nodded, he spoke. "My name is Bailey. I'm an ambassador from my Federation to theirs. We defend ourselves when attacked, but we don't seek conflict with anyone. If you'll talk to us, explain your grievance—"

The Dassik snarled. *"I am Force Leader Grun of the proud and undefeated Dassik nation! I explain myself to no one. You will tell me where the betrayers' homeworld is or you will be destroyed!"*

Kirk traded a look with Bailey. "This has a familiar ring, doesn't it?" he murmured. The lieutenant gave a gallows smirk in return. Despite the similarities to their first encounter with the *Fesarius*, they both knew that this was no mere test.

Facing the viewer, Kirk raised his voice. "We cannot give you information we don't have."

"You are in this system for a reason. Tell me what you know!"

"You can scan the system for yourself, Force Leader Grun. There are no habitable worlds here. There haven't been for a very long time."

"You waste your breath, Captain. So I will relieve you of it and take the information from the carcass of your ship!"

Grun's visage vanished, and the screen now showed the three ships breaking formation and opening fire on the *Enterprise*. "Sulu, evasive maneuvers!"

The helmsman was already initiating the move before Kirk ordered it. Even so, he managed to dodge only the majority of the enemy fire. "Return fire, all phasers! Stand by torpedoes."

The lights and the steady hum of the bridge computers fluctuated. "Power drain, Captain," called Gabler.

"They are attempting to disrupt our power systems," Spock said. "A similar method to that used by Balok three years ago. Deploying countermeasures."

Fortunately, three years had been enough time for Spock and Scott to develop improvements to the ship's power systems, allowing them to counter the effect. Still, three against one was not a fair fight, and the *Enterprise* took a pounding despite Sulu's best efforts. The Dassik ships took damage in return from the *Enterprise*'s phasers and torpedoes, but they sustained no critical damage, and they dodged nearly as well as Sulu. It would take only one lucky shot to change the balance. Unfortunately, the Dassik got lucky first. A shield fluctuation triggered by one ship's barrage opened the door for another ship's disruptor fire to penetrate, tearing into the flank of the secondary hull and causing power loss throughout the port side of the ship. "Port thrusters failing," Sulu announced. "Cutting starboard to compensate. Switching to impulse power."

Thrusting on impulse gave them speed and power, but less precision in their maneuvers. It gave them some distance and a brief lull, which hopefully would give Scotty's teams time to reroute power, but which reduced their ability to alter course swiftly enough to dodge the Dassik's fire. The three boxy craft were able to flank the ship from multiple directions, circling like vultures and making it impossible for Sulu to keep the weakened port shields away from them. That is, until he somehow managed to adjust the impulse vernier fields to vector the thrust directly sideways and fly the ship port flank forward, keeping ahead of the pursuers. Three ships only defined a plane, and as long as Sulu kept the sideways *Enterprise* ahead of that plane, all fire would fall on their starboard side. Of course, that meant the navigational deflector was useless; the weakened shields would have to bear the brunt of any micrometeoroids they might collide with. Hopefully they wouldn't hit anything that would do more damage than a disruptor bolt.

But flying sideways made the *Enterprise* an ungainly beast, and soon the Dassik ships took advantage of that in an unexpected way: They broke apart. "Each large vessel appears to be an agglomeration of smaller craft," Spock announced. Soon, the *Enterprise* was facing eleven ships of various sizes, and the smaller ones had an advantage in speed and maneuverability, managing to slip ahead of the Starfleet vessel and bombard her weakened side. *"We've got most of the portside shield power back up,"* Scott reported from below, *"but it's a temporary patch. The less of a beating we have to take, the better the chance it'll hold."*

"Not an option right now, Scotty," Kirk told him as the deck shuddered under the barrage of disruptor fire.

The sound of an explosion came over the open comm line. "Scotty, are you all right?"

"Ah, bloody hell, and we barely had it fixed! Sorry, Captain, there goes your deflector patch!"

The ship shuddered under renewed fire, more of which was penetrating the shields. "Sulu, evasive at your discretion! Concentrate fire to port!"

"Aye, sir." The helmsman multitasked efficiently, temporarily abandoning his attacks on the largest ships to direct all the *Enterprise*'s fury at the ones that posed the greatest threat. The fierce barrage spattered against the nearest ship's deflectors until they were left in tatters, allowing deadly energies to tear through. Several modules were critically struck, their connecting struts severed until one octahedral module sheared off, exploding a moment later. The remaining hulls of the vessel were largely intact, but it was no longer able to maneuver or pose a threat. Sulu followed Starfleet rules of engagement to the letter, promptly abandoning the attack and redirecting fire to the other hostiles.

But the other ten ships merely intensified their bombardment with their plasma bolts and power disruption fields. And soon another wrinkle was added. "More cubic missiles, sir," Spock said. "Attempting to overwhelm us with radiation."

Kirk could see the spinning cubes on the viewer. Unlike the highly visible buoys, they were dull gray, their lethal emissions invisible to the human eye. *"Captain, we can't take much of this radiation in the shape our deflectors are in,"* Scotty told him over the open comm line.

"Can we break to warp?" Kirk asked. A part of him hated to retreat from a fight, but he had no desire to risk his crew when he didn't even know what they were fighting for.

"Even if we could get past them," Scotty said, *"we've got cracked crystals in two dilithium relays. Between that and the unstable power systems, even odds we'd be lost in a wormhole."* A new barrage struck the ship. *"My team's preparing to swap out the crystals now, but it'll take at least six minutes."* Again the vessel shuddered.

"All right," Kirk said. "If running's not an option, that leaves hiding. Sulu, before they can complete their englobement, get us to the Jovian, maximum impulse."

As Sulu acknowledged, Bailey moved forward to face Kirk. "Captain, what are you planning?"

"We'll hide within the Jovian's magnetic field. It'll disrupt their shields and sensors."

"And ours as well!"

"Then at worst, we'll be even again. And if anyone can get our sensors to work in that soup, it's Spock and Uhura. If we have to, we'll just scare up a telescope and look out a window."

"With respect, Captain, you're taking an enormous chance ceding the high ground to them. You put our back to that planet and we'll be well and truly trapped."

"I see it differently, Lieutenant. We'll be holed up just long enough to make repairs and devise a new strategy."

"If we don't get cooked passing through the planet's radiation belts!"

Kirk peered around him. "Sulu, do you have the radiation belts plotted?"

"Still compiling the scans, sir. There's a lot of energy bleed."

"Do you think you can dodge the worst of them?"

The helmsman straightened. "Absolutely, sir."

"This is a mistake, Captain," Bailey pressed on. "We should break for the Trojan planet, put its mass between us and the Dassik while we break to warp."

"Even at maximum impulse," Kirk countered, "it'd take nearly ten minutes."

"At least we'd be in open space, free to maneuver."

"And they'd be free to continue their attack."

"Captain, our priority is to find Balok. We can't do that if we're trapped here, waiting for the Dassik or the radiation belts to finish us off."

"We can't do it if they destroy us either, Mister Bailey. I'd hoped that by now you would've learned the value of patience."

Perhaps that was a low blow, but it did the trick. Bailey flushed, but lowered his gaze, chastened at seeming like a hothead again on this bridge of all places.

"Mister Sulu, proceed," Kirk ordered quietly.

As Sulu flew the ship into the giant planet's intense magnetic field, the sensor plots on the wall monitors became so much static. Soon, only the optical feed on the main viewer still functioned, though solely through Uhura's heroic efforts to clear the distortion. Thanks to her, they had a spectacular view of the vast world looming before them, a brilliant orb of white interspersed with bands of pale blue, green, and yellow. Here in the star's habitable zone, the Jovian was too warm to support the ammonia compounds that gave Jupiter its red and brown tinges. Its large moons, torn by craters and tectonic rifts, drifted across its face as the ship soared through the mini-system they comprised. Disruptor bolts still hit the ship, but with diminishing intensity as the magnetic disruption threw off the attackers' aim. "Optical tracking shows the Dassik taking up positions on magnetic field perimeter," Chekov reported.

"Berserkers or not, they're smart enough not to dive into this soup," Sulu muttered, his wry tone belying the tension in his shoulders as he watched out for radiation spikes and unaccounted-for moonlets.

But Sulu's skills served them well. Before much longer, he'd managed to pull ahead enough to lose the Dassik around the curve of the planet, then promptly veer onto a new course. Kirk ordered all exterior lights doused to make the *Enterprise* harder to track optically. By the time the eight remaining Dassik ships had maneuvered to engird the Jovian, Sulu had secreted the ship beneath a small, irregular moon, hidden from their visual sensors.

"Scotty, have you got those crystals replaced?" Kirk asked.

"They're good, sir. But no way can we go to warp from here. The magnetic and gravitational fields are too strong to allow a warp field to form. If we want to get out of here, sir, we'll have to get past these raiders first."

"We'll figure that out later, Scotty. For now, let's focus on repairs."

"Gladly, sir."

Bailey let out a held breath. "I guess I was wrong, sir. We made it."

Kirk clapped him on the shoulder. "We made it *in*, Lieutenant. That was the easy part. The real challenge will be making our way back out."

Three

The planet sang to her.

Nyota Uhura's assignment, nominally, was to study the nameless Jovian's magnetic field in order to devise countermeasures for its interference, and to monitor all signal bands for evidence of Dassik activity. As far as optical scans could determine, the mysterious raiders were still lurking in the system, two reassembled ships searching the space around the Jovian while the pieces of the other searched the rest of the system in case the *Enterprise* was hiding somewhere else.

But studying the magnetic field meant listening to its radio output, and to Uhura, that was music. Just now, the *Enterprise* was in the right position to detect one of the planet's decametric radio storms. The innermost large moon, churned into a volcanic hell by the tidal kneading of the Jovian's gravity, constantly erupted conducting gases into the intense magnetosphere, creating a plasma torus like the one that engulfed Jupiter's moon Io. The moon plowing through that plasma created intense magnetic waves that drove a cyclotron maser effect at the planet's poles, generating a storm of radio emissions even more potent than the system's star could produce. Every time the orbiting starship passed through the edges of the masers' emission cones, the radio noise filled Uhura's ears, sounding like crashing surf or a fierce downpour surging against the roof of her childhood home in Kenya during the long-rains season. Sometimes she heard shorter S-type bursts instead, a swift Geiger-counter crackle, each individual pop of which was really a swiftly descending tone, a narrow-band signal dropping rapidly through the radio spectrum. If Uhura listened closely enough, she imagined she could almost make out the descending tones within each split-second crackle.

Between the storms, the planet's song was quieter, but there was still a pervasive white noise with its own subtle surge and flow, like the susurrus within her ear when she cupped a hand to it, but with frequent sharp bursts of noise from the planet's intense lightning storms. As she listened, she imagined she could hear patterns within it.

Except the more she listened, the less convinced she became that all those patterns were imaginary.

"I can't pin it down," she said when she asked Spock to listen for himself. "But there seems to be a faint pattern underneath the static. A steady beat, like something's generating power. And there are faint spikes that sound almost like signal leakage."

Spock considered her words. "You're sure it's not just an artifact of the lightning storms?"

Uhura appreciated his tone—not skeptical, since he knew her abilities and her judgment were solid, but simply procedural, asking her to confirm for the record that everything had been considered. "It's not lightning, sir," she said. "But I can't be sure what it is. Maybe you could run a scan?"

Spock frowned. "Ship's sensor resources are needed to scan for Dassik activity."

"Only those facing outward from the planet, sir," she countered reasonably.

After a moment, he nodded. "Very well. The sensor

teams have other responsibilities, but I can perform the scan myself."

Spock initiated the scan as a background function at his station while he performed other tasks, including a review of the repair status report that Commander Scott had come to the bridge to present. But soon something caught his attention and he craned forward to peer into his hooded viewer. "Interesting," he said after a time.

Kirk, who had been sitting quietly in the command chair, turned around. "What is it, Spock?"

"Scan results from the planet below, Captain."

The captain rose from his chair as the science officer transferred the graphics to the science station's upper screens. "I only see clouds," Kirk said, raising his brows inquisitively.

"Indeed. But those clouds form certain predictable patterns arising from the interplay of thermal, convectional, and rotational forces. The patterns I am detecting here are subtly abnormal."

"Abnormal how?"

"As if something in the troposphere below the clouds were causing subtle disruptions in normal atmospheric convection and heat flow." Spock turned to face the captain, cocking an eyebrow. "Something large, expansive, and most likely, at least partially solid."

Kirk stared. "You don't normally find anything solid in the atmosphere of a gas giant, do you?"

"No, you do not, aside from dust or ice particulates. Generally there is no solid surface at all, only a hydrogen atmosphere growing progressively denser until it transitions into a liquid metallic stage, surrounding a deep solid core of degenerate matter."

"Can we scan deeper? Identify what's causing the effect?"

"We should be able to. Although there is considerable interference with our equipment, we can obtain thermal readings from the planet's interior. However . . ." Spock called up the appropriate sensor feed on the right-hand wall screen. "Sensors show nothing there."

"You're sure that's not due to the interference?"

"The readings are averaged over several minutes, allowing interference patterns to be filtered out. Where there should be some sort of structure affecting the convection patterns, there is nothing detectable."

Kirk was beginning to smile for the first time today. "Then we've got a bona fide scientific mystery on our hands. And maybe a clue to what Balok sent us here to find." Kirk turned to the conn. "Mister Sulu, can we drop a probe into the atmosphere without the Dassik noticing?"

"Uh, yes, sir," Sulu said, "but it wouldn't do much good. The winds in the troposphere are intense, well over a hundred meters a second. And one lightning strike at those magnitudes would fry its systems. A probe would have no chance down there."

"Hmm." Kirk pondered. "Then I don't suppose a shuttlecraft would do any better?"

"No, sir."

"So in order to find out what's going on down there . . . it would take something with strong enough engines to fight the winds and strong enough shields to withstand the lightning."

A grin was starting to form on Sulu's face. "The *Enterprise* can handle it, sir."

Scott stepped forward. "Hold on a minute, Captain. My people have put a lot of hard work into getting this girl up and running again after the battle. I'd rather not see it all undone."

"What's the matter, Scotty? Can't the *Enterprise* handle a bit of bad weather?"

The engineer lifted his chin with wounded pride. "Well, of course she can, sir. She's easily got enough power and shielding. The hull repairs are completed, and thruster power is good." Scott was smiling now, eyes lighting up at the challenge. "We could tie in the inertial damping accelerometers to thruster control for smoother wind cancellation . . ."

Kirk grinned. "You go take care of that, Scotty. Dismissed. And have fun."

"That I will, sir!" Scott left the bridge at a run.

"Batten down the hatches, everyone," Kirk ordered. "There's going to be some rough weather." Taking his own advice, he returned to his chair. "Mister Sulu . . . take her down."

———

"Aye, aye, sir!" Hikaru Sulu said, trying to keep his grin to reasonable proportions and failing utterly. He'd taken on a number of piloting challenges in his years at the helm, and he'd become intimately familiar with how the *Enterprise* performed in almost any circumstance—even flying her in a planetary atmosphere once or twice. But he'd never had the chance to explore what this beauty could do in an atmosphere as redoubtable as a Jovian's.

Sulu took her down gently at first, to minimize the risk of detection by the Dassik ships above. He dropped her more quickly through the ionosphere, though, since a prolonged stay would be too disruptive to the sensors and the navigational deflector, and any electromagnetic disturbance caused by the passage would probably blend into the planet's overall radio noise. At this altitude, and for some distance below, the atmosphere was still little more than a dirty vacuum. Yet Sulu was beginning to feel a trace of wind buffeting the ship as he sank her through the stratosphere. It increased as they reached the upper haze layers, which were kilometers deep even in this relatively thin portion.

Once the haze cleared, the cloud belt he was aiming for appeared a rich, vivid blue, tinged here and there with the yellow of sulfur clouds. He steered toward the center of the belt, where the wind speed would be lowest. The *Enterprise* sank through a few dozen more kilometers of clear hydrogen and methane, the sky becoming increasingly blue above them. Sulu was only now really beginning to get a feel for the scale of this world. Soon, in the distance, the elevated zones of water-ice clouds began to rise up to the north and south, enclosing the ship in an immense canyon with walls of brilliant white. As the ship sank past the sulfur clouds, leaving the yellow and green tinges behind, the blue tint below faded as the thickness of atmosphere between them and the lower cloud belt diminished. Now the ship was sinking through dense white clouds of water vapor just like those on Earth, except that these were immensely deeper. Lightning flickered in the distance, and later—sometimes seconds, sometimes minutes later—the thunder from a storm the size of Earth could be heard through the hull over the increasing roar of the atmosphere rushing past. The lightning storms here were more frequent and intense than on Jupiter, thanks to the warmer, wetter atmosphere.

Finally the ship emerged into the clear air below, a hydrogen-methane mix whose pressure at this depth was several times Earth's surface pressure and whose temperature was just right for liquid water. It was raining, the thick overcast reducing visibility, so Uhura set the screen to enhance the light. Through the haze of raindrops—drops that would just keep falling until they evaporated in the hotter depths and rose back up to the clouds—a vast, dark shape was faintly visible. It seemed like another cloudbank, but it couldn't be, not down here. As Spock had said, there should be nothing but bottomless clarity for thousands of kilometers down.

"What's going on here?" Sulu was startled at the sharp exclamation. He hadn't even noticed Doctor McCoy entering the bridge. "Jim, are we where I think we are? What could possibly have possessed you to dive inside a—What in heaven's name is that?"

Sulu's eyes followed McCoy's and everyone else's back to the viewscreen. The immense dark shape was looming closer now—close enough to see light and color within it. It resembled a vast greenhouse dome, but the scale of it was unimaginable. Startled by the collision alarm, Sulu hastily called up the maneuvering controls on his panel and put the ship into a dive. The dark shape rose up in the viewscreen, seeming to take forever, growing ever closer . . . Sulu was convinced they should have hit by now, but he simply wasn't grasping how vast it truly was. What had seemed like individual windows on its surface now resolved into entire massive arrays bigger than the

Enterprise. Finally the path ahead was clear and the ship flew on with a dark, metallic world as its ceiling, with only open sky below.

"Spock, how big is that thing?" Kirk asked after a breathless moment.

"Approximately one thousand, one hundred and eighty kilometers in diameter, sir."

"One thou—Spock, there are moons smaller than that!"

"Indeed. However, this structure is far less massive than a moon of its size. Most of it appears to be hollow."

"Is it . . . floating?" McCoy asked. "Like a blimp?"

Spock shook his head. "Negative. Although the object's construction appears unusually light for its size, spectroscopic readings suggest a standard oxygen-nitrogen atmosphere within. Even at these pressures, the surrounding hydrogen-methane mix is lower in density."

"The ship's handling lighter, sir," Sulu observed. "I think we're flying through the antigrav field that's holding it up."

"I concur," Spock said.

Once the *Enterprise* came out from under its god-sized umbrella, the rain had diminished and the clouds had thinned—or rather, the ship had traveled so far that it had left the bad weather behind. The screen was still enhancing the light, but Sulu was able to see much farther than before. And what he saw were more of the massive shapes—flattened spheroids so huge and distant that it was only possible to make out the vaguest hints of surface detail through the blue haze of atmosphere, like mountains on the horizon. Sulu saw conduits stretching out from the spheroid they had passed beneath, cylinders thicker than the *Enterprise* but seeming as flimsy as spider webs on this scale, stretching in the direction of the other modules but soon diminishing to invisibility. Sulu put the ship into an arc, confirming that the web of moon-sized structures extended as far as the eye could see in all directions. They extended for a fair depth as well, with at least three distinct tiers visible.

Finally the arc brought them around to face the original module again, and Sulu had raised the ship slightly above it to get a clearer look. Indeed, the top of it seemed to be an immense, clear dome, but the vista within was like an entire continent at twilight: towering mountains, broad rivers, dark seas, forests in exotic colors, patches of light that could only be cities. A whole land mass floating inside a Jovian atmosphere.

"Fascinating," Spock said, and he'd never sounded like he meant it so sincerely. "These structures extend as far as sensors can scan. Just the ones I can detect, if their internal arrangement resembles this one, could collectively hold a habitable volume equal to a half-dozen typical M-class planets. And from my earlier observations of the cloud patterns, it may well extend most or all of the way around this planet." He paused for effect. "This one Jovian could contain within it a surface area comparable to half the member worlds of the Federation combined."

"You're kidding," McCoy exclaimed. "All that inside one planet?"

"A Jovian planet has a much greater surface area than a terrestrial one, Doctor. Jupiter's Great Red Spot alone is large enough to hold several Earth-sized worlds. And the habitable surface area of Earth is less than a quarter of the total. Not to mention that these modules may well have multiple layers of habitation, multiplying the effective—"

"Okay. Okay, Spock, I get the point. But it's just so . . . staggering. Are these things inhabited? Dozens of worlds' worth of people all living here? Why?"

"Recall that these structures were undetectable from orbit, Doctor, even though they should by rights have a much more pronounced effect on the planet's circulation and cloud patterns. They must be deliberately obscuring their signature by some means. The logical conclusion is that they are here for concealment."

Kirk stepped forward alongside the helm station, and Sulu could see him stroking his chin. "And we know of a certain civilization that makes a habit of concealment . . . and has a knack for building monumental structures."

"Indeed," Spock replied. "The modules do appear to be arranged in a hexagonal lattice not unlike the domes of an orbship—though on a far more immense scale, of course."

"Then we may have found what we were looking for," Kirk said. "Though we never could've imagined it would be like this. Lieutenant Uhura, open hailing—"

The *Enterprise* trembled as it was dragged to a halt. "Tractor beam," Spock called.

"Everyone stay calm," Kirk said. "We know they're wary of strangers, and we're not here to provoke them. Uhura, hailing frequencies."

"Open, sir."

"This is Captain James T. Kirk of the *U.S.S. Enterprise*, to those responsible for seizing our vessel. If you are af-filiated with the First Federation, please be aware that we carry the ambassador from the United Federation of Planets aboard this vessel. Our mission here is peaceful, and we mean you no harm. Please respond."

The only response was a screeching feedback and a flickering of the lights and console indicators. "Powerful sensor beams," Spock reported. "Scanning every system. Again consistent with the *Fesarius*'s technology."

"You'd think Balok would've called ahead to let them know we were coming," Sulu muttered to Chekov.

"Do you think this is another test?" McCoy asked. "Maybe they want to see if we can break free."

"They have issued no threats, Doctor," Spock replied. "And logically, if they tow us to a containment facility, we shall encounter them in person, which is our goal."

"Bones does have a point, Spock," the captain said. "Balok didn't trust our declarations of our good intentions until we got the upper hand and still didn't become aggressive." He returned to his seat. "Mister Sulu, full impulse. Try to break us free. Mister Chekov, modulate the deflectors."

Sulu poured on all the power he could and every trick he knew, trying to rotate the ship to present the minimum profile to the beam, giving it as little as possible to grab on to. But it made no difference. "It seems to be coming from all directions, sir!" he called over the rising whine of the engines.

"Modulation not working!" Chekov called. "This is not a conventional tractor beam. Some kind of magnetic effect . . . drawing on the planet's own magnetic field. We cannot fight a whole planet, sir!"

"Sulu, stand down," Kirk said. "Let's save our power until we get a chance to use it. Maybe once we get to where they're dragging us, we'll be able to knock out their emitters."

Soon the tractor effect directed them toward a smaller

module than the others, similar in shape but only (only!) a few dozen kilometers across. Unfortunately, there were no specific tractor emitters to target. "The entire web of connecting conduits appears to play a role in generating the field effect," Spock declared. "We cannot compromise enough of the system to free ourselves."

A hatchway opened for them, its six triangular leaves unfolding much like the larger ones within the *Fesarius*'s hull. The ship passed through into a vast, mostly empty hangar. Sulu could make out exotically shaped but recognizable mooring facilities for hundreds of ships, and that was just in the nearer portion of the yawning chamber. But few of the visible docks were occupied. Perhaps they had deliberately brought the *Enterprise* to a place where few other ships would be around?

The ship trembled a bit as the hangar's own tractor beams took over from the external beam. Sulu jumped at the opportunity, firing up all thrusters, but the transition was too smooth, and the new beams were from so close at hand that their pull was just as strong. "Can we target their emitters now?" McCoy asked once Sulu explained this.

"And go where?" Kirk countered. "The hatch is closed. I doubt we could blast our way out without endangering the ship, and if we did, we'd still be at the mercy of the external tractor field. Besides, I'm no longer sure this was meant to be a test. Balok's game gave us a chance to win. This is as unbeatable as the *Kobayashi Maru*."

The doctor chortled. "Says the one man who ever beat it. I thought you didn't believe in no-win scenarios."

"I believe in choosing the right game. Right now, I don't think we'll score any points if we resist them any further. If this isn't a test, then we need to try to put them at ease."

More power fluctuations struck the bridge. "How are we doing so far?" the doctor asked.

"Compensating," Spock said. "But the interference beams are even more powerful than those of the *Fesarius*. They are disrupting our deflector shields."

"Kirk to engineering. Scotty—"

"Detecting a transporter lock on the bridge," Spock interrupted just as sparkles of light began to appear in the air beyond Sulu's helm console.

"Security to the bridge!" Kirk ordered as the guards already present drew their phasers. The swirling points of light coalesced into a boarding party of at least half a dozen burly creatures of various species, not all of them humanoid—but all of them armed.

The rules of engagement when an armed party boarded the bridge were clear: stun first, ask questions later. The guards fired as soon as the confinement beams faded, but the boarding party was already in motion, dodging the beams deftly. The largest one merely stood there, letting the phaser energy bounce off its armored carapace before returning fire and felling one of the guards.

Sulu spun his chair and kicked out at one of the boarders, knocking the gun from his hand. He then pushed to his feet and jabbed at the attacker's face, but the sleekly built, blue-skinned alien dodged the blow and spun, swinging at Sulu with a strong, whipping tail. He blocked it like a high kick, but realized his mistake as soon as he began his follow-up move—a move predicated on the assumption that the opponent was on one leg and unbalanced, which this fellow wasn't. Rather than falling to the deck, the alien grabbed Sulu's arms and flipped him. He came down hard against the bridge rail, banging his head and shoulder on the deck.

Sulu tried to stay conscious and drag himself back to his feet. Through the flashes of light in his vision, he could see Kirk and Spock holding their own in hand-to-hand, with Spock using some impressive Vulcan *Suus Mahna* moves to send one opponent over the rail in front of the science console. But Gabler and the guards were already down, McCoy was covered and offering no resistance, and Chekov fell to an enemy weapon a moment later. The aliens controlled the sole entrance to the bridge, preventing reinforcements from arriving. Kirk and Spock were surrounded, back to back . . .

"Stop!"

The unfamiliar voice drew Sulu's gaze toward an alien he'd missed before: a female, daintier than the others, attractively humanoid but with a sleek, short-furred, elongated head, silvery-gold skin, and enormous, deep blue eyes. She was at once compelling and intimidating, instantly commanding the scene with a single word. All the boarders held their fire, and even the bridge crew fell silent, waiting.

The blue-eyed female strode through the bridge slowly and deliberately, pausing to transfix every conscious member of the crew in her gaze. When her eyes locked on Sulu's, they seemed to fill his vision and he lost track of time . . . of space . . . of himself for an uncertain interval.

Finally, after surveying Kirk, McCoy, and Uhura, her gaze settled on Spock and held there for several moments. "They are not enemies," the female finally told the other boarders. "They are like us—pursued and in need of sanctuary."

She moved in closer to Spock, gazing even more deeply into his eyes. "Especially this one. He has no place he considers a home."

"Madam," Spock said. "If I may ask . . ."

"Do not fear," she told him. "You need not be alone any longer."

Four

"Sensors still detect no sign of the *Enterprise*, Force Leader," Dral reported.

"Keep searching," Grun ordered.

"Sir . . . the ships have searched everywhere. They are nowhere else in the system."

"Then they are below," Grun told his second, gazing out at the pale blue-white orb that taunted him like his father's ruined and sightless eye.

"We have taken optical sightings on the gas planet's orbital space from every angle, with no detections. Force Leader, is it not more likely that the enemy escaped to warp already?"

"Rrah!" Grun flung out a hand, striking Dral across his narrow face. "All your sensors and simulations. A hunter relies on instinct, Dral! You must know your prey!"

He rose and stepped toward the viewscreen. "This Kirk is fierce and devious. Even with his weak and primitive ship, he was able to bloody one of ours and escape our englobement. Such a warrior will not flee from a battle. He lies in wait, plotting some infernal strategy against us."

"Against three cluster ships? More than fifty of our finest hunters? He would have no chance!"

Grun cuffed him again. "*If* we are ready! But if we grow complacent . . . if we trust in instruments and readings, decide he is not here and turn away, exposing our backs to him . . . that is when he will have his chance. We must deny him that chance, do you see, Dral?" He pointed to his two good eyes. "Our hunters already skirt against the territory of this . . . this second Federation. Further confrontations with their Starfleet are inevitable. Even if they are a separate power from the betrayers, they are still allied with them, and so they will oppose us. So we must show them we are strong! We must not yield if we wish the powers of the galaxy to respect us. Therefore, we must remain vigilant, however long it takes. This Kirk is bold, to use a giant world's radiation for cover. But bold fighters are not patient fighters. He will grow tired of hiding, and he will strike rashly, exposing his throat for us to slit!"

Dral bowed. "As you say, Force Leader." But Grun could tell he was not convinced. Dral belonged to what Grun considered an overly intellectual breed of Dassik, too cold, calculating, and cautious to have the hearts of true hunters. Grun despised their type, and Dral had confirmed all his beliefs about them. For all his pretentions of intelligence, his overly analytical mind made him a fool. At least Grun could rest assured that Dral would be too inept to challenge him successfully for control of the pack.

But that would only happen if this mission failed. And Grun was determined to succeed. Patience was the key. The Dassik understood patience. For millennia, his once-mighty people, the former masters of this space, had been stranded and toothless, stripped of the mobility and power that had once been theirs. Yet they had remembered. Through their hate, they had kept their history alive, their tradition and commitment unforgotten. All Dassik remembered there was a galaxy they had conquered through hard struggle and then had stolen from them through an act of treachery—an act that had left their great race imprisoned, humiliated, and abandoned to extinction.

Yet the Dassik would not settle for oblivion. Their dedication to winning back the stars remained, even as the millennia passed. The crucible of their exile had made them more determined, more shrewd, more inventive, until finally they had achieved the power to reclaim their birthright and rebuild the means to reach the stars. Dral and his ilk would say it was their own science that had achieved this, but they would have been useless without the predatory focus and hunger of the ancient Dassik soul. Patience and unyielding commitment had brought them the power to reclaim what they had lost—and to punish those who had stolen it from them.

Yes, Grun understood patience. It was a skill a younger brother needed to master—the ability to watch and wait for one's opportunities. He had been a dutiful junior member of the pack led by his elder brother, Grnar, and though he had seduced his brother's females on many an occasion while Grnar was away in space, he had remained discreet about it, taking his pleasures where he could and making no attempt to challenge Grnar for control. Instead, Grun had waited for Grnar to achieve a heroic death at other hands, then rightfully claimed his brother's holdings and concubines as his own. He had hunted down and slain Grnar's killer with vigor so that none would question his loyalty, but the secret truth was that the alien had done Grun a favor. Grnar had inherited their father's cruelty toward his own blood kin. Half of Grun's scars had been inflicted in his youth before he ever saw combat. Yet he had still triumphed in the end, for he understood how to wait.

Smiling, Grun met the gaze of the giant blue-white eye before him. He knew he would not fail. Kirk would strike soon. He could not have the patience of a Dassik, the patience of a younger brother. He must be getting very bored right now, with nothing to do but wait.

"I am Chief Protector Nisu Miratuli," the golden-skinned female told Kirk once he had identified himself as the commanding officer. "You may address me as Nisu. I apologize for our use of force, but we must always remain vigilant against invaders. Would you do less if you detected an uninvited presence aboard your vessel?"

Kirk studied her. "You have a point, Nisu. But it goes both ways. You weren't invited here. And we didn't try to get inside any of your . . . habitats. We were attempting to hail you when your tractor beam seized us."

Nisu nodded. "These are fair objections. But please understand. We have taken great care to shield our Web of Worlds from outsiders, so the sudden arrival of a vessel in our midst naturally provoked caution." She looked around. "But you may rest assured that your personnel are only stunned." McCoy, never one to take strange aliens at their word when it came to medical matters, was already bending over the fallen personnel to make sure. "And now that I am confident your intentions are not hostile, there need be no further conflict between us."

"I'm glad to hear it. What changed your mind?"

"You're speaking our language," Uhura said, stepping forward to study Nisu more closely. "Captain, the translators aren't engaged. She's speaking English." To Nisu again: "Are you a telepath?"

The alien woman bowed her sleek, furred head. "I am a Kisaja. My people's gifts allow us to bridge gulfs of understanding. I cannot read your inner thoughts without your cooperation, but by your willingness to communicate, you have opened the language centers of your minds to me. Indeed, that is part of what told me you are not invaders."

"A shame you weren't aboard the *Fesarius* three years ago, then," Kirk said. "It might have avoided a good deal of inconvenience."

Nisu seemed discomfited for the first time. "My first responsibility is to this community."

"She's right, Jim," McCoy interposed. "They're heavily stunned, but nothing serious. Without knowing the details of how their stunners work, I'm more comfortable letting them sleep it off than trying to bring them around with stimulants. But I'd like to move them to sickbay for monitoring."

"Of course," Nisu said. Despite her professions of friendship, she still acted as though she was the one in control of the situation—which, admittedly, she was. "My protectors will assist you in the transfer."

"Thanks, but that won't be necessary," McCoy said, not trying very hard to keep the edge out of his voice. Not that it would've made much difference with a telepath, Kirk thought.

But Nisu merely stepped back in acquiescence. "As you wish." Still, she monitored the operation as McCoy's medics arrived to begin the transfer.

Though she seemed well-intentioned, Kirk disliked the ease with which the Kisaja woman and her boarding party had taken the bridge. That had happened too many times on this tour. Kirk resolved to speak with Commander Scott about installing additional bridge defenses. Perhaps some kind of automated phaser module . . . and possibly a secondary entrance, to make it more difficult for intruders to control access to or from the bridge.

Once the doctor had escorted his patients into the lift, Nisu approached Kirk again. "I think we should start over, Captain Kirk. And so I welcome you to the planet Cherela—safe haven for the First Federation."

Kirk gave her a diplomatic smile. "On behalf of the United Federation of Planets, I thank you for your gracious welcome—and for your use of the stun setting."

Nisu's smile grew sardonic. "I can see it will take some time to make amends for this rough beginning. Perfectly reasonable; we of the First understand caution toward strangers."

"But we aren't strangers, Nisu," he told her. "As I said in our initial hail, we carry the United Federation's ambassador to your First Federation."

It was a moment before the Kisaja replied. "Yes, Captain, I am aware of Commander Balok's outreach efforts."

"Balok's efforts," Kirk repeated. "Are you suggesting that he did not have authority to act as he did?"

Another hesitation. "Let us just say that building a relationship must go in stages. We did not expect a circumstance in which your representatives would arrive at Cherela before we deemed the time to be right. Thus, we were not prepared to welcome you. Again, I apologize for the misunderstanding."

He offered a diplomatic smile. "I find that communication is the best antidote to misunderstandings. If we could meet with your leaders and discuss our reasons for being here . . ."

Those vast eyes transfixed him for a brief moment, probing. "Yes . . . I see you have questions that weigh heavily upon you. Cherela has always been a haven for those in need; we cannot turn you away now. I will arrange a meeting."

———

Rather than ask them to entrust their molecules to an alien transporter system, Nisu invited the delegation from the *Enterprise* to take the scenic route, traveling to the nearest full-sized "world module" (as she called it) through the Web's conduit shuttle system. Kirk accepted gladly, leaving Sulu in command of the ship while Scott concentrated on further repairs. He had brought Spock and Bailey with him, along with Uhura, wishing for an interpreter he could rely on, as opposed to one who might have her own motives for selective translation. Security guards Nored and Prescott completed the party. They accompanied the Kisaja and her team aboard the docking station, where most of the armed contingent broke off to return to their duties. Nisu and two other protectors—the blue, tailed male and a reptilian humanoid—led the *Enterprise* party into a cylindrical shuttle that looked more like a flying craft than the subway-type car Kirk was expecting.

Indeed, once they were secured, the craft launched from its berth and flew through the hangar's interior atmosphere until it passed through a permeable force field into the wide conduit beyond, which stretched out ahead to the vanishing point. Once they were within the conduit, the shuttle began accelerating rapidly. If not for its inertial dampers, the occupants would probably have passed out from the g-forces. Overhead, beyond the conduit walls, the clouds could be seen moving past at a rate that was already astonishing and still increasing.

"The conduit interior is a vacuum," Nisu explained. "Its coils magnetically accelerate and guide us. It is an easier, safer way to reach distant world modules than pushing through Cherela's dense atmosphere at hypersonic speeds."

"How do you prevent the exterior pressure from crushing the conduit?" Spock asked.

"There are multiple layers of shielding and structural bracing between this shaft and the outside. The view you see is actually a projection on the inner walls." She gave a faint smile. "As you learned in your encounter with Commander Balok, we are skilled at illusion."

"Why do you use these tubes at all," Kirk asked, "instead of relying on transporters?"

Nisu's smile widened. "We have no shortage of time here in the Web. No need for haste. And the Bogosrin get annoyed when their fellow First don't stop to appreciate the fruit of their labors."

"Bogosrin," Bailey echoed. "I've met some of them before, seen a bit of what they could do. But I never imagined anything on this scale."

"This is their home star system. The Web is the work of millennia, made possible by their skill and their generosity."

Spock raised a brow. "Then the devastated planet in Cherela's Trojan point . . ."

"Was their original home," Nisu affirmed. "But they had grown beyond it before the end came."

"What exactly caused that end?" Kirk asked.

"We will discuss that in time. For now, look ahead."

They had traveled unexpectedly far in mere minutes. Ahead, Kirk could see a world module already nearly filling his forward field of view. Even so, it was still some distance away. At over eleven hundred kilometers across, approaching it was like descending toward the surface of a highly oblate planetoid, except that the upper half was a transparent dome. From this angle, roughly level with the "equator" of the module, he couldn't see much within.

As they closed in on the world module, the shuttle braked hard, so that by the time they passed through the force curtain into the habitat within, they were flying slower than the speed of sound. Now the shuttle's wings extended and it became a true aerial craft. Below them was a vast ocean dotted with craggy islands, each one of which was lush with yellow-green vegetation. Above, the dome provided light, but either the entire surface amplified the faint light from above or its internal light sources were so numerous and distant that they faded into an indistinct glow blending with and brightening the cloudscape beyond. So it was like flying over the surface of a planet, except that it was far more flat, with the ocean seeming to stretch to infinity. On Earth, the horizon was typically around four to five kilometers away for an observer on the ground; here it was more than two hundred times that. He could see the shapes of the habitat's great islands stretching clear to the point where they disappeared into atmospheric haze, much like the world modules outside.

"This module re-creates the pelagic environment of the planet Syletir," Nisu said. "The world modules of the Web re-create environments from many different worlds. This is one that no longer exists as a living planet. The life you see below you is all that survives of Syletir."

Spock raised a brow. "Are there other worlds represented within the Web that no longer survive in the galaxy outside?"

Nisu's gaze held Spock's, unwavering. "Yes. All of them."

"It's some sort of . . . living museum?" Uhura asked.

"No," the chief protector told her. "It is a sanctuary."

The shuttle was now descending toward a sizeable land mass in the center of the module's ocean. They neared a high, hemicylindrical cliff of granite, atop which a city came into view, its high white towers glistening in the light from above. It was one of the most beautiful vistas Kirk had ever seen, and he could understand why the Web dwellers had chosen to show it off to their visitors.

Their destination was a large complex of towers perched vertiginously atop the narrow crag of land at one end of the cliff. The shuttle passed through one more pressure curtain to alight in a hangar within one of the broader, lower towers; the force field was presumably there to protect the interior from the strong winds at this altitude. Once the shuttle had touched down, Kirk rose and followed Nisu and the others to the exit. He felt lighter on his feet, realizing the gravity here was reduced; the shuttle's internal gravity must have adjusted to this module's local gravity so gradually that he hadn't even noticed his weight changing.

Outside the shuttle, several dignitaries stood waiting. Three appeared to hold special prominence, judging from their matching clothing adornments and the way the others held back behind them. Of the three, one was a male Fesarian, tan-skinned and a few centimeters taller than Balok, with bushy black eyebrows. His bald pate was ringed with a golden headdress more elaborate than Balok's captain's circlet and matching his golden robes. Next to him was a member of the blue, tailed species, a female whose short magenta hair came to a sharp widow's peak. She was adorned in a lightweight gold-and-white tunic cut much like a tennis dress, leaving her long, lissome arms and legs exposed. The third dignitary was large and somewhat ursine with slim, conical horns rising vertically from the head. From Bailey's description, Kirk presumed it was a Bogosrin. He wore simpler, more utilitarian attire including a multipouched vest, mostly brown with only a few bits of gold piping.

Nisu stepped between the two parties. "Captain James Kirk, Commander Spock, Lieutenant Nyota Uhura, Lieutenant Anne Nored, and Ensign Louis Prescott of the *United Star Ship Enterprise*, and Ambassador David Bailey of the United Federation of Planets, allow me to introduce the Triumvirate of the First Federation." She introduced the Fesarian male first. "This is Tirak of the Linnik people, the great benefactors of the First." Kirk traded a look with Spock and Bailey. *Linnik*—at last they had a real name for Balok's species. Nisu went on to introduce the large Bogosrin male as Lekur Zan, and the tailed female turned out to be Aranow of the Tessegri species. The others around them were members of the Council of the First, the legislative body comprising representatives from every module. The councillors present were mostly local, from this and adjacent world modules. But the triumvirs were the joint chief executives of the entire Web, beamed here from nearly halfway around Cherela for this meeting.

"It's a privilege," Aranow said to Kirk, "to be a triumvir

now, when newcomers arrive. When they arrive in peace. That hasn't occurred in my lifetime. In the lifetime of anyone here. It's most exciting." She spoke quickly, seeming to outpace her own thoughts, and her tail twitched like that of a hungry house cat. Kirk wondered if it was merely the excitement of the moment or if she was always like this.

"The privilege is ours, Triumvir Aranow," Kirk told her. "What your peoples have built here is . . . well, it's possibly the most incredible find in Federation history. We never dreamed that something this extraordinary, or so many thriving civilizations, existed in First Federation space."

Aranow exchanged a look with the other triumvirs. "We have reasons for our secrecy, Captain," Triumvir Tirak said. Despite his boyish build, the Linnik's attitude and the lines of his patrician face suggested considerable age. "As you should know, having brought the Dassik directly to our doorstep."

Kirk met Tirak's gaze evenly. The Linnik stared back with a poise and solemnity that belied his juvenile features. "With respect, Triumvir, we detected no sign of Dassik pursuit when we traveled to this system. The Dassik were already searching this space, hunting you down. They would have reached this system eventually. And even if they did somehow follow us, I assure you they have no knowledge that . . . *this* . . . is down here," he finished, gesturing all around them.

"You discovered it," Tirak countered.

"But only after descending beneath the magnetic belts," Spock pointed out, "and only thanks to the exceptional sensitivity of our communications officer's hearing." Uhura flashed Spock a smile, which of course he did not acknowledge.

Aranow stepped between Kirk and Tirak, breaking the tension. "We know you had no ill intent," she said. "And you're here now. So we should welcome you."

Lekur Zan nodded. "True. We don't get to show the place off much. You want to continue the tour? There's a lot more to see."

The triumvirs and their Council escort led the *Enterprise* party out of the hangar and across a skywalk that gave them a glorious view of the island continent on their right and the endless ocean on their left. Overhead, a thunderstorm was now raging in Cherela's perpetual clouds, but here under the dome, it was clear and placid. Kirk could see a cloud bank hovering over the distant mountains in the continent's interior, but its flickers of lightning were mere sparks in comparison to the atmospheric turmoil outside. He wondered what the air circulation patterns were like inside a vast, domed habitat like this.

"I take it from your earlier remarks, Triumvir Tirak," Spock said, "that the Dassik are connected to the reasons for your secretive existence?"

"They are the entire cause of it," the elderly Linnik replied. "We, the Tessegri, the Bogosrin, the Kisaja, and others . . . all of us were once their slave races. They spread across this sector, conquering worlds, and they would tolerate no rivals to their power."

"Like us," Aranow said. "My people, the Tessegri, were born to wander. To travel. Seek. Acquire. It took us to the stars. And we met the Bogosrin. They were great builders. Covered their world in vast cities. Built great stations in orbit. Carved them out of asteroids."

"We were older than they were, actually," Lekur Zan said in a low-pitched drawl. "But we hadn't discovered warp drive. We just built our own worlds here."

"And we wanted what they had," Aranow said. "Their technology. Their resources. They were glad to trade. But we got pushy. Greedy. It led to conflict."

"A long war," Lekur put in. "We were winning."

Aranow threw the big triumvir an amused glare. "Both sides were losing. Didn't do anyone any good. Especially when the Dassik came." Her edgy intensity became subdued. "They were more brutal than anything we could imagine. More ruthless. Our wars were play to them."

"But the Linnik came too," Lekur went on. "They were small, timid, easy to overlook, but that gave them freedom to move around and whisper in our ears. They convinced us that to survive, we had to make peace with each other. Once we stood together against the Dassik, we learned that we could accomplish more together than apart."

"Is that why the Dassik refer to you as 'betrayers'?" Spock asked Tirak, who nodded. "That would imply some particular relationship or obligation which they believe you to have violated. And I cannot help but note the similarity of names."

"We were their first slaves," the Linnik triumvir explained. "Their name is from our language. It means 'predator'—a label they embraced with pride. They subordinated my ancestors for centuries, forced them to invent new technologies to help them conquer other worlds. Our 'betrayal' was only that we refused to be the loyal slaves and passive victims they needed us to be."

"They brought us together in resistance," Aranow went

on. "We the travelers, Bogosrin the builders, Kisaja the listeners. And the Linnik behind it all, whispering, guiding, uniting us in hope. Together, we grew stronger. Held our own."

"But the Dassik only grew more ruthless in reaction," Tirak said gravely. "When the Tessegri, the Bogosrin, and their allies proved unyielding, the Dassik formed a terrible resolve to devastate all their worlds. To render the sector lifeless, as an example to all others who would resist. And they would use my people's gifts to do it. We decided we could not stand for this."

"But what could you do?" Bailey asked. "I mean, you could talk to people, foment resistance, but you're so . . ."

"Small? Helpless? Yes . . . Aranow and Lekur are kind, but to our shame, we tolerated the Dassik's predations for far too long before we finally began to resist. We allowed our physical weakness to be an excuse for inaction. Only later did we realize that we had the advantages of intelligence, patience . . . and deviousness. We could plot in secret, work behind the Dassik's backs to build a safe refuge for the peoples they planned to exterminate."

"Cherela," Kirk interpreted.

"Yes," Tirak replied. "By good fortune, the Bogosrin provided the opportunity we needed. A race of skilled engineers and habitat builders, with a Jovian planet close by, sharing their temperate orbit."

"My kind had already built a few outposts here in Cherela's atmosphere," Lekur said. "For research, and just for the challenge. We like challenges." The Bogosrin face couldn't exactly smile, but Kirk saw a gleam in Lekur's eye that he knew very well. He imagined Scotty would hit it off marvelously with this fellow. "But they were primitive and crude next to what you see around you. We needed the genius of the Linnik to design all this, as much as they needed our strength and, let's face it, our location."

"We worked in secret for years," Tirak said, "as the Dassik began their campaign of extermination. The Bogosrin built what we designed, working deep beneath Cherela's clouds—enduring conditions harsher than the rest of us could survive to create new homes where we could all thrive. The Tessegri organized escape routes for refugees and smuggled them here unseen. The Kisaja used their mental gifts to pass information to the resistance and to obscure the Dassik's perception of our efforts."

"We saved as many as we could," Lekur rumbled. "But far too few." The big Bogosrin shrugged. "We'd only built a few world modules when the Dassik finally swarmed through this system, blew up everything else we'd built, and bombed our homeworld to rubble."

"We . . . saw that," Kirk said. "We're very sorry."

Lekur waved it off. "Long time ago. It was just one of our homes anyway, by that time. And just one of the countless homes the Dassik wiped out. Once they'd left the system, we went right to work mining the moons and asteroids to build more modules, bigger ones, for the rest of the refugees. Giving them a place they could hide, a place they'd be safe from the Dassik."

"And the rest of us were grateful for it," Nisu said. "Because the Dassik would not rest until all the civilizations in our alliance were exterminated. In their minds, our tolerance, our inclusiveness, was an abomination. To them, it was the natural order of things that all species should battle to dominate or destroy one another."

"That's why we thought they were gone," Aranow said.

"After we were wiped out—or they thought we were—they turned on each other. We picked up signals. Lots of fighting. Lots of fighting for a long time. Generations. Then less and less, then nothing. We thought they all killed each other off. Or weakened each other, until someone else could finish them off."

"So in time," Tirak said, "we felt safe to travel in space again. We turned the ships and weapons they left behind into tools for our own defense. Even the Dassik's own fearsome reputation came to serve us, a face we could present to outsiders to frighten off those who meant us harm. In these ways, we were able to reclaim the territory the Dassik had taken from us."

"A territory full of dead worlds," Bailey replied. "What is there left to defend?"

"Our birthright," the Linnik triumvir replied with intensity in his rough tenor voice. "Others may have come to take this territory, but it was ours to begin with. We were the first peoples in this space. The purpose of our great alliance is to preserve that legacy—a Federation of the First."

Kirk and the others traded a look. At least that was one minor mystery solved. It seemed natural enough that a displaced people would cling to their territorial birthright as a symbol of identity.

"And yet you remain here," Kirk said as the skywalk ended and they passed into the next tower. "Hidden inside this gas giant. If the threat is gone, why haven't you come out into the galaxy? Repopulated your territory?"

"Too many of our old worlds are still too poisoned, too damaged, to be livable for millennia to come," Lekur said. "That was how thorough the Dassik were."

"And there are other threats," Aranow said. "Other powers came in. Other wars were waged. Kalandans. Shenchorig. Promellians."

"And other refugees fleeing from their wars," said Nisu. "The First Federation could offer them something they could find nowhere else in the galaxy: sanctuary. Invisibility."

Lekur led them into a large chamber containing a holographic display of the entire Web of Worlds, which indeed spanned the entire girth of Cherela and a significant distance north and south of the equator. The individual world modules, artificial habitats the size of continents, were tiny circles in the display. Lekur manipulated the control column beneath the projection, bringing up magnified views. He selected one specific inset image, and the entire chamber around them transformed to match, immersing them in a realistic simulation of the environment. In this way, Lekur proudly showed off many of the Web's terrains one after the other: a majestic forest of red-leafed trees that dwarfed Earth's sequoias; a broad grassy plain so flat and wide it made Iowa seem hilly; a sulfurous, volcanic landscape where it seemed nothing could live, but where cities of obsidian spires could be seen; a hollow module that was nothing but open sky and kilometers-high towers with large winged aliens flying among them. "Whatever your world is like, we can build it for you. Repopulate it with samples of your native flora and fauna. We have thousands of species here that are extinct elsewhere in the galaxy. Many of our modules aren't even populated—they're purely nature preserves. Safe from the dangers of the galaxy beyond."

"What about the dangers of being inside a Jovian atmosphere?" Kirk asked. "Those winds and lightning storms are nothing to sneeze at. And holding all these worldlets up with antigravs—what if something goes wrong?"

"Don't underestimate the brilliance of Linnik design," Tirak said proudly, "especially when supplemented with the knowledge of dozens of other civilizations. The Web is a perfect homeostatic system—self-sustaining, self-repairing, drawing on the planet's own magnetic field for its power."

"That's right," Lekur said, shutting down the holographic environment projection and returning the chamber to its normal appearance, with the schematic of Cherela once again hovering in its center. "Every module has its own independent levitation and life-support systems. And even if one were to fail, it could draw on the others around it. As for the wind and lightning, we draw on those for power too. They make us stronger, not weaker."

"And yet all this remains virtually undetectable from orbit," Spock said. "Your thermal and magnetic signature is masked, your signal leakage all but nonexistent, and your influence on the planet's circulation patterns is suppressed."

The Bogosrin nodded. "All part of the camouflage. Everything's balanced, nothing wasted. We live in harmony with Cherela, and she hides us in return."

"But you're not completely invisible," Uhura said. "We picked up signal leakage from orbit. We noticed that the cloud patterns were off. That's how we found you."

Lekur made an uneasy grumbling noise in his throat. "Yes, we have some minor fluctuations occasionally. Once in a generation, really. Only to be expected in a system that's twelve thousand years old. We swap out all the parts, of course, keep everything new, but sometimes we lag behind a bit. It's sheer chance you were here when it happened. And as you pointed out, you'd never have heard the signal leakage if you hadn't been orbiting so close." He turned to Kirk. "Not very sane to go for a bath in that radiation soup."

"We didn't exactly have a lot of options," the captain replied.

"Yes," Tirak said. "The Dassik. We are all fortunate that they have not yet followed you down."

"Our camouflage has held for twelve millennia," Lekur countered. "It won't fail us now."

"There," Aranow said. "You can see the value of being hidden here."

"For a little while, maybe," Kirk said. "But for twelve thousand years? Don't you ever feel that old Tessegri wanderlust? Want to go out into the galaxy and explore?"

Aranow shrugged. "Why should I? There are hundreds of worlds to explore here. More than a lifetime's worth to get to know. There are still modules I've never been to."

It seemed to Kirk that she answered a bit defensively, as if trying to convince herself as much as him. "But what about new places? New peoples?"

"Our cultures grow and evolve over time, as any do," Tirak said. He gestured to encompass the module they occupied. "Visit Syletir in a hundred years and it will not be the Syletir it is today." Aranow nodded, seeming reassured.

"And we do occasionally gain new members," Nisu said, stepping forward. "Refugees from lost worlds. Sometimes they make their way here . . . sometimes we seek them out."

"Is that part of the function of the orbships?" Spock asked.

"Yes," Nisu replied. "To seek those in need of our help, or those who might help us. The more friends we have on our borders, the safer we are from invasion."

"But you don't trust your friends enough to invite them home," Bailey commented.

Tirak responded in kind to the edge in the lieutenant's voice. "Trust must be earned, Lieutenant. And that takes time. Our relations with your Federation of Planets are still tentative. Normally we do not invite alien ambassadors into our space as . . . readily . . . as Balok did."

Kirk studied him. "You sound as though you disapprove of his action."

The Linnik gave a calculated smile. "That is between Balok and us, and he has not yet seen fit to return to Cherela."

"He was under Dassik pursuit," Bailey reminded the triumvir. "I'm sure he wouldn't want to risk leading them here."

"Unless he has already done so."

"A moment ago, you were accusing us of doing so."

Tirak maintained his mask of diplomacy, though Kirk could sense the effort it took. "I grant that we cannot yet be sure who is responsible. But understand: We must guard our borders carefully. The galaxy beyond is full of threats. Now that the Dassik are back, attacking our ships and our people, we must be more cautious than ever."

"The Dassik are attacking other ships and peoples as well, Triumvir," Kirk pointed out. "They pose a potential threat to our Federation and its allies. So we have a mutual interest."

"That is true," Nisu pointed out. "You have fought the Dassik and seen the aftermath of their attacks on others. We have received the *Fesarius* crew's report on their battle, but it could be of value to study your records of the attacks. We might learn something of use in defending against them."

Kirk considered. "Under our present circumstances, an exchange of information about the Dassik seems like a good idea. Triumvirs, may I suggest we all adjourn to the *Enterprise* to review its logs? Perhaps share a meal while we're at it? Now that you've extended us the hospitality of showing us your Web of Worlds, I'd be happy to return the favor and show you my ship."

"Yes!" Aranow cried, then caught herself and went on, only slightly more subdued. "I think that would be lovely. Don't you, Zan? Tirak?"

"I'm always interested in new technology," Lekur said.

Tirak was slower to respond. "Very well," he finally agreed. "Aside from the intelligence on the Dassik, it is only appropriate to acquaint ourselves with our guests. After all . . . you may be here for some time."

Five

Nisu insisted on accompanying the triumvirs on their tour of the *Enterprise*. Although she could sense that Kirk and his crew meant them no harm, it was still her obligation to protect them. And she had to admit there was a certain appeal to seeing a place that was new not only to her, but to everyone else on Cherela. To be sure, there were members of the First who traveled beyond Cherela's clouds in orbships to visit the First Federation's various research outposts, mining stations, and the like; but those places still used the familiar designs of Linnik-Bogosrin technology, and contact with outsiders was kept to a minimum for fear of exposure. As a rule, the First preferred to remain on Cherela, where the life and culture of their worlds survived. The sight of the battered, barren worlds they had once called home was too depressing. Nisu had never even considered leaving Cherela; the barrenness of the void was too disturbing for one like her, who thrived on her connection to living minds. So the opportunity to visit an alien starship that had come to the Web was rare and intriguing.

Triumvir Aranow relished the experience the most, devouring the sights and sounds and smells of the *Enterprise*, its stark, angular chambers and corridors with their vivid colors and minimalist design sense, and its crew with their bright, crisp uniforms—although she wondered aloud why the males insisted on covering their legs in those drab, restrictive black garments rather than freeing them for easy movement like the females did. She also pressed Kirk eagerly for the details of his many adventures and discoveries, though her excited chatter made it difficult for him to get a word in.

For his part, Triumvir Lekur was most interested in the ship and its technologies, and he bonded right away with Engineer Scott, who proudly showed off the *Enterprise* as though he'd designed her himself. Tirak, however, was less impressed, noting the inferiority of most of Starfleet's technologies—except for their weapons, whose effectiveness was clearly demonstrated in the data from the ship's battles with the Dassik. The triumvir pointed out that the First Federation had not needed to advance its weapons technology greatly because it usually avoided combat. Kirk insisted that his people's weapons were meant for defense only, reminding Tirak that a civilization that did not rely on concealment needed other means to protect its people. Tirak had other concerns about the treatment of the United Federation's citizenry, though, questioning the predominance of humans and males in the ship's crew complement, particularly in its command echelons. Kirk explained it as mere happenstance, referring to sister vessels with more diverse command crews, but conceded that there was room for improvement. Nisu could sense his sincerity, and she appreciated his ability to admit imperfections in himself and his people. But Tirak was clearly unconvinced.

Once the triumvirs and Nisu had beamed back to the regional governmental headquarters, Aranow attempted to soften Tirak's resistance. "I like them. They'd make a good addition to the community."

"Hmm," Lekur mused. "Do you think they'll want

their own world module? Not quite enough of them to justify it, but we could make a small one."

"You would have them live among us?" Tirak challenged.

"The Web has welcomed refugees for millennia," Aranow reminded him.

"Those we have vetted carefully. Those we have invited, in the knowledge that they posed no threat. These are armed interlopers who have brought the violence of the outer galaxy to our doorstep. Who may have brought the *Dassik* to our doorstep. How can we trust them? If they are to remain at all, they must remain sequestered."

"*If* they stay," Nisu reminded him. "Pardon my interruption, Triumvir, but surely the matter has not been decided yet."

"That's right," Aranow said.

"Well, we can't let the galaxy know about the Web," Lekur countered.

"They can be trusted," Aranow told her Bogosrin counterpart. "Remember what Kirk said? The Prime Directive? Noninterference. We can ask them to respect our secret. And they will."

Tirak shook his head. "While I am uneasy with letting them remain, I fear releasing them even more. You saw how much pride they take in being explorers, how they boasted of their discoveries. The Web is surely the greatest discovery they have ever made. I do not trust them to keep our secret."

Aranow's tail twitched. "Would that be so bad? To be known? To be able to travel? See the galaxy?"

Lekur put a massive hand on her back. "Our ancestors saw the galaxy, Ara. It saw them back. And it hunted them down and devoured them." He turned her to face him, his powerful, clawed digits handling her bare blue shoulders as delicately as they would his most sensitive tools. The laconic Bogosrin, a sturdy, dependable member of the Triumvirate for over a dozen election cycles, had taken to the much younger Tessegri like a daughter. Or perhaps more like a son. Bogosrin females were significantly bigger and sturdier than their males, so massive that they generally had to walk on all fours. They considered it an insult to be treated delicately. "Besides, what do they have out there that we can't build better in here?"

Aranow looked up at him, her eyes wistful. "The stars."

"Pah. A star's just a Jovian that ate too much hydrogen and got a mighty case of heartburn." His words evoked laughter from Aranow.

But Nisu could still sense her uncertainty about compelling the *Enterprise* crew to remain. "There is another concern, Triumvir Aranow," the chief protector said. "The Dassik. They will not give up easily. If we allow Kirk and his crew to leave, we could be sending them to their doom."

"Worse," Tirak added, "the Dassik may capture and question them, forcing them to reveal our existence. Then we would surely be conquered, and all that we have built would be destroyed." Nisu fidgeted, uneasy that Tirak made it seem they spoke as one. He had been her mentor once, taking her under his wing and keeping her with him as he rose through the Council to the Triumvirate. At first, she had been honored, revering Tirak as a member of the species who had saved her own people and so many others from extinction. It had blinded her for far too long to his ambition, to his willingness to manipulate others for his own advantage. She had done her best to separate herself from him, to learn to think for herself, and she did not enjoy the fact that he still regarded her as an automatic ally.

"That reminds me," Lekur growled. "I've got to get back to riding herd on those repair crews. Letting the atmosphere regulation break down at a time like this . . . sheer incompetence." Lekur Zan was normally the most easygoing of individuals, except when shoddy engineering was involved.

Aranow clutched his hand, though she had nowhere near the strength to hold it if Lekur didn't let her. "Come on, Zan. You're a politician, not a builder. All these cycles, you still forget."

"Hey. I'm a builder to the core. I just build policy these days. And now I need to go build terror in the hearts of the repair crews so we can get rid of those anomalies in the clouds. Lazy mother-clingers, should've gotten a simple circulation problem fixed by now." He rumbled deep in his throat, and Nisu could feel the floor vibrate under her feet. "I just hope these new Dassik are as stupid as the old ones were."

Nisu met his gaze, projecting reassurance. "Do not worry, Triumvir. We are not defenseless, and we have had twelve thousand years to prepare. If they descend here, we can make them just as helpless as we made the *Enterprise*. If need be, we can tear their ships apart."

Lekur was reassured, but Aranow was not. She studied Nisu carefully. "Will we do the same to the *Enterprise*? If Kirk refuses to stay?"

"Not while they are aboard it," Nisu told her. "Believe me, I want them as friends as much as you do."

Aranow bit her lip. "I suppose. Still, I'd feel bad for Spock. The only one of his kind among us."

Nisu winced at her words. She had felt Spock's deep loneliness on the starship's bridge—his sense of belonging nowhere, of being torn between two worlds. Beneath his surface layer of reason and control, she had sensed deep pain, doubt, and a lack of hope for the future. It had been Spock's outcast state that had touched her heart and persuaded her that the intruders deserved compassion rather than hostility. Nisu had lost her own parents when she was young, casualties in a freak storm that had torn apart an old, under-maintained conduit while their shuttle had flown through it. That loss had broken her out of her complacency and led her to devote her life to guarding against threats from within and without. But that vigilance had done little to assuage her own loneliness, the same loneliness that had left her vulnerable to Tirak's manipulation. Spock was a kindred spirit, and it saddened her to think of condemning him to a life even more solitary than her own.

Tirak, typically, showed no such concern. "We must consider our own community foremost, Aranow. We are the First, the rightful occupants and defenders of this space. Countless lives depend on our ability to protect them from external threats."

"The *Enterprise* is not a threat," Aranow insisted.

The elder Linnik gazed up at her. "That assumption is a threat in itself, Triumvir."

"So what are you saying? You don't want them to leave. You don't want them to stay. What else is there?"

Tirak kept his own counsel. But Nisu did not like what she sensed beneath his silence.

The Web of Worlds kept forcing Jim Kirk to reevaluate his sense of scale.

When Kirk had come to the Tessegri world module at Triumvir Aranow's invitation, it had initially appeared to him through its overhead dome as an expansive cityscape surrounding a large interior green space, like a more circular version of Manhattan Island with a disproportionately large Central Park. But he had forgotten that the module was over a thousand kilometers across. Once Aranow had met him and begun to show him around, he'd realized that every structure he'd seen as a building was in fact an entire arcology, an enclosed, ziggurat-shaped city unto itself. Even the narrowest "alley" between arcologies was an open tract wider than Central Park, largely greened over but crosshatched with numerous broad, tree-lined boulevards and overhead light-rail tracks. It wouldn't be an insult to call the Tessegri a pedestrian people; the boulevards were filled with sleek, long-limbed, tailed bodies in various shades of blue, eschewing the light rail and aircars favored by the other First species in the crowd and simply running or jogging toward their destinations, or merely moving for its own sake. As a rule, they wore little, for their constant exertion kept them warm; Aranow's limb-baring, semibackless tunic was comparatively modest. The boulevard where Kirk and Aranow jogged now was more like a skywalk writ large; visible in the distance, some of the tracts between argosies formed immense, gently sloping ramps descending to lower levels of this three-dimensional megalopolis. But the glimpses of the lower levels that he could see in the distance showed that they were not dark or gloomy; the arcologies and boulevards were designed to admit abundant light into the spaces below, often by reflecting it off the arcologies' great windows.

Even the arcologies' interiors were well lit and high vaulted, with trees and small parks within them. They were also quite roomy, allowing the Tessegri plenty of space to move around. This was fortunate, since there were plenty of Linnik ambling around as well in their metallic robes of various hues, and Kirk suspected that a lot of them would get tripped over if they didn't have plenty of room to give the racing Tessegri a wide berth. For his own part, Kirk had trouble keeping up with Aranow as she led him into one of the largest arcologies and up a wide, spiraling ramp to the top, kilometers above. Thankfully, even the Tessegri had limits to their energy; the gravity in the ramp shaft was reduced to a fraction of normal, making the ascent fairly easy. A turbolift would have been simpler, but Tessegri liked to move.

Still, Kirk was panting when he finally caught up with Aranow on the roof of the arcology. "Too much . . . time sitting . . . in the big chair," he told her with a strained grin once he was close enough that the strong winds up here wouldn't steal his words away. "Though don't . . . tell Doctor McCoy . . . I admitted that. Whatever . . . you brought me here for . . . it had better be—"

He broke off, rendered speechless as he finally saw what was beyond Aranow, beyond the edge of the roof. This arcology was one of the higher ones in the inner portion of the megalopolis, and it afforded a clear view of the enormous savanna within its confines. Again his mind had trouble adjusting to a view without a horizon. "It's a lot like where we evolved," Aranow said. "The Tessegri. Except without the predators. We keep those in another module. Not really authentic this way," she added with a shrug. "But we like a place to move around free. Without getting eaten."

Kirk nodded. "Always a plus."

"Not like you can do, though. Out there. Space. Now that's openness. That's freedom."

He smiled. "I thought so. When you said you were happy just to explore the Web . . . I got the feeling that was just what a triumvir is supposed to say."

"Oh, no. I'm happy here. So many modules I haven't been to yet. Long time before I visit them all." Her tail swished behind her, unsettling the skirt flaps on either side of the vertical slit that accommodated it. "But sometimes I wonder . . . what then?" She looked upward, and Kirk followed her gaze. The clouds had broken above the dome, and though the thick white haze above still diffused the sunlight (while shielding them from outside eyes and sensors), there were enough kilometers of methane intervening to tinge the sky bright blue.

"There are always the orbships," Kirk said.

"They build them too small," Aranow replied. "Inside, I mean. I know they're huge outside. Of course they're huge outside. But I mean the rooms. Halls. A few roomy parts—not enough. You know, you've been on one." He nodded. "Besides, they just patrol the borders. Mine the asteroids. The ruins. Places we know. Not very interesting. Sad, but not interesting." She sighed, still gazing up at—and through—the Jovian sky. "Sometimes I think . . . it might be nice to see something . . . something no First has ever seen. Not just me. Anybody."

"I know the feeling," Kirk said.

Aranow lowered her gaze again. "Just a fantasy. It's dangerous out there. We can't draw attention—not just for us, but for the others. The younger cultures. Refugees. We have to protect them." Kirk nodded. "And we have all we need in here. Plenty of space. Plenty of room to move. Look around! Huge! Lots of hugeness. Silly to feel cramped."

He turned to study her. "So if you like to move around so much, why take a job as a triumvir?"

"Oh, we travel. The Web doesn't have a single capital. We move seasonally. The Council. Region to region. Every region gets its turn." She shrugged. "Not every species likes to move around. Better we come to them."

"Don't tell me—that was the Tessegri's idea."

"And the Kisaja's. They figured it was more equal. If nobody was more central. And the Bogosrin's. It let them build more capitol buildings. And the Linnik's. It fits the way they organize in cells." Aranow grinned. "Synergy. The way of the Web."

"Hmm, I guess you've been together so many millennia that it comes naturally to you. We younger races have to work at it more."

"Oh, don't misunderstand—we argue plenty. Any family does. When you're really close, it's okay." She paused, seeming uneasy about something. "And it's not like Tessegri all agree. We argue among ourselves. All the species do." She looked at him. "And humans? Do you all get along?"

"Not at all. We disagree about a great many things—both among ourselves and with other Federation members. But we've learned to respect each other's right to disagree, and not to deny others' value simply because they don't share our views."

"We try to do the same," Aranow said. "But sometimes . . ."

Kirk frowned. "Aranow, is something wrong?"

"Wrong?" She laughed. "Of course not. Everything's fine. Hey, come on!" Suddenly she was running off, waving at him to follow. "I'll show you the lower levels! Best restaurants in the module!"

The captain hesitated a moment more, then shrugged it off and ran after her. Aranow's bright mood was infectious, and he felt renewed confidence that everything would work out all right. He studied her sleek form as she raced ahead of him. Her shape was different from a human's, especially in the legs and elongated feet, but not that different. Underneath that tail was a pretty fine—

Down, boy. She's a planetary leader. Matters are complicated enough without an interstellar incident. Now is not the time.

He picked up his pace to catch up with her. He wanted to avoid that particular view, and he had a lot of energy to burn off. But she laughed and pulled ahead effortlessly again. This time, what lingered in his mind was her smile.

Ne-Kewii watched through the groundcar's windows as Triumvir Aranow raced ahead of the outsider captain. She fidgeted, ruffling the feathers of her silver wings as best she could in the tight space. "He's isolated," she said. "We should move in."

"No," Kasan Tor rumbled, his deep Bogosrin voice resonating through the car's spherical frame. "Aranow is too close. In more ways than one, it looks like." He growled. "The triumvirs didn't waste any time getting their hooks into these outsiders. There'll be no getting to them now."

"Don't be so sure," Ne-Kewii said. "Aranow's not like the others. She's new, not as set in her ways. Maybe we could get to her, given the chance. And maybe these outsiders are the way to do it." She kept watching the captain. His species didn't look so different from Linnik, just bigger and more angular. They weren't nearly as frightening as a Dassik, say. "If there's any chance, we have to act soon, Tor. You think security around the triumvirs will be this lax once the dying begins?"

"It's not like there's a set timetable for this thing," Kasan told her.

"Exactly. It could start tomorrow for all we know. We need their ship, Tor. With or without their cooperation."

"If they're in with the triumvirs, it'll have to be without."

"Is that a good idea? Would we even be able to fly their ship?"

Kasan straightened, wincing in annoyance as his horns bumped into the roof of the car. "We might have to," he said. "If they don't go along, they'll have to stay behind and die with everyone else."

Six

Nyota Uhura was grateful that Spock had offered her the chance to accompany him and Nisu on their tour of the Kisaja world module. She had the sense that the first officer had invited her as much as a chaperone as anything else, given Nisu's obvious interest in him. But that was between the two of them, and Uhura could hardly blame the Kisaja protector for her fascination with Spock. As for herself, the communications officer welcomed the opportunity to observe the Kisaja people in large groups and learn something of how they balanced verbal and telepathic communication.

The Kisaja habitat was dimly lit, mimicking the light of the cool red dwarf under which they had evolved. The low lighting helped explain their oversized eyes. But it was a warm and comfortable environment, dominated by a single vast sea that served as a heat sink. The Kisaja habitations were concentrated on the shorelines of the many artificial islands and fjords that had been sculpted into the world module's synthetic bedrock. A gregarious people, the Kisaja lived in close quarters by choice and freely shared their community with Linnik, Tessegri, and others. The architecture was closely packed but airy and spacious, with abundant walls of glass or transparent aluminum to give the Kisaja as many open sightlines to one another as possible, facilitating their gaze communication. Some areas were partitioned and hidden to allow for privacy when it was desired—though it was clear that what the Kisaja considered private differed from the human or Vulcan norm. The many swimmer-filled shorelines and floor-to-ceiling windows left no doubt that, as with many species that could see into one another's minds, the Kisaja saw little need to hide their bodies from one another. If anything, it seemed to Uhura, modesty in a Kisaja was expressed more by averting one's own eyes, in order to conceal what was beneath the surface, than by wishing others to avert theirs from what was on the surface.

But it was nothing Uhura hadn't seen before, allowing for slight variances in humanoid anatomy, and she soon found herself more intrigued by what she heard than by what she saw. Though the city's occupants routinely locked eyes with one another as they passed, on many occasions they stopped to exchange words as well—fragmentary conversations to human ears, seeming to start in the middle and leaving out much that had presumably passed unsaid, but still fully and fluently verbal. "Why do the Kisaja retain the ability to speak at all," she asked Nisu, "given how easily you commune telepathically?"

The golden-skinned security chief smiled at Uhura, though taking care to keep the direct gaze of her huge blue eyes to a minimum. "For one thing, to attract the attention of someone looking the other way," she replied with a shrug, pointing out the obvious without judgment or condescension. "Or to call over a distance or around corners, when line of sight is not available. But it is more than that, of course. The spoken word is more . . . linear, more specific, than what we share telepathically. Gaze communication can be approximated in words. If, for instance, I wished to tell you in English what another Kisaja had conveyed to me through a glance, I could offer a reasonable approximation. But there would be differences in detail, in emphasis; and many nuances and abstractions would be left out."

"Like how the music and performance of a song can communicate things the lyrics can't," Uhura interpreted.

"An excellent analogy," Nisu said. "You can find meaning in each independently of the other . . . but the song is not complete unless they are both present."

The tour was a heady experience, and Uhura was both disappointed and relieved when the trio returned to the conduit car that had brought them here. Once they had entered the conduit and accelerated away from Kisaja, Spock addressed their escort. "I am curious, Nisu. We have seen the modules re-creating the homes of the Tessegri, Bogosrin, Kisaja, and other First Federation member worlds, as well as nature preserve modules like Syletir. Yet though we see Linnik among the inhabitants of every module, they seem to have no module representing their own homeworld. Why is this?"

Nisu paused before replying. "The Linnik rarely discuss their origin world. They were already Dassik slaves when the rest of us met them. I suppose theirs was the first world the Dassik destroyed." She brightened. "But they are an adaptable people, as one would expect from such great intellects. They have made the entire Web of Worlds their home. They reside in the subterranean complexes of numerous habitat modules, where they can monitor their functions and keep them maintained. There is a Linnik warren not far from here, underneath the Altecla nature preserve. Would you like to see it?"

"I would indeed," Spock affirmed. Uhura nodded as

well. As much as her head danced with Kisaja linguistics and semantics, the chance to learn more about Balok's secretive people was irresistible.

Nisu flew them on a complex course through the conduits until they emerged within a module terraformed as a vast desert. She angled the craft toward a small cluster of domelike buildings not far from the module's rim. Once they had landed in a hangar dome, the Kisaja led the *Enterprise* officers underground into a warren of low-ceilinged tunnels and chambers, the spaces delineated by latticed dividers and curtains in the Linnik style. Uhura heard the sounds of children at play, and soon they emerged into a large rounded chamber with play sets and a padded floor, where several juvenile Linnik were playing. One was chasing the others around, wearing some sort of mask and making snarling noises that were almost obscured by the high-pitched shrieks and giggles of the rest. Adult Linnik looked like hairless children to begin with, so their children were astonishingly tiny, like newborns that could run and talk and laugh. Uhura found them unbearably adorable.

Their reaction to the new arrivals was not reciprocal, though. The children's flight led them nearly to Spock's feet, and they looked up at him, shrieked, and scattered, crying, "A Dassik! A Dassik!" The pursuing child dropped his mask and joined their flight—and Uhura could see now that it was skull-like, narrow, and sallow-featured, a stylized representation of a Dassik face. She quashed an inappropriate burst of humor at the thought that she could understand how the children had mistaken Spock for one of them.

The children rushed over to a triad of adult Linnik,

two male and one female, who had been supervising their play. While the males comforted the children, the female strode forward to confront the newcomers belligerently, even though she was no bigger than a human five-year-old. "What is the meaning of this? How dare you come in here and scare the children?"

"There is no need for concern, Caregiver," Nisu assured her. "These are visitors from the starship of the—"

"I know who they are," the caregiver said. "Outsiders. Fighters. Bringing the Dassik and their savagery to our skies. Stay back, children!" she warned, though the children were moving forward again, gazing up at Spock and Uhura with open curiosity now that the fantasy terror of being chased had dissipated. Nyota smiled at one tiny girl who smiled back with a gap-toothed grin. But the caregiver threw herself in front of the child and gave Uhura the stink eye. "Don't bare your teeth at them, you predator!"

"Caregiver!" Nisu cried. "That is uncalled for. These people are victims of the Dassik's violence. Their worlds, their ships are in jeopardy. They came to our space seeking answers and were forced to hide here from a Dassik task force. They are on Cherela for refuge and assistance, the very things we exist to provide. Your lack of welcome is shameful."

The caregiver was chastened, glancing at the children as if considering the example she was setting for them. "My apologies, Protector." She turned more grudgingly to Spock and Uhura. "And to you as well. Of course all who seek refuge are welcome here," she recited as if by rote.

Nonetheless, she made excuses that the children's playtime was over, herding them away over their groaning objections. As with children everywhere, their curiosity outweighed their fear when given the chance. Unfortunately, as the caregiver's behavior reminded Uhura, the same was not always true of adults.

"Perhaps," Nisu said to the Starfleet officers, "it was unwise to come here without notice. You must forgive our people; it has been quite a shock to discover that the Dassik are no longer a harmless relic of our past." She glanced down at the mask that still lay abandoned on the playground. "It has reawakened certain . . . old habits of thought. Our way is welcoming, though. I am sure our people will remember that."

"Indeed," Spock said. "However, perhaps you are correct that an unscheduled visit is needlessly disruptive. It is not our wish to create any discomfort for your people. Let us return to the aircar."

Uhura was disappointed that Spock had given up so easily, but as they walked back to the aircar, the first officer began to question Nisu. "This event has reminded me that there are certain anomalous aspects in your people's account of the Dassik's history. I am hopeful that you can provide clarification."

Nisu hesitated, and the lieutenant began to understand why Spock had felt it best to continue this conversation alone rather than in the presence of a crowd of Linnik. "What do you mean?" the Kisaja finally asked.

"Your people apparently have no explanation for how the Dassik disappeared twelve thousand years ago."

"We assumed they had simply wiped one another out. Turned on their own kind when their other prey was exhausted."

"That assumption is clearly not reconcilable with their

continued survival today. Which raises the questions of how they survived and why they did not resume their aggression until now."

"Those are questions we cannot answer."

"Which is itself an anomaly. The First Federation has controlled this region of space for millennia, patrolling its borders, mining its systems, and constructing scientific outposts. And yet, in all that time, you never discovered either an explanation for the Dassik's disappearance or any evidence that they continued to exist?"

Nisu was quiet for a time. "Perhaps," she finally said, "there were some questions we were too afraid to ask."

Once they reached the conduit car, Nisu spoke again. "Before we leave Altecla, Spock, there is something I would like to show you out in the desert. It is a matter of scientific interest that I think will intrigue you." She glanced at Uhura. "You need not accompany us, Lieutenant. I sense your fatigue and your desire to digest and organize the observations you have made today. Let me arrange to have you beamed back to the *Enterprise*."

Uhura could not dispute her insights, but she still glanced back and forth between Nisu and Spock. Could he handle this woman without a chaperone? "If you think that would be all right, Commander?"

Nisu turned to Spock as well . . . and she did not look away. Neither did he. After several moments, he turned back to Uhura. "Yes, Lieutenant, thank you. You may return to the *Enterprise*. I shall follow presently."

Uhura held his gaze for a moment, wishing it could do as much good for her as for a Kisaja. "All right, sir," she finally said. "Thank you." *You're a big boy. And it's none of my business . . .*

Twenty minutes later, Spock and Nisu stood atop a rocky crag overlooking a broad, flat expanse of desert terrain. Overhead, a thunderstorm bigger than the Earth poured torrents of rain upon the dome, surrounding them with a waterfall sky. But here inside Altecla, it was scorching hot and the air stole the moisture from their skin.

The loose white attire Nisu had donned for their visit to Kisaja was suitable for this occasion as well, but Spock was in full uniform and experienced no discomfort. Altecla's climate was much like the one in which his species had evolved. If anything, these were the most agreeable conditions he had experienced in months.

The view down below was as extraordinary in its own way as that above. Approximately one hundred meters away, a creature like a cross between a sidewinder snake and a giant millipede was undulating across the hard ground at some speed, twisting its body so that only a few of its feet touched the burning surface at any moment. Through the binocular sensor device Nisu had provided, Spock could see that its feet were tapered to bifurcated points to minimize the contact area. What the creature fled from was even more remarkable. It looked like a cross between a lizard, a peacock, and a cross-country skier. Its hind limbs ended in elongated feet that were, to put it bluntly, organic roller blades. It spread its broad, feathery tail membranes to form a sail, adjusting its tack to change course as the wind blew it forward, and it used a pair of forelimbs that functioned like ski poles for maneuvering and extra speed. As it drew near the sidewinder, it used one of the forelimbs to stab at it, trying to pin it to the ground, but the sidewinder dodged and veered sideways, forcing the predator to change course, furl its sail, and rely on its forelimbs to push it forward. Even without the wind, it was able to get up considerable speed.

"Fascinating," Spock said. "Animals with rotary anatomical features are virtually unknown in nature, due to the difficulty of the neural and circulatory connections."

"The bearings in the sailskater's feet," Nisu explained, "are accretions of a chitinous material that grow into a spherical form."

"Indeed," Spock said. "I am aware of similar such formations, such as the pearls secreted by Terran oysters to encase irritants."

The Kisaja continued. "They're held in place within the foot hollows in which they grow; they're slightly too large to fit through the opening."

"Are they lubricated?" Spock asked. "The expenditure of moisture in this environment would be untenable, I would think."

"The material forming the bearings and the groove surface is extremely low in friction."

"How do the creatures locomote in the absence of flat or stable surfaces?"

"There are muscles that can compress to lock the bearings in place, allowing them to walk normally."

The wind had shifted, enabling the sailskater to overtake the sidewinder at last. Spock observed the violent scene with clinical detachment. "Indeed a remarkable find," he told Nisu. "But why did you choose this biome to bring us to?"

"You asked to visit a Linnik warren."

He turned to her. "I observed our course. We bypassed

a number of other modules to reach this one. Statistically, it seems likely that there would have been a warren nearer to Kisaja than this."

She faced him without equivocation. "I wanted to bring you here, Spock."

"For what reason?"

"You are from a desert world, are you not?"

"Yes."

"I thought you might . . . appreciate the chance to visit a place that could feel like your home. I know that . . . you find a sense of belonging elusive. If you were—that is, if circumstances did not allow the *Enterprise* to leave anytime soon, then . . ."

The first officer spoke uneasily. "Your people's generosity is commendable, Nisu. Yet you need make no special effort on my behalf. The idea of 'belonging' is a sentimental one. It is not the Vulcan way to concern ourselves with such things."

Her gaze did not waver from his. "Uhura and I spoke of the limits on what words can convey. I know there is far more going on inside you than you are willing to speak of, Spock. I know you feel adrift. You sense no viable future path, and you are lost. As lost as any of the peoples who have come to Cherela seeking refuge."

He turned away. "Your compassion does you merit, Nisu. But my need is not so profound as that. I am merely experiencing a degree of uncertainty as to my long-term career prospects. The question of my ultimate goals in serving Starfleet has recently been raised, and I have found the answer elusive. It is a matter that requires further contemplation—that is all."

Her hand rested on his shoulder. With most others, he

would have been reluctant to allow that, but for Nisu it was a less intimate gesture than the gaze they had already shared several times. He could not deny that there was an affinity between them, however hesitant he had been to acknowledge it. "Those words ring false against what I feel from within you. Perhaps you do not realize what is truly behind your sense of rootlessness. If you would allow me to look deeper . . ." He stepped away from her touch. "Please, Spock. It is my life's work to protect . . . to help those who need me. I feel a need in you."

"I am a Vulcan. My only need is logic."

"No, Spock. That is your aspiration. And to achieve it, you need to face and overcome the emotions that hold you back from it. I only offer to help you understand what it is you need to face."

He turned to her again, though she kept her eyes lowered. "You offer far more than that, Nisu," he told her bluntly.

"I would be glad to give far more than that," she acknowledged. "But I offer no more than you are willing to accept."

Spock considered it. Certainly being here, in this desert so much like home, had brought his uncertainties about his place in the universe closer to the forefront of his mind. While he was confident that he could control them with meditation, surely it was logical to avail himself of the assistance of another telepath—one who would not judge him as a Vulcan would.

Rather than speaking, he touched his fingers to Nisu's chin, tilting her face upward. Accepting the invitation, she raised her deep blue eyes to meet his.

Spock did not perceive how much time passed before

his clarity returned, but once it did, his face and Nisu's were much closer than they had been before. The fabric of her light robes just barely brushed against the xenylon weave of his uniform tunic as they breathed in sync. "There," Nisu said. "*Koon-ut-kal-if-fee*. A betrayal. A broken bond."

He stepped back, startled. It was not his proximity to Nisu that had troubled him, but rather the other connection that it—and her words—had just reminded him of. "T'Pring," he said at length. "She was to be my wife—a marriage arranged from childhood. She . . . decided that my Starfleet career made me an unsuitable choice."

"And she compelled you to do something you hated in order to break that bond. Something that would have destroyed you."

"She evoked an ancient combat ritual that is rarely undertaken in these civilized times. She appointed Captain Kirk as the adversary I had to kill. For a brief period, I believed I had succeeded."

"At which point you wanted nothing to do with that . . . woman." Nisu was quietly furious. But Spock understood the cause of it, through the memories she had shared in exchange for his—memories of her own deep grief at being orphaned as a child, a grief that had compelled her to become a protector in hopes of sparing others from such sorrow. The death of others was something she took personally.

"I am not vindictive toward T'Pring, Nisu. While her methods were deplorable, her reasons were understandable. As long as I am in Starfleet, I am an unsuitable bondmate for a Vulcan woman."

Nisu moved closer. "Yet you were bonded for most of

your life. You grew up assuming that, in time, you would be wed. That you would have a family, a legacy among your people. I can tell that this is something the Vulcans prize highly."

"Yes," Spock conceded. "Granted, my own experiences with family have been . . . turbulent. Divisive. Yet I had allowed myself to anticipate that, given the opportunity to raise children of my own one day, I might be able to avoid the mistakes made by my own father."

The Kisaja smiled. "Don't we all?"

"It was never a matter I considered at any length," he protested. "My focus for the past two decades has been on my career as a scientist and a Starfleet officer."

"Yet the quiet certainty of the marriage bond was always there for you, so solid that you didn't need to think of it. Now, though, it is gone . . . both the mental connection itself and your image of who T'Pring would turn out to be. And so you are alone, adrift. You wonder if you will ever find a bond to replace the one you lost. It may not be in the forefront of your thoughts, Spock, but it is there. An emptiness, a doubt in the back of your mind. A fear that you will never be able to leave the kind of legacy that is so important to your people."

Spock wanted to protest that fear was illogical. But it would be just as illogical to deny the validity of Nisu's insights. She was no Leonard McCoy, seeing what he imagined he saw as filtered through the human prejudices he stubbornly cultivated. Spock had allowed her into his thoughts, and this was what she had found.

As he considered her words, he realized that they could explain much. On several occasions within the past year, Spock had allowed himself to be drawn to a woman, perhaps more so than was wise or rational under the circumstances. With the Romulan commander Charvanek, it had been understandable that he would be drawn to a member of an offshoot culture of the Vulcans. With the Sarpeidon exile Zarabeth, his emotional control had been somehow compromised as a consequence of time travel. Yet how to explain his rather embarrassing flirtation with Droxine of Stratos, who had offered little of interest beyond her considerable aesthetic appeal? His reaction to her had been an anomaly he had struggled to reconcile for months now. Nisu's hypothesis finally provided a logical explanation. A Vulcan male whose betrothal bond was severed as abruptly as his own had been might experience an instinctual urge to replace it. This urge could provoke a heightened interest in eligible members of his preferred sex, particularly if it went unrecognized.

But none of those women had been suitable candidates for bonding, whether due to biology or to circumstance. Nisu was another matter. She was not Vulcan, but her telepathy might well make her compatible. She did not subscribe to the Vulcan way of life, but neither did his own mother. If marrying outside his species had worked for Sarek, then possibly . . .

Spock shook himself and stepped away from Nisu. "You may well be right," he told her in a rough voice. "The instinctive need to seek another bondmate may indeed be influencing my behavior. Yet if that is the case, it is all the more reason why I—why *we* must resist what is happening here. It would be unwise to give in to it recklessly, without due consideration."

She masked her regret well. "Of course. That is only

reasonable. Now that we both know where things stand, we can take our time deciding what comes next."

"Moreover," he reminded her, "it remains uncertain how long the *Enterprise* will be on Cherela. Once the Dassik siege is resolved, we will need to resume our mission."

This time, Nisu turned away, keeping her gaze from his. "Yes," she said, her tone noncommittal. "Yes, the future does remain uncertain." She turned back to him, only briefly catching his gaze. "But it is good that you know . . . that for as long as you are here, Spock, I will be here as well."

Pavel Chekov tried not to scream as he fell from a ledge kilometers above the ground.

He did this by codifying all the reasons he had for not screaming. One: He wasn't falling very fast. The low gravity in this world module saw to that. But since he was falling, he was by definition in free fall, or at least nearly so due to air resistance, and thus it felt the same as a plummet under higher gravity. Since the air here was fairly dense, the slower wind against his face still felt strong.

Two: In case of emergency, his wingsuit's antigravs would stop his fall.

Three: His wingsuit had wings. They weren't very large, but they didn't have to be in this gravity and atmosphere. All he needed to do was get them into the right orientation and he would be fine.

Four: He didn't want to embarrass himself in front of Lieutenant Sulu.

The helmsman was, in fact, yelling, but his were

shouts of enthusiasm. He'd started out falling freely too, not because he didn't know how to avoid it, but because he wanted to. His assurances that this would be fun—outright lies, Chekov now concluded—were the only reason the young ensign was in this situation in the first place. The *Enterprise* was trapped here for who knew how long, the Dassik were still lying in wait for them, and they were grossly outmatched if the Web denizens turned out to have ulterior motives; but Sulu was acting as if he were on shore leave, and somehow he'd managed to get Chekov roped into it too. Now Hikaru had spread his wings, effortlessly achieving the right configuration of this alien getup the first time out, and was soaring like a bird while Chekov still struggled to break his own fall.

"*Just relax!*" Sulu called over the helmet comm. "*Spread your arms and legs and let the wind do the rest!*"

Doing the former was out of the question, but Pavel could at least try the latter. He tumbled at first, but with his limbs spread-eagled, the membranes of the wingsuit—two on his sides, extending from the arms on short struts, and one between his legs—soon caught the wind and guided him into the correct position. He was gliding, and it actually felt pretty good—first from sheer relief, then from the realization of what it was he was doing. He tried flapping the wings to get some lift, but it seemed to make him sink again.

"*That won't work!*" Sulu called. "*You're just spilling wind when the wings are slanted. You need to use your hands and feet to adjust the membranes, like the flaps of an aircraft. Maneuver until you hit an updraft.*"

Sulu soared down to parallel Chekov's glide path and

showed him how to do it. Soon Chekov had enough control that he could follow Sulu to where the most likely updrafts were, given the architecture of this world module. It was a complicated and beautiful megastructure, which Chekov was able to admire now that he didn't need to focus so much on not falling. The winged Fiilestii had built their module's interior in a way that reflected their aspirations more than their origins. The whole place was open sky with vast towers spearing upward through it for kilometers. Each tower was shaped like a narrow conical shaft piercing the centers of multiple horizontal disks. But each disk was hundreds of meters in radius and dozens thick, getting larger as they descended. The Fiilestii's homes, workplaces, and other buildings were within or atop the disks, each of which was surfaced with vegetation from the Fiilestii's long-lost homeworld. While most of the Web's world modules were like gigantic, flat stretches of planetary terrain that spread to the limits of vision, this was like a collection of miniature ones stored on giant spindles.

In the air between the towers, hundreds of life-forms soared from disk to disk, some commuting, others strictly having fun. The Fiilestii population was comparatively small; as avian predators, they needed large territories and couldn't abide having too many of themselves in one place. They were almost outnumbered by the Linnik, Tessegri, and other tourists who came here from their own world modules—and now the *Enterprise*. *Not tourists,* Chekov reminded himself. *Explorers. The captain ordered us to explore the Web and its customs. Just my luck I got assigned to the module where flying is the custom.*

The shape of the towers made the updrafts complicated, but Chekov did his best to follow Sulu's lead. As usual, the helmsman steered him true. Pavel's initial fear had mostly given way to exhilaration at being in flight, and the view was truly spectacular. He was glad Sulu had brought him here. Over the two years and change since Chekov had been promoted to bridge duty, the helmsman had done his best to broaden the young Russian's horizons beyond his work. Sulu was so energetic and driven, with so many interests, that Chekov sometimes found it intimidating, but generally he was grateful to Sulu for pushing him to try new things. (All except food. He didn't share the lieutenant's interest in exotic cuisine, but Sulu kept up his urging.)

Chekov overcorrected a turn and found himself flailing and sinking for a few moments before he caught himself. *"You're still too tense, Pavel!"* Sulu called from some distance above him. *"I brought you here to relax. You've been on edge for months, ever since your old girlfriend came aboard."*

"I have not!" he said. "Well . . . I have been thinking about Irina lately. Whether I have become too fixated on work to have room for other things. Whether it might be possible—" He broke off. "No. I am dreaming! It would never work!"

"You won't know that if you don't give it a shot."

"How do I give it a shot when I am on the *Enterprise* and she is . . . wherever she is?"

"Do what I did last year. Take an extended leave."

"I'm still an ensign! I don't have that much leave time built up!"

"Then take a temporary ground posting. Whatever. If

Irina's stayed on your mind this long, then it's worth doing something about it!"

A brilliant flash of light distracted him—perhaps mercifully—from Sulu's suggestion. He blinked away the afterimage of the vast lightning bolt that had struck the dome in front of him. "I thought the dome was supposed to dim the lightning!" he called.

"It did!" Sulu said. *"That one was huge! Do you have any idea of the amount of energy in these storms? You could wreck a fleet with it!"*

More lightning was striking the dome now as the storm intensified. Beyond, Chekov could see one of the conduits connecting this module to its neighbors; it was swaying under a fearsome wind. He reminded himself that the conduits were made to handle that kind of stress, that the modules were built to channel the lightning into their batteries. He tried to relax and concentrate on the flight.

But as the minutes passed, the storm only grew fiercer. Something odd seemed to be happening to the angle of the dome rim. "Sulu! Am I getting wobbly or is the module . . . swaying?"

A pause. *"I think it's swaying."*

"It's supposed to do that, right? And the antigravs compensate so we don't feel it?"

"I guess so." Several more lightning strikes punctuated his sentence. *"Still, maybe we'd better land and talk to someone."*

"Good idea!"

The two of them banked toward the nearest tower, aiming their glide path toward the edge of one of the disks. But as they neared it, suddenly Chekov felt something yank him downward. He was falling! And this time, so was Sulu. The wings were no longer holding enough air to do more than slow their descent.

For a frightening moment, it looked like they were about to collide with the edge of the thick disk. But they just barely slipped under it and fell toward the top of the next disk, hundreds of meters below. And they were falling fast. *The antigravs will kick in,* Chekov reminded himself. *The antigravs will kick in the antigravs will kick in the antigravs will—*

"Kick" was the right word. The wingsuit antigravs did engage, but too weakly to prevent a crash landing. Following Sulu's lead, Chekov spread out as wide and flat as he could, depending on the thick air beneath his wingsuit membranes to provide what cushioning it could. Still, he hit hard and tumbled. The ground cover was thick and soft, but the landing still hurt.

Groaning, he tried to sit up—and found he couldn't! He struggled into a seated position, but it was a strain, and it left him woozy as the blood rushed from his brain. His helmet pressed down uncomfortably on his head. He pulled it off, and it fell hard to the ground.

"What's happening?" Sulu asked as he struggled upright in turn.

"The gravity," Chekov said. "The module's antigravs must have failed. We're feeling Cherela's full gravity at this altitude. Maybe . . . four and a half times Earth's."

"No," Sulu said after testing it out for a moment. "We couldn't even move then. This is no more than two g's. The system must still be running at a reduced level." Chekov felt his innards sink, and from the look on Sulu's face, the helmsman felt it too. "But it's fluctuating."

"Sulu—those antigravs are what hold this module up against its own weight. If they fail . . ."

But Sulu was looking up at the enormous disk that filled the sky above them. The module was undoubtedly swaying now, and a deep groaning sound was audible all around them. "What I want to know is . . . what's holding *that* up?"

Seven

"*The gravity fluctuations are getting worse, Captain,*" Sulu reported over the comm. "*I don't know how much longer this module can hold up.*" The ominous sounds of structural strain under his voice, and the alarmed crowd chatter that followed them, told Kirk that his helmsman had good reason for his concern.

On the viewscreen, Triumvir Lekur reacted differently. "*Nonsense, Captain Kirk. The Fiilestii module has 'held up' for over a thousand years. This is just a localized antigrav failure. We're already redirecting power from neighboring modules to shore it up until we can repair the storm damage.*"

"*I don't know if that's going to be enough, Captain,*" Sulu called. "*If anything, the wind and lightning are getting stronger! The locals I've talked to say they've never seen it this bad, not at this altitude, anyway.*"

"Triumvir," Kirk said, "maybe you should order an evacuation as a precautionary measure."

"*We know what we're doing, newcomer!*"

Spock stepped forward, speaking with a calmness Kirk would be unable to manage at the moment. "If nothing else, Triumvir, removing the populace from the module would reduce the load on the strained antigravs."

The big Bogosrin snorted, seeming a bit abashed. "*Of course, you're right. Only sensible. Rrr, take a damn lot of work, though. Not densely populated, that one, but still it's over a million people.*"

Once Lekur had issued orders to set the process in motion, Kirk said, "The *Enterprise* can help. If you'll release us from the hangar, we can—"

"All due respect, Captain, there's nothing your people can do that can't be done better by the thousands of more experienced engineers and crisis managers we have here. You don't know the Web."

"You said it yourself, it'll take a lot of work to evacuate the module. We can use our transporters and shuttlecraft to help out."

Lekur bowed his head. *"Right again. Forgive an old builder his stubborn pride. To have this happen when we have visitors . . ."*

Kirk smiled. "Forget about it. I'll just—"

"Captain!" It was Sulu's voice, but nothing followed it save the sound of screams and a loud metallic groaning.

"Sulu!" There came a series of sharp percussive sounds, then nothing. "Sulu, come in! Lekur, what the hell's going on there?"

"We have a video feed," one of the triumvir's technical aides said. Uhura sent the feed to the main viewscreen, reducing Lekur's image to an inset window. The view was evidently from a camera atop one of the Fiilestii towers looking down and out at the other towers beyond. At first, the view looked normal, until it zoomed in and Kirk realized that material was falling off the disks' surfaces in one direction—water, sand, loose objects. The people atop the disks were clinging for dear life or trying to scramble for entrances into the interior. The entire module had tilted, the camera along with it.

"My God," Kirk said. There were no handrails at the rims of the disks; the winged Fiilestii had no need for them in the normal low gravity of the module. Kirk and the bridge crew watched in horror as a group of Linnik, small but recognizable in their loose, shimmering garments, tumbled toward the edge. A restraining force field snapped into visibility, catching them—and then giving way, not designed to cope with the increased gravitational pull. They plummeted off the side.

To Kirk's relief, they then vanished in swirls of light. *"Emergency transporters engaged,"* another of Lekur's aides announced with even greater relief. *But what about Sulu?* Kirk wondered. Had he gone over the edge as well? Had he been retrieved in time?

"Chekov to Enterprise! *Come in!"*

"Kirk here! Chekov, where's Sulu?"

"I'm right here, Captain," Sulu's voice came, sounding breathless. *"Dropped my communicator. We're inside the structure, but I'm not happy being here."*

"Captain," Chekov interrupted, *"if the module isn't leveled out, the strain on the towers will—"*

"Understood! Lekur, let us out of this hangar! We need to get there now!"

"Captain," Spock told him, "the Fiilestii module is forty percent of the way around the planet. We cannot get there in less than an hour without exiting the atmosphere and risking detection by the Dassik."

"Then we'll risk detection! Lekur, come on, man!"

"There's a better way," the Bogosrin said. *"We'll beam you. Send your matter stream through the conduits."*

Kirk blinked. "Beam the *Enterprise*?"

"Easy to do, with the power of Cherela to draw on."

"That would be inadvisable, Triumvir," Spock said. "The *Enterprise* was beamed across space by an advanced transporter once before, during an encounter with a Kalandan outpost. The vessel was reassembled fractionally out of phase, resulting in a nearly catastrophic engine malfunction."

"Kalandans? Ancient history. Our transporters are much better. And it's not across space, more like station to station. We'll have more control over reassembly."

"There's no choice, Spock," Kirk said. "Not while our people are in danger. Lekur, do it!"

"Standing by," the second aide said at Lekur's prompt. "Please drop all your deflector screens and depolarize any hull-reinforcement fields so they won't interfere with the dematerialization."

"Do as she says," Kirk told the bridge crew. He hit the shipwide intercom button. "All hands, this is the captain. The entire *Enterprise* is about to be beamed to the site of an emergency. I'm assured there's no danger, but it might be best to shut down any nonessential systems and . . . try to hold still. Stand by."

"Scott to bridge! Captain, beam the whole ship? I've barely got everything back in alignment after that Kalandan mess! And you know how dangerous it is to beam antimatter! If it isn't kept carefully segregated in the particle stream, we could end up with some of our pieces missing, even blow up on reassembly!"

Now he tells me. "No choice, Scotty! Just batten down the hatches and pray!"

"Ready, Captain," Spock announced moments later.

"Lekur, go!"

The overhead and outer bulkheads of the bridge began to shimmer and sparkle. The effect closed in on Kirk until everything around him was dissolving into dancing light. The whine of the phase transition sang through the air, engulfing him, growing deafeningly loud, as though the particles of the *Enterprise* were screaming in his ears as they were torn apart from one another. Then phosphenes clouded his view as his own retinas began to disintegrate. It was the slowest dematerialization he'd ever been through. His entire body tingled and grew numb.

After an uncertain time in limbo, he felt the tingles again, saw the shimmers, and the bridge re-formed around him, a crystal fairyland of dancing light gradually giving way to solidity. Kirk's ears kept ringing even after the transporter hum had faded, and he blinked away afterimages in his eyes. "Scotty, are we in one piece?"

"*Checking . . . aye, antimatter containment reads nominal. It'll take a full diagnostic to be sure of the rest, sir.*"

"Later, Scotty." On the viewscreen, he could see the Fiilestii module. The conduits around it were visibly whipping about in the fearsome winds, winds that buffeted the *Enterprise* as well. "Deflector shields up! Rahda, get us in range of that module!" The relief helmswoman acknowledged and brought thrusters to bear to counteract the winds. Kirk could now see that the module itself was rocking with stately slowness. Lightning speared down from the vast storm bank overhead to strike the dome and the snaking conduits. "Lekur, how's that antigrav reinforcement coming?"

"*We're getting it leveled out,*" the triumvir told him. "*The antigravs are still weakened, but we can ease—careful, Mnorgrel, don't let the flow rate surge!—ease the stress on the towers. They'll still be overloaded, but at least in the direction they're designed to cope with. Should make things safer until we can get the people out. Rrrh, Mnorgrel, what did I just tell you?"*

"All right." Kirk hit the intercom again. "All hands, prepare to assist in mass evacuation. Ready all shuttlecraft to transport rescue parties to the Fiilestii module."

———

"Enterprise to Sulu and Chekov," came Kirk's voice. *"Stand by for transport."*

Sulu took Chekov's communicator. "Negative, Captain!" he said. "We're needed here, evacuating the building." Another deep rumble made Sulu look around at the wide hallway, making sure its walls and ceiling were still intact. The module may have leveled out again, but a structure this large was almost fluid, and stresses were still rippling through it. "There's been some structural buckling. People are trapped in the side that was higher up."

"Understood. Just get out of there as soon as you can."

Sulu could hear the reluctance in Kirk's voice—not only at having to leave his crew in harm's way, but at not being there himself. The captain's willingness to risk himself on the front lines regardless of regulations was part of the reason why Sulu admired the man so much. But Sulu himself could do no less.

"Sulu, over here!" Chekov beckoned to him, studying his tricorder readings. It was a strain to walk in this gravity, but they were managing with a little help from their wingsuit antigravs. "There are over fifty people trapped in here."

The tricorder readouts supplemented the evidence of Sulu's own eyes. The door to the chamber beyond was stuck, its frame warped as the disk buckled under its own unbalanced weight. "Stand back." He drew his hand phaser and set the dial to its highest intensity. The deadly particle beam burned through the door quickly, taking less than thirty seconds to carve a hole. The Fiilestii, Linnik, and others within poured out as Sulu and Chekov urged them to stay orderly and avoid the burning-hot edges.

"What's going on?" asked a Linnik female in green robes. "Is it the final collapse? So soon?"

Sulu didn't know what she meant. All he could do was try to be reassuring. "It's a temporary antigrav failure. We're evacuating as a precaution."

"Temporary. That's what they always say." The childlike alien hurried away, muttering, "Maybe now they'll have to listen."

There's one in every crowd, Sulu thought. He soon forgot the encounter in the press of search and rescue. He and Chekov located and freed a few hundred more trapped Web denizens over the next half hour. It was exhausting work in this gravity, but they couldn't stop to rest. Sulu hoped Doctor McCoy would have something for his sore knees and ankles . . . and hips . . . and back . . . and neck . . .

For one brief, glorious moment, Sulu's weight dropped and he felt free. *At last! They fixed the antigravs!* But a second later, weight returned, more crushing than ever, and slammed him to the floor. It hadn't been gravity cancellation he'd felt, it had been free fall. Far from being fixed, the antigravs had cut out completely for a second and then engaged again at a weaker level than before. The building creaked and shuddered around him, absorbing a new set of stresses.

What did that Linnik say, Sulu thought, *about a final collapse?*

"It should have worked," Lekur insisted on the viewscreen. *"Somehow the instability is growing faster than we can cancel it out. We just can't feed enough power to this part of the network in time, not without compromising adjacent modules."*

"So power's all you need?" asked Bailey, who had arrived on the bridge minutes before and now stood alongside Kirk's chair.

"Not all, but it's the main thing."

Bailey turned to the science officer. "Mister Spock, could the *Enterprise* gravity system be interfaced with theirs, to feed them the extra power?"

Both of Spock's brows went up. "Lieutenant, the module is thousands of times more massive than the *Enterprise.*"

"I remember flight training, Spock—the gravity and inertial damping systems are designed to counteract thousands of *g*'s if necessary. So the power's there. At least enough to shore up their own systems."

"If the instabilities are increasing exponentially, pouring more power into the system may not be enough to stop them."

"But it'd hold them for a while, right? Enough to get the people out, at least."

"We have no way of knowing if our systems are even compatible with theirs. There could be unpredictable fluctuations. The feedback could damage the ship."

Bailey was growing impatient. "Don't you have anything to offer besides worst-case scenarios, Mister Spock?"

"Lieutenant," Kirk said, urging calm. Bailey quieted down, but his urgency remained. So Kirk asked on his behalf, "Spock, what are the odds of damage to the *Enterprise*?"

"I have insufficient data to compute the odds."

"So you can't say for sure this won't help," Bailey spoke up.

"But we can't say for sure it will," Kirk countered. "Bailey, I understand your urgency, but we mustn't act in haste. We won't be any use to the people we can save if we wreck the ship trying to do too much."

The younger man stepped toward him. "Captain, I'm not the same hothead who served on this bridge three years ago. I've learned a lot about First Federation systems in that time. I'm confident that this can work. Yes, there's a risk, but there was a risk when we answered Balok's distress call too. We did it because trying to help was the right thing to do."

Kirk studied Bailey for a moment. The intensity he remembered was still there, but it was more tempered and seasoned now, just as he had always hoped it would be one day.

The captain turned back to his first officer. "All right, Spock. If anyone can make this work, it's you and Scotty. So let's make this happen."

But once he'd filled in his chief engineer, Scott's reaction was rather less confident. *"Aye, we've got the power, sir, but keeping the energy flow stable will be like riding a bucking bronco covered in engine grease."*

"Scotty, I know you'll rise to the occasion. We have to try."

"Aye, sir."

After another few moments, Spock announced, "Calculations complete. Sending now."

"Received," Lekur's aide said a moment later. *"We verify. Ready for interface."*

"Now, Mister Scott," Kirk said.

"Hold on to something," Scott warned. "Here we go—mark!"

Kirk felt his weight fluctuate for several seconds, then it stabilized again. "Interface established," Spock reported. "Power transfer under way."

"Antigrav power increasing," the aide announced.

"Compensating for fluctuations . . . holding steady . . ."

"See?" Bailey said. "I told you it'd work."

Then an alarm went off. "Instabilities accelerating," Spock announced.

"Scotty, more power!" Kirk called.

"No!" cried Lekur. "Captain, the added power is intensifying the instabilities! Your systems' phase isn't matching with ours, it's going out of sync!"

But it was too late. An alarm sounded as the world module suddenly heaved. The Enterprise, gravitationally bound to it, shuddered in resonance. "Captain, two more antigrav units have blown out!" Spock called. "The module is tilting again."

Sulu and Chekov had reached the second disk from the bottom when the world tilted around them and the groaning of the tower increased sharply in pitch and volume. "Everybody move!" Sulu cried, and all pretense of an orderly evacuation was abandoned. He and Chekov hurried the evacuees down the increasing slope of the floor toward the center shaft as fast as they could in this gravity, taking the rear themselves. The floor continued to shudder beneath Sulu's feet. Each time it sank a little more, he was convinced it would be the last time. He only prayed these were the last people in the disk.

Once he and Chekov reached the center shaft, the ceiling above them had already cracked open as the raised half-disk began to tear free. He and Chekov dodged falling debris as the floor sank faster, the spry ensign outpacing Sulu. Hikaru saw the floor in front of him beginning to crack and put on a final burst of speed to catch up with Chekov, who'd just crossed over in time. He made a running leap just as the floor gave way. He fell short, his midsection colliding with the edge, and scrambled for purchase as he slid back. Chekov dove forward and caught him by the upper arms, straining against Sulu's twice-normal weight.

But then the building lurched and sent them both toward the edge. Sulu looked down. Beyond his dangling feet, the broken disk segment had crashed into the bottommost disk below it and caused it to begin giving way as well. The noise was deafening, and a cloud of choking dust rose to obscure Sulu's vision as his feet flailed for purchase.

Then something pulled Chekov back, lifting Sulu along with him. When the dust cleared, he saw they owed their rescue to a Bogosrin female, one of the largest sentient beings Sulu had ever seen. Lifting them both had been easy for the giant bearlike alien, who set them down on her broad back. "Hold on," she rumbled as she began loping forward quadrupedally. Sulu clung to her clothing for dear life.

Luckily the Fiilestii built big to accommodate their wings, so the Bogosrin was able to fit in the spiral stairwell. They descended as rapidly as the evacuees before them would allow, finally emerging into the open air. They weren't safe yet, though, for the lowest disk still formed an enormous roof above them. "Go!" Sulu cried. "Everyone, fast as you can, get out from under!" He and Chekov jumped off the Bogosrin's back so as not to slow her down, then did their best to hasten the others along. The Linnik in the crowd had the hardest time moving swiftly, but the other species seemed to be reflexively solicitous toward them, taking their hands to pull them forward or lifting them bodily and carrying them, protecting them like the children they resembled.

Luckily they were on what was now the downhill side of the building; as the raised half of the bottom disk broke free and crashed to the ground alongside them with terrifying speed, it damaged nothing but the evacuees' nerves and maybe their hearing. But now the building was unbalanced, with more weight on the downslope side. Its collapse was inevitable. The deep straining and cracking sounds kept getting louder, and Sulu knew that once the tipping point was reached, it would be fast. He flipped open the communicator, coughing in the dust. "*Enterprise*, stand by for transport, wide beam around this signal!" Wide beam to get as many as possible and to take their motion into account. But he knew that beaming up a moving target was an iffy proposition.

Still, miraculously, the building held up until everyone was clear, as far as he could tell. But he and Chekov didn't make it very far before the noise from behind grew deafening. Instinct told him to keep running, but he had to look back to make sure he was running the right way. So he saw the stunning, horrifying spectacle of a tower kilometers high disintegrating under its own weight. It didn't topple like a felled tree, for it was too big and brittle; it only moved a slight distance sideways before it broke apart, its disks pancaking down on one another. A tremor rippled outward through the ground and he lost his footing, twisting his ankle. He was far too close. The impact of the building would be like a series of explosions, sending out deadly shrapnel and powerful atmospheric shock waves. At this distance, he'd be a dead man.

Then someone was pulling him up, dragging him backward as he watched the tower collapse in on itself. Just before the shock wave hit, his rescuer pulled him behind something, a large metal sheet that must have fallen from an adjacent tower and sliced into the ground at an angle. Shrapnel pummeled the metal sheet and some fragments pierced it like bullets. It teetered over him, pushed back by the shock wave, but it held. He looked around; Chekov was there too, along with a number of the evacuees. He looked up to see who had saved him and beheld the familiar face of Anne Nored. "Thanks," he got out.

"You're welcome," the brown-haired security lieutenant said. "Are you able to walk?"

"I don't think so. Not under these conditions."

Nored looked at Chekov. "Get him back to the *Enterprise*. I'll help with the other evacuees."

Sulu stared as she pulled herself to her feet with surprising ease. "How are you doing that?"

Nored gave a wistful smile. "Carter and I once spent four months on a relief mission to Pangea." Sulu was surprised. Nored rarely spoke of her engagement to Carter Winston, who had been the Federation's wealthiest philanthropist before his disappearance five years ago. "It's a high-gravity mining colony. I wouldn't want to live there, but it was one hell of a workout."

Sulu felt he should say something. "He . . . was a great man. I'm sorry."

Nored shook her head. "It was a loss to the galaxy, not just me. So I haven't let it define me. I joined Starfleet to keep on helping people, like he did."

"Lucky for me," Sulu said with a grin. "Just stay away from the towers. The rest could come down at any time." She nodded thanks and loped away. Fortunately, there was a lot of space between the towers, so no domino effect was likely—and this area, where a tower had already fallen, was probably a safe place to be. He hoped the remaining evacuees had the sense to keep as far as they could from the towers that still stood.

But as Chekov called the ship for beam-out, Sulu looked around through the blowing dust and saw that not everyone had been spared from the shock and shrapnel. Some of the bodies around them were not moving. Some had been torn open by flying debris.

As the transporter beam took him, he felt guilty about escaping with only a twisted ankle.

Kirk was relieved to hear that Sulu and Chekov had beamed aboard safely. Outside, the immense module continued its slow lurching. One of the conduits stretched taut and broke loose at its connection point. The conduit snapped back like a whip, tearing itself apart, and three conduit shuttles full of evacuees were flung out. One was able to level out under its own power, setting a course for the *Enterprise*, the nearest safe refuge. But the other two were damaged from collisions with the conduit walls and tumbled out of control. "Get tractor beams on those shuttles!" Kirk ordered. The beams snagged one of them, but the other was too far; the atmosphere attenuated the beam, and the shuttle plummeted down toward the bottomless darkness below. There must have been at least thirty people in that shuttle. The thought tore at Kirk's gut.

But there was no time now for grief. "Lekur, how many left to evacuate?"

"At least thirty thousand. Our transporters are taking over a hundred a second, but the module won't last long enough at this rate. We can't trust the conduits anymore, and we've already beamed in every airborne ship we can spare."

Kirk looked up. "Do they have tractor beams?"

"Some do."

"Then let's use them to hold the module up."

"It's too vast! It won't handle the strain!"

"We need anything that can buy us time!" Grimacing, Lekur nodded. Kirk turned to the helm. "Rahda, get us up above the dome. Uhura, are those Web shuttles in the bay yet?"

"Twenty more seconds, sir."

It took longer than that to get into position. To allow the tractor beams maximum spread, Lieutenant Rahda parked the ship several kilometers up, just below the cloud ceiling. Mighty winds pummeled the *Enterprise* while lightning snapped against its shields. "Tractor beams on!" Kirk ordered. "Maximum power, maximum spread!"

Rahda had already extended the targeting scope from the helm console, peering into it to aim the tractor emitters. The ship trembled as the beams latched on. The screen projected a ventral camera view. The tractor beams, eerily visible as discontinuities in the rainfall, spread out in a cone and latched on to as much of the dome as they could hold, but it was still just a fraction of its area. Around the *Enterprise*, nine smaller ships used their own tractors to shore the world module up at its edges. At all the contact points, triangular chunks of transparent aluminum began to tear free from the dome, windows sucked out of their geodesic frames by the beams and tumbling upward under their pull. Many of them were blown free of the beams by the wind, looking like fountains of glass spewing upward. The ruptures would be letting the outer atmosphere rush in, increasing the internal pressure dangerously, but the interior volume was vast enough that it would take minutes. With luck, everyone would be out by then.

Beneath the dome, the scene was terrifying. One by one, the vast, beautiful pagoda-like towers were collapsing in on themselves in mighty explosions of dust and debris. Fires were burning and a gray-brown miasma filled the air. "Kirk to transporter room. Are our security teams still in the module?"

"Yes, sir," came Lieutenant Kyle's voice.

"Kirk to evac teams! Stand by for beam-out!"

"Not yet, sir!" came Nored's voice. *"There's still . . ."* Her voice dissolved into choking. *"Still work to do."*

"You've done more than enough! It's getting too dangerous down there."

More choking. *"Understood."*

He switched the channel back. "Now, Mister Kyle!"

A moment later, the ship experienced a sudden, sharp tremor, then a continuous, unsteady shuddering. "Captain, the module is beginning to buckle," Spock called. "The strain from the tractor beams is ripping it apart!"

"Kyle, have you got the team?"

"Aye, sir. The last of them are aboard now."

"Good. Lekur, how many people left?"

"Still about ten thousand! You've got to hold it longer!"

"Scotty, can we get any more tractor power?"

"I can barely keep what we have! We've already blown two dilithium circuits. We've got no safety margin. And the shields are taking a pounding from the lightning."

"Hold her together another ninety seconds, Scotty!"

A bolt of lightning penetrated the shields, its voltage so intense that it jumped over all the circuit breakers, causing electric arcs to coruscate across the bridge consoles. The lights flickered and the ship trembled. The targeting scope sparked and buzzed from the inside. "Rahda, look out!" Bailey cried, pulling her away from the helm console just before the scope blew. Bailey himself took the brunt of the hit, collapsing alongside Kirk's chair.

"Medical team to the bridge!" Kirk ordered just as Rahda moved to Bailey to see to his condition.

But other concerns presented themselves once the static cleared from the main viewscreen. "Scotty, we're sinking!"

"Impulse engines are offline! That behemoth is pulling us down! We've got to cut her free, or we'll be dragged down with her!"

"Use thrusters! Keep us aloft!"

"It'll only slow us down!"

"We just need another minute!"

By now, the medical team had arrived to take Bailey to sickbay. A jolt ran through the deck as the thrusters kicked in, but as Scott said, it only decreased their descent by a small margin. Huge chunks of debris were tearing loose in the tractor beams now, flying up toward the *En-*

terprise. Kirk's instinct was to order full ventral shields, but the lightning from above posed a greater threat. They'd simply have to live with some hull damage.

But the debris sucked up by the beams was a symptom. The uneven stresses were twisting and tearing the world module apart. A mighty construct, larger than a hundred cities, enduring for thousands of years, and now it was breaking into rubble, imploding from the atmospheric pressure. "Spock," Kirk said quietly. "Life readings?"

"Fewer than a hundred," Spock replied. A moment later . . . "Now none."

A heavy sigh escaped Kirk's throat. "Release tractor beams. Get us out from under this storm." He dreaded asking the next question. "Lekur. How many did you get out?"

The Bogosrin's head hung low. *"Not enough. At least thirty-six hundred people were still in there."*

Kirk absorbed the news solemnly. "Triumvir . . . I'm sorry. We did everything we possibly could."

"You did more than enough, Kirk." Lekur's voice was an ominous growl. *"It was your power transfer that overloaded the system! If you'd left well enough alone, we could've gotten everyone out in time!*

"Those deaths are on your head, Kirk. And you will be held to answer."

Eight

"Force Leader Grun. You are ordered to proceed at once to the Ranth sector and resume the hunt for orbships. We can no longer afford to have three cluster ships out of action in pursuit of a quarry that may not even exist. The hunt for the Linnik is too urgent."

Grun seethed inwardly at the orders. The image of War Leader Vraq on the command pod's viewer was distorted and laden with static, presumably due to the interference of the giant planet's radiation belts. But his voice was recognizable enough, and his identification codes were valid. And Vraq's cold condescension, that haughty turn of his head, was just what Grun would expect from someone in his position. After a lifetime of orders from his father and brother—orders that had usually been accompanied by blows or been tailored to cause him humiliation—Grun had developed a deep-rooted resentment at being compelled to do anything against his wishes. He understood the urgency of their mission against the treacherous Linnik, but he despised being lectured about it.

But he had also learned to keep his resentment buried and avoid exposing his true intentions until the opportunity to strike presented itself. If he could not find and destroy the *Enterprise* to avenge the Dassik blood it had spilled, he would find some other way to compensate for this stain on his pack's prestige.

Still, losing Kirk galled him. The same childhood that had trained him for patience had also trained him for persistence. Since nothing had come easily to him, since there had been obstacles to his success at every turn, he had learned to stalk his quarry with tenacity and never let go until he achieved victory. To be forced to walk away from a goal he had set himself was galling.

The final straw was the smug look on Dral's face. "Shall I ready the ships for departure, Force Leader?" he asked, his words deferential but his tone insolent.

Grun swallowed his bile and his pride with it. For the moment, as so many times before, he would have to tolerate a setback. But it was harder now. He'd thought he was finally free of such humiliations, and yet . . .

He took a breath, readying himself to give the order, schooling his tone to ensure he would not sound as defeated as he felt. But before he could get the words out, monitor officer Remv called, "Force Leader!"

Grun would have jumped at the interruption even without the urgency in Remv's tone. "Speak!" he said, striding over to the third-tier officer's console.

"I have detected anomalous emissions from the planet, sir. Here." Young Remv magnified a sector on his screen. The view became dominated by a turbulent storm bank, one flickering with intense lightning. Below it was a graphic displaying energy spectra from the selected region. "The storm makes readings difficult, but some of these energy bursts suggest more than lightning. This spike here, and this here . . . they resemble the output of an overloading warp reactor. And these gravimetric fluctuations suggest artificial gravity generation, possibly a tractor signature."

"Yes!" Grun cried. "They are down there. The *Enterprise*! We cannot leave now, not when we finally have the spoor!"

But Dral shook his head. "I see nothing in these readings. Just noise. It is a foolish hunter who strikes at the wrong time because his ears mistake the rustle of tree branches for the step of his prey."

"Must you question everything, Dral? Can you never simply act?"

"When I am sure of what action is wise. We are not berserkers anymore. That is what caused our downfall the last time! Now we must be more shrewd."

"More cowardly, you mean. Talking and debating endlessly as an excuse not to strike!" Grun turned to his subordinate. "Remv, tell me. Could this be just random noise?"

Remv quailed at the fire in his voice. "No, Force Leader! I know the pattern! It is artificial, upon my life!"

Grun clapped his shoulder. "Good hunter."

Dral sneered. "He sees what you command him to see! All that proves is that he fears you!"

The commander turned to face his subordinate, looming over him. "And you do not, Dral?"

"No!" Dral stepped back. "You wish me to act? Then I will act. Force Leader Grun, you are a hyperaggressive fool whose obsessions have blinded you. You are defying a direct order based on a delusion! You are no longer fit to lead this pack!" He drew his disruptor. "And so it falls to me to take over your—"

Dral broke off, silenced by the realization that he had been a complete idiot. At least, that was how Grun liked to interpret it. Perhaps the second had realized nothing. But as usual, his insistence on talking rather than simply acting had doomed him—as had his preference for technologically advanced weapons over simple, honest blades.

He had left Grun plenty of time to reach the hidden button in his gauntlet that set off the concealed charge in Dral's disruptor. The shaped detonation had blown out backward and turned the rear half of the disruptor into shrapnel, which drove itself clear through Dral's body armor and into his heart.

"Now then," Grun said to his horrified crew, nonchalantly resting a leg atop Dral's twitching frame as the former second bled to death. "Where were we? Oh, yes. Tell the third cluster ship to set course for the Ranth sector. The rest of us will rendezvous with them when our mission is completed." He glanced down at Dral, meeting his eyes, where a faint spark of life still lingered. "Is that a satisfactory compromise, Second? Surely we do not need all three ships now that we know where our quarry lies. Not when we hold the high ground."

Dral expressed his approval by finally dying.

"Good! Then it's settled." He turned to his security officer. "Rhuld. You are now promoted to second. Have your predecessor escorted out of the command pod."

Rhuld gave a toothy smile of gratitude and approval. "Yes, Force Leader," he said. "Shall I ready the ships for atmospheric entry?"

"Your enthusiasm is commendable, Rhuld, but there's no hurry. We know they're down there, but they have plenty of room to hide. Let's send down a scouting party in a pilot vessel first—take the lay of the land. Once we've got their exact position, we can take them out with an economical strike."

"Yes, Force Leader. I am yours to command."

He liked the way that sounded. *I should've killed Dral weeks ago.*

"Oh, depths," Linar cursed as she saw the single Dassik cluster ship enter warp, leaving the other two behind. "I really thought that would work."

She turned to see Choda patting the flank of "Mister Hyde," as Balok had taken to calling his Dassik simulacrum ever since Ambassador Bailey had come aboard the *Fesarius*. "Don't fault our oversized friend here for his performance. We programmed the voice accurately from the signal intercepts the *Jesoliar* relayed. And the 'interference' should have kept them from getting a good look, same as always."

"It's not the same," Linar reminded the *Fesarius*'s lead engineer. "We've never had to use him to fool actual Dassik before." Balok's usual approach to hide the puppet's imperfections was to feign a dense, roiling atmosphere, which added to the sense of alienness and mystery, at least with outsiders who hailed from standard oxygen environments. But the Dassik knew perfectly well that their kind breathed air as clear as the Linnik's, requiring the use of the signal interference dodge instead. Although Linar reflected that it could have been worse. If "Hyde" had been aboard Balok's pilot vessel when he had fled days before, they would not have been able to attempt this deception. She wondered whether Balok had actually planned for this contingency or if it had simply been a lucky outcome of his erratic decision-making. With Balok, it was often hard to tell.

"But it must have worked," Choda pointed out, "or none of them would have left. And they'd probably be looking for us now." The *Fesarius* was staying safely out of sight in orbit of a dwarf planet in the outer Oort cloud of Cherela's system, running dark to blend in with the comets and planetesimals out here. The sheer volume of the cloud was enough to minimize the chance of a searching ship coming across them, unless that ship extrapolated the vector of the fake transmission they had sent.

Linar shook her hairless head. "Whatever the reason, Choda, we've failed to lure the Dassik away from Cherela. I doubt any more staged orders will do the trick, and Dassik aren't the sort to respond to distress calls."

The science head, young Almis, came over from his sensor monitor station. "What worries me," he told his fellow executive officers, "is the timing. It's hard to get clear readings from this distance, but something happened a short while ago to generate a neutrino burst from Cherela."

"Cherela itself?" Linar asked. "Not the sun?"

"From the planet," Almis confirmed. "Which suggests that some kind of high-energy event has happened involving the Web."

"Or the *Enterprise*," Choda said. The Dassik's intership communications had made it clear that the humans' starship had reached this system and disappeared around Cherela, suggesting that it had found its way down to the Web. That in itself was disturbing enough. For all of Ambassador Bailey's agreeable qualities, his people were still large, aggressive, and more inquisitive than was good for the First. What if, in their recklessness, they had done something to tip off the Dassik to the secret Cherela's clouds had hidden for millennia?

Linar wished she could send a signal home and ask

what was happening. But it was a fleeting impulse. Staying low and quiet to avoid detection was second nature to her. That she had even considered the possibility was proof that she'd been too influenced by Balok and his intrepid ways. *Curse that tranya-addled fool*, she thought with long-suffering affection.

But where *was* Balok? It was natural enough that he'd fled the battle; that was the preferred reaction of any Linnik, given the chance. But instead of coming back, he'd simply vanished—and he'd apparently sent a transmission to the *Enterprise*, one that had led them to Cherela, for reasons Linar could hardly fathom. Her frustration with the commander had never been so acute. He was supposed to save his deceptions for outsiders, not his own crew! What madness had possessed him?

All Linar could do was wait. If Balok had sent the *Enterprise* here, it stood to reason that he would come himself, sooner or later. She just hoped that, when and if he arrived, he would not find himself at the mercy of the Dassik cluster ships. Something as small and fast as a pilot vessel might be able to slip past them using Cherela's bulk and its radiation field for concealment—so long as they stayed together rather than splitting into cells. But if he pulled off a stealth approach to Cherela, then the *Fesarius* might never detect him, given his evident lack of interest in contacting his own crew.

It made no sense to Linar. There was nothing Balok loved more than the *Fesarius*. This orbship was his home, even more than Cherela. What could possibly be urgent enough to transcend that?

"Bailey will be fine," McCoy reported to Kirk when he could finally get away to check in on sickbay. "The shrapnel didn't penetrate too deep, and the burns are minor. And I've already released Anne Nored—she suffered only mild smoke inhalation and some muscle strains. Determined girl, that one."

"I'll remember that," Kirk said. Nored was a fairly recent transfer to the ship, and this was the first time she had really been tested in the field. He was glad to know she had what it took. The way things stood, he would take his successes where he could get them.

Bailey sat up to greet Kirk as he entered the recovery ward. "Captain."

"I'm glad to see you're recovering, Lieutenant. Rahda asked me to pass along her thanks."

Bailey nodded. "I was glad to help, sir. What's our status?"

He delivered the depressing litany. "We're in bad shape, I'm afraid. We blew the starboard impulse manifolds and all but two dilithium circuits. The inertial dampers are burned out along with the tractor emitters. Deflectors are at minimum power. The lightning fused the port nacelle intercoolers, and a chunk of debris damaged the starboard Bussard intake."

"I see," Bailey said after a moment. "So we have no warp drive, no impulse power, and hardly any shields?"

"That's right."

"Meaning if we try to leave this place, the Dassik will make short work of us."

"In our current state, we could barely get out of the atmosphere."

"How many were lost in the module collapse?"

THE FACE OF THE UNKNOWN

"From our crew, nobody, thank heavens. From the Web, it's upward of thirty-eight hundred." He tried not to make it sound like just a number. It was obscene to reduce so many sapient lives, so many unique personalities and memories and aspirations and dreams, to a mere statistic. They were the lives James Kirk had failed to save . . . lives he might even have cost. But there was no way to put into words what that meant to him. All he had was the hideous inadequacy of arithmetic.

Bailey closed his eyes in acknowledgment of the loss. It was a while before he spoke again. "What . . . what's the reaction from the First?"

"Chaotic. They're preoccupied right now with the emergency. They have to relocate all the refugees, and they're still working to stabilize the Web. The loss of a module has imbalanced the system, created new stresses, and they're working to restore the balance. They're afraid that if the Web's equilibrium is too badly compromised, they won't be able to cancel their thermal and atmospheric signatures, leaving them detectable from space. And that would bring the Dassik down for sure."

"Is there anything we can do to help, sir?"

Kirk winced at his plaintive expression, then let out a heavy sigh. "They've rejected our offers of assistance. They don't want us anywhere near their systems. We're floating in open atmosphere now, the calmest air we can find, thousands of kilometers from the nearest module." He took a breath. "Next time they contact us, it'll probably be to demand my surrender for trial."

Bailey stared. "You, sir? No. No, Captain, it was my idea to interface our systems. This whole thing . . ." He took several sharp breaths, almost gasps, as the weight of his words sank in. "This whole thing is my fault. All those people . . ."

"No, Lieutenant. The decision was—"

Just then, the red alert klaxon sounded. Kirk ran to the wall and hit the intercom. "Kirk to bridge. Report."

"*Spock here, Captain. The First have sent an atmospheric craft. They are attempting to board the* Enterprise."

"I'm on my way." He ran from sickbay, with Bailey close behind, ignoring McCoy's protests. Kirk felt the deck shudder beneath his feet. Flipping open his communicator, he said, "Kirk to bridge. Are we under fire?"

"*Affirmative. They attempted to override our deflectors again, but our countermeasures were effective.*" The deck trembled again. "*They are now resorting to cruder methods.*"

"Shield status?"

Scott's voice came on the channel. "*Weak, Captain. Barely enough to stop a transporter beam, let alone a weapon. We're doin' all we can to boost it, but they won't hold long at this rate.*"

"*Correction, Mister Scott,*" Spock said. "*Their transporters are more powerful than anticipated. The beams are breaking through now. Multiple parties, Captain, including one near your—*"

Spock's voice broke off as the sound of weapons fire came over the channel. Kirk ran faster, but as he rounded the corner toward the turbolift, he saw a security team at the next intersection, pinned down in a firefight. Ensign Zhang spotted him and Bailey and called, "Sirs, stay down!"

Kirk drew his own phaser and hugged the wall, sidling over to the guard's side. "How many?" he asked her.

"Six of them. Stun weapons, but powerful ones." The bronze-skinned ensign tilted her head to indicate Crewman Konaka, who lay unconscious with a nasty burn on his red tunic. Gilbert and al-Rashid had dragged him to safety on the other side of the intersection.

"Give Bailey a weapon," Kirk ordered.

Gilbert tossed a phaser to the lieutenant, who held it warily. "I don't want to fight them, sir. Now, least of all."

"Neither do I, Lieutenant, but they've boarded my ship—again. If we have to fight, you need to be ready."

Bailey grimaced. "All right," he finally said, but he took care to ensure his phaser was on light stun.

Kirk peeked around the corridor. The boarding party was the usual eclectic mix of Firsts, and once again, Nisu was in the lead. That meant they probably knew he wasn't on the bridge.

The bridge. He raised his communicator again. "Spock, are you there?"

"Apologies, sir," Spock's voice came over the continuing weapons fire. *"It was necessary to find a more protected position."*

"Good thinking. I have a plan to deal with this."

"Captain Kirk!" It was Nisu's voice calling out. "I know you're there. Order your people to stand down!"

"You've illegally boarded my ship, Nisu!" he called back. "If *you* stand down, then we can talk!"

"You are not the wronged party here, Kirk! In the name of the Council of the First, I hereby order you, James Kirk, to surrender to lawful arrest! You are to be tried for your acts of this day. If you turn yourself in, we will leave your ship and crew unharmed."

Zhang hefted her phaser. "Don't worry, Captain. We

won't let them take you." She readied herself to jump out into the corridor.

But Kirk touched her shoulder with his fingertips. "Stand down, Ensign. Everyone, stand down!" he repeated more loudly.

"Captain, what are you—"

"I mean it, Spock!" He took a deep breath, released it. "Nisu! Tell your forces to stand down, and I'll turn myself over!"

A moment later, the sounds of weapons fire halted. "It is done," Nisu said.

"I'm coming out." He stepped forward slowly, hands raised, and once he was in view, he knelt to place his phaser on the ground. He gestured to the security team to fall back. Down the corridor, Nisu and her people moved forward gingerly. "You promise my crew won't be harmed?"

"They were only following your orders," the chief protector said. "And many of them acted commendably to save lives." At least the contempt she radiated was reserved for Kirk alone.

By the time Nisu's protectors pulled back his arms to cuff him, Spock had arrived in the corridor. "Spock, just in time."

"Captain." The Vulcan turned to the Kisaja. "Nisu, this is unnecessary. I implore you to reconsider."

"I cannot do that, Spock. This is greater than either of us. The safety of our home has been threatened. That overrides all other considerations."

"If Captain Kirk believed that," Spock countered, "then we would still be fighting you. We would never have risked our ship to come to your aid in the first place."

"Spock," Kirk said. "They're within their rights. I made a bad call. I'm not going to hide from the consequences."

Spock stared at him. "Jim . . ."

"You have the conn, Mister Spock. Keep my crew safe."

———

Kirk was taken back to the cliff-top government building in the Syletir world module, but this time there was no grand tour. As he was led in restraints along the skywalk between the hangar and the administration tower, he saw crowds of Linnik, Bogosrin, Fiilestii, and others gathered to watch, held back by cordons and security personnel. They shouted and hissed at him as he and his escorts went past, and while there were too many overlapping voices for his translator to parse clearly, he picked up enough. They blamed him, blamed his crew, for the destruction of the Fiilestii module. Some cursed him for bringing the Dassik, screaming that it would surely lead to the destruction of the Web.

Kirk had heard Spock and Uhura's report about the xenophobic reaction they had received in the Linnik warren. It was not the only such incident his crew had reported in their exploration of Cherela's world modules. But such reactions had been infrequent, and he had dismissed them as anomalies—until now. The captain realized that he had been so drawn to Triumvir Aranow's fascination with space that it had blinded him to the other Firsts' fear of it. Out there, the Dassik and other predators had devastated their worlds, their kinfolk, and it was only by retreating here beneath the clouds that they had survived. Their dread of the destroyers had been so entrenched in their psyches that the Dassik had remained their default bogeymen for countless generations, the face of fear itself to this very day. And now the real Dassik loomed overhead, searching for them, one lucky break from finding them and inflicting their ancient horrors once again. That fear must have been lingering below the surface of all the friendly Firsts his crew had met. As a basically decent people who took pride in the safe refuge their home offered, most of the Firsts had resisted that fear and tried to be welcoming. But all it had taken was one tragic incident in which outsiders had been implicated to make that free-floating fear coalesce into open xenophobia. It was a pattern all too familiar from human history, Kirk reflected.

Once inside the administration tower, Nisu unceremoniously escorted him to a meeting chamber adjacent to the triumvirs' situation room and left him there under guard to await their convenience. It was a long wait, and Kirk's attempts to make conversation with the protectors were met only with icy silence. They wouldn't even meet his eyes. Kirk tried not to fidget; it seemed disrespectful under the circumstances. But he had never been good at sitting still.

After a while, Kirk began to wonder if the triumvirs were intentionally making him wait as a show of contempt. But he realized that might be uncharitable when he felt a deep rumble through his feet. The world module wasn't shaking or swaying, but there was definitely a vibration, one not unlike those he'd felt going through the *Enterprise*'s deck during the storm. Whatever was keeping the triumvirs from seeing him, it wasn't just capriciousness or spite.

Kirk saw one of the protectors—a member of the Niatoko, as the reptilian humanoid species was known—step away and talk on his comm for a moment. When he returned, Kirk ventured to ask the burly brown protector, "Is anything wrong?" The Niatoko might as well have been a statue for all the response Kirk got.

He repeated the question once Triumvirs Aranow and Tirak finally arrived. "It is nothing to concern you," the latter said, his voice soft but cold.

"Just the storms," Aranow elaborated, unable to resist speaking even though she was reluctant to meet his eyes. "A temporary instability in the weather grid. Zan—Triumvir Lekur is attending to it."

"A consequence of the destruction *you* caused, Captain Kirk," said Tirak. "The loss of a world module disrupts the equilibrium of the Web, the careful atmospheric and thermal balance that maintains our concealment. As a result, Cherela is experiencing unusually powerful storms."

Kirk frowned. "With all due respect, Triumvir . . . wasn't it an unusually powerful storm that caused the collapse in the first place?"

"Individual such storms occur often," came the Linnik's hard-edged reply. "But they are not subsiding as they normally would. We will restore equilibrium in time. *We* know what we are doing."

Kirk quashed his impulse to fire off a retort. He didn't have the moral high ground here. "All right," he said. "I just want to be sure my crew will be safe."

"We won't let any harm come to them," Aranow said.

"So long as they follow the laws of the Web," Tirak added. "And cooperate in our legal proceedings against you."

"Our Prime Directive requires us to respect local laws.

I promise you, there won't be any interference with your legal process."

"Very well," Tirak said. "You will be remanded to the Nepara penal module until your trial can be scheduled. At the moment, more pressing matters occupy us."

"Wait . . . how long a delay are we talking about here? The *Enterprise* crew has other responsibilities, a larger mission to get back to."

"That is something they will no longer have to concern themselves with."

Kirk stared. Aranow turned away, which was more revealing than the controlled expression on Tirak's lined but boyish face. "Now, hold on! Nisu assured me you wouldn't penalize my crew for my actions! You can't hold them here as prisoners!"

"It's not like that," Aranow said, speaking more slowly than he'd ever heard her. "They'll be free to travel wherever they want . . . within the Web. Hundreds of worlds to explore. Enough to last them a lifetime."

"You've seen the mood out there," he countered. "Would my crew be safe if they left the ship?"

"We cannot let them go now," Tirak said. "Not when our concealment is so vulnerable. We must preserve the secret of our existence."

Kirk's jaw stiffened. "You never intended to let us go, did you?"

"It's for their own safety," Aranow said. "Your crew. Their ship is crippled. They couldn't survive. Not against the Dassik." Her eyes roved around the room, focusing everywhere but on his face. "The anger will die down in time. Then your people will be safe here. Free and safe, for as long as they live."

He stepped forward until she couldn't look away. The big Niatoko advanced on him, but Tirak halted the protector with a gesture. Kirk met the Tessegri's eyes imploringly. "Aranow . . . there's more to life than safety."

Her gaze hardened. "That's the kind of thinking that gets people killed."

Nine

The *Enterprise* was in rough shape. Commander Scott was doing all he could to repair the vessel, but there were limits. Many of the spare dilithium crystals installed to replace those burned out in the battle with the Dassik had been burned out in turn themselves, so that the remaining reserve of crystals and relay components was only sufficient to repair half of the power circuits. The nacelle damage, meanwhile, was the kind that would take a spacedock to repair properly. A makeshift job could be done; it was, of course, a bad idea to design a starship that could not restore its own warp capability at least well enough to reach a repair base. But restoring the nacelle to combat specs, ensuring that it would not weaken or blow out during pursuit or battle, was beyond what the crew could achieve without external support and replacement parts.

The irony was that the *Enterprise* was currently *in* a dry dock, one belonging to a highly advanced, warp-capable civilization with abundant resources and technical skill. They had been permitted its use for shelter from the elements following Kirk's arrest. Yet they were prohibited from using its facilities to perform any actual repairs.

"*It is a matter of security,*" Nisu explained—or rationalized—over the bridge viewscreen when Spock requested assistance. "*Neither your safety nor ours can be assured if we allow the* Enterprise *to leave Cherela at the present time. To ensure your cooperation, we must regrettably make an exception to our hospitality and decline your requests for repair assistance."*

Spock steepled his fingers before him, his elbows resting on the arms of the command chair. He studied Nisu's visage on the viewscreen, although he could sense nothing from its digital re-creation of her eyes. Her tone and manner were clear enough, though. The Kisaja chief protector was stiff and formal toward him, treating him like a stranger. The trust that had formed so easily between them before was suspended, if not destroyed. Perhaps Nisu believed she had been too hasty in extending it to him.

But such personal matters were beside the point in the current situation. He kept his own tone suitably formal as he replied. "We have no intention of leaving Cherela without our captain. Yet you have not only confined the *Enterprise* to this dock, you have confined its crew aboard the ship itself. How long do you expect this state of affairs to continue?"

Her reply was measured. *"You are welcome to stay as our guests for as long as may be needed. However, given current . . . tensions, it is best if you remain aboard your own vessel for the time being. Once tempers have cooled, you will again be free to travel anywhere you wish within the Web—supervised, of course, for your safety until . . . until you become more familiar with your new environs."*

He considered her words. "Very well. Your . . . hospitality is appreciated, Nisu. I intend to demonstrate to you that we are still worthy of it." Her expression did not waver. Taking the hint, he went on, "For the moment, though, we must concentrate on our repairs. Spock out."

On the upper deck to Spock's left, Lieutenant Bailey clenched the hand rail tensely, displeased that Spock had closed the channel before allowing him to speak. "With all due respect, sir, you're not just going to give in to them, are you? They have the captain prisoner! We should be mounting a rescue, not arranging for tourist visas!"

Spock turned the command chair to face the young human and held his gaze calmly. "Mister Bailey, you, more than any of us, are familiar with the First Federation citizens' proclivities toward defensiveness and caution. Many of them are already holding us accountable for the Fiilestii collapse. How do you suppose they would react to an armed raid on our part against their government facilities? At this point, our best option is to avoid antagonizing the local authorities until their tempers have had a chance to cool, as Nisu said. Perhaps then we can negotiate for the captain's release."

Rising from the chair, he went on. "In the meantime, our priority must be our own vessel. We are badly damaged in a hostile physical environment, our relationship with our hosts is tenuous at best, and the planet remains under siege from above. Whatever course of action we take, we shall need an intact ship to carry it out. We need our shields, our weapons, and our engines."

"Aye, sir," Scott said. "And when you say engines . . ."

"Warp and impulse, Commander."

"Wait a minute," Bailey said. "Why would we need warp engines? We can't abandon Captain Kirk!"

"Think it through, Mister Bailey. The First Federation's technology surpasses ours significantly in many respects, and their resources here on Cherela surpass ours insurmountably. Rescuing the captain would accomplish little if we lacked the ability to leave this planet upon doing so."

That silenced the young ambassador. After a moment,

he descended the steps and spoke more softly. "You're right, Spock. I'm sorry. It's just . . . I'm the one they should've taken. It was my suggestion to tie our power to theirs. I was reckless, and it cost thousands of lives. I'm still as much of a hothead as I ever was. And the captain shouldn't be punished for that."

"First of all, Mister Bailey, we do not yet have a complete enough assessment of the event to say for sure that our actions were responsible. Second, even if they were, the responsibility is not yours. It was the captain's choice to act on your suggestion."

"But you don't understand, Spock. I played on our history. Three years ago, he convinced me it was worth taking risks to help others. I used those same ideas to sell him on my plan because I knew it would resonate."

"Even so, Captain Kirk does not blindly follow the suggestions of others, nor is he easily manipulated by nostalgia. He acted on your proposal because *he* concluded that the risk was worth taking. Had he not deemed it so, he would have rejected the plan."

"And come up with something better."

"Or nothing at all. Captain Kirk is not infallible, Lieutenant. He makes his share of mistakes. But he does not dwell on them. Instead, he focuses on moving forward and avoiding their repetition in the future. Do you understand, Mister Bailey?"

After a moment, Bailey nodded. "Yes, sir. I understand."

As soon as Koust saw the enemy vessel emerging from the haze, he opened fire.

He had been ready, determined not to be taken by

surprise. This planet's endless expanse of ugly blue haze threatened to lull a hunter's senses into complacency, but Koust would not fall victim. He knew he was here to prove himself or die in the attempt. Or possibly both. He had almost died several times merely getting this far; the fierce winds and lightning in this planet's upper atmosphere had almost torn his pilot vessel apart. But his flying skills and sheer determination (with, admittedly, considerable help from the vessel's sturdy construction and overpowered engines) had brought him through that challenge, and now he faced his next enemy without fear or hesitation.

But his reflex to fire had been hasty. He had failed to gauge the actual size of the object he approached, thinking it much smaller and closer than it actually was. His disruptor bolt dissipated, scattered and absorbed by dozens of kilometers of hydrogen and methane, before it reached its target. The structure was huge, larger than any space station Koust had ever seen. He swore an oath and flew toward it even faster. He had sacrificed the element of surprise; he had to make up for it by closing to an effective combat range. One of the betrayers or their allies would no doubt run away and wait for another chance to sneak in, but a Dassik hunter charged in fearlessly and counted on his enemy's shock and alarm at the sight.

Before Koust could make it very far, though, his ship was caught in a tractor beam and dragged to a halt. He tried every move he knew to break free of it. But then his controls began to shut down, their power disrupted by some external interference. He was caught from all directions, it seemed, and there was no enemy in range to fire upon. He fired at the distant station anyway, hoping enough energy would get through to do at least some damage.

Then he heard his hull groaning and screeching as the beams began to pull it apart. "No, I will not be defeated like this!" Koust cried. His mission was too important. The secrets of the betrayers were nearly in his grasp! He could not let them conquer him so easily. He was better than that. The Dassik were so much more than they had been in ancient times. He had to prove that now, to earn survival for himself and his people.

But his power systems were still shutting down, his weapons useless, his hull starting to disintegrate. There was only one way left to gain a victory over the betrayers. And so he reached for the self-destruct controls. It seemed redundant with the pilot vessel shrieking its last around him, but a torn-open vessel could still be studied for Dassik technological and military secrets. A vessel blown to atoms could not. And in this dense atmosphere, the self-destruct warhead would cause a mighty fireball, shock wave, and electromagnetic pulse, perhaps enough to inflict some damage on the standoffish foe. Thus he would score a blow against the betrayers, leaving a wound that those who came after him could exploit.

But before Koust could key in the destruct sequence, he felt himself dissolving in a transporter beam. The enemy would not even grant him this victory.

As soon as he was whole again, he roared. Looking around for his enemy, he spotted a tall female with a short-furred golden head and vast blue eyes. She stood on the outside of the confinement chamber that now held him. "Release me!" he demanded. He drew his dagger and struck at the clear wall between them with its clubbed hilt. Repeated blows had no effect, so he inverted it and pried at the door seam with the blade. "I will kill you!" he cried, though his assault on the door had no effect. Finally he drew his disruptor pistol and fired at the female's face. But the weapon was dead.

The female tilted her head. "Forgive me for not responding in your language," she said in the tongue of the Linnik. "Your hostility creates a resistance to communication. Are you familiar with this tongue?"

Of course—one of the legendary Kisaja. He had not been convinced they were real. "Yes," he replied in the same inferior language. Its sounds and forms had changed somewhat since the races had last met, but the form she used was archaic enough that he could follow it.

"Good. Tell me: How much have you seen?"

"Enough," Koust replied. "Your base hidden under the clouds. So this is where the Kisaja went to ground. One more refuge for the cowards of the 'First Federation.' But now we know it is here. We shall seize it and strip the location of the betrayers themselves from its databanks! Then we will hunt them for sport!"

The Kisaja female retained her control, but Koust could see her tension subsiding. "I see. You know nothing. But of course, we cannot return you now." She gestured to a subordinate at a console. "Perhaps with another race, we could come to an understanding. But with you—"

He pre-empted her. "There can be no understanding between us. Not until you understand we are your masters."

The female actually smirked. "You're just as insecure and bullying as the Dassik ever were. I've really had enough of overconfident types today." She turned to her minion. "Why not put him in Nepara, next to our other guest? See how well they get along." The two of them chuckled, and moments later, Koust felt himself dematerializing again.

He arrived in a chamber large enough to hold his pilot vessel, under a broad, clear dome that looked out onto the blue emptiness. To his outrage, he had been rematerialized naked, stripped of all his armor and weapons. But a simple jumpsuit materialized next to him, and once he donned it, he found it was exactly his size, as though the transporter beam had taken his measurements and instantly synthesized a garment.

Walking to the edges of the chamber and surveying the view through the dome, he saw he was atop a saucer-shaped structure reminiscent of the forward hull of the Starfleet ship Grun was seeking, though significantly larger. It hung alone in the vast, empty sky. Three heavy cables, no wider than his waist, stretched out from its edges and vanished into the distance. As far as he could tell, there was nothing beneath the structure either. Certainly it was nowhere near the immense station Koust had seen before.

"Do not move." The voice made Koust whirl. In the center of the room, an elevator platform was rising from a circular gap in the floor. A Kisaja male appeared, this one with silver head fur and purple eyes. He was accompanied by two enormous guards of species Koust didn't recognize and would have taken for animals if not for the sidearms they bore. Koust began to charge, but the guards brought their weapons to bear faster than he would have expected from creatures of such bulk. He came to a halt. "You can gain nothing by resisting," the Kisaja said. "As you've seen, you're worlds away from anywhere. This is the Nepara penal module, and I am Mure, its warden. No one enters or leaves this place unless I will it. There is no escape."

"There is always death."

Mure gave him a condescending smile. "If that were what you wanted, you wouldn't have stopped just now. Perhaps you're not as mindlessly savage as the rest of your race—though I doubt it. Now come with us."

The weak creature's insult rankled him, but he would not give his jailer the satisfaction of confirming his beliefs. Grudgingly, Koust let them lead him onto the elevator and down into what he now recognized as a prison. He tried to get a sense of the place, but the guards blocked his view with their bulk, and it didn't take long to reach his cell. It was a simple enough cell, its walls translucent with transparent portions. The guards dematerialized the door, pushed him through, then rematerialized it, sealing him in. The cell's accommodations were basic but comfortable, a luxury suite compared to his bunk aboard the cluster ship.

And he had a neighbor. A human neighbor, a male with sandy hair and bright eyes, dressed in the same kind of gray jumpsuit as Koust.

"Welcome," the human said. "I'm Jim Kirk. So what are you in for?"

Within a day, and with help from statements issued by the Council's Kisaja press secretary, the mood within the Web of Worlds began to calm. The arrest of Captain Kirk had allowed the populace to feel that justice was being pursued, and the Council's statement urged the people to remember their customs of friendship toward refugees and not to hold the *Enterprise* crew responsible for the decisions of its captain. It was not an ideal sentiment, in Spock's view, but it was sufficient to allow Nisu to grant the crew permission to leave the ship, albeit under protector escort at all times.

Spock advised the crew to take advantage of this new freedom. "Many of you have already spent time as tourists, making connections among the Web dwellers," he announced to the department heads. "See where those connections can lead you. In a community this large and diverse, there must be dissent. It is logical to expect that in the immediate wake of a disaster, those who bear grievances against the sitting government will be emboldened. Seek out those who do not agree with the party line. Particularly those who have engineering skills or access to starship technology—as well as those who understand the Web's tractor systems and how to subvert them. It is still my hope that we can resolve this situation diplomatically. But in the event that we cannot, we must be ready to act."

Once the crew had begun mingling, it didn't take long at all for a dissident faction to approach them. Spock had been concerned that the protector escorts would be an impediment to such contacts, but it turned out that one of the escorts was herself a dissident. Ne-Kewii, a Fiilestii who had survived the module collapse, made contact with Lieutenant Sulu to pass along a message. The Fiilestii warned that the collapse of her module was only the beginning, and she invited the *Enterprise*'s senior officers to a meeting in Kenaibrara, one of the Web's nature preserve modules, if they wished to know more.

Spock attended the meeting in the company of Sulu and Bailey. Most of Kenaibrara's volume consisted of a tropical rainforest dominated by enormous trees with giant, disk-shaped leaves in hues of magenta and violet. Spock found the humidity most uncomfortable but endured it stoically. Sulu, who numbered botany among his many interests, was far from stoic, reacting to the exotic foliage with considerable enthusiasm.

Ne-Kewii led them to a small clearing within the forest, then took to the air to ensure the area was clear of eavesdroppers. "All clear," she announced as she landed in a quadrupedal crouch and folded back her silver-feathered wings. Spock was reminded of the Greek mythological creature called the sphinx, until Ne-Kewii rose into a more upright posture, resting on her haunches and using her wingtips for added support. "I have sent my partners the signal. They are on their way."

Moments later, two more Web denizens emerged into the clearing. One was a Bogosrin male, stockier than Lekur Zan and with golden rather than dark brown fur. "This is Kasan Tor," Ne-Kewii informed them.

Spock nodded to the Bogosrin. "Commander Spock of the *Enterprise*. My colleague Lieutenant Sulu, and Ambassador David Bailey."

A hearty tenor laugh erupted from the small, silver-robed figure behind the Bogosrin as he stepped forward into full view. "Mister Bailey needs no introduction. Do you, my friend?"

Bailey's face split into a grin. "Balok!" he cried, striding forward to greet the *Fesarius* commander. "I was worried about you! Where the hell have you been all this time? What was with the cryptic messages?"

"One question at a time, please," Balok intoned, still laughing. "I do apologize for the theatrics, but the circumstances made it necessary to keep the triumvirs from knowing of my return. I needed freedom of movement so that I could coordinate with my friends in the underground." He chuckled. "If you'll pardon the expression. It doesn't quite make sense in these surroundings, does it?"

Ne-Kewii flexed her wings and hissed. "You laugh too easily, Balok. Sometimes at most inappropriate things. Or have you forgotten what has become of my home ground?"

"Certainly not," Balok went on, abruptly displaying a steel and solemnity that were quite incongruous on his childlike, gap-toothed countenance. "I'm here, am I not? I brought them, did I not?"

"Yes, he did," Kasan Tor said, addressing his words to Ne-Kewii. The Fiilestii dug her foreclaws into the soil and stilled herself.

Sulu stepped toward her, offering a mollifying gesture. "I was on the module when it fell," he told her. "I saw it all. Believe me, we understand your loss."

Ne-Kewii appeared to appreciate his words. "You are not the ones to blame," she said. "And my people have lost our home before. The First Federation used to be about reaching out to the homeless and lost, giving them safe refuge. But these days, we've become too insular. The government values concealment above all else. They're so concerned with protecting our physical existence that they don't realize how much they've eroded our soul."

"Come on, Ne-Kewii," Kasan said. "You promised you wouldn't turn this into an ideological thing."

"I'm just saying—"

"I know. I could quote it from memory, you've said it so many times." The Bogosrin turned to Spock. "The point is, all this hiding is endangering our physical existence too. The Web has become a greater danger to itself than any invader could be."

"Please elaborate," Spock invited.

"What happened to Fiilestii wasn't your fault," Balok said.

Bailey looked up sharply. "It wasn't?"

"No, my friend, no. It was the end result of instabilities that have been building up for a long time."

"More or less, yeah," Kasan said. "Could've happened anywhere, but it hit there first. Will happen again if we don't change our ways."

"What is the nature of these instabilities?" Spock asked.

"You know how we hide ourselves, right?" the Bogosrin went on.

Spock nodded. "You modify the circulation and thermal distribution of the atmosphere, as well as the dynamics of the planetary magnetic field, to cancel out the effects of the Web's presence within them."

"In brief, yes," Balok said. "Now, tell me, Mister Spock, speaking as a scientist: Does that sound like a stable system to you?"

Spock raised a brow. "The First possess a greater understanding of the relevant technologies than I do. However, it has occurred to me to wonder how such suppression of the atmosphere's natural circulation could be maintained over the long term without negative consequences."

"Well, here's your answer," Kasan replied. "It can't."

Bailey frowned. "I don't get it."

"I'll make it easy for you," the Bogosrin went on.

"There's a whole lot of energy in Cherela's atmosphere. A lot of heat and movement. You want to make the Web invisible, you have to control that energy, make it flow the same way it would if the Web weren't there at all. But you have to *use* energy to do that. And that energy, that heat, gets added to the atmosphere. So you have to make that energy invisible too. Which means you have to use more energy, which—"

"I see," Sulu said. "Sooner or later you hit a point of diminishing returns. All that energy keeps building up in the system until you can't hide it anymore." Spock was reminded that Sulu had served as an astrophysicist before transferring to flight control.

"It's much more complex than that, Lieutenant Sulu," Balok told him. "There are ways to balance the system— to recycle the energy back into the grid, or to let it leak out at levels too low to affect the weather. But this Web of ours is an immensely intricate system whose concealment depends on maintaining many different kinds of equilibrium at once. Imagine your mythical Atlas balancing the world on his shoulders." The Linnik commander grinned. "Now imagine him as a juggler."

"And the atmosphere's even more intricate," Ne-Kewii said. "The builders of the Web were so confident they could master all its complexities, but that was pure arrogance."

"Now, be fair," Kasan growled. "My forebears—and Balok's—did an impressive job with the Web. The problem is that the system they designed worked at the size they originally built it. Over the millennia, as we kept building more and more world modules, it put more strain on the system and the atmosphere. We've tried to upgrade the atmospheric regulation systems, the magnetic and gravitational control networks, and so on to keep pace with the growing demands. But again, it comes down to heat. The more modules there are, the more waste heat they generate, and the harder that is to contain."

"And the larger and more complex the system gets," Balok added, "the more opportunities there are for Atlas to fumble—for components to fail or to interact in ways that create progressive instabilities."

"Instabilities both in the Web and in the atmosphere it occupies," Spock interpreted.

"That's right," Kasan told him. "And they feed back on each other. These storms we've been getting lately, the flaws in the concealment grid that let you detect us . . . the government insists they're just a natural fluctuation like Cherela's had many times in the past. But they've been getting steadily worse for years now. There's a trend the Council won't admit to, because it would mean admitting that continuing to build up the Web *and* keep it hidden indefinitely is a failed policy. *Ghrrr,* now it would mean admitting that their policies *caused* the destruction of Fiilestii, and they'll never admit to that."

"So we . . . we didn't cause the module to collapse sooner?" Bailey asked with great relief in his voice.

"Hard to say, really," Kasan said, oblivious to Bailey's sense of culpability. "The situation there was profoundly unstable. The storm, the gravity failures, the structural upheavals . . . there were so many volatile things happening at once that it's impossible to pin the final collapse on any one factor. The triumvirs want to think your gravity feed caused the system overload because Lekur can't believe his precious systems could go that wrong on their own. But at most, it was the final push that toppled an already-failing system. If it hadn't been that, the next lightning strike might've pushed things over the edge."

"And if Captain Kirk hadn't attempted to hold Fiilestii with tractor beams," Balok said, "it might have collapsed even sooner. I, for one, believe that far more people would have died without the *Enterprise*'s involvement. Captain Kirk is being made a scapegoat when he should be called a hero." He smiled up at Bailey. "You all should." Bailey smiled back, clasping Balok's shoulder.

Spock raised his brows. "I am sure the crew of the *Enterprise* will appreciate that sentiment as much as the ambassador does. However, I assume it was not the sole reason you requested this meeting. You believe we can do something to advance your cause."

"That's right," Ne-Kewii said. "Your interests coincide with ours. Together, we may be able to save the Web from its current leadership."

"I must inform you that our Prime Directive forbids us from taking sides in internal disputes. We would certainly be willing to mediate negotiations between you and the sitting government, but if you seek to solicit military assistance in a coup, that would not be possible."

Balok laughed raucously. "Oh, yes. A war. Just what we need when the Web is already starting to tear itself apart around us."

Kasan Tor's reply was more sober. "Mister Spock, we've lost modules before, but never as suddenly and violently as Fiilestii, and never when the system as a whole was so overloaded and close to failure. Fiilestii's collapse was just the beginning of the avalanche. It's left a hole in the grid that was keeping the atmospheric forces in check, and what's left is too unstable to hold them in. If we don't make some drastic changes, then all of Cherela's repressed fury is going to break free and tear the Web apart with storms that will make the last one look like a gentle drizzle."

"What kind of changes are you talking about?" Sulu asked.

"The only way the Web can survive, Mister Sulu," Balok said, "is if we stop trying to suppress the atmosphere's response to our presence within it. We have to let the natural forces flow freely and find a new equilibrium, one that we're an integral part of rather than one we're fighting against."

"I see," Spock said. "A simple, elegant, and obvious solution. But one that would permanently alter Cherela's cloud layers and thermal profile, thus advertising the Web's existence to outside observers."

"Exactly," Ne-Kewii said. "Hiding here is killing us."

"But the Dassik are out there," Sulu pointed out.

"Yes, they might find us," Balok said. "But we are stronger now than we were twelve thousand years ago, and they . . . well, they are weaker than they were. And if we do nothing," he finished with a shrug, "then soon there will be nothing for them to find in any case."

"I presume you have made the government aware of your conclusions," Spock said.

"We've tried many times," Kasan replied. "They don't want to listen. They're so afraid of what's out there that they refuse to believe our findings. They dismiss them as 'fearmongering speculations.' The only scientists they're willing to listen to are those who tell them what they want to hear."

"Are you hoping we can convince them?" Sulu asked. "I mean, if it comes from outside, not just from people they've already dismissed . . ."

"They won't listen," Ne-Kewii said. "It doesn't matter what the source is. Their power is based on their success at keeping us hidden. They'll never admit they've been wrong to do that. They'll absolutely never admit their own policies are murdering the Web."

"And let's face it," Kasan said, "considering they just threw your captain in jail and refused to let you leave, you're not exactly high on their list of people to trust right now."

"Yes, they are fearful," Balok said, his voice as serious as Spock had ever known it to be. "Fearful of outsiders. Fearful of losing power. Fearful of being proven wrong. We have become a people too enslaved to our own fear, and it is destroying us. But that is exactly why I believe humanity can help us."

Spock studied him. "The tests you conducted," he said. "You were assessing more than the threat we posed to the First Federation."

"Quite right, Mister Spock. That is how I presented the program to the triumvirs, of course, but I had an ulterior motive. Since our own government would not accept the truth, I knew we needed allies. We needed the help of someone who offered not merely technological advancement, benevolence, and mercy, but some deeper, more ineffable quality as well." He turned to Bailey. "It was you, David, who showed me that quality at last—the quality that led me to invite you aboard as an ambassador."

The lieutenant shook his head, nonplussed. "What quality, Balok? What was so special about me?"

"Your fear."

It was not the flattering answer Bailey expected. "Excuse me?"

Balok chuckled at his reaction. "Of all the stalwart officers on your bridge, as you faced my Mister Hyde and his deadly ultimatum, you were the most fearful. The one least in control of his terror, most ready to lash out at the thing you feared."

"Gee, thanks."

Balok took the lieutenant's hand in his own far tinier one. "And yet, in time, you learned to overcome that fear. More, you volunteered to face the very thing you had feared so much before—even to reach out a hand of friendship to it. And when I offered you an opportunity to get to know us better, you leaped at it. The same passion that fueled your fear, the same dissatisfaction with your lot in life, was transformed into the ambition to learn and grow. All it needed was a shift in direction from a negative response to a more constructive one.

"Through you, friend David, I learned that fear could be overcome. I saw how humans had the capacity to learn from their fears and failures and transform them into strengths. And I hoped that you, and your people, could help our leaders learn to make the same transformation in themselves."

Bailey was dumbstruck, blinking rapidly. Sulu chuckled and thumped him on the back. "Always knew you had it in you, kid."

The younger lieutenant cleared his throat. "But if that's so, Balok . . . why didn't you just bring me here? Why keep me out on the *Fesarius* for three years?"

"What's the matter? Didn't you like my ship?"

"Come on, Balok, enough joking around." The Linnik commander merely stared up at him with a very boyish pout. "Okay, I like the *Fesarius* fine. Now will you answer the question?"

"Oh, very well," Balok said after a further moment's pondering. "But surely you can see that with a culture as . . . well, as timid and committed to concealment as ours, I couldn't just bring you here and solve our problems with one lecture. I knew it would take time to convince them you were safe and trustworthy. And I couldn't let on what my deeper goals were, of course. I was trying to be subtle. I thought I would have much more time to influence matters, to nudge the triumvirs until they were ready to learn from your example. To strengthen the ties between our Federations to a point where they would trust you enough to accept your aid. I had expected that to be the work of decades, perhaps generations."

"Decades? You were gonna string me along for decades?"

Balok ignored the lieutenant. "But matters have become urgent far faster than we anticipated. Especially with the Dassik suddenly showing up again. Which is a whole other story in itself," he finished with a hint of unease.

"So we may be forced to take more radical action," Kasan said before Spock could question Balok further. "We can help you repair your ship. Ne-Kewii can smuggle the parts aboard if you tell us what you need. Then, once you're ready, we can sabotage the tractor system long enough to let you get away. With some of our representatives aboard, that is."

"That way," Ne-Kewii added, "we can inform your

Federation of the Web's existence and make a formal request for aid. Once our secret is out, the government will have no reason to cling to its suicidal obsession with concealment."

"That's the optimistic outcome," Kasan said. "More likely they'll keep debating and denying until the Web is torn apart around them. At the very least," he said, his gruff voice growing more solemn, "your Starfleet can help resettle those who get away, and some of our cultural legacy will survive."

Spock could appreciate his sentiment, but at this point, everything the dissidents said was merely hearsay, and at least in Ne-Kewii's case there was a clear ideological motive behind it. "I would appreciate the opportunity to review your scientific data on the system instabilities you describe," he said. "Naturally we must verify your findings before we decide on a course of action."

"Of course," Balok said. "Take your time, Mister Spock. It's not like the world is coming to an end or anything, after all. Oh, wait. Yes, it is."

Kasan handed Spock a data cartridge. "Here's our original research. Feel free to compare it against the copies on the Web's information network. Whatever our problems, at least we have free speech."

"For now," Ne-Kewii interposed.

"But decide fast, Mister Spock—before we all run out of ground to stand on."

Ten

Kirk's fellow prisoner had not been very neighborly so far. The Dassik soldier had given up little beyond his name, Koust. He seemed youthful to Kirk, despite his cadaverous features and booming voice. His intense energy and pent-up rage reminded Kirk somewhat of the young David Bailey—not to mention the young Jim Kirk. But that rage had been an effective barrier to communication in this case. Koust had pegged Kirk as an enemy, the commander of the ship that his pack hunted, and the fact that they were both prisoners did not affect that perception. "You are Federation," he had insisted, unimpressed by Kirk's attempts to clarify the difference between *First* and *United.* "I am not a fool. You will not win my confidence. I will not tell you anything to pass along to your treacherous masters!" Stimulating conversation with a fellow prisoner was off the table, then.

Still, for the most part, this was one of the most clean and humane prisons Kirk had ever been thrown into. The accommodations were comfortable, there were reading and viewing materials available, the meals were adequate and healthy, and he was beamed to an exercise yard daily—although it had quickly become evident, in his first visit to the yard, that the rest of the prison's population blamed him for the destruction of Fiilestii and would gladly take his punishment into their own hands. Thus, it had been necessary to keep Kirk in protective isolation. The prison warden, a purple-eyed Kisaja male named

Mure, clearly held Kirk in the same contempt as the inmates did, judging from the willies Kirk felt when Mure's gaze transfixed him for even a moment. But the warden followed the letter of his responsibilities and took the necessary steps to ensure Kirk's safety, though he made it clear enough that he did so grudgingly. Kirk assumed the same was true for Koust, given that he and the Dassik were the only two inmates in the isolation wing. But their shared pariah status had not led to bonding.

This was not in itself an intolerable state of affairs. Though Kirk was gregarious by nature, he had schooled himself to discipline over his long years in Starfleet. There was a part of him that valued solitude and quiet contemplation, and he had nurtured that side of his character during his time at the Academy, enabling him to excel in his studies at the cost of being perceived as a humorless bookworm. Perhaps he had taken it a bit too far, but he had deemed it necessary to keep his more passionate and unruly side in check. In time, friends like Gary Mitchell and lovers like Carol Marcus had helped him to open up once more and find a healthy balance between the sides of his character. But his quiet, studious side still served him well in the solitary role of a starship commander, and it aided in coping with the solitude of his imprisonment now.

Still, there were more lives at stake than his own. Opening communication with a member of the Dassik, understanding what they believed and what they sought, could be key to resolving the current crisis and preventing a clash between the Dassik and the UFP.

So Kirk had continued speaking to Koust, attempting to make some sort of connection. He had monologued about his own life, his ship, his friends and colleagues, the worlds he had visited in the Federation and beyond. He had spoken of his youth on the farm in Iowa, of his father and mother and their own illustrious Starfleet careers, of his great-grandparents who had served aboard the *U.S.S. Pioneer* during the formative years of the Federation, of the more distant ancestor who'd commanded a lunar base and the one who'd been on an early manned mission to Venus. He had hoped that, by directing the conversation toward his own family history, he might encourage Koust to do the same. Warrior peoples often took pride in their lineages, and tales of the past would presumably be less strategically sensitive than current information.

Indeed, it was clear that Koust was tempted to react at times. Yet the young hunter held himself in check and revealed nothing. Kirk was surprised. The Firsts had characterized the Dassik as a feral people, relying on brute force and intimidation to compel more intelligent, disciplined species like the Linnik and Bogosrin to achieve the refined work of building a starfaring civilization. But then, those were tales passed down from twelve millennia in the past. Perhaps the Dassik had changed, or perhaps the tales had distorted the facts. At least he learned that much from Koust's silence . . . though it underlined how much more he was failing to learn.

The real test of Koust's refusal to speak was under way when Kirk was beamed back to his cell from his exercise period the following day. He arrived to find Mure standing outside the transparent wall of the Dassik's cell, transfixing him with his gaze. Next to the Kisaja stood the diminutive figure of Triumvir Tirak, looking on in fascination as Koust sweated and shook, groaning through gritted teeth as the warden pressed him telepathically. Reflexively, Kirk pounded against the dividing barrier. "Stop it! You're hurting him!"

Mure did not react, but Tirak looked up at Kirk in irritation. The Linnik triumvir stepped around Mure's bulkier form to get closer to the captain. "Our methods inflict no pain," Tirak insisted. "The Dassik is causing his own distress by resisting. Once he cooperates, he will no longer suffer."

"Every torturer in history has said the same thing," Kirk shot back. "It's easy to inflict pain if you can pretend it's not your own fault."

"Says the man whose crew attempts to help him evade his culpability for the death of thousands."

Kirk's gaze didn't falter. "If a fair trial concludes I am responsible, then I will face the penalty for that. But what has he done to warrant this treatment?"

"He is our first Dassik captive. We require intelligence about their numbers, their resources, their distribution. Our survival may depend on it. And as I said, our methods cause no harm—only his resistance does."

"If it's so humane, Tirak, then why haven't you done the same to me?"

The triumvir's expression made it clear he was tempted. Still, he said, "The crime you committed was well documented. My fellow triumvirs feel you have been cooperative . . . and they do not wish to court the disapproval of your Federation."

"You don't agree?"

It was startling to see such bitterness on such a childlike face. "I fear they are deaf to the anxiety of the masses. We are in the midst of a crisis—Dassik threatening us from above, disaster striking from within. The people are frightened. More, they are angry that this chaos has been brought to our safe haven of Cherela. This is not a time for tentative measures, for the slow and careful grind of the justice system. The people need prompt assurances. They need the source of their fears dealt with swiftly and decisively."

"How, Tirak? By turning them against any convenient enemy? By firing them up to inflict cruelty on others? That's not calming their fears, it's feeding them."

"I know what my people want, Kirk. I know what they need. My only goal is to give it to them—in spite of the restrictions imposed by laws formulated in gentler times."

"So you admit that what Mure is doing to his prisoner is against the law. Do you hear that, Warden? You're under no obligation to obey an unlawful order! Mure!"

The Kisaja's huge violet eyes finally released Koust—and came to rest on Kirk. For a moment, he felt what Koust must have felt, the overpowering pressure on his mind. Even without resistance, it was invasive, violating, humiliating. More than that . . . he could feel the hatred that motivated it. While the effect lasted, he despised himself as deeply as Mure despised him. It was brief, but it left him shaken once the warden broke his gaze. Kirk understood: The warden was a willing accomplice. Tirak had simply given him permission to do what he had wished to do anyway.

"I'm still a witness," Kirk gasped. "You can't frighten me into keeping quiet about this. So unless you plan to kill me . . ."

"We have no death penalty, of course," Tirak said. "We are not barbarians. Still . . . if you were to die, it would resolve the matter of Fiilestii without the need for a time-consuming trial, or for testimony that might confuse the people at a time when they need clarity."

"You have very little faith in your own people, Tirak."

"Oh, I have great faith in their principles, Captain. I know they would never tolerate anything so primitive as an execution—not at the hands of a First." His gaze drifted over to Koust's cell. "Of course, one cannot expect anything but primitive violence from a Dassik. See the hatred in his gaze. Even now, after you have defended him, he clearly wants you dead. If he were to get loose somehow . . . well, naturally we would take all necessary measures to subdue him, but conceivably we might not put him down in time. Tragic, to be sure, but it would simplify matters enormously."

Kirk saw the glance that passed between Tirak and the warden, and he understood that this was not a hypothetical discussion. Getting through to Koust had just become more urgent than ever.

"The dissidents' conclusions appear to be sound," Spock told the rest of the senior staff seated around the table in the main briefing room. "Their theoretical model is more mathematically rigorous and more consistent with the documented evidence—presupposing the accuracy of data gathered before our arrival—than the model that serves as the basis for the government's policies. While the government model may have been sound for the original Web, it has failed to adequately account for the exponential increase in system chaos that has accompanied its growing size and complexity over the centuries. The dissidents' model predicted a world module collapse consistent with what we observed at Fiilestii, as well as the continued instability of Cherela's atmosphere in the wake of that collapse. Their overall conclusion is most likely sound as well. The module collapse has triggered a runaway instability in the Web's structural, magnetic, and gravitational balance and in Cherela's atmosphere as well. The only way to reverse that instability is to shut down the process that is driving it, namely the atmospheric and magnetic regulation that keeps the Web concealed. If that does not occur within a fairly short span of time—years at most, possibly months—then the complete destruction of the Web of Worlds is inevitable within two decades."

McCoy was torn between horror and relief. "Then Jim wasn't responsible!" he said.

"Correct," Spock told him. "However, convincing the triumvirs of that will be difficult. They are aware of this research and choose to dismiss it."

"And these dissidents are hoping," Lieutenant Uhura said, "that if the Web is revealed to the Federation anyway, it will obviate the need for concealment and force the government's hand."

"Correct."

"I have to ask," the communications officer continued, "what about the Prime Directive? We're not supposed to take sides in a local dispute."

"Even if there's a whole civilization at stake?" McCoy protested, his eyes wide. "Not just one—dozens of civilizations! We can't just stand by and let them destroy themselves!"

"Certainly not while they still hold Captain Kirk!" Chekov added.

"As it happens, Doctor," Spock went on, "I was about to make that very point. For every regulation, there is an exception. That can be particularly true of the Prime Directive, given that each contact will be unique. Captain Kirk has always understood this."

"But you haven't always agreed with him," McCoy riposted.

"Each case must be judged on its own merits, Doctor. In this case, I am not convinced the Prime Directive applies at all. Given that the government of the First Federation is holding us here against our will, that classifies them as a hostile power. General Order One does not prohibit us from defending ourselves against hostile acts. This is why, for instance, we were able to intervene in the war between Eminiar VII and Vendikar once our own crew was targeted for destruction.

"Therefore, I conclude that we are legally entitled to do whatever we must to liberate our ship and crew. If that means collaborating with the dissidents who are also at odds with the government, then that is a permissible choice."

McCoy leaned forward. "For once, Spock, I like the way you're thinking. But what about rescuing Jim? Surely boarding our ship and taking its captain prisoner is a hostile act too."

"Undoubtedly, Doctor, and I will take proposals for Captain Kirk's rescue under advisement. But there is another consideration. If we do free the captain, escape Cherela with the dissidents, and then assist them in publicizing the Web's existence and pursuing their ends through diplomatic channels, it would likely be weeks or months before any significant results could be expected.

However, given the growing instabilities within the system, I estimate a fifty-six percent probability that another world module will collapse within three weeks—and a forty-one percent probability of such a collapse within two weeks. The dissidents' plan might save the majority of the Web, but millions of lives could be lost in the interim."

"Is there a point to all this, Spock?" McCoy demanded.

"The point is that the sooner we can act, the better the odds for the Web. And we are at the greatest liberty to act so long as the government does not perceive us as an active threat—which they surely would the moment we attempted to rescue Captain Kirk. I am sure the captain would agree that the preservation of the Web is a higher priority than his own liberation."

McCoy opened his mouth to argue, then stopped himself. He could not dispute that Kirk would always place others before himself.

"Wait a minute," Sulu said. "If the Prime Directive's off the table, then can't we do more? Say, maybe find a way to break into their control systems and shut down the concealment protocols? We could save them ourselves."

"That would be difficult, Lieutenant," Spock answered. "The dissidents understand these systems far better than we do and have been unable to achieve the same ends."

"But we could offer a new perspective," Uhura said. "Mister Spock, you know everything there is to know about Federation computer systems. Maybe you could come up with some tricks they haven't tried."

Spock shook his head. "Their systems are more advanced than ours. There would be too great a risk of failing or even inadvertently worsening the problem."

"There's also the risk from the Dassik," Bailey put in.

"Balok didn't seem to think they were that great a threat, but we've seen how fragile the Web is, how little disruption it would take to cause another catastrophe. At the very least, we'd have to draw the Dassik away from this system before exposing the Web to discovery. If we just shut down the concealment grid now, the Web would be conquered or destroyed within days."

"Could be," McCoy said. "May be. Up against millions of lives that will probably be lost if we don't do something."

"Then let *me* do something," Bailey urged. "I'm the ambassador, right? Let me try to reason with the First's officials. If we offer independent corroboration of the dissidents' findings, maybe we could convince them to take the threat more seriously. In combination with the offer of Federation protection," he went on, "maybe it could change their minds."

McCoy snorted. "Not likely. A politician's a politician, anywhere you go in the galaxy."

"At least we could try."

"With all due respect to your abilities, Mister Bailey," Spock said, "I am concerned that we may have already expended what diplomatic capital we have with the triumvirs in our attempts to negotiate the captain's release. If we wish them to grant us an audience, we would need a way in." He pondered. "Perhaps if I approached Nisu and reasoned with her, it might carry some weight. She would be able to sense my sincerity."

"Wouldn't she be able to sense it in the dissidents too?" McCoy asked.

"The dissidents have strong sentiments against the sitting government. That may color any Kisaja's perceptions of their thoughts. As I lack an emotional bias on the issue, I may be able to convince Nisu, whereupon she could help persuade the triumvirs to consider your petition."

McCoy grimaced. "Weren't you the one just saying time was of the essence?"

"Indeed I was, Doctor. But we can do little until the *Enterprise* is repaired. Until then, we must make the most constructive use of our time that we can. And that means pursuing every avenue at our disposal."

McCoy's grudging silence indicated his acceptance of Spock's argument. Still, the first officer could see the skepticism in his pale blue eyes—the unspoken conviction that if Kirk were here, he could devise a better plan than Spock could manage. Privately, Spock conceded that the doctor was probably correct. Once again, he found himself thrust into command of the *Enterprise*, at a time when his sense of his inadequacy for that position was stronger than ever.

But perhaps reminding Nisu of their prior discussions, of her attempts to help him and his act of faith in sharing his concerns for the future with her, would aid in convincing her to trust his message in turn. Not, perhaps, an entirely honest way to deal with a being who had been consistently benign and considerate toward him. But it would be misguided to place sentiment above the survival of the *Enterprise* and the Web of Worlds. Surely Nisu would see the logic of that . . . in time.

"I am grateful that you came to see me," Nisu told Spock as they sat together. She had chosen to combine their meeting with a meal at what she described as the finest vegetarian restaurant in the Tessegri world module—a promising sign in the wake of her aloof, mistrustful reaction toward him earlier. They sat on a terrace overlooking the interior of one of the module's great arcologies, an indoor city as brightly lit and lively as any urban area Spock had ever seen. "I wish to apologize for my coldness toward you before. It was wrong to let recent events drive a wedge between us. You were not responsible for what occurred, Spock. Once I had time to process my shock and anger, to look beyond them, I was able to realize what a difficult position you must be in now . . . forced once more to take on a responsibility you do not desire, and in a time of such crisis."

"Your understanding is appreciated, Nisu," he told her. "But the responsibility remains the same, regardless of its impact upon me. I know you understand that. I do not believe it was easy or desirable for you to board our ship a second time and place Captain Kirk under arrest. You did what your duty required of you under the circumstances."

"I have no regrets about that." Her sharp tone softened a moment later as she granted him a concession: "If he does prove guilty under the law, that is."

"It is gratifying that you keep that in mind."

"I didn't come here to talk about your captain, Spock." She placed her hand atop his. "It's important to me that *you* know you are still welcome here in the Web. Whatever the future holds . . . this can be a home for you, if you let it."

"A most . . . hospitable sentiment, Nisu," Spock replied. His gratitude was genuine, but he could not indulge it now. He withdrew his hand, steepled it against his other one, and continued in more businesslike tones. "However, it presupposes that the Web will continue to exist. I have come across research that casts that supposition into doubt."

He went on to speak to Nisu about the dissidents' research, dissembling about how and where he came across it. It was not a lie; he had personally tracked down the research on the Web's information network and evaluated the data presented therein, data identical to what Kasan Tor had given him. He merely omitted mentioning his direct contact with the dissidents themselves.

Still, Nisu's gaze soon hardened as she recognized what he was describing. "We are of course aware of these allegations. They are based on faulty data and assumptions. They're the work of fearmongers who spin doomsday scenarios as a way of protesting the Council's policies."

"I understand why you would have reason to doubt the objectivity of dissenters within your own society, Nisu. However, I am concerned only with scientific truth. You may trust me when I tell you that I have analyzed these findings in considerable detail and find them to be persuasive."

"What would you have us do, then? Shut off the defenses that have kept us safe and hidden for twelve thousand years? Expose ourselves while a Dassik blockade circles above us, ready to attack?"

"You have the orbships for protection."

"They are few, and they are miners and freighters, not combat vessels."

"They are still powerful, and intimidating in their way. If nothing else, you could surround Cherela with your radiation buoys."

Nisu laughed. "This planet is already surrounded by an intense radiation belt. It provides some defense, but not enough, or you would never have made it through."

"True—but the radiation belt does not actively pursue

starships and block their progress. And other defenses could be easily devised and implemented. The advantage of the First Federation is its compactness. It would be far easier, and require far fewer vessels, to defend the Web than to defend a comparable population living on multiple M-class planets."

"And the sheer concentration of people and resources, all openly here in one place, would make it an irresistible target for the Dassik. They will stop at nothing to avenge themselves upon us. At least now, with the Web a secret, we can permit some traffic between Cherela and the stars beyond. Once that secret got out, the Dassik would not allow us a moment's peace. We would be truly besieged here."

"Unless you could negotiate a peace with the Dassik."

"They are incapable of it. Do you think we never tried? It is the Kisaja way to seek communication. But the Dassik were too savage, too low in intelligence to be persuaded. They corrupted my ancestors' abilities, used them as overseers—slaves to help the Dassik control the rest of the slaves." She sighed, gathering herself. "I apologize for my display of emotion, Spock. The scars of our history run deep. When each generation can feel their parents' pain directly . . . it lingers."

"I understand, Nisu. However, that awareness of the distant past must not blind you to the threat the entire Web faces in the present."

"The present—and future—of the Web is my overriding concern as well. I know what you cannot know, Spock, what I pray you will never know: how terrible it is to see one's entire homeworld destroyed. Our concealment is the only thing that has saved us from that fate."

"It saved you twelve millennia ago. It does not follow

that modern threats require the same solution—or that a solution that worked once under different conditions cannot become a danger in the present.

"All I ask is that you allow me to present my findings to you. No dissident rhetoric, no polemics or appeals to emotion, simply the raw science."

After a moment's consideration, Nisu agreed. Spock led her through the data, the equations, and the results of his simulations as they dined. Spock had only a small salad and finished it off as efficiently as he could, wishing to minimize the distraction from his presentation. Nisu listened patiently, asking cogent and reasonable questions, until he reached the point where he demonstrated how the dissidents' model predicted a collapse like that of Fiilestii. "And thus you see that the very attempt to cancel the instability of the antigrav system by channeling power from elsewhere in the Web actually amplified the chaos within the system and—"

"Stop!" Nisu said, looking at him angrily. "No bias, no polemics? Please. All of this is just to try to convince me that your captain was not to blame for the deaths of nearly four thousand people!"

Spock frowned. "While that is a corollary of these findings, it is an incidental point. It has no bearing on the underlying mathematics—"

"Don't lie to me, Spock. I can feel it within you. You're not objective when it comes to the welfare of your captain. He is the one unwavering certainty in your life. You'd do anything to rescue him."

"Nisu, you have seen for yourself how the evidence leads to these conclusions. You raised no objection prior to this point."

"All I have seen is that you've constructed a theory that fits what you want to be true. Numbers can be made to say anything, Spock. It's what's in your heart that tells the tale." She rose stiffly from the table. "To think I was willing to believe you sincerely wished to confide in me. You're no better than any other outsider! Playing on our connection to use me for your own ends! Is it any wonder we hide from the likes of you?"

Nisu ordered one of her lieutenants to escort Spock back to the *Enterprise*, refusing to speak with him again. Spock was nonplussed by her burst of emotional volatility. It was surprising to see in an individual who had seemed so reasonable and level-headed before—and to receive such hostility from one with whom he had experienced such a close rapport.

But later, when he relayed the conversation to Bailey in the lieutenant's guest quarters aboard the *Enterprise* (leaving out the more private elements), the young human grasped the situation readily. "She's afraid, Spock. Afraid of what she doesn't understand and can't control. She's so afraid of taking chances on the unknown that it blinds her to the danger that's right beneath her feet."

"Hmm. Then perhaps you were correct," Spock said, "and I should allow you to attempt to persuade the Council of the First."

Bailey chuckled. "Actually, Mister Spock, after what you just told me, I've changed my mind. I mean . . . the Kisaja are the ones who are supposed to be good at listening, at empathizing. If even she's too paranoid to open her mind, there's no way the triumvirs will listen to me. They didn't even want me to be here."

"Still, at least the attempt should be made."

"Fine. I'm willing to try, Spock. But we're going to need some other plan to save the Web if and when I strike out."

Spock quirked a brow. "Yes, Mister Bailey. I had already concluded that myself."

Bailey studied him. "You're going to find a way to override the Web controls, aren't you? To shut down the concealment grid ourselves?"

"I cannot confirm that supposition."

"But didn't you say that would risk making things even more unstable?"

"I now believe that to be a manageable risk. And the risk of inaction is greater."

"And what about the Dassik?"

"The First Federation has defenses, such as the radiation buoys, which it chooses not to deploy around Cherela in order to maintain concealment. I believe the risk from the Dassik would also be manageable. But the collapse of the Web of Worlds if we do nothing is not a risk—it is a virtual certainty."

"Then I know what Balok would say," the lieutenant replied, setting his jaw. "Do whatever you have to. Even if it means bringing down the government."

Kirk did not have to wait long for Tirak and Mure to make their move. He was near the end of his next solitary session in the exercise yard, a spacious rectangular chamber at one edge of the saucer-like prison module. Overhead, an arched skylight followed the curve of the outer shell and afforded a splendid view of Cherela's atmosphere, which was currently roiling with another vast thunderstorm. The skylight was thick enough to damp the clamor of the thunder to tolerable levels, but even so, Kirk almost missed the sound of the transporter beam behind him. Just in time, he whirled to see Koust materializing meters away, with nothing between them but empty air. The young Dassik soldier was panting, but not from exertion as Kirk was. From the haunted look in Koust's slitted eyes, Kirk could tell he had just been undergoing another mind-probing session with Mure, surely fighting the intrusion with all his might. And now, when the Dassik was at his most beleaguered and enraged, they had given him a target he could strike at freely—one who was already fatigued from a lengthy workout. Kirk wondered how Mure intended to justify the "accident" that had put them both in the exercise yard at the same time. Perhaps he would blame it on the electrical storm.

"Koust, wait," Kirk attempted, but the Dassik was already charging. It was clear in his eyes that there was no chance of negotiation. If the towering predator got a solid grip on Kirk, he was as good as finished. So he had to strike preemptively. He dodged right and aimed a roundhouse blow at Koust's head. But the Dassik moved fast, grabbing his arm and swinging him around into the nearby wall. Kirk's right shoulder absorbed much of the impact, but the blow to his head was still jarring. Dazed, he slid to the floor.

He recovered in time to see Koust running at him, pulling back a fist to slam into him with pile-driver force. He barely dodged the blow, which left a dent in the cushioned flooring. Kirk rolled to his hands and knees and kicked out sideways, driving his right foot into Koust's temple. The Dassik's hand shot out and clamped crushingly hard around his right leg. Kirk twisted his torso forward and fired several quick punches into the nerve cluster below his opponent's shoulder, finally managing to relax Koust's grip. He then delivered another kick to his foe's pointed chin, dazing Koust enough to let Kirk break free, tumble to his feet, and gain some distance. Running hurt; he'd avoided a broken tibia by maybe one second, but his leg was far from undamaged.

Koust didn't stay dazed for long, and in moments he was lunging forward again. He moved lightning-fast, slamming Kirk into another wall. The Dassik pulled back his right arm for a killing blow to the neck, but Kirk was able to block it in time and twist it aside, delivering a nerve-cluster blow that caused the arm to fall limp.

But Dassik, it seemed, were ambidextrous—or at least this one was. Koust readily pulled back his left arm to finish the job the right had begun. Kirk slammed his right fist into Koust's solar plexus, then jerked it up to impact his chin again. Koust staggered back and Kirk leaped free, shaking out his hand and praying that none of his fingers were broken.

Amazingly, the Dassik was still on his feet, striding toward Kirk with undiminished purpose. Kirk was impressed with his endurance . . . and unsure whether he could stop this giant.

Luckily, Kirk was now in position to use the exercise machines for cover, darting behind them and dodging to keep them between himself and the Dassik as the latter attempted to circle around them. "Koust, listen to me," he urged. "I know you're hurt. I know you're frightened. But you need to think."

"I fear no one!" the young warrior cried. "Least of all you."

"I'm not your enemy, Koust. Think about it. I know they've hurt you, enraged you. You want revenge. But think, Koust. Why would they fill you with rage and then send you here? Send you after me? Is that something they would do if I were their spy?"

Koust paused for a moment, then shook it off, lunging for Kirk and getting himself tangled in the cables of one of the machines. "No. You *are* my enemy! Your ship battled ours!"

"Only in self-defense, like I'm doing now. But we prefer to solve our problems with talking. And so do most of the people in the First Federation. But right now, they're frightened and angry, just like you. They want to find someone they can lash out at, someone they can blame for all their problems. They imagine that if they make them go away, then their problems will go away too.

"That's why Tirak and the warden sent us here, Koust. They want us to be those someones. They want you to kill me so they'll have an excuse to kill you. So they can use their people's anger for their own advantage. So they can earn their people's gratitude and obedience without having to do the hard work of actually solving their problems."

Koust finally wrenched himself free. "Why should I trust you, human?" he demanded, circling the machine.

Kirk was about to retreat behind another machine— but he stopped himself. "Because I'm ready to trust you, Koust. I've been watching you. You haven't said much, but I can see you watching, listening, thinking. I'm convinced you're more than the mindless savage the Firsts think you are." Taking a step forward, he lowered his hands and spread them out to his sides, palms open. "And I'm willing to stake my life on it."

Koust watched him warily for a long moment. Then the Dassik erupted. Almost faster than Kirk could see, Koust's left hand was around his throat, holding him aloft. Kirk struggled to break free . . . then simply struggled to breathe.

But then those wiry, clawed fingers were gone from his throat, and he was able to gasp for air once again. He found himself on his knees . . . and there were those same fingers, extended to help him to his feet.

Kirk placed his hand in Koust's and clasped it firmly as the Dassik drew him upward. "It takes great courage," Koust said slowly, "to choose not to fight when you are in clear danger."

It was meant as praise for Kirk . . . but also as a declaration of the Dassik's own intent. In that spirit, Kirk clapped Koust's shoulder and nodded. "Yes. It does."

"Then it is time," Koust told him, "that we finally talked."

Eleven

At last, the *Enterprise* was nearly shipshape once again. It did Montgomery Scott's heart good to see the system readouts returning to normal one by one. The Web dissidents had been of great help, managing to create high-quality replacement parts to Scott's specifications and even improving on them in some cases.

The tricky part had been repairing the port nacelle without the Web officials catching on. The *Enterprise* was designed so that most repairs and maintenance could be done from inside the hull, but the damage sustained by the port Bussard collector and intercoolers was extensive enough to require EVA maneuvers to complete the large-scale structural work. It was tricky to find ways to pull that off while making it look like merely superficial repairs. The dissident engineer Kasan Tor came up with a clever solution, designing some of the larger replacement parts to be easily assembled from smaller components so that they could be smuggled through the maintenance conduits inside the nacelle and pieced together *in situ*. Scott had to admire the technical ingenuity of these folks.

And so he was in a receptive mood when Commander Spock and the dissident Ne-Kewii (the one who looked like a griffin, or maybe a sphinx—a griffosphinx?) approached him in private with a proposal that would let him repay the dissidents for their help. Still, what they asked of him was rather . . . monumental. "Override the whole weather-control grid?" he asked in a stunned whisper, cognizant of how his voice would echo through the engineering complex if he raised it too loud. "Across the whole planet at once? You don't think small, do you, Mister Spock?"

"We must scale our plans to fit our problems, Mister Scott."

The engineer grinned. "Very well said, sir. D'you mind if I quote you?"

While they waited for Spock's eyebrow to come back down, Ne-Kewii spoke. "I'm still not sure you can find a way when we've been unable to find one for decades," she said. "The problem is immensely complicated. The systems that keep the Web and the atmosphere in balance are made up of thousands of different components, one in every module. They interact and overlap one another for redundancy, but each one is independent, and any one that goes wrong can be overridden by the others around it. There's no way to infect the whole system with a virus, no single central control we can take over. There would need to be a coordinated effort from dozens of control centers at once." She ruffled her silver wings. "We don't have enough people to mount such a widespread takeover even with your crew's help, and it would be too violent. We're trying to save lives, not take them."

"Also," Spock observed, "a violent takeover would run the risk of damaging control systems we need intact. And if our forces failed to capture a sufficient number of control centers, the implementation would not succeed."

"Well, certainly," Scott said. "If you wanted to go in with guns blazin', you'd be talking to Sulu now instead of me. So what can we do instead?"

"If we cannot take over the control systems physically

or with a computer virus," Spock said, "perhaps we could devise a way to take them over remotely planetwide."

"That's been considered too," Ne-Kewii said. "The system has countermeasures against remote take-over. The original builders were very cautious, and understandably so."

"But those countermeasures are only designed to account for methods known within the First Federation. They may be vulnerable to methods you have never before encountered." Spock turned to Scott. "Specifically, Mister Scott, are you conversant with the techniques which the Romulans used during the Earth-Romulan War to gain remote control of enemy vessels?"

Scott's eyes widened. "Aye, I've read about those. Cost us a lot of good ships before we found a way to beat it." He chuckled. "Oh, they had some mighty devious ways to sneak a subspace signal past a ship's defenses, get right into the core processors. I'd be surprised if anyone from the FF had ever seen the like."

"Excellent," Spock said. "Then if Ne-Kewii provides you with the specifications for the Web's control systems, you could assist us in adapting the Romulan protocols accordingly?"

The engineer chuckled. "I certainly could, sir. And may I say, it's a plan worthy o' Captain Kirk himself."

"I sincerely hope so," Spock replied. "For it may be the captain's only chance of survival."

———

Nisu Miratuli cursed herself for a fool. She had been so blind, thinking Spock could be trusted to understand the importance of the Web just because she imagined him a kindred spirit. She'd compromised her duties as a protector out of a desire for relief from a lifetime of loneliness.

People always assumed Kisaja were so happy, so connected. Most of the time, that was true. It was the nature of her people to form easy bonds, to empathize and identify with others. But a Kisaja protector was another matter. Her job required her to deal mainly with the angry, the disturbed, the antisocial—those who endangered the safety of those around them. Constant exposure to such minds, to personalities defined by a sense of disconnection or antagonism toward the world around them, inevitably left its mark on a Kisaja's psyche. Perhaps, Nisu thought, that was why Warden Mure had allowed the "accident" of timing that had placed Kirk and the Dassik prisoner in the exercise yard at the same time. She had no hard evidence to refute the warden's report of a sensor malfunction and scheduling mix-up, and he had been cooperative toward the oversight team she had sent in to ensure the prisoners' safety. But she had sensed something in Mure that had made her uneasy—because she recognized that it was also within herself.

If anything, the psychological impact of the work might be harder on a Kisaja like Nisu, who had been prone to depression and loneliness ever since her parents had been violently taken from her. The downside of psionic sensitivity was that other Kisaja often found it difficult to be near someone in such a dark state of mind. Although they had done their best to comfort and reassure Nisu, she had always suspected it was more for their own benefit than hers. In the streets and public buildings of the Kisaja module, she had often felt the need to keep her eyes downcast, to retreat from public gaze and gravitate toward enclosed and isolated areas, so as not to trouble others with her own psychic burdens. That was probably why she'd become a protector in the first place: She was already predisposed to understand those with darker states of mind.

Still, the solitude took its toll, and she often wished to find someone who could understand and ease it for her. She had found Spock's emotional restraint and logical discipline of thought to be a haven of peace—yet when she had sensed the isolation, uncertainty, and repressed sadness lying beneath his control, it had touched her heart and made her too quick to trust him. Hearing him advocate the paranoid theories of the dissidents had been the rude awakening she'd needed. At first, she'd assumed he had simply gone fishing for anything that could help him absolve his captain of four thousand murders. But then she'd reminded herself of her earlier folly in making assumptions about Spock. What if he hadn't stumbled across the dissidents' theories by accident? It stood to reason that the doomsday sect would see the *Enterprise* as a lifeboat off the sinking ship they imagined the Web to be—or worse, a means to recruit outside help to "save" the Web by overthrowing the Council and the triumvirs. They would try to make contact. Maybe they already had.

She had therefore placed Spock and the rest of the *Enterprise* crew under increased surveillance and begun doing the same for those Web citizens they interacted with—including her own escort staff. Kisaja couldn't normally read beyond surface thoughts without consent, and it wasn't ethical to probe deeper without judicial authorization, so anyone who had a disciplined enough mind could hide dissident sympathies from her.

Such paranoid thinking wasn't normally the way of the First, and if Nisu's hunch hadn't paid off, she would probably have had to answer to the board of ethics. But they were dealing with outsiders, and as Tirak so often reminded her, outsiders were dangerous. Yes, the doomsayers within were a serious threat, but multiple outside forces were already disrupting the Web's careful balance, creating unrest of a sort the safe haven of Cherela had not experienced in millennia. They had to be checked before the instability grew even worse.

And Nisu's extra vigilance had proven necessary. The surveillance revealed that the escort Aluu Ne-Kewii and several others were meeting regularly with certain suspicious persons within the Web as well as with Spock, Scott, and Bailey. Those three Starfleet officers were occasionally seen meeting directly with the suspicious individuals as well—and in time, it became clear that one of those individuals was the long-absent Commander Balok, whose secretive return to Cherela seemed to confirm Triumvir Tirak's long-standing suspicions of Balok's dissident sympathies.

All of these persons of interest were seen traveling to evenly spaced locations all over the Web, often carrying unknown equipment that was no longer with them upon their return. Nisu knew that the dissidents advocated the shutdown of the Web's concealment protocols. She knew that it would require coordinated action across the entire Web at once. Until now, the experts had assured her it was a logistical impossibility. But that had been before the wild variable named Spock.

She was there waiting for him the next time Spock and Balok attempted to plant a device in an isolated area near one of the local control centers that regulated the Web's equilibrium. She had her most trusted protectors with her, and the two saboteurs promptly found themselves surrounded. Her tech expert quickly confirmed that the device was some kind of remote computer override programmed to shut down the Web's regulation of Cherela's atmosphere. "I knew you were an iconoclast, Commander," she said to Balok. "But I did not expect you would go to these lengths."

"Of course not," Balok replied with a defiant grin. "Most people expect only shortness from Linnik, not length."

"This is not a matter for your jokes!"

"The joke, my dear Nisu, is your own belief that you are the one protecting the Web. None of my jests can rival the absurdity of that."

"You have always been defiant, willful. You truly expect me to accept you as a champion of the First?"

"Oh, I assure you, my interests are entirely selfish. If we lost the orchards of the Renetran module, why, there would be no more *tranya* to drink! I ask you, what would be the point of going on in a universe like that?"

Tiring of Balok's irreverence, Nisu turned to Spock. "It is you who truly disappoint me," she said. "Do you have any idea of the danger of attempting to override the Web's control grid?"

"I do," the Vulcan replied with that insufferable surface calm, which she could tell was just as much a lie as ever. "But that danger can be managed, while the greater danger of failing to act cannot."

"And you would be so reckless, so arrogant, as to endanger entire worlds based on your own belief?" Nisu shook her head. "I thought you of all people would know better, Spock. You who seek only knowledge and under-standing, not authority."

He met her eyes, and there was urgency in his. "I do not act from belief, Nisu, nor from pride. It is my conclu-sion as a scientist, based on logical analysis and deduc-tion, that this is the only way to save the Web of Worlds. It is the beliefs and fears of those you follow that endanger it. I implore you not to let their arrogance and self-interest blind you to necessity."

The most painful part was that he sincerely believed what he said. There was no point in arguing further. "Spock of Vulcan, Commander Balok, I arrest you for the crime of attempted sabotage against the Web of Worlds." Once she bound their hands and advised them of their legal rights, she turned Spock back around to face her. "I had hoped you would make the Web your lifelong home, Spock, but not in this way. At least you will be reunited with your captain."

Spock didn't flinch under her gaze, which was sur-prising. Though she wasn't intentionally exerting the full pressure of a Kisaja's gaze, her anger was such that it would be difficult for anyone to bear looking into her eyes right now. But Spock was not transfixed or even visibly affected. His willpower must have been remarkable. "Your actions, Nisu, may have just ensured that all of us will spend the duration of our lives here," he said. "But none of those lives will be very long."

Balok sighed. "But on the bright side, they don't serve *tranya* in prison. So at least it will feel long."

———

The sight of Spock's face cheered Jim Kirk enormously. But his spirits fell again when he saw that Spock was attired in the same drab prison jumpsuit as himself and Koust. "I take it this isn't a rescue," he said as the guards escorted Spock into Kirk's cell.

"No, I'm afraid not," Spock replied as the wall was resealed behind him. "Are you well, Jim?"

Kirk replied with a sardonic twist to his lips. "I am, but it's despite the best efforts of Triumvir Tirak. He and the warden attempted to arrange a little accident involving my neighbor here. Oh, Spock, this is Koust, fourth-tier warrior of the Dassik. Koust, Commander Spock of Vulcan, my first officer and science officer."

Koust merely gave Spock an appraising look. The Vulcan reciprocated, though with a touch of puzzlement. "I see. Then does this mean the Dassik are aware of the Web?"

"Alas, not yet," Koust replied. "The cowards seized me before I could report back."

Kirk stared at his Vulcan friend. "I thought you'd be more surprised to find me on good terms with one of the Dassik."

"You do seem to have a knack for finding common ground with initially hostile individuals, Captain. I am more concerned at the news of the attempt on your life. Are you in continued danger?"

"Not from that," Kirk said. "The incident has brought increased scrutiny from Nisu's people. Assuming she's not also in Tirak's pocket . . ."

"I am confident in Nisu's integrity. She is misguided in some respects, but fundamentally honest."

"I'm glad to hear that." Kirk looked around at their environs. "Frankly, I'm more concerned about the way this place keeps rumbling and swaying. Assuming that's not just something they do to alarm the prisoners."

"No, Jim. The instabilities in the Web are worsening." He went on to explain how the Web's own methods of concealment were endangering its survival. "The simulations show conclusively that Fiilestii's antigravs would have become just as unstable even without the *Enterprise*'s intervention. Indeed, had we not been there, more lives may have been lost."

The words lifted a weight from Kirk's heart. "I can't tell you how relieved I am to hear that, Spock. Thank you."

The science officer went on to describe the measures he had attempted to correct the instability and how that attempt had led to his and Balok's arrest. "I expect Commander Scott and the dissidents to continue their efforts to implement the plan, but they will be under increased scrutiny. Much of the populace of the Web has been gripped by an irrational fear of outsiders in the wake of recent events—a fear that has only been exacerbated by Triumvir Tirak's rhetoric."

"Yes, I've been made painfully aware of that." He threw a wry glance at Koust.

Spock followed his gaze. "I find it interesting that the triumvirs have not seen fit to inform the public that they have a Dassik prisoner," he said. "Their ability to overcome and contain one of the enemy—if you will pardon my characterization, Mister Koust—might serve as a symbol to placate their fears."

"I'm not sure placating their fears is what Tirak wants, Spock," the captain replied. "He seems more interested in pandering to them."

Koust stepped closer to the barrier. "And they would not wish their people to know of me so long as I remain alive. They fear I would expose the truth about the Linnik . . . and the crime they committed against my race."

———————

Tirak stood in front of Balok's cell with his arms crossed, a smug grin on his face as he appraised the current state of the *Fesarius*'s captain. "So, Balok. All your rhetoric about opening our society . . . tearing down the walls in which we imprisoned ourselves . . . and this is where you end up. I would think you of all people would appreciate the humor."

"If you think this is the ending, Tirak, then you are laughable indeed," Balok replied. "You can't make the dangers to the Web go away by silencing those who acknowledge them."

"The dangers to the Web are the very outsiders you insisted on drawing here!" the triumvir shouted. "You brought the human starship here intentionally, and I have no doubt you led the Dassik here when they pursued you." Tirak leaned closer, narrowing his eyes. "Or was that just as intentional? Did you lead them here in hopes of exposing the secret? Discrediting the Council?"

Now Balok did laugh. The incongruity of the triumvir's priorities was so startling that he couldn't help it. It would be pointless, the *Fesarius* captain supposed, to explain that the Dassik had already been in Cherela's orbit when he reached the system, or to describe the exceptionally clever ploy he had used to slip past them. He would save that tale for a more receptive audience, ideally over a bowl of *tranya*—assuming he ever got the opportunity.

Unsurprisingly, though, Tirak misunderstood his reaction. "Don't deny it, Balok! I know you broke into the Council's secure files. You know how we defeated the Dassik."

"Yes, I did." This was a feat he was happy to boast about. "When we first learned of the Dassik's return, I needed to understand what the *Fesarius* would be facing. And I had my suspicions deriving from hints in the ancient lore, the myths we were told as children. Really, it was an elegant solution. I don't see why you're so afraid to let it be known what our ancestors did."

"How can you not recognize the danger? If the other races knew that we were siblings to the Dassik . . . that we differ from them only through neoteny . . . they would fear what we have the potential to become."

"Or are you more concerned that they'd fear us for what we were willing to inflict on an entire species for the sake of our own survival? We were quite the scourge even without towering bodies and sharp claws."

"Either way, they would mistrust us. They would turn on us."

Balok shook his head sadly. "Really? After twelve thousand years of peaceful cooperation and trust, you believe our fellow Firsts would reject us so easily?" He sighed. "I am sad for you, Tirak. All you know is fear, and so you assume that is all others are capable of."

"And you and your dissident friends do not promote fear? Spreading lies about how the Web is doomed to destruction? Fomenting panic to undermine the state?"

"The danger we point out is within ourselves, a fault in our own practices. And that gives us the power to do something about it, something more effective than just hiding from it. But you're so afraid of admitting your own policies are the problem that you'd rather risk the destruction of the Web. Fear is what dooms us—our fear of being seen, our insistence on staying hidden from the galaxy even though the need passed a hundred centuries ago. But rather than overcome that fear and take a chance on joining the rest of the galaxy, you'd rather intensify it—stir up even more fear and paranoia to distract from the real problem."

"The Dassik are out there even now!" Tirak insisted. "They will destroy us. If not physically, then by destroying the foundations of the people's trust in the Linnik. I will not allow you to reveal the truth!"

This time, Balok merely shook his head instead of laughing. "You really think I care about what happened thousands of years in the past? The past is over, my friend. It's gone. That's why they call it the past. What's important is the future. Not what we did before, but what we'll do next. And how much 'next' we have left to do it in."

"Our heritage is what defines us, Balok. We are the First."

"And we have long welcomed others who were not the First. The Fiilestii were some of the last to join our Federation. Yet now you use them as your rallying cry against outsiders. Can't you see the problem there?"

"It doesn't matter if it makes sense, Commander. It's what the people need to hear. Frightened people need clear, simple reassurances, not complicated truths."

Balok looked him over with contempt. "Which is no doubt why you're so eager to make the people afraid. It makes them so much easier to control—especially when you don't have the truth on your side."

"So the Dassik and the Linnik are members of the same genus," Spock said as he slowly paced the cell, organizing and interpreting what Koust and Kirk had explained to him. "At first, a single species like the Dassik, large and predatory. But a mutation led to a neotenous offshoot, the Linnik. Their extended juvenile period enhanced their neurological development, giving them higher intelligence while preempting the emergence of the heightened aggression and physical defenses of the adult Dassik form. Thus, the Dassik were able to enslave them and compel them to use their intelligence and fine motor skills to build the Dassik's civilization and eventually their starfaring capability."

"That is correct," Koust said without pride. "The early Dassik were . . . crude creatures. They could have achieved little without the Linnik's cunning. And that was their eventual downfall."

"From what Koust tells me," Kirk explained, "the Linnik eventually developed a bioweapon that would have the same effect on Dassik biology as their own mutation. The Dassik who were exposed to the compound gave birth to children who never grew up. That is, they matured sexually and were able to reproduce, but they never matured in other ways, never developed the Dassik's size or aggressiveness. They were no bigger or stronger than the Linnik themselves, and so once the mature Dassik died out, their neotenous offspring couldn't pose a threat. The Linnik were able to take control of their ships and weapons and overpower them easily."

"But they did not destroy them."

"Not all of us," Koust said. "Even in our diminished state, they were too weak for that."

Kirk threw him a look. "Or maybe they saw too much of themselves in what you'd become. Maybe they hoped you'd become like them someday."

"In either case," Koust grudgingly went on, "they stranded us on an uninhabited planet, far from the space we had ruled. They left us there and forgot about us."

"Not entirely," Spock pointed out. "They retain legends of the Dassik menace to this day. You are the monsters in their tales to frighten children. Their ship commanders use your image and reputation to intimidate potentially hostile outsiders."

Koust's ghoulish features took on a disquieting grin. "Really! Perhaps I should be flattered. Or perhaps I should be angry that they stole our very faces from us and kept them for their own use."

"Even so," Spock went on, "the Dassik clearly did not remain neotenous. How did you revert to your original form?"

"The betrayers brought that on themselves," Koust told him. "Kirk thinks they hoped we would become like them one day? Well, we did, though not as they expected. Like them, we grew more intelligent. We learned to reason, to build, to invent. But we did not lose our aggression or our resentment at what had been inflicted on our race. We learned, invented, and experimented, and finally we found a way to reverse the mutation. We could grow into adult Dassik again—but with the same intelligence we had gained in our exile. And so, in time, we were able to reinvent spaceflight on our own."

"Whereupon you resumed your ancient practices of

raiding and conquest," Spock replied dryly. "Could you find no better application for your empowered intellects?"

"We are not what we were, Vulcan! Yes, we are still hunters. That is a part of our nature that was denied to us for too long by the betrayers, and so we must not abandon it now that we are ourselves again. But we are not the undisciplined brutes of the past. We seek to be strong, yes, but only to hold our own against the powers of the galaxy. To win respect and make it clear we are no easy prey for Klingons or Romulans or whatever else is out there."

Kirk had heard much of this from Koust before, but there were questions the young hunter had not yet answered to his satisfaction. "Forgive me, Koust," he said, "but that doesn't explain your belligerence toward the First Federation. You're not trying to win their respect, but to inflict revenge. Do the modern Linnik, let alone their allies, deserve to be punished for the actions of their forebears twelve millennia ago?"

The Dassik growled. "You do not understand, Kirk. What we seek is more urgent than mere revenge." He paused, fidgeting, before he continued in a quieter voice. "Our reengineering of our genes . . . it is unstable. Fewer Dassik survive to adulthood with each generation. In order to fix the problem, we must understand what the betrayers did to us originally before we can reverse it for good. Without that knowledge, the Dassik will truly go extinct."

Kirk stared in horror at this revelation. He glanced over to Spock, seeing the solemn, unspoken empathy in the Vulcan's eyes, and drew strength from it. "Koust . . . I'm sorry. That's a terrible burden to bear. But . . . the Linnik didn't let you die before. If they knew . . ."

"We did try, Kirk. We swallowed our pride and attempted to contact their leaders. But they would not even admit that our species were kin. They will never face what they did to us. Not willingly. Not unless we take the knowledge from them by force." He glared at Spock. "I see your disapproval, Vulcan. Do not judge us. It is no greater than the violence they inflicted on our entire race."

The rumble that ran through the prison complex served to punctuate Koust's bitter words—and to change the subject rather decisively. "Clearly there's a lot of bad blood here," Kirk said, "and we're not going to work through it right now. For the moment, I think we need to focus on our more immediate survival." He smiled. "How about it, Spock? You up for another prison break?"

His friend pondered. "In the interests of salvaging our relations with the First Federation, I would ideally prefer to seek our release through proper legal channels. However, under the circumstances, our odds of surviving long enough to gain release in that fashion are slim. Escape is the best option." He looked over at the neighboring cell. "Is Mister Koust to be included in our escape?"

"Absolutely. We jailbirds have to stick together."

"Very well, then. That gives us more options."

Koust stared at them both. "You speak as if breaking out of prison were something you did every day."

Kirk traded a wry look with his first officer. "Sometimes it feels that way. But on the plus side, I'd like to think we've gotten pretty good at it by now."

"Perhaps," Spock acknowledged. "However, it might prove more efficient in the long run if we improved our skills at staying *out* of prison in the first place."

In the wake of Spock's arrest, Montgomery Scott ordered Sulu and Bailey to continue working with the dissidents to install the remote override devices in the Web's control network, while Scott and his engineers continued to focus on repairing the *Enterprise*. But the dissidents' efforts soon ran up against a new problem. "The triumvirs are inflaming the people against us," Ne-Kewii snarled once she and Sulu had returned to the ship after an abortive foray. "Tirak has announced that we are responsible for causing the disruptions. He has called us terrorists, employed by outside powers to attack the Web from within."

"We were almost caught by an angry mob," a still-breathless Sulu added, slumping against the bridge railing while Ne-Kewii paced on the upper deck behind him. "It's getting ugly out there, Mister Scott."

"Aye," the chief engineer replied with a nod. "I've heard from the dock administrator—it seems she's under pressure to kick us out or let us be boarded. She's a good egg, refusin' to bend to them, but I'm hopin' we'll be in good enough shape to brave the winds before much longer, so we can take the heat off of her."

"Your regard for our people is commendable, Scott," Ne-Kewii said. "If only our own leaders had the same decency. I have heard reports of an 'accident' in prison that threatened your captain's life. With the people's anger growing worse, I fear for his safety and Mister Spock's."

Scott absorbed the information gravely. "Well, then. All the more reason to get the *Enterprise* back in fightin' form as soon as possible. Since it seems the crew won't be goin' anywhere in the current climate, that means we'll have more hands to do the work here."

"You are not in this alone, remember," the Fiilestii told him. "Commander Balok is in prison as well, and he may also be in danger. My people have resources we can use in an escape."

Scott was reluctant to ask others to endanger themselves on his own crew's behalf. But with one of the dissidents' own leaders at stake—particularly a fellow connoisseur of fine libations such as Balok—how could he deny them? Besides, loath though he was to admit it, the *Enterprise* was not yet ready to go to the aid of its captain and first officer. So what choice did he have? "All right, then. As of now, Mister Sulu, our priority is to break the captain and Mister Spock out of jail and bring them safely home."

"Aye, sir," Sulu said. "And if I may say so, it's about damn time too."

"That you may, Sulu. And you speak for both of us."

"Grun, you fool!" War Leader Vraq's image on the communications screen was much clearer this time—and far more unpleasant for Grun to behold. *"Allowing yourself to be duped by that crudely faked transmission. That . . . thing looked nothing like me! There is no excuse for this incompetence!"*

Grun seethed at his superior's dismissal. "But, War Leader, this proves I was right to remain! There *is* something important here that the betrayers wish to divert us from!"

"And that gave you the right to disobey what you believed were my orders?"

"I—well, of course I suspected trickery immediately, War Leader! So naturally I—"

"Naturally you contacted my squadron and requested verification of the orders?"

"That . . . that was the task of the cluster ship I sent to you!" Grun extemporized. "More urgent discoveries demanded my attention. Our scans affirmed that there is more down there than just the Starfleet vessel. There are multiple energy sources below the clouds—some of them quite large."

He cursed that fool Koust for not returning from his scouting mission. Grun was not troubled by the loss of Koust himself, who had been a member of Dral's subtier and thus a potential threat to Grun's authority. But it meant he still lacked necessary intelligence on the enemy below the clouds. Grun hadn't wanted to risk losing more warriors and pilot vessels, and automated probes would never survive the harsh atmosphere. And he certainly wasn't foolish enough to take what remained of the cluster ship down against an unknown enemy in unknown conditions.

"If you have found the enemy, then why have you not struck?" Vraq demanded.

"The conditions make it difficult to narrow down their locations amid the vastness of the planet, War Leader. We could waste all our firepower on an ocean of hydrogen and do no damage to the enemy. But my sensor officer is working to refine his scan algorithms. In time, he will be able to deduce the pattern and determine where the targets can be found."

In fact, Remv was having more trouble localizing the targets than Grun let on. More anomalies had been found, but they were proving too erratic to allow a positive fix. If the failures continued, Grun could simply kill Remv, but he wasn't sure if anyone else in the cluster ships' remaining crew possessed a comparable skill level with the instruments. Yet admitting to Vraq that he needed outside help would be a confession of weakness and a probable death sentence for himself.

"*Tell him to work quickly, Grun, for your sake,*" Vraq boomed. "*My squadron is en route to your location. Clearly a great secret lies within the gas planet—one that is too big for you to handle on your own. If you succeed in locating this enemy by the time we arrive, it may mitigate your failure. So commands the War Leader!*"

Once the screen went dark, Grun bellowed and paced within the tight confines of the command pod, ignoring the terrorized looks from the crew. Expecting to be eviscerated by an enraged Force Leader at any moment might finally provoke some measure of competence from them.

After his rage subsided to a low simmer, Grun pondered the dilemma. He had to find a way to conquer the betrayers before Vraq's squadron arrived. He had to ensure that history would see him, not that posturing, condescending Vraq, as the savior of the Dassik. And patience would not serve him anymore. He would need something quick and decisive. If only there were a weapon that would let him strike at the enemy without knowing their precise location . . .

"Yes!" he roared. "I have it!"

Rhuld ventured closer, perhaps heartened by Grun's suddenly improved mood. "What is it, Force Leader?" the second asked.

"The solution, Rhuld! A way to bring the betrayers to

their knees *now*, without waiting for reinforcements that may come too late." He did not bother to specify for what they might be too late; all that mattered was to instill a sense of urgency in the crew.

"I await your insight, Force Leader."

That was a nice bit of sycophancy. Grun approved. "You have studied the histories of our ancient wars, yes? Before we took to the stars?"

"What there is of them, sir. But much of it is mere legend."

"The names and events, maybe, but not the tactics. Not the weapons. Do you remember the weapons used in ocean warfare?"

He explained the modification to the cube missiles that he had in mind, and Rhuld's eyes widened. "It is a bold idea. But . . ."

One thing Grun was not patient with was hesitation in his men. "But what, Second?"

"Force Leader . . . what you suggest is . . . there would be very little control. If the betrayers are down there, we run the risk of destroying them before we can obtain the information we need from them."

Grun snarled. "Fah! You sound like your predecessor. All second-guessing and doubts, no commitment to act! We must take risks if we are to win!"

"Force Leader, what we risk is the future of our entire race. If ever there was a cause for caution—"

He struck Rhuld across his sniveling face. "For cowardice, you mean! We do not need their secrets. We are as smart as they are now! We made ourselves dangerous again, lifted ourselves out of the planetary muck again, without needing them to hold our hands! It is our strength, our ruthlessness, that will let us win! Do you understand?"

Rhuld lowered his head. "Of course, Force Leader. I exist only to serve you."

Grun smiled. "Yes, you do. Now carry out my orders! And if it means the destruction of everything down there in the clouds . . . then so be it!" *So long as it comes at my talons instead of Vraq's!*

Twelve

"I have it!" Koust said. "The two of you pretend to get into a fight, and when the guard comes in, you jump him."

Kirk and Spock exchanged a long-suffering look. *Amateurs*, Kirk thought. "Koust," he said apologetically, "the Web has only been isolated for twelve thousand years."

"So . . . you think they'd know that one."

"It seems likely," Spock told him.

"Perhaps one of you could pretend to be ill." The others both stared at him. "What?"

Kirk sighed. "Let's face it, we don't have a lot of options here. I mean, there's no door. Just a wall they beam in and out. Now, if there were some way to break it . . . maybe find a way to detach one of the cots and smash it into the wall . . ."

"I'm sure the cell is designed to prevent such actions," Spock said. "Besides—if we did break out of this cell by force, we would never be able to reach the transporter controls before being intercepted. Our escape will require finesse and subtlety."

"Well, that's something the First would never expect from the likes of Koust and me," Kirk said. "So what did you have in mind?"

That brow went up again. "I am considering options."

No further ideas were forthcoming for a time—which was just as well, for the guard, a massive Niatoko with dark brown scales, came by a few minutes later. Once he (or she, for all Kirk could tell) had departed, Spock furrowed his brow. "The guards appear to make their rounds once every forty-seven minutes."

Koust stared. "How can you know that without a chronometer?"

"You get used to it," Kirk told the Dassik. "Go on, Spock."

"Has that particular guard been on shift before during your incarceration?"

"Yes. They're on a four-shift rotation."

"How many times did he go past before I arrived?"

"Maybe a couple of dozen. Why?"

"Excellent," Spock said. "That means his long-term memory stores an image of this cell with only you present within it." He took a deep breath. "It is possible that if I concentrate, I may be able to influence the guard telepathically to see that image when he next passes. In effect, I can make myself invisible to him."

"You mean the same mental suggestion technique you used on Eminiar and the Kelvan settlement. Make the guard think we've escaped." He frowned. "Are you sure that trick will work on this species? So far, your results have been hit and miss."

"I cannot be certain, but what I intend here is simpler than in those cases. Rather than imposing the specific concept of our escape, all I need do in this case is to restimulate a sense memory that has already been reinforced through repetition."

"I don't understand," Koust said.

Spock turned to him. "Since this guard has only seen me in this cell once, after seeing the captain alone on multiple occasions, he will subconsciously expect this cell to have only one occupant. My presence is still a novel aberration in the long-term pattern. All I have to do is apply a slight telepathic pressure to the guard's mind, making him see what he habitually expects to see and overlook the new input. Namely myself."

Kirk was grinning now. "But the guard will still remember you're *supposed* to be here, right?"

"Indeed. I will only affect his sensory perception."

"So he'll look in the cell and see you gone. Thinking you've escaped, he'll come in to investigate. And then you can come up from behind and whomp him."

Spock raised a brow. It wasn't often that Kirk let his Iowan upbringing slip into his speech. "I was assuming I would use a nerve pinch, not a 'whomp.'"

"We can't be sure a nerve pinch will work on his species either."

"Perhaps not," Spock said. "But the less overt disruption we cause, the better our chances."

Kirk nodded. "Right. Finesse and subtlety."

"So how," Koust wanted to know, "do we finesse our way to the transporter chamber?"

"The guard should have access," Kirk said. "You can extract the codes from his mind, right, Spock?"

"In theory."

"Then let's do it."

Spock moved to sit cross-legged in the forward corner of the cell, where he began to meditate, preparing himself for the mental effort to come. And preparing Kirk and Koust as well, as he explained it. He advised them to do their best to ignore him, which would be easier if he made no sound or motion until the guard came. Though if anything, his preternatural stillness made it hard for Kirk not to stare at him.

Once the guard appeared in the viewport, Kirk gave the burly alien his best innocent look. The guard hesitated, seeming puzzled. Kirk forced himself not to glance over at Spock. "What . . . where is the other one?" the guard said.

"What other one?" Kirk said in the most pure and guileless voice he could muster.

As anticipated, the guard opened the cell and came in to double-check it. He looked around the whole cell, including the corner where Spock crouched, but did not acknowledge the Vulcan's presence. The guard whirled on Kirk. "Where did he go?" the reptilian guard cried, looming over the captain menacingly.

Just then, Spock's hand appeared on the guard's shoulder and squeezed.

Nothing happened.

The guard whirled, lashing out at the unseen intruder, but Spock had already ducked. Whereupon he struck the guard forcefully in the solar plexus, then shot his other fist upward into the Niatoko's jaw with a force that seemed to originate in the ground beneath him and travel through his body. The guard fell as though poleaxed.

Koust cheered. "*That* was a mighty whomp!"

"Please, Mister Koust," Spock said, massaging his knuckles while Kirk relieved the guard of his sidearm. "We should salvage what subtlety we can."

The rest of the plan went more smoothly. Using the guard's keycard and the codes Spock plucked from his mind, they freed Koust, whereupon the threesome made their way to the guard post at the end of the corridor. "We should try to find where they're holding Balok," Kirk whispered.

"Provided that the opportunity presents itself," Spock agreed.

A second guard, a reddish humanoid with backswept spines instead of hair, manned the post. Kirk tucked the sidearm into his waistband and strode forward casually, smiling at her. "Excuse me. Hello. I was wondering if you could tell me where to find the commissary."

Not that he expected the guard to fall for it; she just needed to be off-balance for a moment, unsure if he posed a threat. By the time she recognized him and pulled her sidearm, he had already whipped out the other guard's weapon and brought it to bear. She froze, setting down her weapon at Kirk's instruction. Spock moved behind her and used the nerve pinch, successfully this time. Spock went to work on the guard post's computer, using the first guard's access codes. "I have Commander Balok's location. I have accessed the surveillance network and guard allocations. I shall clear a pathway to Balok's cell and from there to the outgoing transporter station." He relieved the second guard of her weapon, and they set off.

"And how am I supposed to fight without a weapon?" Koust hissed.

Kirk threw him a look. "The way you bluster about your fearsome Dassik battle prowess? Aren't your bare hands and teeth enough to let you take down an army?"

"Of course," Koust countered. "But I don't want to make you look too weak in comparison."

Spock looked back and forth between them. "Fascinating."

Soon, they reached Balok's cell, where they found the *Fesarius* commander sitting quietly with his eyes closed. Once Spock had opened it, Kirk moved inside. "Balok!"

The Linnik opened his eyes, focusing slowly on Kirk. "What is it?"

"Balok, it's Kirk. We're here to get you out. Are you all right?" Had Mure "interrogated" him as well as Koust? If it came to that, Kirk was grateful that Balok would be easy to carry.

But after another moment, the commander smiled and rose smoothly to his feet. "I'm fine. Shall we go?"

Kirk traded a look with Spock. The commander's lively attitude was nowhere to be seen. But Kirk supposed that imprisonment could do that to a person. The best thing for Balok was to get him to freedom.

Luckily, Spock's efforts to create a safe path were up to his usual standards of thoroughness. "You know, I think this is actually going to work," Kirk said after the foursome had passed through several more nice, empty corridors, untroubled except by the intermittent rumbling and swaying of the module around them. "A victory for subtlety and finesse." He swiped the keycard to open the next door.

Beyond which were the sounds of phaser fire. Kirk looked around the door frame—just in time to see the tail end of a messy firefight. Sulu, Prescott, Nored, and several others from the *Enterprise* were caught in a crossfire with three guards, while behind them, a trail of stunned bodies led back to a large hole blown in the wall.

"Hey!" Kirk called, dividing the guards' attention. This let Sulu break from cover and advance to a better position, but two of the guards promptly resumed firing on his team while the third diverted fire to Kirk's location. The captain returned fire and ducked back behind the door. He traded a glance with Spock—who had already

shoved Balok behind the other side of the door frame—
and dove across the doorway, firing wildly at the guards,
drawing their fire so Spock could lean out and stun one of
them. Kirk got off a shot at a second guard just as her gun
barrel came to bear on his head. The guard convulsed and
the beam went astray, grazing Kirk's ear. The action distracted the final guard enough for Sulu to take him down.

Once the coast was clear, Kirk stepped forward, facing
his delighted crew. He sighed and shook his head. "Honestly. I can't take you people anywhere."

"Captain!" Sulu beamed. "Mister Spock!" He laughed.
"I should've known you'd find your own way out."

"Jim!" Kirk's eyes widened as Leonard McCoy's head
peeked out from behind Prescott's burly frame. "My God,
am I glad to see you!"

"Bones?" Kirk laughed. "What the devil are you doing
on a strike team?"

"What do you think?" McCoy groused. "You always
manage to get into trouble without me. Somebody's gotta
keep you alive."

"Captain!" Sulu's eyes widened in alarm as Koust
emerged behind Kirk. The young helmsman raised his
phaser rifle, followed by his security team. "A Dassik!"

"Stand down!" Kirk said forcefully. "This is Koust. He's
a fellow prisoner, a victim of an assassination attempt.
And he's agreed to work with us to escape." The phaser
barrels wavered, but only slightly. "If we want to get out
of here, we need all the help we can get. So lower your
weapons. That's an order."

Sulu and the guards lowered their weapons, though
they kept a close eye on Koust. The Dassik looked at Kirk.
"You keep your word after all, human."

Jim smiled. "We have our moments." He looked to the doctor. "Bones, any injuries?"

"Zhang's stunned," McCoy said, kneeling over the black-haired ensign. "I'll have her on her feet in a minute," he added as he applied his ubiquitous hypospray to her neck. "No casualties on the Web side, but they'll have headaches from the phaser stuns, and Sulu dislocated that guy's shoulder," he said, nodding at a fallen Tessegri. "I'd like to treat it, if we have time."

"If you can make it fast, Bones." As McCoy hurried over to the guard, Kirk looked around, puzzled. "Balok? Where are you?"

The *Fesarius* captain stepped out from behind the door frame, where he'd been the whole time. "I'm fine. Shall we go?"

Kirk turned to Sulu. "Lieutenant, where's our ride?"

Sulu gestured over his shoulder. "A couple more blown walls back that way," he said. "It's a Web-built aircraft, designed for this atmosphere, so it's plenty fast. Uhura's aboard now, keeping it ready for a quick getaway."

"Uhura?"

"She helped us fake our clearances and track protector activity."

"All right, let's start moving out. Bones, wrap it up!"

"That's what I'm doing!" McCoy barked, and indeed he was literally wrapping the Tessegri's shoulder with tape. Kirk sighed.

"Captain," Spock said, "we will no doubt face resistance from the protectors, now that we have drawn their notice. How will our escape craft evade their magnetic tractor fields?"

Sulu grinned. "Same way we got here, sir. The dissidents know a few tricks."

"Then let's go," Kirk ordered. These must be the same dissidents Spock had told him about, the ones who'd promised to help the *Enterprise* escape Cherela. He just hoped they wouldn't exhaust their bag of tricks getting the rescue craft back to the ship. Otherwise this escape might all turn out to be moot.

———

Sulu was beginning to regret his confident boast to the captain. The dissidents' tricks had worked well enough on the approach, when the protectors hadn't known they were coming and Uhura had been able to ensure they avoided drawing attention. But getting away from the prison while the protectors were actively trying to restrain them was a different matter. The escape craft was an actual airplane, given lift by a pair of compact, adjustable wings. Since it was designed to operate exclusively within Cherela's immense atmosphere, there was no reason for it to waste energy relying on antigravs when there was so very, very much dense air available to provide buoyancy. It had powerful thrusters to propel it at supersonic speeds—a necessity given the vast distances it had to cover—but as a strictly aerodynamic craft, it had limited maneuverability, complicating Sulu's efforts at evading the Web's tractor field. The plane had magnetic deflectors that let it resist that field, but their charge was finite and diminishing quickly each time the tractors' grip closed in on them once more. Sulu had done his best to keep the craft moving unpredictably to confound their attempts to focus the tractor effect, but he was pushing the vehicle's performance envelope. "Recommend we take her above the ceiling, sir," Sulu said to Kirk.

The captain looked out at the looming clouds above and frowned. "Looks like there's a storm brewing in there. Can this type of aircraft take it?"

"It's a risk, sir, but if we can get above it, we'll have cover to lose pursuit." All they needed was a few minutes out of sight. In an atmosphere this vast, it would be hard for the Web forces to intercept them if they didn't know where to look. If the escapees could blend in with normal Web traffic, the recreational and short-range aircraft that didn't use the conduits, then they'd be free and clear to reach their rendezvous with the dissidents and get smuggled back aboard the *Enterprise*. By which time, Sulu hoped, the captain and Spock would have a plan for getting away from Cherela and the Dassik. But that was a problem for later.

Kirk turned to his first officer. "Spock?"

The Vulcan pondered. "If we stay below the clouds, the risk of recapture approaches certainty. We must make the attempt."

Kirk nodded to Sulu. "Do it."

"Aye, sir," Sulu said, grinning as he angled the plane upward, battling the wind. Lightning flashed before him, taunting him, and he grinned wider. "Just try it," he told the storm.

A deep, raucous laugh sounded over his shoulder. He saw the Dassik, Koust, reflected in the windscreen as a flash of lightning illuminated him, the image reminding Sulu of Munch's *The Scream*. "Force Leader Grun told us you humans were cowards," he said. "I think I was lied to."

"About that and a lot of other things, I'd wager," Sulu told him.

"Ahh, so you're a gambling man too?"

"I like a challenge."

"Then I wager you can't get us through that storm alive."

Sulu stared at him in bewilderment. "What do you get if you win? You'll be dead with the rest of us!"

"But my death will bring me victory!" Koust said. "That is its own reward."

"But what do *I* get from you if you lose?"

"You may demand what prize you will."

A console alarm beeped, warning him of a static charge buildup in the clouds ahead. It figured that the Web dwellers would build their aircraft with lightning detectors. He banked left, steering away from the charge concentration, but when the lightning bolt came, it arced dangerously close to the plane. He needed to get better at reading the clouds. "Okay. If we live, then you teach me Dassik fighting styles."

"Armed or unarmed?"

Sulu threw him a quick glance. "Do you use swords?"

Koust laughed and clapped him on the shoulder. "My friend, are you sure you aren't part Dassik yourself?"

The blow almost cost Sulu control of the aircraft. "Hey, watch it. No fair trying to make me lose."

"I thought you enjoyed a challenge."

"Koust," Kirk said. "Sit down and let the man fly."

The young predator grumbled, but he complied. Sulu was relieved. The winds were picking up sharply, and it was a struggle to keep the plane level. He wanted to get up above the storm, but the instruments showed a massive charge concentration building up right overhead, stretching for some distance. Sulu realized he'd forgotten to account for the scale of things on a Jovian world. Here, even a small storm was the size of a continent.

A continent with an attitude. A gust of wind kicked the plane upward, too close to the static charge. An immense lightning bolt struck the aircraft's tail, deafening him. He could feel the kick through the fuselage. Ears ringing, Sulu checked the readouts. They flickered, but they were holding. The plane's magnetic shielding had protected it from the worst of the lightning.

But it did have some effect. "Jim!" McCoy called. Sulu turned to see him crouching beside Balok, who seemed to be having a seizure.

Immediately, Kirk was by their side. "Balok? Are you all right? Bones . . ."

McCoy was already deploying his medical scanner. After a moment, he stared at it in dismay. "Jim—this isn't Balok! It's a mechanism!"

Indeed, there was a distinctly mechanical quality to the way "Balok" was jerking around. Spock examined the false Linnik for a moment, then found some kind of deactivation control, which he operated. The robot fell limp. "The same technology as the Dassik simulacrum aboard the *Fesarius*," Spock said. "Though more lifelike, presumably because Balok did not have a live example of a Dassik on which to base his model."

"Do you think Balok faked his capture?" Uhura asked.

"Negative, Lieutenant," Spock said. "This is the First's own technology, so surely their prison officials would have been able to recognize it. Besides, I was with him at the time of his arrest, and I can attest that his behavior was far more . . . idiosyncratic . . . than the simple, repetitive responses demonstrated by this apparatus. We know the *Fesarius* simulacrum was teleoperated by Balok himself, not unlike the Redheri infiltration drones we recently encountered on Sigma Niobe II. But this unit was programmed to operate autonomously, either because of the vast distances between world modules or to preclude the detection of control signals."

Kirk frowned. "Then it must have been substituted by Warden Mure. Probably on Tirak's orders. And they couldn't have known we'd escape, so it must have been Nisu they were trying to fool. They've taken Balok somewhere else, and they don't want the Council to know about it."

"Then he is likely already dead," Koust said. "As they intended the two of us to be. With our 'accident' under investigation, they could not risk another in the prison itself."

"I'm not ready to accept that," Kirk told him. "Tirak may hate outsiders, but Balok is one of his own. Hopefully that still matters to him. And once we get back to the *Enterprise*, we can try to find out where—"

But then another lightning bolt struck, and another. Sulu put the plane into a dive, instinctively trying to get away from the source of the bolts. But he still wasn't reading the clouds well, and he realized too late that he was heading straight toward another charge concentration. And the shield was still running at high power, bleeding off residual charge from the strike. If it was leaving a trail of ionized air behind the craft, then—

The previous lightning bolts had been mere sparks in comparison to what struck the vehicle now, using its ionized wake as a conduction path. Sulu wrenched his eyes shut against the blistering light from outside, but it dazzled him even through closed eyelids. When he opened his eyes, he saw that the controls had gone dark. The throttle wouldn't respond. And the plane was in a dive, spiraling out of control.

"Sulu!" Kirk cried, pulling himself forward. "Get those engines going again!"

Sulu jabbed at the reboot control, but only a few status lights came on. He used what he could, trying to get into the system and reroute control to backup circuits. But nothing happened. "There's too much damage!" He ducked under the console and pulled open the maintenance cover. "If I can reroute manually . . ."

It was a desperation move. It might take minutes to identify the intact systems and cross-connect the circuits. And every second, the aircraft fell deeper into the atmosphere. There was nowhere to crash, but before long the pressure would crush the fuselage like a discarded drinking cup. Sulu's ears were already popping.

He struggled to get some power to the engines, but soon enough it became clear that there was no time. "I'm sorry, Captain," he said. "There's just no way—"

The plane lurched. Sulu flew forward, banging his forehead on the console. He cursed and rubbed his head, but through the substantial pain, he gradually came to realize that they'd stopped falling. *What did we land on?* he thought woozily.

Noticing that the others were staring out the ports in amazement, Sulu pushed through the fog in his head, staggered to his feet, and followed their gaze out and upward.

There, hanging a few dozen meters above them, were four enormous balloons. He followed their tethers downward and saw that they emerged from hatches in the nose, the wings, and presumably the tail of the aircraft. Sulu chuckled. "Sorry, Koust. You haven't won the bet yet."

"We're not out of this alive yet either," Koust pointed out.

"Fascinating," Spock said a bit breathlessly. "Presumably helium-filled. A last-ditch emergency measure."

"Great," McCoy said. "Finally they do something sensible! Why couldn't they put those on the habitats too? Then we wouldn't be in this mess."

"The sheer amount of helium required in that case would be prohibitive, Doctor," Spock replied.

"Speaking of being in a mess," Uhura said, "any chance of restarting the engines now that we have a breather?"

"I'll see what I can do," Sulu said.

But before he could get anywhere, the craft shuddered again and started to move. The magnetic sensor screen was barely working, but he got enough to know what was happening. "Damn. The tractor field's got us, sir. Countermeasures are down."

"Those balloons saved our lives," Kirk said, "but made us an easier target. Any chance we can fix the shields and slip free?"

"No way, sir. The power's too depleted. Sorry."

Kirk set his jaw. "Then we'd better get ready for a fight."

The balloons soon snapped free from the force of the wind as the tractor field pulled them at high speed toward whatever their destination was. Sulu had brought spare weapons for Kirk and Spock, and then some; he believed in being prepared. But he glanced uncertainly at their Dassik guest. "Captain?"

After trading a look with Koust, Kirk nodded. "Give him a phaser. But lock it on stun."

As Sulu complied, Koust asked, "What's wrong, Kirk? Don't you trust me?"

"I trust you not to kill *us*," Kirk replied. "I don't want you killing any of them. Whatever the Linnik's ancestors may have done to your people, the individuals out there aren't responsible for it. Our mission's to save their lives, whether they want it or not."

Koust grumbled, then gave Kirk a sullen look. "Very well. I'm a soldier. I follow orders. I will *stun*." He grimaced as though the word left a foul aftertaste.

The captain turned his attention to McCoy, seeing that the doctor was prepared to fight. Kirk knew that McCoy's code would not allow him to take a life even to save his own—but a doctor understood that sometimes one had to inflict some degree of pain or damage to a body in order to heal it. He stood ready to do what needed to be done. But Kirk hoped it wouldn't come to that. "Bones, it's best if you stay back. We may need a doctor before this is done."

The doctor's eyes met the captain's. "Understood."

Kirk turned to the communications officer. "Uhura, you might want to stay back too. Leave it to the fighters."

"With all due respect, sir . . ." Uhura deftly, pointedly locked and charged her phaser rifle. "I've had my fill of being frightened."

"Thank you, Lieutenant," Kirk said, respect in his eyes. "I'm glad to have you at my side."

Once armed, there was little they could do to get ready short of breathing deeply, keeping their muscles loose, and trying to stay calm. It was some distance to their destination, though, and the long wait made that last part the hardest of all.

Finally, a shape came into view ahead of them. "It's another hangar module," Sulu said. "Not the same one the *Enterprise*'s in; that's too far away. But basically the same design."

Kirk leaned forward, studying the approaching module. "So the inside should be in free fall but have a breathable atmosphere."

"Probably, sir."

The captain turned to address the crew. "Then we have a chance to break free before the plane docks. As soon as we're inside, we blow the hatch and bail out."

"What?!" McCoy cried. "And flail around in zero gravity?"

"No. Push off as hard as you can when you bail out. Our momentum should carry us to the hangar wall. From there we can try to make our way to a working vehicle. Just angle yourself to minimize air resistance. Like skydiving."

"Blast it, Jim, I'm a doctor, not a paratrooper!"

"Just follow my lead. Now, everyone, get ready."

Sulu moved toward the hatch and waved his team forward. "Prescott, Zhang, take point. Mister Koust, go with them."

"Yes!" Sulu wasn't surprised that the Dassik was pleased to be leading the charge, but he hadn't done it for Koust. Bottom line, however charming the young hunter may have been in his rough way, Sulu considered him the least trustworthy and most expendable member of the team. And from what Sulu had seen of the Dassik, he'd probably make quite a lot of noise and be a good distraction from the rest.

"Nored," Sulu went on, "you and I will cover the rear."

That would be a vital position, since by that point the Web forces would have caught on and begun responding. He wanted his best person there with him, and after his experience in the Fiilestii module, he was convinced that was Anne.

As the plane passed through the hangar door's containment field into the breathable atmosphere within, Sulu nodded at Lou Prescott. The burly guard opened the hatch and leaped out, with the lanky Zhang Xiaolu and the eager Koust following close behind. Kirk and Spock went next, then Uhura and McCoy, with Anne Nored and Sulu being the last to leave the aircraft—aside from the Balok dummy, of course. Sulu wondered if it would be needed as evidence later, but it would be an impediment to take with them. Hopefully it would be safe where it was.

No sooner had Sulu pushed off the lip of the hatch than he felt himself being yanked sideways. He saw the others heading for the far wall as planned, but by a stroke of bad luck, the plane must have shifted in the tractor beams and he'd been caught in one of them. The focused gravity beam was pulling him toward it, and he soon fell ahead of the aircraft. There were multiple beams focused on it, balancing one another, but he was caught in the gravity of just one, literally falling toward it—which meant he was moving faster by the second. If he didn't act fast, he'd splatter into the hangar wall just as if he'd fallen off a cliff.

Even as the thought formed, Sulu swung the phaser rifle up and blasted in the direction he was falling, continuing to fire until he blew out the tractor emitter. But it was too late. He was going too fast. And his phaser could do no more good, since its beam had no significant recoil. Instinctively, he spread-eagled himself to maximize air resistance, wishing he still had on that wingsuit from the Fiilestii module. The move slowed him a little, but he was drawing too close. He could tell he wouldn't decelerate enough in time. All he could do was thrust his legs forward and attempt a parachute landing fall, hoping to absorb enough of the impact force that it would merely put him in sickbay for a few weeks rather than killing him outright.

But then he saw a shape soaring toward him. It was a Fiilestii, wearing the colors of a protector. The winged alien was matching his speed and course, and the pilot in Sulu was intrigued to watch how she angled her wings and body to compensate for the lack of gravity to counter-act lift. (He was pleased with himself that he could rec-ognize Fiilestii sexes from a distance. The difference in plumage patterns was subtle.)

Sulu offered no resistance as the Fiilestii protector caught him, tossed his phaser rifle aside, and flapped her wings fiercely to veer them sideways and reduce speed. But he was just playing possum until the right moment. When it came, he pulled his phaser pistol from his belt and stunned the protector at point-blank range. They were still heading toward the hangar wall at an angle, but at a slow, easily survivable speed. Sulu pushed off the protector's body, sending himself toward the wall and the Fiilestii back out into the open air, where she tumbled la-zily. He flipped, bent his knees as his momentum carried him into the wall, then launched back toward the others.

The rest of the team had reached a vacant docking structure, which they were using for cover as the protector team flew toward them in an inspection pod, two of them leaning out the side hatches to fire their stun weapons. Three more protectors were riding some kind of main-

tenance sleds, basically open platforms with clear cowl-
ings at the front and waldoes extending forward, ridden
in a motorcycle-style crouch with the arms in the waldo
sleeves. The waldoes were designed for fine manipulation,
able to handle the protectors' stun rifles as well, allowing
the sled riders to pin the *Enterprise* team down in a crossfire. Zhang had already been stunned, her second time
this mission, and McCoy was futilely trying to get out in
the open long enough to get a tricorder scan of her vitals
before she drifted too far from the docking structure. Kirk
pulled the doctor back behind a strut just before a stun
bolt would have taken him down.

But Sulu realized his mishap could be a lucky break.
The nearest sled rider had turned his back to Sulu, apparently discounting him as a threat. If he struck fast, he
could make the most of it. Luckily he was heading in the
right direction to intercept the sled—*if* he timed it right.

He stayed in a headfirst, arms-back dive posture as
long as possible for maximum airspeed, drawing closer.
Seeing what he was doing, Koust let out a fearsome battle
cry and fired wildly at the sled rider to distract him. When
the time came to swing his own phaser forward, Sulu
made the shot count; as the protector's body fell limp,
the sled stopped thrusting, letting it stay on course long
enough for Sulu to intercept it. Well, almost. He lunged
out for it and barely managed to snag the protector's foot,
his momentum almost pulling the humanoid off the sled.
Luckily, the protector's arm snagged in the waldo sleeve.
Sulu was able to clamber over his body and reach the sled
before the protector slipped free completely.

The controls were intuitive for anyone of humanoid
build, so Sulu was quickly in motion, though he almost

lost the waldo's grip on the protector's firearm. He saw that the others were still keeping the inspection pod and other two sleds occupied with a steady phaser barrage. Spock fired fewer shots than the others, but they counted more; as Sulu watched, the Vulcan's precision aim picked off one of the protectors leaning out of the pod. But another one caught her stunned colleague, pulled him back into the pod, and took his place. Prescott came out from cover, taking advantage of the brief lull, and opened fire on the pod. But the new protector was a Tessegri, her quick reflexes letting her hit him with a grazing blow to the arm before he could hit her. Prescott's phaser rifle floated free from his limp right arm, and he weakly strained for it with his left, making himself a more exposed target in his dazed condition. Before the Tessegri could take Prescott out completely, Sulu stunned her, then played the rifle's beam into the pod's cockpit through the open door while Uhura pulled Prescott to safety. The pod swerved toward Sulu, its windshield blocking his fire. He applied maximum thrust on a collision course, pushing himself back and out of the sled at the last second. The impact smashed the sled and cracked the pod's windshield, but the larger vehicle held.

Sulu was still traveling toward it at a fair clip, though, and as it twisted sideways from the impact, he snagged the door frame and fired a few more shots into the cockpit with his phaser. He scored one more sure hit and a glancing blow, but then had to duck as another protector opened fire on him. Pushing free, Sulu twisted around, dialing his phaser up to high power at the same time. He fired freely at the inspection pod's thrusters, causing what damage he could as he drifted clear.

A stun beam shot by his head from behind, close enough to make his scalp tingle. Tipping his head back, he saw that one of the two remaining sleds was arcing toward him, its rider trying to get a bead. Adrift and ballistic, there was no way Sulu could dodge. But then a phaser bolt struck the protector, who convulsed, sending his next shot flying wild. Sulu looked left and saw Uhura lowering her phaser rifle and giving him a blinding grin. *Talk about stunning,* Sulu thought, grinning back.

A moment later, once he'd snagged the approaching sled and dislodged its unconscious operator, Sulu saw that Kirk and Nored had the third sled rider pinned down, while the remaining conscious protectors in the pod were trapped there by fire from Koust and Spock. A shot from Nored took the sled rider in the leg, convulsing her and putting her sled in a spin that allowed Kirk to get a decisive stun shot off. Settling himself into the second sled's control seat, Sulu went after the pod again.

They were ready for him this time, though. The pod still had enough maneuvering control to rotate toward him, and stun beams lanced out through a small hole they'd burned into the damaged windshield. His own stun beams bounced off the windshield, having no effect. But he was able to keep them distracted long enough for Kirk to kick off from the docking frame, grab on to the pod, force the hatch, and take out the rest of its occupants with a spinning dive-and-fire maneuver that would only be possible in freefall.

Sulu picked up Kirk and took him back to the others, snagging Zhang along the way. "*Victory!*" Koust was crying at the top of his lungs.

"We're not out of the woods yet," Kirk called back.

Even as he spoke, a transporter chime sounded. All around them, new protectors beamed in—dozens of them, all armed and armored. Sulu recognized Nisu and her elite team at the head of the group. No sooner had they materialized than shots rang out, stunning Prescott, Nored, and Koust. A different kind of beam lashed against Sulu's sled, sending St. Elmo's fire across its surface. He instinctively pushed free before receiving a full shock, but he was left adrift. He saw that Kirk had leaped free just in time and taken Zhang with him. Sulu heaved a sigh of relief, not wanting to know what that beam would've done to her on top of two stun shots.

"Have them stand down, Kirk!" Nisu cried. "We outnumber you by millions. You can't escape."

With a heavy sigh, Kirk let go of his weapon and let it drift away. "Stand down," he ordered. Sulu chafed at the command, but knew it was pointless to keep fighting. He let his phaser go as well. One of Nisu's protectors jetted over, using thrusters in his suit, to secure it and him.

In moments, the whole team, conscious and otherwise, had been rounded up and placed in handcuffs, floating before Nisu. Her huge eyes focused on Spock, and even just getting the peripheral effect of her gaze held Sulu enraptured. "This was foolhardy," she said. "The Web is something greater than you can understand. You cannot bring it down."

"We . . . do not wish to," Spock said, struggling against the hypnotic effect of her stare. "Whatever Tirak has claimed . . . we are not your enemies."

"And that makes your folly all the more dangerous." She broke her gaze on Spock to look around at the group. "Where is Balok?"

"We don't know," Kirk told her while Spock caught his breath. "If you check inside the aircraft, you'll see that the Balok we thought we liberated is a fake."

"What? That makes no—"

She was cut off as the hangar module heaved and tolled like a bell. Floating in midair, the protectors and their captives were spared from the former, but the acoustic shock was like a physical blow.

As the echoes died away, Sulu heard Kirk's voice through the ringing in his ears. "Nisu, what's happening?"

She looked away, heeding an inner voice while new, more distant thunder boomed from outside. Whatever it was, it was no storm. "Explosions in the atmosphere. Near our modules, though none has been hit."

"The Dassik?" Kirk asked.

"We are not sure, though—"

Another blast made the module heave and pounded through their bodies. Sulu realized he and the others were beginning to fall toward the bottom of the hangar, though it felt the same as weightlessness. The hangar's antigravs were failing! The ships were beginning to plummet from their docks as well. The shock of their impact, and any explosions that resulted, might tear the whole hangar open. Not that Sulu would still be alive to care at that point.

"Emergency beam-out, all life-forms!" Nisu cried. The delay that followed seemed endless to Sulu as the deck flew closer. But the beam took him just as he heard the ships beginning to crash.

Thirteen

Nisu rematerialized and struck the floor, though with much less force than she would have struck that of the hangar; the transporter had corrected for most, but not all, of her momentum. Rolling to her feet, she found herself in the regional security center. Her eyes immediately went to the big hologram that displayed situational status. It was bad. High-yield fusion charges were going off within a few thousand kilometers of each world module. There had been no direct impacts yet, but some had come dangerously close, producing sizeable fireballs and shock waves. The modules were shielded against their electromagnetic pulses—no worse than one of Cherela's larger lightning strikes—but radiation could pose a hazard. And multiple habitats were showing atmosphere breaches and structural damage.

Worse, the antigrav network was showing increasing instability, with the close call in the hangar being merely a symptom. The status reports in her earpiece told her that the engineers were working hard to maintain the balance, but on top of the lingering instability from Fiilestii's collapse, this bombardment was a serious complication to their efforts.

"Depth charges," came Kirk's voice. Turning, Nisu confirmed that Kirk, Spock, Sulu, McCoy, and Uhura had materialized along with her team. All of them were clambering to their feet, but the protectors made it first and ensured the five outsiders were secure at gunpoint. "They're dropping depth charges into the atmosphere."

"Essentially, yes, Captain," Spock said, perusing the readouts of the blast pattern. "They would appear to be the Dassik's cubic missiles, set to overload and undergo fusion explosions. They've narrowed down the module positions, but not precisely. They seem to be attempting to inflict what damage they can."

"Maybe they're hoping to knock out the Web's camouflage systems," Lieutenant Sulu observed.

"Or just setting off bombs for the hell of it," added Doctor McCoy.

Kirk looked around at his diminished party. "Where are the rest of my people?" he demanded.

"I called for emergency beam-out," Nisu told him. "That means that injured or unconscious subjects are automatically directed to a medical facility. They will be safe and cared for."

"I'll be the judge of that!" McCoy exclaimed. "Take me to them right now!"

She transfixed him with her gaze. "You are in no position to make demands!" She held her stare a moment longer, then broke it off when she realized his respiration had slowed. Some susceptible individuals could have their attention so transfixed by a sufficiently intense Kisaja stare that it even affected their autonomic nervous systems; essentially they forgot to breathe. Nisu had never before been angry enough to ramp her stare up to that level. It disturbed her, the degree of disruption these outsiders had brought to her ordered world.

While Kirk made sure his physician was all right, Spock studied the status display. "The bombardment is exacerbating the Web's instabilities. If they find their range and begin striking the modules directly, the impacts could trigger a cascade failure in the grid. In which case the entire Web of Worlds will tear itself apart."

"Don't!" Nisu cried, whirling on him. "Don't use this as an excuse to sell me your lies! The Web has always been here. It will always be here! We will deal with this!"

"How?" Kirk demanded. "By hiding? Squeezing your eyes shut and hoping they go away? That's what got you into this situation in the first place, Nisu. The Dassik know we're down here now. They aren't going anywhere. Not until they get what they want from your people."

"Maybe . . . maybe we can modify the atmosphere grid. Make it appear we have been destroyed."

"They've seen through that illusion already," Lieutenant Uhura said. "If you disappeared again, they wouldn't take it at face value."

The ground heaved beneath them. Nisu refused to take the timing as a sign. But Kirk seized the moment to step forward. "The time for hiding is over, Nisu. The only way to stop the Dassik is to face them. And that's something we know how to do. Please . . . let us help." He moved one more step closer, lowered his voice, and projected a sincerity she could feel was genuine. "All we've been trying to do all along is help."

The reports on the data stream were growing more distressed. Modules all over Cherela were feeling gravity surges, even those that weren't taking damage from the explosions. People were beginning to die in tube accidents, building collapses, atmospheric ruptures. The instability was growing worse despite everything the engineers attempted.

An urgent signal came through on both her earpiece and the holographic display. A detonation had gone off alarmingly close to one of the world modules. In the display, the fireball expanded nearly to the module's dome before convection made it roll upward, and moments later the dome buckled around the point of near-contact and began to cave inward. The superheated hydrogen and methane rushed in and mixed with the oxygen within, igniting into flame—a vast torrent of blue fire that poured into the dome with terrible, majestic slowness.

"My God," McCoy breathed.

Kirk turned to Nisu, whose eyes were wider than ever. "Is that module populated?"

After a moment, the Kisaja blinked. "It . . . no, it is a nature preserve. The subarctic biosphere of the planet Niatok. But if there are tourists . . ."

"The sheer volume of atmosphere is great enough to shield them for now," Spock said. "The hydrogen and methane are lower in density than the internal atmosphere, so they will not reach ground level, and it will take time for the thermal and pressure effects to propagate. Evacuation should be possible." He paused. "However, if we do not act quickly, they may have nowhere to evacuate to."

No, Nisu thought, unable to process all of this. *This can't be. The Web is my home. The Web is safety. The Web has always taken care of me.*

Suddenly Spock was there, his eyes transfixing hers almost like a Kisaja's. He was with her in thoughtspace. *Ever since your parents died?* he urged. *Remember—how did it happen?* Unwillingly, her mind went to the memory: the freak storm out of nowhere, the conduit overwhelmed and torn apart, her parents' skulls crushed in the turbulence before the emergency balloons had deployed.

The storm, Nisu. How many more freak storms have there been over the past few generations? Don't you see? Your parents' death was a symptom of the growing instabilities the Web's concealment grid created in the atmosphere. It was a tragedy that could have been prevented if the government had not been so intractable in its determination to stay hidden.

"No!" she sobbed, wanting to look away, but she couldn't break the link.

I understand your fear, Spock told her. *You were alone. You were lost. The Web offered protection, security. You needed to believe it would always keep you safe. The prospect that it could die is too terrifying to contemplate.*

I realize now that we have both been paralyzed by fear of the future. We look ahead and see no clear path that will let us avoid unwelcome change, and so we quail at the thought of facing what lies ahead. But that is illogical. The future will come whether we wish it or not. Change will come. Therefore, we must accept it and adapt to it, so that we may assert some control over where it takes us.

You must not let your fear prevent you from taking that control, Nisu. The First Federation has relied on fear for too long, and it has become a trap. You must move beyond that fear, as I must move beyond my own doubts and face whatever the future brings. This is not a threat you can hide from, Nisu. It must be faced openly if the Web is to survive.

Spock released Nisu from the link, but still her eyes held his a moment longer. Then she shook her head and turned to Kirk. "I will take you to the triumvirs," she said.

"But the First are in no mood to trust outsiders right now. You'd better have a good plan if you want them to listen."

"All I have is the truth," Kirk said. "We'll just have to hope it's enough."

Nisu squeezed her eyes shut, praying she wasn't making a huge mistake.

———

"Are we hitting anything?" Grun demanded. He hovered over Remv's shoulder, struggling to divine some meaning from the readouts on his console, but he remained entirely dependent on the monitor officer to explain them to him.

"It is . . . difficult to tell, Force Leader," Remv replied with a quaver in his voice. "The detonations worsen the interference."

"Get me results, Remv! Your life hangs by a thread as it is."

"J-just give me a moment, please! I have an idea!" Remv worked his console frantically. "Ah!" he exclaimed after a moment. "There! The detonations create shock waves in the atmosphere. When the waves hit obstructions, it alters their pattern. Whatever form of concealment these objects use must not be calibrated to cope with—"

"Fewer words, Remv!"

"Sir, the blasts are letting us detect the objects more clearly! We can improve our targeting!"

"There!" Grun cried, clapping his shoulder. "I knew I was right not to kill you! Show me, show me!"

Remv did something to the controls to make the readouts show. The objects that appeared were still vaguely defined, fragmentary, but it was possible to begin divining their form and pattern. "They're immense!" Rhuld cried.

"And look," Remv added. "They go beyond our scan range. They could extend clear around the planet!"

"Yes," Grun said, his heart racing with the thrill of the hunt. "At long last, we have hounded the betrayers to their nest! Now they are at our mercy! Increase the bombardment until they surrender!"

"But, Force Leader, look!" Rhuld said, indicating the readouts. "The grid is fluctuating. The modules are beginning to lose their support in the atmosphere. Our bombardment must be destabilizing their balance. If we strike too aggressively, the whole system would collapse!"

And if we hesitate, Vraq will arrive and steal my glory. This victory had to be Grun's and Grun's alone. He would allow no one to overshadow him ever again. "Let it collapse, then," he replied with a sadistic laugh. "A fitting fate for those who left our race to die!"

"Force Leader, without the knowledge they possess, our race *will* die!"

"Do not question me, Rhuld!" Grun cried, smacking him across the face once more. "I know how things stand. We will bombard them until they have no choice but to beg us for mercy. They will give us whatever we ask in exchange for their lives. And then . . . we will have no need to grant them those lives."

Grun could see the continued doubt and hesitation in Rhuld's eyes, but his second was too cowardly to continue to question. He could have hoped for a higher caliber of warrior, but under the circumstances, with Vraq's squadron drawing nearer by the moment, he preferred Rhuld's quick and unquestioning obedience.

"Make ready for another bombardment," he commanded. "Target the enemy installations! We will not relent until the betrayers are broken for good!"

Once Nisu and the five from the *Enterprise* materialized in the transport center of the Syletir module's government complex, the Kisaja quickly led them out onto the skywalk that led to the central tower. Kirk slowed to take in the spectacular vista beyond—the vast ocean and its islands, preserving forms of life found nowhere else in the galaxy, and the looming storm clouds that had suddenly become a secondary threat.

The sky lit up above them. The dome quickly polarized to block the worst of it, but Kirk's eyes watered, and he tried to blink away the searing afterimage.

Once the light faded, it was some moments before he realized McCoy was shaking his shoulder, goading him forward. "Well, what are you waiting for? Come on!"

"Sorry." He picked up the pace.

But the doctor peered at him closely as they strode together. "Okay, what's bugging you?"

It was a moment before he spoke. "I'm just . . . overwhelmed by the sheer magnitude of it all, Bones. To have so many worlds riding on what I decide . . . I've never felt so much weight on my shoulders."

"Bull," McCoy said. "You've made decisions that affected whole worlds before. Even ones affecting the history of the whole Federation."

"But the stakes were more distant then, more abstract. Here . . . I can *see* the worlds that could live or die based on what I do next."

"These worlds are dying just fine without your help, Jim. Right or wrong, you have to do something."

Kirk nodded and resumed his course toward the central tower at a run.

Once inside the tower, as they neared the situation room, the sentries spotted the approaching group and reacted with alarm, brandishing their weapons in near panic. Kirk heard cries of "We're under attack!" and "Protect the Council!" before one of the sentries, a Tessegri male, had the presence of mind to shout "Halt, all of you!" at the approaching party. Kirk was grateful for that, at least; the protector held his firearm with such agitation that he had feared the Tessegri would simply start shooting.

But Nisu stepped to the front of the group. "Stand down, Initau! These people are with me."

"But—but Triumvir Tirak said they were attacking the Web."

"Tirak says many things. That is his job. Yours is to obey my orders. Now stand down and let us pass."

"But they're outsiders!"

"Look around you, Initau. Did your kind evolve here? Did mine?" The floor swayed and rumbled beneath them once more. "Surely now, more than ever, it is obvious that none of us truly belong here."

Finally, the sentry stepped aside, and the others followed suit. Nisu looked to Kirk. "Now we must face Tirak himself. Be ready."

As promised, once she led them inside, the older Linnik male was already storming toward them, no doubt alerted by the earlier ruckus. "You!" he exclaimed, gesticulating furiously at Kirk. "This is your fault!"

He met Tirak's eyes head-on. But this was not the time

to confront him over his secrets. "That's right," Kirk said. "Much of this is my fault. So let me help fix it." The triumvir froze, the wind taken from his sails.

Brilliant light flashed. Kirk realized that the roof of the situation room was a high, clear dome showing the sky beyond, a sky roiling under the shock of another detonation. A gravity fluctuation pulsed through the room: a harrowing sensation of falling, a feeling of crushing weight, then normality again, all within seconds. "Tirak." It was Aranow, resting her long blue fingers on the older triumvir's arm. "We don't have time. The bombs are getting closer. Let them help."

"Is that Kirk and Spock?" Lekur bellowed from across the room, where he'd been immersed in the status displays, not even noticing the drama. "For *hrunh*'s sake, get them over here now!"

That settled it. In moments, they were all assembled around the massive array of display holograms showing the escalating situation. "They're getting their range now," Lekur said. "We're boosting the emergency shielding as fast as we can, but with the fields so unstable already, it's a fight. And if we divert too much energy, we won't be able to damp the fluctuations in the Web."

"Can't you shoot down the bombs before they hit?" Kirk asked.

"We're not equipped for combat," Aranow said. "We don't need to be. Nobody ever found us before."

"The *Enterprise* is," Kirk said. "Put me in contact."

"It is not our way to depend on outsiders," Tirak insisted. "Especially ones who have betrayed our trust."

"The depths with politics!" Aranow cried. "We need help. Who cares how it looks? I vote yes."

"Me too," Lekur said. "Doesn't have to be unanimous. Call your ship, Kirk."

———

Montgomery Scott was immensely relieved to see Captain Kirk on the viewscreen. He had been trying his best to talk his way through the bureaucracy and get permission to help, but the dock foreperson had been too reluctant to risk the disapproval of the angry masses. Scott had been on the verge of abandoning diplomacy and ordering Lieutenant Rahda to blast the ship free of the hangar.

Even so, he would have been setting off without most of the command crew. He looked around the bridge: Chekov manned the science station, Elizabeth Palmer sat at communications, Frank Gabler monitored engineering, Manjula Rahda worked the helm, and Jana Haines filled in at navigation. All good people, or they would not have been aboard the *Enterprise*, but they were not the people Scott was accustomed to relying on when the fate of worlds was at stake.

So it did his heart good to see that, despite all the odds arrayed against them, Kirk and Spock had once again muscled their way right to the top and convinced the authorities to cooperate. He never should have doubted what those two could accomplish.

Once Kirk had relayed his intentions, Scott acted promptly. "Rahda, get us into the open air."

"*Scotty,*" Kirk asked once the helmswoman had acknowledged and complied, "*are you up to taking on two Dassik warships?*"

"I wish I could say yes," Scotty told him, shaking his

head. "Shields are still a bit iffy, and the port warp engine's still half-assembled."

"*Warp drive's beside the point, Scotty,*" Kirk said. "*You won't be needing it.*"

"But in its current condition, if it takes too much damage, a power imbalance could build up and take out half the secondary hull."

A pause. "*All right, then avoid direct confrontation. Instead, try to intercept the depth charges and detonate them in the upper atmosphere.*"

"Aye, sir."

A surge of turbulence struck the hangar just as the *Enterprise* passed through its doors. Rahda hit the thrusters to swerve and accelerate clear, but a sharp thump and scraping groan resonated through the ship's superstructure. Scott glanced at the engineering station; the status readouts showed minimal damage, nothing a few new hull plates and a coat of paint wouldn't fix.

"That's risky too, sir," Ensign Chekov said as the lowering storm clouds came into view through the forward port. "Our phasers will be attenuated in this atmosphere. We will have to get pretty close."

"Torpedoes?" Scott asked.

"They are not designed to maneuver in these winds, Commander. Again, we would need to get close."

"*Scotty,*" Kirk said, "*you know what's at stake. Do what you have to do to protect these people.*"

Scott straightened with pride. "Absolutely, sir. We'll find a way. These First folks may not have been the most hospitable hosts lately, but that doesn't mean we're going to let them down."

"*We know,*" Triumvir Aranow replied. "*Maybe it's more than we deserve. Fortune run with you,* Enterprise."

We'll need it, Scott thought as he studied the view ahead. The fusion charges were ionizing the atmosphere, adding more charge to the lightning storms that were already intensified by the Web's atmospheric effects. Lightning raked the shields as the *Enterprise* flew toward the clouds—lightning on a Jovian scale, plasma arcs so huge they dwarfed the starship. The vessel trembled. If this lasted much longer, Scott thought, they'd be better off facing the Dassik.

Especially with the ionization disrupting the ship's sensors. The Web's sensor systems were better designed to cope with Cherela's atmosphere, so it was a relief when the Triumvirate's staff provided the *Enterprise* with a real-time feed to help them track the Dassik's cubic depth charges. "Down here is the best place to do it anyway," Chekov observed as he studied the feed in Spock's hooded viewer. "They're dropping the charges from a midrange orbit—as close as they can get without the radiation belts frying their systems." An evasive course around the radiation belts, like Sulu had used to get down here in the first place, would've made an effective bombardment pattern impossible. "It takes a few minutes for the charges to spiral in."

"So even if we went out there and took those ghoulish beasties out now," Scott said, "we'd be letting a number of bombs slip by us. Better to pick 'em off down here."

"More dangerous, though, sir," Chekov replied. "All else being equal, it would be better to set them off in space. No shock wave, no fireball, not much EMP—just a nice, quick flash of deadly gamma rays."

"Aye, there's that, lad," Scott replied. "But who doesn't love a good fireworks show? Lieutenant Rahda," he ordered, "light up the sky."

The staff in the situation room cheered as the *Enterprise* detonated one of the cubes in the middle cloud layer, far from its target. But with the atmospheric ionization disrupting communications, Kirk waited on tenterhooks until the readouts confirmed that the ship was intact. He reflected on the nastiness of the weapon design the Dassik were using. Normal fusion weapons would just fizzle out if they were destroyed, since it took a precise sequence of events within a precisely configured vessel to trigger the nuclear reaction. When the *Enterprise* had blown up Balok's initial cube buoy three years before, its explosion had been conventional, less damaging than the radiation the cube had already been emitting. But the Dassik must have rigged their cube missiles with failsafes that triggered a fusion detonation if they registered tampering or imminent destruction. So the *Enterprise* would have to endure numerous close-range nuclear explosions, their effects amplified by atmosphere, in order to save the Web. And worst of all, he wasn't there in the center seat.

"There has to be more we can do, Spock," he said. "The First Federation has all this technology, all this power. I can't believe all we can do is sit here and watch."

"Perhaps we could employ the Web's transporters," Spock suggested.

Lekur Zan grunted a negative in the back of his throat. "Been tried. The things are shielded. Maybe we could push through if the atmosphere weren't so ionized, but that's not happening anytime soon." He shook his massive horned head. "And we can't get them in the tractor fields until they're too close. We'd set them off, and the interaction with the magnetic fields would make the EMP even worse."

"Could we move?" Sulu asked. "Lower the world modules deeper into the atmosphere so they'd be harder to reach?"

"If we had a few days to calculate the field configurations," Lekur said. "As it is, it's a struggle to keep all the modules afloat at all. The last thing we need is to destabilize the network even more."

Lightning flashed again, not a single flash this time but a sustained barrage of dozens of strikes against the Syletir module's dome. The power flickered in the situation room and another gravity fluctuation made Kirk's knees buckle. "Generator overload," one of the technicians explained once the power came back. "Compensating with network power feeds . . . transferring to secondary generators."

"What a crazy place to build a civilization," McCoy grumbled. "If the Dassik don't kill you, your own weather will!"

Kirk looked up sharply, meeting his eyes. "Bones, you're a genius!"

"Well, yes, but what'd I say?"

But Kirk directed his next words at his first officer. "Spock, the lightning. This planet's got enough power in its lightning storms to vaporize whole fleets of starships. If the Web's systems can harness the planet's magnetic fields as a tractor beam, can't they harness that electrical energy as a weapon?"

Spock frowned. "Unlikely, Captain. Vacuum is an insulator. It would require an electric arc of immense potential to leap across the gap from Cherela to one of the Dassik vessels. Even if we could generate that level of voltage in one strike, it would more likely arc to a nearer ground such as one of the inner moonlets—or, more probably, the Web itself."

The ground heaved beneath them as the network of modules struggled to maintain equilibrium. "Which is having enough problems as it is," Kirk said. "All right, bad idea."

"Wait," Lekur said. "Maybe there is a way to direct the lightning on a smaller scale, to take out the fusion charges. It would be hit-or-miss, but it could give us a shot at defending ourselves instead of depending on the *Enterprise*."

"Do what you can," Aranow told him. Tirak merely stood by sullenly, continuing to give the outsiders a suspicious glare.

Spock was still absorbed in thought. "Captain . . . perhaps you were on the right track after all. Cherela's electrical activity may be constrained by its atmosphere, but its overall field of influence extends much farther into space."

"The magnetic field!" Uhura said. Kirk was not surprised that the insight came from the person who had discovered the Web by listening to Cherela's magnetic emissions.

"Indeed," Spock replied. "And contained within that field, trapped as if in a magnetic bottle, are enormous quantities of charged particles from the primary's stellar wind."

Uhura nodded. "The radiation belts."

Now Sulu was grinning. "Radiation belts intense enough to fry the circuits of any ship that gets caught in them. Or worse."

Kirk's eyes darted between his helmsman and his first officer. "Can the outer magnetic field be modified from down here?"

"In fact, its source is far below us," Spock said, "in the metallic hydrogen core of the planet. And the Web is designed to interact with that field, to draw on it for power and stabilization, and to influence its patterns so that the presence of the Web remains disguised." Spock began to pace, eyes darting as he worked through the computations in his head. "It should be possible to use the Web's own magnetic network to modulate the shape of the planetary field, thus redirecting the radiation belts. With sufficient precision, we could concentrate the radiation on the Dassik ships, which would be the equivalent of striking them with an intense particle beam barrage. Even a diffuse bombardment would scramble their sensors and control systems, if not burn them out entirely. If concentrated sufficiently, however, it could be a devastating weapon."

Now Kirk was smiling. "One that would surround this entire planet and draw on its power." He spun to face the triumvirs. "There'd be nowhere the Dassik could hide."

"Are you mad?" Tirak demanded. "You primitives have jeopardized the Web enough through your clumsy tampering with forces you cannot comprehend. Now you wish to tamper even more? You will doom us all!"

"The required degree of modification would not be as great as that involved in repositioning the Web," Spock said. "It would be comparable to the process Triumvir Lekur is currently undertaking to harness the lightning storms."

"Which is working," Lekur reported, "to an extent. We've taken out two charges, missed two more we've tried for." The big Bogosrin growled as the ground heaved beneath them once more. "But we can't do both. It's one or the other."

Tirak shook his head. "We cannot listen to these outsiders and their aggressive ways. We have survived for twelve thousand years by keeping to ourselves, not pushing outward. We should focus on the immediate threat of the charges."

Nisu stepped forward. "That's a stopgap, Triumvir. The source of the threat is the Dassik. We have to neutralize that threat or they will simply strike again." Tirak seemed surprised, even angry, that the Kisaja was not supporting him.

"She's right," Aranow said. "We can't stay timid. We have to stand up, face this threat." She met Kirk's eyes, then moved to his side, her hand clasping his shoulder. "Trust Captain Kirk. Trust Spock. They know how to face the world. How to face problems. Not just how to hide and hope they go away."

Tirak held Nisu's gaze a moment longer. But she remained calm, confident, and defiant. Finally, Tirak sighed. "I have no choice, then. Assuming it can be done."

"That's a big assumption," Lekur said. "Spock, you're wrong, it's bigger than the lightning. That we can do on a local scale, a few control nodes at a time. For what you're talking about, we'd need to modify the whole global network at once, a coordinated effort. That's complicated enough to do normally. Now we've got control nodes down, power relays damaged or lost, and the teams in the various control centers struggling just to coordinate efforts to keep the Web together. I don't think we can do it under these conditions."

"You could," Spock said, "if you had a means of gaining centralized remote control over the entire network at once."

Nisu stared at him. "Like the remote transmitters you and the dissidents were planting to take over the grid!"

"Exactly. What did you do with the transmitters you confiscated?"

"They have been secured as evidence pending . . . your trial." She glanced away.

"Then they are intact?"

"Yes."

"Excellent." Spock turned back to the triumvirs. "The dissidents should still be in possession of the remaining transmitters you have not yet managed to find, and they have been trained in their use. With cooperation between the government and the dissidents, we should be able to position the full complement of devices and implement centralized control."

"How convenient," Tirak said, eyes narrowing. "Your plan requires letting your fellow criminals take credit for saving the Web of Worlds. And who knows what they could do once they have full control of our grid?"

"If we install the override transmitters in the actual control centers, rather than nearby, the interface could be two-way. Control could be implemented from this location, under the Triumvirate's supervision."

"So you claim. What's to stop you from overriding our control from your ship?"

"Damn it, Tirak!" Kirk cried. "Stop thinking like a politician. You're a triumvir. Your job is to protect everyone in the First Federation, not just the ones you agree with. All right, maybe you and the dissidents have different ideas about what the Web needs. But you're both trying to protect it—because you both love it as your home, your community. You're not enemies just because you have different points of view." He gestured skyward. "Do you know why the Dassik are attacking you so relentlessly? Because they fear you!" Tirak stared in disbelief, but Kirk barreled on. "That's right, Triumvir. Your big, scary bogeymen you use to frighten small children—they're as scared for their own future as you are! They reversed the genetic change your ancestors imposed on them, but it's unstable." Aranow stared, startled by his words. Had she not known? Koust had said his people had contacted the Council . . . but Aranow was its newest member.

"I don't know what lies you're spinning, Kirk," Tirak attempted.

But the captain pushed on. "Fewer Dassik are born with each generation. They're heading toward extinction if they don't find the answers. And only your people have the knowledge to save them. But in your fear of them, you've rejected them, hidden from them, and so they feel they have no choice but to take the knowledge by force. Your fear is killing both of you! And it doesn't have to happen."

"What are you saying, you lunatic?" the older Linnik cried. "Do you want us to fight them or make peace with them?"

"Right now, they're too angry to make peace. Too afraid. You have to stop them to save yourselves. But you have to do it by putting aside your fear of the people in your own society who disagree with you. And then, once you've managed to do that, maybe you can do the same with the Dassik, so that an attack like this doesn't happen again."

Nisu stepped forward. "Tirak, I don't understand what he's claiming about us and the Dassik. But I do know that our own people are not our enemies. The enemies are the people out there trying to destroy all of us. They don't care what side you or the dissidents are on. So do you want to stay politically pure, or do you want to contribute to actually *solving* the problem?"

"Tirak, come on," Aranow said. "What else can we do?"

The child-sized triumvir reluctantly looked to the huge Lekur. "Zan? Will it work?"

The Bogosrin grumbled. "Don't like the idea of relying on alien tech. But if it can do what Spock says, we have to try."

"Very well," Tirak said heavily. "Contact your dissidents. We will sort through the lies later."

The ground heaved once more. "If there is a later," Aranow said.

Fourteen

"Come on, faster! We're not goin' to make it!"

"We're at maximum airspeed already, sir!" Lieutenant Rahda told Scott even as she worked the helm controls to try to coax a bit more speed out of the engines. The *Enterprise* was already trembling from the rush of air across its shields as it forced its way through Cherela's atmosphere, fast enough that a corona of blue flame now engulfed the ship, obscuring the forward view. The vessel had already taken a pounding from the charges it had successfully intercepted so far, and it hadn't been designed for these conditions; but it was holding together impressively well nonetheless. Scott had expected nothing less of his baby.

If her speed could not be increased further, then Scott would just have to push a different performance envelope. He turned to the weapons subsystems station just starboard of the viewscreen, which was manned now that the ship was at red alert. "Mister Lemli, I need the tightest, most intense phaser bursts you can manage—we need more range."

The crew acknowledged his orders, but they had little time to work. The next cube was only seconds away from reaching the minimum altitude at which it could be safely detonated. When the moment came, he had no choice but to order, "Fire!"

On the tactical plot, the beams lashed out across the distance, leading the target by just enough, or so Scott hoped. Attenuated by their passage through the atmosphere, the beams had no effect at first, but finally, seconds later, the cube detonated. "Damage to the Web?" he called.

"The nearest world module has sustained a major atmosphere breach," Chekov reported. "Antigravity failing— no, wait, it is stabilizing at a weaker level." He sighed in relief. "There should be time to evacuate. But . . . but a smaller module of some kind, maybe a hangar, has fallen. Hard to get life readings, but . . ." He trailed off.

"Don't dwell on it, lad. Move on to the next one."

"We may not be able to get to the next one, sir. The problem is that the Dassik are in orbit and we're stuck in this soup. We can't go fast enough to keep up. Not without breaking atmosphere."

"Which would open us up to direct attack."

"Yes, sir." Chekov shrugged. "But we're not that much better off down here. At least then the shields wouldn't be strained fighting the atmosphere and the blast effects."

"Just fighting disruptor fire," Scott replied pointedly.

"At least we could maneuver. All we have to do is hold out until the captain and Mister Spock can carry out their plan."

Scott considered. The idea of using the planet's entire magnetic field as a weapon may have been daft, but he had seen Kirk and Spock pull off madder schemes. The engineer knew better than to underestimate what talented, determined people could pull off in a crisis. And surely that went for the people around him now. He may not have known this lot as well as the usual bridge crew, but they had comported themselves with distinction, and he had no reason to doubt that they would rise to the occasion as well as any who wore the arrowhead.

So let them rise, then, he told himself. Scott turned forward, taking a deep, cleansing breath and releasing it. "Lieutenant Rahda," he said, "take us into space."

"So you're finally forced to admit we were right!" Ne-Kewii declared smugly from the comm screen, on which she appeared adjacent to David Bailey.

"We admit no such thing," Triumvir Tirak told the Fiilestii dissident. "The bombardment is creating the instability."

"Even now you try to cover the truth! Captain Kirk, you can't seriously expect us to reveal the location of the remaining remote devices to these—"

"Quiet, both of you!" Kirk cried. "Like a friend of mine said," he went on, nodding at Aranow, "we've got no time for political posturing. We're all in the same sinking ship."

"Kirk's right, Ne-Kewii," Bailey said, stepping forward. *"This is the Web's only shot now. All of us together, like it should've been all along."* The young ambassador turned his gaze firmly on Tirak. *"But we need everyone, sir. You have to release Balok from prison. We'll need his expertise— and the dissidents will need the gesture of good faith. Ne-Kewii's not the only one who'll be suspicious."*

"Haven't you heard?" Tirak asked. "Balok escaped with Kirk and Spock."

"No, he didn't," Kirk said. "Someone from the prison substituted a mechanical decoy for him. What we rescued was a puppet. Presumably to hide the real Balok's transfer to a secret location."

"Preposterous! Even now you spin lies to discredit this administration!"

"He speaks the truth, Triumvir," Nisu said, her tone making it clear that she did not expect the news to surprise Tirak. "My people have confirmed the decoy's presence in the escape craft. And I, for one, was not informed of any substitution—even though the prison operates under my authority. Only you, Triumvir Tirak, can supersede that authority."

Tirak relented under the scrutiny of Nisu and his fellow triumvirs. "Very well. Balok has been securely transferred to an undisclosed facility. He may be in possession of classified data of the highest sensitivity. It was necessary to . . . investigate the matter under the most extreme security."

"Coward! Liar!" Ne-Kewii cried. *"How do we know Balok is even still alive?"*

Kirk was about to intercede, but Bailey beat him to it. *"Listen to me, both of you. I care about Balok as much as anyone. He's my friend, my mentor. So I'm afraid for him too. But there are bigger things at stake. Balok helped teach me—in his own way—how to control my fear, rather than letting it control me. And that's what we all need right now. Let's focus our fear where it really matters. The rest can come later."*

Tirak's jaw tightened. For a moment, Kirk was afraid he'd misjudged the triumvir's willingness to kill a fellow Linnik. But then Tirak relented. "Very well. I will order Balok's release."

If anything, he'd given in too easily, and that gave Kirk cause for concern. "Mister Bailey," he said, "I recommend you oversee Balok's release and escort personally. You have the dissidents' trust, and it wouldn't hurt for Balok to see a friendly face."

"Aye, sir," Bailey said, his eyes thanking the captain.

Kasan Tor lumbered into view on the screen. *"For the same reason, Kirk, I'd prefer you send one of your people to coordinate with us. So there won't be any trust issues."*

Kirk turned to his helmsman. "Sulu, you've worked closely with them. Go."

"Aye, sir." He got coordinates from Kasan and headed off.

Spock addressed Uhura. "Lieutenant, I shall need you here, supervising the teams. This operation will require precise coordination and timing."

She nodded. "Aye, sir."

"Nisu," Kirk went on. "Have one of your people take McCoy to that hospital where our people are being held. Bones, get them all up and running, even Koust. We need every hand."

"Right, Jim."

Kirk clapped the doctor on the shoulder, then turned back to Nisu. "The remotes you're storing as evidence. Take me to them."

The Kisaja threw a glance at the triumvirs, then looked back to Kirk. "Come."

"Jim." Aranow moved closer, clasping his hands briefly. Her tail trembled. "Our worlds are in your hands."

"Wonderful. No pressure." Impulsively, he kissed her. He kept it quick, but figured a Tessegri would like it that way. Aranow blushed purple, but she was smiling. With a grin and a wink, Kirk broke into a run after Nisu.

She led him out of the central tower and across a sky-walk to the security section. Powerful winds struck them as they hit the open air, forceful enough to blow them sideways. Kirk flailed out and grabbed the windward railing, catching Nisu with his other hand. She pulled herself to the railing, and they both held on as they strove forward.

Kirk looked out over the rail and beheld a terrifying sight. An immense tsunami, maybe a hundred meters high, was surging toward the cliffs below them. They were well above it, but still he felt an instinctive need to move faster, to escape before it hit.

"The charge that detonated outside!" Nisu cried. "It must have triggered a shock wave!" Given the enormous scale of this world module, Kirk realized, it must have taken this long to reach the government center.

Kirk's instinct to run proved justified. When the tsunami crashed into the cliffs below, the whole island trembled. It struck Kirk that the geology of this artificial world might be artificially light, even hollow; it couldn't absorb the impact of that great mass of water as well as the real thing.

The quake continued, and to add insult to injury, the skywalk and its occupants were struck by a mighty gust of hot wind as the air pushed ahead of the tsunami was forced up the side of the cliff at enormous speed, heated by its compression. Kirk lost his footing as the skywalk began to buck and twist beneath him. Nisu's slender frame took the worst of it, and Kirk lunged forward to catch her before she fell, saving her from cracking her head open on the railing. "Stay down!" he yelled as the wind continued to roar past, spattering them with droplets of moisture and pebbles and grit torn from the cliff face. They made their way forward as quickly as they could on all fours. Kirk reflexively tried to shield her with his body, but she would have none of it.

But as the skywalk continued to twist and groan, Kirk could see it beginning to break loose on the far side. He and Nisu had no choice but to straighten up and run as fast as they could. As they neared the doorway at the far end, one of Nisu's protectors, the big armored one, trod forth to assist them.

Just then, though, the skywalk heaved up beneath them like a wave, a crack forming in its arched surface before them. "Go!" Kirk shoved Nisu forward over the hump and into the arms of her teammate—at the cost of losing his balance and falling back. He struggled to regain his footing before the crack grew too wide to jump over.

But then a pair of strong arms wrapped around him from behind, and suddenly he was airborne, soaring in an impossibly wide arc over the gap. He stumbled on the landing but his rescuer held him up and carried him forward into the tower, Nisu and her colleague following right behind. They skidded to a stop just short of the far wall. Kirk spun to watch the bridge tearing free and collapsing into the chasm.

Panting, he turned to face his rescuer. His eyes widened at the sight of Aranow's bright-eyed, blue-skinned face. "You," he managed. "That was . . . how . . . ?"

She shrugged. "Strong legs and a tail. You flat-butts have no balance. Figured I could help."

"Triumvir," Nisu said, "you shouldn't be in harm's way."

"Everywhere's harm's way now. Like Spock said. I couldn't just sit around," she went on, turning back to Jim. "I have to move. Have to help."

He turned to face her, clasping her shoulders, and smiled. "Well, I'm very grateful that you did."

Aranow's eyes widened. "Oh! And I had to do this." She cuffed him on the side of his head.

"Oww!" He stared at her.

"For kissing a triumvir in the situation room," she proclaimed, though her smirk belied her affronted tone. "Most inappropriate."

"Understood," Kirk said, rubbing the side of his head. "It won't happen again."

But Aranow didn't let the moment linger. "Come on!" she cried, grabbing Nisu's arm and pulling her forward. "No time for gabbing! Let's get those remotes!"

"Triumvir," Nisu said, "the other way."

"Right." Aranow reversed direction without missing a beat, pulling Nisu past Kirk with a gust of air. He followed in their slipstream, grinning.

———

"The remotes are being distributed," Uhura reported. "Teams are on their way."

"Excellent," Spock replied. "Status of the captain?"

"His team is taking the Tessegri world module."

"Understood."

Spock was somewhat relieved to know that Kirk was away from the Syletir module. The whole megastructure was beginning to sway as an aftereffect of the shock wave and tsunami; the displacement of that much water had unbalanced the module, and the strain on the Web-wide antigrav network was making it difficult to compensate. The floor was already beginning to slant beneath their feet, and Spock was less than sanguine about being in a tower atop a cliff under these circumstances. Triumvir Lekur was supervising the efforts of his engineering teams to stabilize the module, but they were visibly struggling.

Spock held Uhura's eyes, speaking softly. "Advise

Captain Kirk and his team to establish an alternate command post at their location. They may need to take over coordination of the network should we be unable to do so from here."

She allowed her fear to show only for an instant. He regretted requiring the lieutenant to be here with him; he could have sent her to an evacuation ship, something that could hover in the atmosphere and survive if the Web were to collapse. But he knew it was an illogical thought. Such a small craft would be at risk from the storms and would have no safe harbor unless the *Enterprise* prevailed over the Dassik—an unlikely prospect under the circumstances. The *Enterprise* was depending on the success of this operation as much as everyone else. And the odds of that success were materially greater with Nyota Uhura coordinating the operation.

Recognizing this, the lieutenant gathered herself. "Aye, sir." Uhura paused before turning away. "And thank you," she said softly. He raised an inquiring brow, and she continued. "For your calm. Your logic. I draw strength from it, sir."

He responded with only a wordless nod. She smiled briefly before returning to her duty, her manner brisk, professional, and Vulcan-calm. Not for the first time, Spock was reminded of how much respect he had for this woman—a respect that had made him willing to indulge her emotional expressions more readily than those of her peers, even when she teased him, flirted with him, or sang marginally ribald songs about him in the recreation room. He occasionally wondered if her flirtations were in earnest, and if, absent the obstacles of rank and discipline, that might not be such a bad thing.

Before he could pursue the idea any further, Tirak approached him. "There must be something more we can do," the Linnik said, wringing his hands.

"The plan is proceeding apace, Triumvir. Everything that can be done is being done."

"By you, by the dissidents. This is our home. We are the protectors of the First. We are the ones who should be taking action. Perhaps . . . we should try speaking to the Dassik. Engaging with them directly."

Spock was surprised that this man, who had lived his whole life defending his people's commitment to secrecy and concealment, could propose revealing himself to an enemy. It was an encouraging sign of growth. So it was with some regret that he replied, "Under current atmospheric conditions, Triumvir, it would be virtually impossible to send a clear signal. Even if we could expend the resources to devise a relay, I am confident that Force Leader Grun would accept nothing less than your complete surrender and subjugation."

Lekur looked up from where he worked. "Never. We built the Web to be free. We'd rather burn."

Tirak nodded in affirmation. "Of course. That is not what I propose. My thought was that we could merely give the appearance of surrender. In order to stall the enemy while we prepare the weapon."

Not a sign of growth after all, then, Spock thought. "Such an act would contravene all civilized rules of war, Triumvir. After such a precedent, no subsequent surrender in any future conflict would be trusted or accepted."

"Civilized war, huh?" said Lekur. "Who knew?"

"All things are relative," Spock replied dryly.

The staff at Tirak's "undisclosed facility" had resisted releasing Balok at first. Fortunately, the large Niatoko protector that Nisu had sent to assist Bailey had done his job, making it clear that this was a directive of the Council requiring immediate compliance.

When Bailey and the protector reached Balok's cell, they found the *Fesarius* captain transfixed in the gaze of a narrow-featured, green-eyed Kisaja woman with bronze head fur. "Vulo!" the reptilian protector demanded. "Stop what you're doing! This prisoner is to be released at once!"

The woman, Vulo, released Balok from her gaze to face the protector. Balok slumped and gasped for breath, and Bailey ran to him while Vulo said, "No problem, Protector. Just making sure he was ready for release."

Bailey cradled his friend's small, bald head in his hands. "Balok! Are you okay?" The captain's eyes wandered, failing to focus on Bailey or anything else. He had never looked so much like an infant.

Whirling to face Vulo, Bailey demanded, "What did you do to him?"

"I only cured him of the lies you outsiders would have had him spew to discredit the Council," the Kisaja said.

"What are you talking about?"

"It doesn't matter. He'll remember none of it now. Just take him and go."

A tremor hit the module, as if to reinforce the value of her suggestion—although the venomous look she gave Bailey suggested that she blamed him for the disruptions to the Web. He quickly glanced away before he could feel more than the faintest trace of the effects of an angry Kisaja stare.

Instead, he focused on the *Fesarius* captain again. "Balok! Come on, it's me, Bailey. Dave Bailey! You know me, right?"

"Bai . . . ley?"

The human grinned. "Yeah, it's me. I'm here. We're together, just like all those times on the *Fesarius*. You remember? All those word games we played? Those weird mythology videos you liked to show me, the ones that left me so confused?" He laughed, realizing that humor was a likely way to connect with Balok. "You look as dazed as I did. Remember?"

Balok was frowning now, trying to concentrate. Another rumble shook the cell, and the floor swayed beneath them. Balok's mind was still elsewhere, though. "*Fesarius.*"

"That's right, Balok! The *Fesarius*. Your ship. You love that ship so much. And I know your crew wants you to get back to them as soon as you can."

"My . . . ship. The *Fesarius.*" Balok jerked awake as if slapped. Eyes finally locking on Bailey, he beamed and let out a raucous laugh. "Ahh, David, my friend! You said just the right thing!"

Bailey laughed in return, but it was to hide his relief. "Well, I am an ambassador."

"For once, I think I actually believe that," Balok teased back. As the floor lurched and groaned beneath them again, he hopped to his feet with surprising spryness. "Well, what are we waiting for? You seemed pretty keen on leaving a moment ago. You want to stay here, slowpoke?"

Shaking his head in amusement, Bailey followed the

lively commander out the door. But he noticed that Vulo was staring at the revived Balok with some disbelief. Once he caught up to the determined Linnik, he muttered, "What was that Kisaja doing to you? She seems surprised that you remember your own name."

Balok chuckled. "As I said, my friend, you knew exactly the right thing to say. I'll be happy to explain later." The floor shook again. "But I think there are more pressing matters you need to fill me in on first, don't you?"

The lieutenant hastened to fill Balok in as they hurried down the corridor. It surprised Bailey how swiftly those little legs could carry Balok when he was sufficiently motivated. "And the *Enterprise* has left the atmosphere?" the Linnik captain finally asked.

"Last I heard, yes. They're going to try to deal with the Dassik by themselves."

"Against those cluster ships?" Balok shook his head. "They'll be outmatched. We have to get out there and help."

"In what? Your ships aren't built for that sort of thing. Except an orbship, and I doubt the Council would trust you with one of those even now."

"I already have one, my young friend. If I know my crew, they've figured out by now that I came here. The *Fesarius* is bound to be on the outskirts of the system, watching for some opportunity to act. But I doubt they'd have it in them to do something bold without me there to browbeat them into it. So we need to get to my pilot vessel and into space. I'm sure the *Enterprise* will keep the Linnik distracted long enough to let us slip past."

"Can your pilot vessel handle Cherela's weather? It's not all that aerodynamic."

"At the speed I'll be taking off, that will hardly matter. Now get moving!"

Sulu clung to a post as the Vea-Shol module heaved around him, tossed by storms in the atmosphere beyond and in its own suspension fields. *Not this again,* he thought. The Fiilestii collapse had been enough to give him nightmares; the last thing he needed was a reenactment. His eyes scanned the skyline of this largely urban module, watching for towers on the verge of collapse. The sight was oddly reassuring; the skyscrapers here were only a few dozen stories high, maybe a hundred tops, downright tiny next to the Fiilestii towers.

"Too much for you?" Ne-Kewii asked as she pulled him forward. "The brave starship pilot can't handle a little turbulence?"

Sulu stared at the Fiilestii dissident. "You're grinning. I think." It was a bit hard to tell with her anatomy. "Why are you grinning? This is your world that's shaking apart around us!"

"Exactly! Just like we've been warning for years! Don't you see, Hikaru? This is vindication! This—" She laughed. "The scandal will surely bring down the government! A few rotations from now, we'll be running this place."

Sulu gaped. "That's what this is about to you? Still, after all this? People are dying, Ne-Kewii!"

"That's the Triumvirate's doing. We're the ones who'll hold them accountable for it."

"The hell with that! We're trying to stop them from dying in the first place!"

"Oh, of course," Ne-Kewii said with a dismissive wave

of one pinion. "I'm just saying, at least some good will come of the loss of life. The whole Web will finally be forced to see that we were right."

Sulu wanted to grab her and scream that she was out of her damned mind. This small-minded cliquism was the very thing that had brought the Web to the brink of disaster. But he reminded himself that there was no time for that. They had to get the remote transmitter into position, and anything else was secondary. If Ne-Kewii couldn't keep that in mind, then he had to. "Just come on," he said, striding forward.

The sky lit up behind them. For an instant, all he saw were their shadows stretching out amid a field of blinding white light. *Oh, God. One of the fusion charges got through!* "Don't look!" he cried. He squeezed his eyes shut and waited for the red light beyond his eyelids to subside.

Then he spun to look behind him. There, past the skyline and the module dome, a dimming fusion fireball rose languidly through the air. Normally, that would've been a terrifying sight. But here, it was the least of their problems. Before it, a ripple of fractured light spread out across the dome as it shattered under the shock wave. Sulu's eyes widened. "Get to cover!" he cried. He pulled Ne-Kewii under the awning of a nearby building an instant before the sky lit up with blue flame. Just as in that nature module, the high-pressure hydrogen and methane beyond, heated by the blast, had mixed with the oxygen within and combusted. A nice, clinical, scientific explanation. But it looked to Sulu like the wrath of God descending from on high.

After a few moments, he realized he could still breathe. The rupture in the dome was high enough that there was still uncombusted oxygen at ground level. But Sulu knew there would be other problems coming soon. "Come on, we have to get to the control center fast!" Ne-Kewii was blinking, her wide, dark eyes unfocused. "Are you okay?"

"I looked," she said. "The light . . . it hurts."

Sulu waved his hand before her face. "Can you see me?"

"Mostly. With one eye, and it's blurred . . ."

"That'll do. It'll get better, come on, hurry!"

He dragged her into the street, envying her for her inability to get a clear look at the Brobdingnagian blow-torch over their heads. Glancing up, Sulu saw that the tops of several skyscrapers were aflame, ignited by the heat. Windows were blowing out, falling, so he ran faster, dragging Ne-Kewii by her forelimb. A wind was picking up, a hot wind striking down and splashing out through the canyons of the city streets. As they reached an inter-section, a gust blew them sideways, almost knocking them over. But a large window pane smashed down right next to where they would have been. Ne-Kewii shrieked as shrapnel from the pane slashed her. The helmsman checked her out quickly; the bleeding was minimal. She slowed down, moaning, but he cried, "Move, move!" in his sharpest tone.

The hot wind was spreading the flames. The fires seemed to chase them as they ran through the city. Crowds of panicking citizens, an eclectic mix of spe-cies, ran screaming from the buildings, obstacles in their path, oblivious to their need for haste. Sulu saw a small, frail Linnik, or possibly a child, fall beneath a Bogosrin female's paws and be instantly crushed. Ne-Kewii gasped in horror.

Mercifully, the emergency transporters began to engage and thin out the crowds. Sulu had to swerve to avoid the beams lest he be snatched away before he could emplace the transmitter. But the beams came too late for many. They ran under a burning building, dodging and hurdling the broken bodies of citizens who'd desperately leaped from the upper floors. Ne-Kewii slipped in the pooling blood and came up with her free forepaw covered in it. Dozens more screamed from the flame-licked windows, and Sulu could do nothing but drag Ne-Kewii away, keeping his stinging eyes relentlessly forward as he heard the building groan and thunder into rubble, the screams peaking, then vanishing into the noise.

Finally, they reached the control center, which was mercifully free of flames for the moment. Once they were inside someplace relatively quiet, Sulu could hear Ne-Kewii sobbing and choking. He whirled at her, about to shout, *Are you still glad this is happening?* But then he saw the haunted, horrified look in her eyes, the tears streaming from them freely. And he knew there was nothing more to say.

————

"Damn fool place to live! Who ever thought this was a good idea anyway?"

Koust growled in his throat as the physician McCoy kept up the monologue of complaints that he had continued almost without interruption since he had arrived in the secure hospital to obtain the release of the *Enterprise* rescue team. Koust had been surprised and somewhat gratified to be asked to participate in Kirk and Spock's plan, but he was regretting his decision to guard the feeble healer so that the other, more qualified *Enterprise* personnel could be free to pursue their own assignments. McCoy had quailed at first, no doubt frightened of the Dassik, but had relented when a member of the protector force, a strong, gray-skinned Niatoko named Targus, had agreed to accompany them. But since then, he'd kept up an unending chain of complaints about their circumstances, and Koust was increasingly tempted to kill the doctor himself just for peace and quiet.

Their current situation had only exacerbated the doctor's grumbling. The Quapep world module containing their targeted control center would normally have been an easy terrain to navigate. It was a grassland preserve module, largely empty except for the surface entrance to the Linnik warren below, a cluster of low domes spread out some distance apart on the level, grassy plain. But the upheavals in the Web had left the module with a rather severe tilt, or at least it felt that way; since the module's antigrav field was out of alignment with the giant planet's much more powerful pull, the force resisting their uphill motion was stronger than the actual slant of the ground would suggest. And by ill fortune, their destination was almost directly uphill from the module's main transporter terminal, and they'd arrived in the middle of a thunderstorm, making the grass slippery and difficult to climb. Koust lamented the loss of his heavy boots. And they were getting little help from the Linnik themselves; the timid creatures were all huddled within their tunnels, useless in the face of peril. It was hard to imagine that such fearful, weak creatures had brought down the mighty Dassik race—or that the Dassik had been forced to live like them for so many millennia. Koust resented the fact that it was a module full of betrayers he had been sent to save.

"And would it kill them to at least beam us right where we need to go instead of making us slog through all this?" McCoy went on. "No, they said. Too much power, they said. Emergencies only, they said. Like this whole thing isn't one big emergency! Serves them right, living in giant tin cans that need antigravs to hold them up! The ground shouldn't tilt beneath your feet, damn it! Why couldn't these people build on solid rock like any sensible person?"

"Be quiet!" Koust finally snarled. "Save your energy for striving!"

"I'll use my energy however I damn well please, Mister Koust! Staying mad helps keep me motivated!"

Koust blinked, forced to admit the doctor might have something resembling a point. Dassik hunters used battle cries and ritual chants to fire up their passions before a hunt or combat, focusing their energy. Still, Koust couldn't see how the doctor's constant rehearsal of his own fears and weaknesses could do anything more than dishearten him. Not to mention the foolishness of broadcasting those fears and weaknesses to enemies or admitting them to allies who needed to believe they could trust him. Koust and Targus were left knowing that if danger struck, they would be unable to rely on McCoy's courage.

It was bad enough that Koust didn't even know if he should be here. Kirk's and Nisu's people were working to defeat the plans of his own commander. By abetting them, let alone aiding the betrayers, he was committing treason. But he had realized he felt no loyalty toward Force Leader Grun. After all, the leader had sent him to his own probable death after executing his triad subleader. And now Grun was attacking the Web without even knowing how many billions of lives he was endangering. Lives with no ability to fight back, lives that bore no share of the blame for the crime inflicted on the Dassik by the betrayers—indeed, Koust reminded himself, by betrayers who had died millennia ago, whose distant descendants did not even seem to know of their crime. Koust had found himself reflecting on his own words to Kirk back in the prison, his insistence that the Dassik were more than the unthinking savages they had been in the past. Grun's actions were doing little to prove that claim. So perhaps it was up to Koust to deliver that proof. And if the Dassik had matured in their long ages of seclusion, then perhaps the Linnik had as well.

Besides, Kirk, Spock, and Sulu had treated Koust better than Grun ever had. He might not be sure if he should be fighting in the defense of the First, but he had pledged to fight alongside Kirk and follow his orders for the duration of their escape—and since they technically had not yet escaped the Web, Koust decided that pledge was still binding. Kirk deserved that much loyalty. Unlike Grun, he had earned it.

A rumble came from up ahead, something more than thunder. Koust's head spun in that direction. Beyond the Linnik domes were some low, rocky hills with a river flowing out of them. A bank must have given way, for a cascade of muddy water was descending toward them, bringing many rocks and small boulders with it. The pathways between the domes did little to diminish the deluge and even helped concentrate it, and it came on them fast in the high gravity.

"Quickly!" Targus called. "Get in the entrance alcoves!" But the domes around them were quite wide and rounded, and it was a struggle to clamber up toward the nearest alcove even as the water from above began pouring around their feet. Targus had the best grip on the ground due to his weight and the powerful claws of his feet, so he helped push Koust and McCoy toward the alcove. The rocks were now close enough to begin striking them, and Koust raised an arm to shield himself long enough to surmount the corner and pull McCoy to safety. The arm sustained several forceful impacts, and so did his flank, but Dassik bones were strong and the pain merely motivated him. The trio made their way horizontally, relying on the slanted wall of the dome to support their weight, until they reached the alcove and were sheltered from the cascade.

Targus pulled himself up to the alcove corner and tried to swing around, but then a large, sharp stone tumbled down and struck him in the head, felling him. Bright orange blood pooled around his head, a dense fluid that the rain and the spray of the flood did little to disperse.

To Koust's surprise, McCoy was instantly in motion, rushing into the path of the water and stones before Koust could start after him. Seemingly oblivious to the danger, McCoy knelt by Targus and began dragging him to safety—slow going until Koust joined him in the effort, as much to get the fool out of the path of danger as to help the Web protector who was probably past saving.

"Thanks," McCoy said absently as he drew forth his medical tools and began to work. Koust waited impatiently, noting that the deluge was beginning to subside, the rainstorm along with it.

"We must go," he said once it seemed clear. "Leave him."

"He's dying!"

"Then let him! It is a death to be proud of!"

"He can't be proud if he's dead, you fool! Just give me another minute and I can save him!"

"You have other lives to save! Surely one is expendable!"

McCoy's eyes met his with a fierceness that froze the Dassik in his tracks. "He's not dead yet, Mister Koust! One life or a million, I'm not going to surrender anyone to death without a fight!"

Koust recognized that fire in the doctor's eyes. It was the fire of a warrior. He realized he had misunderstood this man profoundly. It had never before occurred to Koust that one could be a warrior *against* death. He had assumed that resisting death was an act of fear. But he could no longer believe that as he looked into McCoy's eyes.

This was the measure of Kirk's kind, he realized. He and his people valued life, cherished it above all. And so they fought for life with a strength, courage, and commitment the likes of which Koust had rarely seen. Indeed, they fought as valiantly for the lives of strangers and enemies as for those of their own kind. Even when they would be safer allowing an enemy to die, they still took the risk of fighting for that enemy's life. What fearlessness that must require!

If this was what it meant to be a warrior in the name of life, Koust realized, he would be a weakling himself if he refused to embrace the challenge.

"Then save him," Koust said. "Let me have the transmitter. I will save this world . . . and the Linnik who inhabit it."

McCoy met his eyes, warily at first—but then he softened, nodded, and handed Koust the device. "Good luck," he said.

Koust nodded. "Victory," he said to his fellow warrior.

Fifteen

For once, Balok had not been joking. The pilot vessel's launch through Cherela's atmosphere had been ballistic, and Bailey had been convinced the little craft would tear apart until it had burst through into the thinner atmosphere layers and finally into vacuum. They had emerged out of the line of sight of either Dassik ship, but given those vessels' bombardment pattern, that would not last long. So Balok pushed the pilot vessel into warp as soon as he was far enough out of the Jovian's gravity well to form a stable field.

"How do you know where to find the *Fesarius*?" Bailey asked once his jaw finally unclenched. "I assume you don't want to send out a general hail and risk attracting the wrong attention."

"I trained my crew, remember?" Balok answered. "They'll be laying low out in the cometary cloud, in a sector that will let them keep an eye on Cherela, but far enough outside the ecliptic plane that they can monitor all approaches to the planet."

"But out from the plane in which direction?"

"Knowing Linar, toward the positive coordinate. She doesn't have my innate contrariness." Balok waved his hands over the control column, giving the vessel instructions. "I'm scanning the cometary bodies in that sector for the best candidates to hide an orbship. I just need to tight-beam a subspace signal to those, and with luck, the *Fesarius* will hear and answer."

Bailey studied him. "So while we're waiting, you want to tell me what that Kisaja was doing to you back in the prison?"

"Oh, that. She was trying to erase a dirty little secret from my memory." Balok gave the lieutenant a quick summary of the hidden history of the Linnik and the Dassik, as revealed by the secret Council files he had unearthed.

"So what was the 'right thing' I said that brought you back? Something about the *Fesarius*?"

The Linnik captain chuckled. "It was something you know all too well, my friend—the first glimpse you ever had of my face, so to speak."

Bailey blinked. "You mean Mister Hyde? The scarecrow?"

"Exactly! It still makes a fine diversion. You see, memories are about associations between ideas and sensations. Vulo tried to purge all my memories associated with the Dassik, but I associate my old friend 'Hyde' more with the *Fesarius* itself—and my memories of my ship are too dear to me for anyone to take away. Even Vulo knew better than to tamper with those. So I just conditioned myself ahead of time by thinking of Mister Hyde when I reviewed what I remembered about the government files on the Dassik. So after Vulo thought she'd severed every mental association that would let me recover that memory, she overlooked the back door I'd tucked away aboard my mental *Fesarius*." He laughed. "I suppose you could say good old Hyde lived up to his name!"

Bailey was saved from the need to react to that terrible pun by a signal from the communications panel. Balok grinned. "There. Didn't I tell you?" Opening a channel, he said, "Balok to *Fesarius*. About time you got here!"

Linar's voice in return was cross. *"We've been here for days, you insufferable—"* She broke off, then sighed. *"Well, I should have known you'd show up just when things were at their worst. If trouble doesn't follow you, you make sure to follow it."*

"I'm afraid you're more right than you realize, old friend," Balok told her. "The Web of Worlds has become unstable. The Dassik bombardment is threatening to destroy it. Our *Enterprise* friends have a plan, but there's no guarantee it will work. So I need you to set course for Cherela and engage the Dassik."

"But, Commander—"

"Now, don't argue, Linar. With what's at stake, the *Fesarius* can't sit on the sidelines any longer."

"I understand that, Commander. But what about the other Dassik?"

Balok blinked and traded a surprised look with Bailey. "What other Dassik?"

The voice of Almis, Balok's chief science and medical officer, took over. *"Commander, we've detected a sizeable number of Dassik warships heading for Cherela. At least six vessels. They're less than an hour away, at best."*

Bailey frowned. "The interference from the bombardment must be blocking the Web's sensors. And the *Enterprise* is too busy defending the planet."

The Linnik captain needed only a moment to think. "New plan, then, Linar. Move to intercept the incoming Dassik force. Send ahead as many buoys as you can to delay them. We should be able to rendezvous with you before they arrive."

"*But—*" Again, Linar stopped herself. "*Yes, Commander. But you'd better get here soon, you old trickster.*"

"Leave a light on for us, Linar. Balok out."

Bailey turned to the captain. "Will those buoys hold them for long? We were able to blow one up with one shot."

"Only because I let you. With their defensive screens up, they can last a while longer." Balok's uncertainty made him look more childlike than Bailey had grown accustomed to perceiving him. "At least, I hope so. And if Cherela's secret is out . . . then anything we do may simply be delaying the end."

Kirk was caught in the middle of a stampede.

The Tessegri were an intelligent, reasonable people most of the time, but like most other species, they could succumb to blind panic, and that was what had happened here. If anything, the Tessegri world module had suffered less than many others: The *Enterprise* had successfully deflected the cube missile that would have detonated near it, and though the planetary-scale thunderstorms outside were growing stronger than ever, they were inflicting little direct damage on the module. But the psychological effect of the storms, in combination with the swaying and gravity shifts within the module and the reports of the devastation befalling other habitats around the Web, had spooked this population of intense, energetic beings into a frenzy. They were racing madly through the wide boulevards between arcologies, not knowing where to go, just succumbing to their species' instinct to run. Hundreds of Tessegri, Linnik, Kisaja, and others had been trampled to death already, and even as Kirk watched, he saw others being pushed off the edges of raised boulevards to plummet into the crowds below, probably causing other casualties on impact.

Beside him, Aranow was shouting, "Everyone, please stay calm!" as loudly as she could, but with little effect; she was barely audible over the tumult of the mob, and they weren't inclined to listen anyway. He could see the tension in Aranow's lean frame, the struggle to resist succumbing to the instinct herself. Nisu had tried spearing groups of Tessegri with her stupefying Kisaja gaze, but those groups had merely been left as sitting ducks for trampling by those behind them, and she'd quickly had to stop trying.

Only Aranow's quick reflexes and Nisu's ability to sense approaching minds had enabled the group to dodge the panicking crowds until they reached their destination arcology. Within, things were better only to the extent that the occupants had already fled for open ground. But those thousands who remained were still in the throes of panic. Doors were smashed open, indoor trees and gardens trampled to ruin. Bodies were strewn on the ground, some moving, others not.

Kirk looked around, seeing large overhead screens futilely projecting what he assumed were instructions not to panic, though he couldn't read the script. He caught Nisu's gaze and shouted, "If we get to a transmitter, can you project your gaze effect over the screens?"

"No," she replied without shouting; he heard it in his mind as much as his ears. "Only face-to-face."

"Damn it!" He looked around, caught sight of one of the massive spiraling ramps that led to the upper levels of the arcology. Tessegri were falling from it too, but its low gravity diminished the damage so long as they didn't fall too far. Which was little comfort for those who did.

"We're here!" Aranow cried, pointing at a self-contained, miniature glass ziggurat within the open space of the arcology. She ran toward it, dodging her panicked conspecifics, and Kirk led Nisu after her, his mind racing.

But their path to the control center was blocked by a crowd of Tessegri, Linnik, Bogosrin, and others who were trying to force their way inside, perhaps in some desperate attempt to fix the problem or save themselves. "Please let us through!" Nisu called.

Some of them jerked around warily. "Get away! We were here first!"

"We have a plan to protect the Web," Kirk told them. "But you have to let us inside!"

More were turning to face them, eyes widening at the sight of the human. "It's Kirk!" one of them cried.

"Kirk?" The others echoed the name one by one, turning away from the control center and focusing on him. "The world-killer!"

"This is your doing!"

"You brought the Dassik down on us!"

"Get him!"

"Kill him!"

The group closed in on the trio, shouting angrily. Kirk was shocked by the barrage of hate; he'd felt the same hostility from Warden Mure and the prison staff, but he hadn't realized until this moment just how widely Tirak had spread his message of xenophobia.

"Stand *down*!" Nisu shouted, bringing her gaze to

bear on the crowd. A few of them slowed, but there were too many, and they were too angry. They surged forward around the ones in her eyes' grip, knocking her over. Kirk caught her and pulled her back to her feet.

"Protect the transmitter at all costs!" Kirk cried. He grabbed the first Tessegri and tossed him aside with a judo throw. A Bogosrin swung at his head; he ducked and threw a sharp kick at his attacker's shin. Nisu stunned the Bogosrin; as the ursine alien staggered, Kirk slammed shoulder first into his chest, knocking him back onto two of the attackers, immobilizing them. Nisu stunned them before they could drag their limbs and tails out from under the Bogosrin's bulk.

More Tessegri were charging Kirk, and his attempt to dodge them was hampered by a couple of Linnik pounding feebly on his thighs. One Tessegri's bullwhip tail caught him in the flank, a glancing blow that sent him tumbling. Once again, he was amazed by how fast they could move. He staggered to his feet, the intense pain in his side telling him he'd probably bruised a rib.

"All of you, stop this instant!" Aranow cried. "That's an order! I'm a triumvir! Really!"

But they were past listening, or maybe they blamed the Triumvirate as much as Kirk for the current danger. Jim pulled her back out of the path of a Tessegri attacker's kick, then surged forward with a roundhouse punch that sent the attacker down for the count. Another Tessegri sent a high kick at his head, but he leaned back enough that it only grazed his scalp. It dazed him for a moment, but he'd been through worse many times before, so he shook it off and lunged at the kicker, felling him with a fist to his gut and another to his jaw.

All legs and tail, he realized. *They aren't used to fist-fights. Good to know.*

Unfortunately, not all the attackers were Tessegri. A more humanoid mob member, red-skinned and spiny-headed, got him in a headlock and wrenched his head back. He wasn't sure, but it seemed the humanoid's teeth were going for his throat. Then a sharp shock went through the attacker's body, knocking Kirk's remaining breath from him as well, and the red-skinned man sank to the floor. Kirk saw Aranow standing there, panting and lowering her tail. "Thanks," he said.

"Owed you. Duck!"

It went on like that for a while, but between Kirk's fists, Nisu's stunner and eyes, and Aranow's increasingly attractive tail, they managed to make it to the entrance of the control center, whereupon Nisu's codes got them inside. They were all bruised and bleeding, but essentially intact. Most importantly, so was the transmitter.

Once he'd caught his breath, Kirk turned to the females. "Can we cancel Cherela's gravity completely? Keep everyone floating in midair so they can't run and fall?"

Nisu shook her head. "It would take too much power. And if the antigrav system failed . . ."

Kirk nodded, then closed his eyes and winced. "Then we have to reduce its power. Turn up the gravity, everywhere but here. Make everyone so heavy they can't move."

Aranow's eyes widened. "But . . . those who fall, or those buried under bodies . . ."

"I know. But it's the only choice!"

Eyes glistening, Aranow nodded. "You're right. Nisu, do it."

"Yes, Triumvir," the Kisaja said solemnly.

It was an incongruously simple operation, the press of a few buttons, the entry of a few override codes. Within thirty seconds, all the Tessegri, Linnik, and others outside were pressed to the ground, immobilized by their own weight. They screamed in panic, but most of them were safe . . . for now.

Loud groans echoed through the vast indoor chamber as the arcology settled under its augmented weight. "Aranow, get on the public channel, try to keep the people calm. Tell them they'll be okay."

She nodded. "Lie. Got it."

"Nisu, let's get the transmitter in place and get this done," Kirk said, "before one of the boulevards gives way." He looked up. "Or something else."

———

The bridge of the *Enterprise* trembled under a barrage of Dassik disruptor fire, thunder crashing with the impact of each plasma bolt. Montgomery Scott strove to ignore it, resisting the temptation to bolt from the command chair and race down to the engine room where he belonged. He reminded himself that it was sound and fury signifying nothing—well, nothing that couldn't be easily absorbed by a spaceframe and inertial damping system designed to handle the intense accelerations of spaceflight. The noise and vibration that got through were little more than the shield and damper generators belching after swallowing the energy of impact, or the rattling of the hull as the plasma bolts' heat flash-vaporized the surface molecules of its protective coating. No, the real signs of peril were in the monitor readouts on the engineering stations to Scott's left, displaying the status of the deflector shields, dampers, power systems, and the like. It was those readings that conveyed the true borderline chaos and showed how close the *Enterprise* was to disaster.

"Rahda, bank sixty degrees to port," he ordered. "Keep our narrowest profile to them. Gabler, full power to starboard lateral shields! Try to get the dorsal saucer grid reinforced in the meantime, they're bound to go after it again!"

"Acknowledged."

Rising into space had made things easier at first. The range of their phasers and torpedoes had become practically limitless, allowing them to pick off the infalling fusion charges like ducks in a shooting gallery—though it had forced them to abandon pursuit of several remaining charges in the atmosphere, and Scott could only pray all of those missed their marks. But their need to concentrate on the remaining charges had left them more or less sitting ducks themselves. The Dassik had quickly divined their intentions and reacted, one warship continuing to deploy charges while the other came about and began firing steadily on the starship, which could only do so much to evade or counterattack without letting the charges through. With the phasers and torpedoes mostly dedicated to intercepting the depth charges, the remaining phaser banks weren't able to block every incoming beam and missile, and two had already fallen to enemy fire, leaving gaps in the ship's coverage. The Dassik had concentrated on those gaps, and the deflector grids in those sections were taking quite a pounding. Scott's teams below were diverting what power they could to those sections, but resources were limited and some rerouting options were off the table due to the unfinished repairs.

And that didn't even take into account how close the starboard warp nacelle was to catastrophic failure. The repairs to the coolant system and plasma flow regulators were still incomplete, meaning that if the nacelle came under heavy fire, it could trigger a backflow of superheated plasma that might overload the conduits throughout engineering and blow out half the secondary hull from the inside. Scott had teams riding herd on the plasma flow rates, manually keeping them steady and venting them when necessary, and Ensigns Gardner and Davis were working on a software patch that would take over the job automatically. But Scott didn't need to be down in engineering to know that it was tough going for his people when the Dassik barrage kept knocking them off their feet and triggering overloads in vital systems, distracting them from the business of keeping themselves whole. He wished he could be down there with them, but Scott knew that the best thing he could do for them was to focus on his task up here on the bridge.

At least most of the phaser banks and torpedo tubes were still working, successfully protecting the Web from further bombardment. But those walking scarecrows were determined sorts. "Sir," Ensign Haines announced, "the lead ship is pulling ahead. It's trying to put the limb of Cherela between us."

"The atmosphere's refracting our phasers," Rahda added a moment later, frustration in her voice.

"Then pour on the torpedoes," Scott said, trying to project calm and reassurance. "Aim them through the outer atmosphere, program their thrusters to compensate. If it shields them, it can shield our torpedoes too."

After a moment, he added, "And raise our orbit, try to regain line of sight."

"That will bring us closer to the second Dassik ship, sir."

The ship rocked again, and a moment later, Scott said, "Do it anyway. Give them a sporting chance for once."

The next few minutes were a struggle to hold the *Enterprise* together under the intensified fire from the second vessel. It took all of Scott's discipline to keep his focus on taking out the cube missiles, even when it meant allowing his beloved starship to endure more damage. But finally, Chekov let out a crow of triumph. "That's it! That's the last missile!"

"And glad I am to hear it, laddie," Scott replied. But his elation only lasted for a moment, since now the other Dassik ship was free to turn its weapons on the *Enterprise* as well, and soon the engineering boards were showing even greater chaos in the ship's systems. Deflector grids were burning out, phaser banks were overheating, computer circuits were being deranged by bursts of particle radiation penetrating the hull, structural members on the outer decks were exceeding their maximum loads and nearing failure. Two compartments had already blown out to vacuum—neither one occupied, thank heavens—and only the emergency bulkheads had prevented worse depressurizations. *Even that sound and fury is starting to feel a wee bit significant,* Scotty thought as he clung tightly to the command chair arms during a particularly fierce barrage.

"Mister Scott," Chekov called from the science station. "I hate to add to our problems, sir, but I'm detecting activity on the fringes of the system. Energy signatures consistent with Dassik engines and weapons—at least a half dozen ships, sir."

Och, not more of them! "Weapons, Mister Chekov? Who or what are they shooting at?"

"That's the good news, sir—maybe. They're not drawing closer at the moment . . . and I'm reading radiation signatures consistent with First Federation buoys."

"Buoys, aye!" Scott's mood was appropriately buoyed by the news. He'd experienced how effective those cubic contraptions could be at holding a ship in place. But how they came to be there was a mystery. The First Federation had done all it could to make Cherela's star system seem abandoned, so it had no defensive perimeter of the sort they maintained around their overall territory.

Which meant that these buoys must have been newly deployed—and Scott knew what type of ship was responsible for deploying them. "Ensign, scan for orbships."

Before Chekov could even complete his scan, Lieutenant Palmer spoke up. "Incoming hail, Commander. It's from the *Fesarius.*"

The bridge shook and the screen flickered as the incoming signal appeared. *"Balok to* Enterprise," said the diminutive captain who appeared on the screen. *"Ahh, Mister Scott. I see you're having your own disagreement with the Dassik. I don't suppose you expect to clear that up anytime soon? Because, you see, we have a rather larger Dassik problem heading our way."*

"Aye, we've detected the incoming ships, Commander Balok. But if you're askin' for our help, I'm afraid that's not an option. The Dassik here seem to have exhausted their depth charges, but they might have other nasty surprises to spring on us. We need to stay here to defend the planet. And our warp drive's in sorry shape anyway. There's no chance we could get out to you in time to make a difference."

Balok sighed. *"I was afraid of that. Well, we'll just have to do our best out here."*

"What with? All due respect, Commander, as impressive as your ship is, she's not built for war."

"Direct confrontation has never been our way, Mister Scott. I've still got a few tricks up my sleeve. There may be a way Starfleet can help us without needing to be here."

The ship rocked again. "Whatever you have in mind, Commander Balok, I wish you well. We'll hold the line here as long as we can."

"You're better friends to the First Federation than we probably deserve, Mister Scott. I hope more of my people will come to see that. Thank you."

Balok's visage disappeared, replaced by the far bleaker sight of the Dassik warships still raining fire down upon the *Enterprise.* This wasn't how Scott wanted it to end. If he had to go down with his ship, he wanted to be below-decks, tending to his precious engines until the last moment. *The captain and Spock had better do something fast,* he thought, *or we're all done for.*

———

The situation room floor was sloping rather severely now, and the tower was experiencing increasingly frequent tremors. *"We're ready,"* Kirk reported via holodisplay from the Tessegri control center. *"Rigged for secondary override control. Let's hope we won't need it."* He glanced down at an indicator on his console. *"I'm reading go on the last module, do you confirm?"*

"Confirmed for go," Uhura reported, clinging to the edge of the console next to Spock. "But we're only reading eighty-seven percent. Four teams report failure."

Spock nodded. Under the circumstances, it was only logical that some of the teams had been unable to position their transmitters or had lacked intact systems to interface with.

"*Make that five,*" Kasan Tor reported heavily over the comm. "*One team was still on Kaibikil when the last charge hit. I . . . think they're dead.*"

"*Damn,*" Kirk murmured.

"*I sent them there myself,*" Kasan said, his voice shaking.

"*Kasan, listen to me,*" Kirk said sharply. "*It's not your fault. They knew the risks and chose to help. We owe it to them, to everybody, to hold it together and make this work.*"

"*You're right,*" Kasan said after a moment. "*We . . . we're ready here.*"

"It's not enough," Lekur Zan growled. He had fallen to all fours to help maintain his balance, an option that came more easily to his species than others. "With that many gaps in the network, we won't be able to synchronize enough of the field manipulators."

"No, we can do it," Uhura said. "It's just a matter of interpolating the gaps in the pattern, adjusting the signal levels to compensate."

"The precision required . . . it'd be prohibitive."

"Let me hear it," she said. At Lekur's stare, she turned to Spock and said, "Let me listen to the radio noise of the field."

"Of course," Spock said, hands racing to set it up.

"*Trust her,*" Kirk said. "*Uhura's hearing is extraordinary.*"

"Indeed," Spock confirmed. "And while my own skills

for acoustical pattern recognition are nowhere near the lieutenant's, my hearing is excellent as well. I will assist you, Lieutenant Uhura."

"If you would, sir."

One of the situation room's Linnik technicians stumbled over across the quaking floor and provided them with headsets to listen on. "These will block outside sounds somewhat," she said.

"What if we need to give you information or instructions?" Tirak asked.

"I will monitor the screens," Spock said. "And only the lieutenant and I will know what needs to be done at any given moment."

Tirak bristled. "We are still the leaders of the First Federation, Mister Spock. We should have a say—"

"We have," Lekur told him. "We decided to let Spock do this. Now stand back, shut up, and let him do it already."

"I couldn't have said it better myself," Kirk put in.

The Linnik triumvir subsided, though without much grace. Deprived of the ability to dominate and control, Tirak had little else to fall back on.

Spock finished setting up the controls and turned to Uhura, who was securing herself in the seat next to his. "Ready."

She nodded. "Go ahead, sir."

He hit the switch, and the radio noise of Cherela roared in his ears. It was an intricate blend of sounds—a symphony, he thought, trying to interpret it as Uhura would, for he was following her lead. A multilayered pattern, surging, pulsing, crackling in complex counterpoint. Studying the readouts on the monitors, he began to recognize which layers of the sound corresponded to which phenomena: the steady undertone of Cherela's magnetic dynamo, the higher, fluctuating harmonics of the Web's destabilizing magnetic field, the percussive pops and cracks of the lightning storms, the distant sizzle of the radiation belts. Faintly, beneath it all, an irregular sputter of wideband noise, multiple different tones discernible: the sound of phasers and disruptors, starships joined in battle.

After taking a moment to get the feel for it, Uhura turned to him, nodding to indicate her readiness. He nodded back. "Captain, we are ready to proceed."

"All remote stations online. It's your show, Spock."

"On my mark," Spock said. "Three . . . two . . . one . . . mark."

Uhura's slender hands worked the console, activating the remote network, tapping into the Web's entire regulation grid and centralizing its control at her station. The fate of hundreds of billions of sentient beings now rested in those hands.

Tentatively, Uhura began adjusting the output of the grid, testing the changes it created in the sound of the planetary field as well as the visual readouts. As Lekur had predicted, it was difficult to regulate at first. The control grid was fluctuating wildly, and without a complete remote network to override it, her ability to compensate was hampered.

But she was an expert at teasing coherence out of fragmentary signals or incomplete information. As she worked, Spock could tell that she was deducing, or perhaps intuiting, how to compensate for the control gaps, manipulating adjacent field sectors to smooth out the spikes, like generating a tone that would modulate a discordant one and bring it into harmony.

Spock worked to adjust the equalization of the audio signal, bringing out the nuances of the Web field network. She gave him no gesture of thanks, remaining focused on the work. No such gestures were required; they were a team, working as one. She simply used the new information to refine her control still further, hands dancing across the console as she counteracted the instabilities second by second, gradually bringing the network into a state, not of stability, but of marginally balanced instability, dependent on her continued attention to hold it steady.

And on that foundation, Spock was able to build. He began working his own controls, like a pianist taking on the main melodic line while his partner played the ostinato. Except his melody was a modulation of that same ostinato, like a minimalist composition. Gently, gradually, he took the dynamic equilibrium Uhura created and nudged it into a different configuration. Uhura adjusted along with him, modifying her performance to maintain each new alteration in the field balance. Every time he changed it, he forced her to recalculate and reconfigure so as to prevent the instabilities from erupting again. But somehow, Uhura kept it steady.

As Spock adjusted the Web's interaction with the planetary magnetic field, he began reshaping the field itself, or at least its outer portion. The changes propagated at the speed of light, so their effects on the radiation belts should be prompt. The nearest belt to the Dassik was below them, between them and the *Enterprise*; indeed, without that barrier, they would probably have closed for the kill already. But the readings indicated that the starship was damaged, leaking plasma and maneuvering erratically. The radiation belt needed to be more than a barrier. It needed to be raised to engulf the Dassik, and quickly, before they could recognize the motion and act to evade it.

But that was simple enough. The stellar-wind protons that made up the radiation belt were circling the planet at high velocity, accelerated and confined by Cherela's intense magnetic envelope. Thus, all that was needed was to reduce the intensity of the field confining them, and they would surge outward under their own momentum. He just had to manipulate the Web's control grid to weaken the magnetic field at the appropriate place.

After explaining this to Kirk and the others, Spock added, "Captain, initiating the field surge will require a major, rapid change in the grid configuration. Its stability will be difficult to maintain after that. There is likely to be renewed turbulence. It is imperative that all the remaining override transmitters remain online."

"Understood. All control stations, stand by. Do whatever it takes to keep your transmitters running."

Spock finished the computations and caught Uhura's eyes, warning her to be ready. She nodded.

"Ready, Captain," he said.

"Do it!"

Spock triggered the field shift. A massive shudder went through the situation room, possibly through the entire Web of Worlds. Uhura scrambled to find a new equilibrium, to keep the surge from escalating until it tore the whole Web apart. Spock heard several control stations reporting problems and Kirk giving orders to all of them, coordinating the efforts to keep the override network intact.

And Spock could not hope or pray, but merely wait and see if the plan worked.

———

"She's bleeding!" Force Leader Grun howled. "Limping like a *rhelkul* lizard with a spear in its side! Just a few more shots and we will tear out her throat! Then nothing will stop me from seizing the final prize while Vraq is still struggling to defeat a few gaudy cubes!"

Grun was so enthused that Remv was reluctant to report the new readings. "Force Leader, we are taking new fire from . . . somewhere!"

"What?" Grun strode over, looming above Remv menacingly. "What fire?"

"A—a proton bombardment, sir. It's like—"

Grun laughed. "A proton beam?! How desperate have they become? That's barely worth bothering with!"

"But it grows more intense! It's not just a beam, it's more like—"

"Silence, Remv!" Grun interrupted. "You panic too easily. A few more shots and—"

That was when the shields failed.

Remv had tried to warn him. True, a proton beam was a primitive weapon—potent but inefficient, limited in range due to electrostatic bloom, and easily deflected by an electromagnetic shield. But that was on the scale of weapons built by sentient beings. A water hose was not much of a weapon either, but a flood could wash away a town. This planet's radiation belts had been large and intense enough to sterilize entire habitable moons—and one of them had somehow risen to engulf the cluster ship.

Grun had never been the type to listen to scientists. But science had a way of exacting its revenge.

The flood of protons muscled its way through the shields, vaporizing much of the hull armor on impact. The ship's systems burned out moments later, including the inertial dampers, so the crew felt the full effect of the explosive vaporization of much of their hull pushing them in the other direction. Remv clung to his seat, but Grun went flying, Rhuld's body breaking his fall. Electric arcs danced across the bulkheads and the hunters' armor, convulsing the command pod's crew with the shock. Remv knew, though, that the command crew had it easy; those in the pods most directly exposed to the bombardment would probably be near death from direct and secondary radiation exposure.

Then the gravity went out and all was darkness. Before long, Remv couldn't tell if he was alive or dead. And he couldn't for the life of him understand how a planet could reach out and smack them down.

"It worked!" Nisu cried. "Both cluster ships have been engulfed in the radiation belt. They're adrift and inactive. Life readings . . . unclear but still present. I estimate low to moderate casualties, but the threat of the ships is neutralized."

"The *Enterprise*?" Kirk asked.

"Damaged but also present. Stronger life readings. Power readings strong and . . . and stabilizing."

Kirk sighed in relief. He was too tired and sore from

making sure the transmitters stayed functional to cheer. "We did it."

"And did you notice?" Aranow said. "The quakes have stopped. I think the Web's stabilizing too."

"It can't be that easy," Kirk said. "Nisu, can you get me the situation room?"

Soon, Spock's voice came over the comm. *"I am gratified to hear you are all well, Captain."*

"Status of the Web?"

"Fifteen world modules have sustained extensive damage, six of them heavily populated. One world module and six minor modules have collapsed into Cherela's depths, but most of their occupants were evacuated in time."

"Most but not all," Aranow said softly, weeping.

"Long-term status?" Kirk asked.

"The Web is still unstable, but the instabilities are being held in check by Lieutenant Uhura at the moment. Triumvir Lekur is supervising the creation of an automated protocol which should duplicate the lieutenant's efforts, but it is a temporary solution.

"You should also be aware that the Web's long-range sensors have detected the approach of at least six more Dassik warships in the outer system. It would seem that Commander Balok and Lieutenant Bailey have rendezvoused with the Fesarius *and are attempting to hold the Dassik at bay with radiation buoys."*

Aranow looked shocked for a moment, but then relaxed. "Well, that's no problem. Not now. We have the radiation belts now. Right? So they can't hurt us."

"Providing the Web holds together," Kirk said.

"Indeed," Spock added. *"The more we employ the radia-*

tion belts as a defense, the more it threatens to destabilize the Web. This is not yet over."

"Then you need to beam us back there," Kirk instructed. "Things are . . . something of a mess outside here. There's no chance we can reach the transport terminal. You'll need to bring us back directly."

"Give us a few moments," Lekur's voice cut in. *"We have a few dozen other urgent matters we're dealing with right now."*

"As soon as you can."

Aranow led Kirk away from the console where Nisu monitored the situation. "While we wait . . . there's one more thing to address. In case we don't . . . if we aren't here to address it later."

"What's that?"

She gave him a wan smile. "I just realized—we're not in the situation room now."

She grabbed his head in her long, strong fingers and pulled him into a kiss full of relief, gratitude, sadness, and need. For once, she didn't rush.

Sixteen

"Why haven't they stopped?" Balok paced the command chamber of his pilot vessel, now docked within its domed hangar and restored to its normal place as the "brain" of the *Fesarius*, as he watched the Dassik squadron fly through the debris of the last cubic buoy and resume its course toward Cherela. "They've seen what the radiation belt did to their ships. They should be running as far and as fast as they can."

David Bailey could not recall the last time he'd seen his friend so unsure of himself. All he could offer was, "They're not Linnik, Balok. Retreat isn't their way."

"But they're hunters. Predators aren't reckless. They only strike when they feel it's safe. This should have worked!"

"Does it matter?" Linar asked. "However many ships they throw at Cherela, we can stop them now! We have an incredible weapon to use against them—the might of an entire giant planet!"

"But the Web is already on the verge of collapse. They need to focus all their efforts on stabilizing it now. Continuing to use the weapon could undermine that."

"They're still not slowing," Almis reported. He paused, listening to a report from his underlings over an earpiece. "Two of them have veered off," he announced hopefully. But as the moments passed, his optimism gave way to concern. "They're on course for a pair of cometary bodies in the outer system. The other four ships remain on course for Cherela."

"Why go after comets?" Bailey asked.

"Oh, no," Balok said. "Remember how they used their tractors to hurl debris at the *Fesarius* before." He turned to his science officer. "Almis, check those comets against the hazard registry."

Bailey saw where Balok's thoughts were heading. Naturally, every advanced planetary civilization monitored the minor bodies in its planetary system and kept an eye on those whose orbits could be most easily perturbed onto a collision course with an inhabited world. It wasn't long until Almis confirmed, "Both comets are on the registry, Commander. It wouldn't take much tractoring to shift them onto impact trajectories."

"So much for the ultimate weapon," Bailey said. "The radiation belts only work at close range. The Dassik can hang back and lob as many comets at the planet as they want."

"Normally," Almis replied, "I'd say the risk to the Web was minimal—the atmosphere would burn up most of them, and the odds of debris hitting a module would be slight. But given how much the bombardment has already destabilized things . . ."

"We need to scare them off," Balok said. "We need to threaten them with something bigger."

"Bigger than a whole Jovian?" Bailey challenged. "What else can you throw at them? The *Fesarius* is all you have, and I doubt any other orbships could get here in time."

The silver-robed commander looked him over. "We have Starfleet as well."

"But the *Enterprise* is crippled. They can't make much difference."

Balok gave a mischievous grin. "I wasn't talking about the *Enterprise*. Come with me."

———

Bailey had always been impressed by the *Fesarius*'s holographic recreation room, but he was surprised to see how well it was able to simulate the bridge of a *Constitution*-class starship based only on Balok's original scans of the *Enterprise* and its data banks. The command chair replica he sat in now certainly felt solid, its textures not unlike the real materials. A recording of the *Enterprise* bridge's actual ambient sounds was looping in the background. The simulator could not replicate people, however, so Balok made sure the visual pickup was focused tightly on Bailey in the command chair—which also served to conceal the rank stripes on his sleeves. His command gold tunic would allow him to pass for the captain of an imaginary Starfleet task force, one whose approach Balok would simulate by using a distant, remote-controlled buoy to emit a suitable energy signature. The rest was simply a matter of Bailey remembering the lines Balok had fed him and delivering them with suitable authority. He hoped he wouldn't succumb to stage fright; the *Fesarius* would be broadcasting his words across the entire system, so that the *Enterprise* and the Cherelan authorities would be alerted to the ploy and able to respond accordingly.

He nodded to Balok, who stood by the holographic control station in the forward port segment of the bridge, out of sight of the imager. "I'm ready. Hail them."

In moments, a fierce Dassik visage appeared on the viewer. All Dassik looked fierce to him, but this one projected an air of exceptional power and authority. "*This is War Leader Vraq of the Dassik Expeditionary Force,*" he intoned in a gravelly basso. "*If you call to give us warning, do not bother. Our cause is just, and we shall not turn away. Attack us if you must, for we do not fear death. But for their own sake, pray that your underlings do not fear it either.*"

Bailey opened his mouth, preparing to meet Vraq's bluster with his own. But he hesitated. Vraq's words resonated with his memories of Kirk's corbomite challenge from three years ago—words he had not been on hand to hear in person, but that Balok had laughingly replayed for him many times over the years. "*Death has little meaning to us. If it has none to you, then attack us now. We grow annoyed at your foolishness.*" Kirk's words had been a bombastic bluff to give Balok pause. But Bailey realized that Vraq was not bluffing now. His people did not fear death in battle because they knew the death of their entire species loomed if they did not learn the secrets the First Federation kept hidden. No threat, genuine or feigned, could outweigh that existential fear.

If this is poker . . . then it's time to put the cards on the table.

Bailey stood, moved over to Balok, and shut down the entire bridge simulation save for the viewscreen, to the Linnik commander's bewilderment. Then he widened the sensor angle and moved back into view of the pickup, still aware that the whole system would be watching. "War Leader Vraq. This is . . . Ambassador David Bailey of the United Federation of Planets. I'm not going to try to scare you off, and I'm not going to fight you. I just want to talk."

"*You would plead for your fellow Federation? Try*

to convince us of the folly of taking on their planetary weapon? Yes, it is formidable—yet they did not wait to deploy it until my ships were in orbit. And that tells me they had no choice but to strike sooner. Which means they are vulnerable. And their weapon's range is limited. A comet's range is not. If you would plead for them, then convince them to surrender."

"Yes—they are vulnerable," Bailey said, drawing an angry glare from Balok. "But so are you. I know what was done to your people, Vraq. I know the danger you face. If you attack that planet, you risk destroying the knowledge that would save your people."

"You would have me believe they would just hand that knowledge over?"

"I believe they might. The Linnik who transformed and imprisoned your ancestors all died twelve thousand years ago. And they hid the truth of what they'd done from their allies . . . and their descendants. Most of the people on that planet now know nothing about what was done to you. They are not your enemies. They are not warriors by nature. They could easily have vaporized your ships with that radiation burst. Instead, they just crippled them."

"Or perhaps they have not yet found their weapon's range."

"What do you have to lose by extending a little trust?" Bailey pleaded. "You said it yourself, the weapon's reach is limited. You have the high ground. You can afford the time to get to know the real situation before you decide. Believe me, acting rashly doesn't usually pan out well."

"And what can you offer us that could possibly change our minds?"

Bailey's eyes went to the other person in the chamber

with him. "A Linnik who knows what was done to you and wants to reveal the truth," he said. "A Linnik who was arrested and tortured for that knowledge, but who still refused to back down, because it went against everything his civilization means to him."

"None of the betrayers ever had such courage."

"Courage is being afraid but doing what you have to do anyway. It's facing your fear and not letting it dictate your life." He met his friend's eyes imploringly. "Isn't that right, Balok?"

The childlike captain quailed at first, but Bailey's gaze remained steadily upon him. Taking a deep breath, Balok tugged on his robes and haltingly stepped forward into view of the sensor. "War Leader Vraq . . . I am Commander Balok of the *Fesarius*, in service to the First Federation. My young friend here is right. We may be a timid people by nature . . . but our way has always been to provide shelter and hope for those whose futures are in peril. The fact . . . the fact that your ancestors created that peril for so many of ours . . . well, it shouldn't matter any longer. You are in need now, and that makes it our obligation to offer you our aid. I know where to find the records of what was done to your people . . . and I am willing to work with you to find a permanent cure."

Vraq peered closely at Balok, narrowing his catlike eyes, and Bailey could see what a struggle it was for the Linnik captain to withstand that predatory scrutiny without retreating for cover. *"And your leaders . . . they would cooperate with you on this?"*

Balok gave a breathless laugh. "Why, of course—" He broke off at Bailey's hand on his shoulder. The lieutenant shook his head, silently imploring his friend that the time for deception had ended. "Well . . . not all of them would. But I believe the others could be convinced . . . *if you showed them you were willing to negotiate.*"

It had the virtue of being honest, which Bailey was convinced was the right way to play it. But he feared it wasn't enough. It would take something more than words from an admitted outsider to give Vraq a reason to stand down. And Bailey was fresh out of cards to play.

"*Enterprise to Dassik fleet.*" It was a new voice, with a brogue Bailey recognized. "*This is Commander Montgomery Scott of the U.S.S. Enterprise to the Dassik fleet. We have scanned the two damaged ships in orbit of the planet Cherela. Both ships have sustained heavy damage to propulsion, weapons, and life support. One ship's shielding was already badly damaged before the radiation burst struck, and our scans show that its crew's life signs are fading. I request permission to beam a team across to provide medical assistance and life-support repairs.*"

Balok chuckled softly. "Of course," he murmured to Bailey. "Reliably altruistic as always."

Another transmission came in now. "*This is Force Leader Grun! I refuse to allow any Federation scum aboard a Dassik ship!*"

"*Force Leader Grun,*" Scott replied, "*that ship's crew will die without swift medical assistance! Many of your own crew's life readings are fading as well!*"

"*Then they will die! It is fitting payment for their incompetence in failing to destroy you!*"

"*Grun!*" roared Vraq, his angry visage still visible on Bailey's screen. "*You are in no position to speak of incompetence, Force Leader! Your reckless attack has threatened to destroy us all!*"

"*War Leader, you cannot be considering backing down! If we grovel before our killers and beg for their charity, we will doom ourselves to death with our weakness. We must keep fighting. Our pride is at stake!*"

"Pride is nothing but the fear of looking bad," Bailey spoke up. "Are you really prepared to let your people die because of fear?"

"*We do not fear you, Federation weakling! We have surmounted all other challenges with patience and relentless will. Now that we know where the secrets are to be found, we will seize them by force!*"

"And how many more of your people will die in the process?"

"*No matter how many glorious sacrifices we must make against this infernal weapon, we will not back down! We will conquer the betrayers, rip the secrets from their throats, and destroy them once and for all.*"

"*Do you hear yourself, Grun?*" Vraq demanded. "*Your bloodlust blinds you. What good is it to chase your prey to the ends of the world if your family has starved by the time you return?*"

"*But, War Leader—*"

"*You are relieved of command, Grun! Second, you will remove Grun from the command pod and take his place as Force Leader. Then you will permit the* Enterprise *to send medical teams aboard your ships.*"

There were sounds of a scuffle from the other ship, ending with the sound of a disruptor blast. A moment later, a new voice spoke. "*War Leader, this is Second—ah, Force Leader Rhuld. It seems that Grun will require medical assistance himself.*"

"*A pity,*" Vraq said with no hint of sincerity. Then he

turned back to Bailey and Balok. *"Ambassador. Commander Balok. I am willing to talk. But it now falls upon you to convince your leaders to do the same."*

The screen went dark, and Balok looked up nervously at the lieutenant. "Why do I get the feeling this may have been the easy part?"

When Kirk had arrived in the situation room with Aranow and Nisu, he had found it somewhat the worse for wear. The floor was slightly slanted, cracks had formed in the walls, and a few consoles and screens had apparently blown out. In the middle of it all, Uhura had sat at a console, fingers racing across its controls as she carried on a running discussion with several technicians around her, working with them to establish new automated protocols that would take over her efforts to maintain the Web's balance. Still, the systems had been intact enough to pick up the broadcasts from the *Fesarius*, Vraq's squadron, and the *Enterprise*. Now Balok and Bailey appeared on the largest intact screen, listening in as the triumvirs debated the issue before them.

"It's a lie, all of it," Triumvir Tirak insisted. "The Dassik try to paint their people as victims in order to justify their own atrocities against us. They must be destroyed at once, before they can take knowledge of Cherela's location to the rest of their people."

"You don't think they've already sent word?" Kirk asked. "Besides, most of their ships are out of range of the radiation belts. And they've got two comets ready to fling at Cherela if they don't like what they hear."

"Exactly why we cannot submit! If we give in to their

threats, we are as good as conquered. And we can concentrate the radiation belts on the comets—burn them up before they hit."

"At the speed they would be traveling," Spock pointed out, "it would not be possible to concentrate enough radiation upon them to vaporize them. At best, they could be deflected toward harmless trajectories, but nothing would prevent the Dassik from launching more comets."

"We have buoys. Orbships."

"And you don't think a massive siege warfare campaign in this system would give away Cherela's existence?" Kirk asked, disbelieving.

"It would be impossible to keep the Web of Worlds concealed in any case," Spock added. "As I have been attempting to explain, the only way to restore the long-term stability of the Web is to halt all efforts to suppress the atmospheric and magnetic responses to its presence. As long as they inhibit Cherela's natural cycles, the buildup of further instabilities is inevitable."

"*He's right,*" Kasan Tor said over a screen. "*We need to find a new balance, one that works with Cherela's natural flow of energies, that adapts to them instead of forcing them to adapt to us.*"

"We're still not sure of that," Lekur told the younger Bogosrin. "We're convinced now we should take a closer look at your findings, but it'll be a while before we've sorted this whole mess out."

"In any case, there's more at stake here," Kirk went on. "The Dassik won't leave you alone if you continue to hide from them. They need the knowledge you have if they're to have any chance of survival."

"And I say again, no such knowledge exists!" Tirak insisted. "You simply take the Dassik's side to discredit this council and conceal your own culpability in our recent disasters."

"The only one who's discredited us is you, Tirak!" Balok called from the screen. *"And by your own actions!"*

"You can offer nothing to back up your accusations, Balok. I am sure of that."

"Only because you had your agent do her best to wipe my memory," Balok charged, drawing shocked looks from Aranow, Lekur, and Nisu. The *Fesarius* captain chuckled. *"Luckily, I still had a few tricks up my sleeve."*

"I can vouch for that," Bailey added. *"Both parts."*

Nisu stepped forward. "Commander Balok . . . are you saying you can prove this allegation? That there are, in fact, records in our own data banks confirming that the ancient Linnik transformed the Dassik in a way that now endangers their survival? And that Triumvir Tirak ordered your memory erased to conceal this fact?"

"Indeed I am, Chief Protector," Balok assured her. *"I'd be happy to show you the sealed records."*

Suddenly, a group of armed security troops stormed into the situation room, headed by Warden Mure. "I'm afraid I can't allow that," Tirak announced, stepping into the center of the room as the protectors surrounded the group.

"Tirak!" Aranow cried, her tail twitching in agitation. "It's true? How could you?"

"I am defending the First Federation, Triumvir. As I have always done. As you are sworn to do."

"By lying? By kidnapping people and wiping their memory? By holding us hostage?"

"You do not understand! No one can know the connection between the Linnik and the Dassik. Not the Dassik, not the First, not the humans. They would see the Linnik as a threat."

"So to prevent that," Balok asked, *"you would* make *us* a threat?"

"I would do what I must to ensure our secret is kept." Tirak turned to his Kisaja associate. "Mure! The human female controls the weapon. Transfix her."

"No!" Kirk cried, reflexively moving forward as Mure locked his purple gaze on Uhura. The nearest protectors raised their guns, but next to what he had just been through on the Tessegri module, it seemed a laughably feeble threat.

But Spock held him back. "No, Jim. We cannot risk a firefight here. The equipment is too essential to maintaining the Web's stability—we cannot let it be damaged."

"But Uhura . . ."

"I have confidence in the lieutenant's strength of will."

Kirk wanted to share his first officer's faith. He could see the defiance in Uhura's eyes, her proud refusal to capitulate. But he knew from experience how overpowering Mure's will could be. "Compel her to operate the radiation weapon," Tirak ordered. "Have her direct it against every Dassik ship in range—and against the *Enterprise* as well. Destroy them all."

"No, you can't!" Kirk roared. "Tirak!"

"Stop this, Triumvir!" Nisu demanded. "This is unconscionable!"

"This will save our people!" insisted Tirak.

"It will damn your people!" Kirk countered. "Even if, by some miracle, you can stop Vraq's squadron from retaliating, you will condemn the Linnik forever.

"Look at yourself, Tirak. Think about why you're doing this: because you're ashamed of what your people did so long ago. You're afraid no one will forgive that crime, even though it was committed in the defense of your people and so many others. How do you imagine that committing yet another atrocity will erase that shame?"

"We kept it buried for twelve thousand years, Kirk. We can hide it again, once we get rid of you and the Dassik."

"Will you get rid of us too, Tirak?" Lekur Zan rumbled. "Is that part of your plan?"

"Lekur . . . Aranow . . . we protect the First together. For so long, we have kept the Web safe and hidden. Surely you can see that this is the best way."

"To hide your guilt?" Aranow asked. "Your crimes? Your lies?"

"We have always thrived by concealment!"

"And it hasn't worked!" Kirk cried. "It's only been a stopgap. It hasn't solved the underlying problems, just let them fester and grow more dangerous. The more you try to hide from consequences, the harder they hit you in the end."

"You know nothing of our world, Kirk! Of our ways!"

"I know what you have it in you to be," Kirk urged. "From Balok, and Aranow, and Nisu. I have seen the best of the First Federation, and I know you are capable of better than this."

"We cannot be that if the Dassik destroy us."

"And I've seen the best in them as well," the captain went on. "Through the example of a Dassik named Koust, whom you set up to kill me, but who proved he was capable of more than that. Who just fought alongside my people and risked his life to save all of yours."

"I don't believe you."

"The fact that I'm standing here proves you're wrong about the Dassik. They're more than murderous savages. Tirak—they're your family. They're no different from you, save for a few genetic quirks."

"They are nothing like us! They must be destroyed! And now we have the means to do it!"

"You do not," Spock countered. "Using the weapon again at the present time would require diverting resources away from the stabilization of the Web. Repeated use could trigger a new cascade failure—particularly if the Web comes under cometary bombardment."

"And even if the Web does survive," Kirk added, "even if you somehow manage to destroy the armada out there, all you'll do is invite more Dassik retaliation. More endless fighting that could doom both your civilizations."

"The Web has endured longer than your primitive civilization has existed! It will not fall now, no matter what the alarmists find it useful to claim." Tirak spun. "Mure! What is taking so long? Destroy the aliens!"

"She is . . . fighting me," the warden grated out. Indeed, Uhura was clenching her teeth and sweating heavily. Her hands trembled as Mure attempted to force her to move them on the controls. "If I . . . push harder . . . I will damage her."

"Damage her, then! It will be the least of their losses."

"And you say you're nothing like the Dassik?" Kirk demanded, furious now. "You're both the same, Tirak. Both with the same potential for peace or war, just like any other species." He schooled himself to calm, aware that he had to defuse the situation to help Uhura. "You *gave* them that, Tirak. The Linnik did. You gave them twelve thousand years to develop and refine their culture. To cultivate their intelligence and reason. They aren't brutes—maybe they never really were. They just want to survive. Just like you, they're afraid, and they're lashing out at the ones they fear. Don't you understand by now that fear is not the answer?"

He turned to the other triumvirs. "Aranow. Lekur. You told me that your races were at war until the Linnik showed you a better way. That it was better to work together than to fear each other. Despite all the harm you had done to each other, you learned to set it aside and cooperate."

"That's right!" Aranow affirmed. "We did."

"It was the start of . . . all this," Lekur added.

Tirak scoffed. "You really think we can cooperate with the Dassik? Look at the ruins of the Bogosrin home-world, a fraction of an orbit away. We can see a constant reminder of what those monsters did to our peoples, our space. *We were the First!* This is our space, won back from the Dassik at great cost!"

"You and the Dassik are from the same planet," Spock pointed out. "Logically, if the Linnik are among the First, then so are they. And if they are not, then you cannot claim the title for yourself without hypocrisy."

"We have always stood with the First!"

"You have stood together in fear. You have been ruled by it—and being ruled by fear can blind you to possibility."

"He's right, Tirak," Balok said. *"There is more out there in the galaxy than fear. There is wonder and beauty and awe."* He took Bailey's hand. *"There is friendship and kindness. There are people who can come together to achieve great things."*

Tirak gestured at his surroundings. "We have achieved the greatest engineering feat in the galaxy!"

"We have built the greatest trap in the galaxy. A trap for ourselves. All beings have limits, Tirak. If we stay wrapped up in our own private worlds, then we can never escape our own shortcomings, our own failings. That's why we need to reach out to others. To trust in their strengths to balance our weaknesses, their perspectives to fill in our blind spots."

"Infinite Diversity in Infinite Combinations," said Spock. "It is when different entities combine, when they complement each other's limitations, that new and great things can be achieved."

"That's what we've done," an uncertain Lekur Zan said. "Found other refugee peoples, invited them to join us. Built new worlds to hold them and made our community larger. Better."

"That's right," Kirk said. "Because the First Federation has always been about more than fear." He looked around at them. "You've known that all along, going back to when you first founded the Web of Worlds—back when it was an ideal, a belief bigger than any physical place." He met Aranow's eyes. "The searchers." Lekur. "The builders." Nisu. "The communicators." Tirak. "The dreamers. All limited by yourselves, but when you reached out and joined together, you became something far greater. And then you kept reaching out and taking in others, growing stronger the more diverse you became.

"It's time to remember what the First Federation used to be about. Not just hiding from danger, but reaching out. Making connections. Building something greater than what you had before."

"With the Dassik?" Tirak asked in disbelief. "They could never belong with us."

"They're a people in need, Tirak, the same as all of you once were. They've lost their homeworld just as you did. Now they're damaged, dying, desperate to find answers that only you can give them. The only reason they feel they have to take those answers by force is because they can't believe you would ever offer them freely."

"Then let's offer them!" Aranow cried. "They're willing to talk. They've said so. They've asked for our help! War isn't our way, Tirak. Even before. Your ancestors didn't kill the Dassik. Just made them peaceful. Made them like you." She reached for him. "Do you want to be like them?"

Tirak's eyes darted. "No. No, I am not the threat. I am protecting us."

"You're mad if you actually believe that at this point," Lekur said. "You're holding your own colleagues hostage, you pitiful man! You're trying to make that poor woman destroy her own ship!"

"Please," Aranow said. "Let's try. At worst, we have a defense now. The radiation belts. But only if we need them," she hastened to add. "We should try peace first. Like we always have."

"*First,*" Balok said, shaking his head slowly. "*We pride ourselves on that. We were here first! It's our ruined wasteland, nobody take it! But that's not all that it means. We are the First Federation. The first known group of races in modern history who joined together in peace and agreed to work together for the good of all. Now we've found another Federation that follows our example. And they don't need to hide from the galaxy, or from their own past, in order to make it work. So maybe we don't either. After all—we were doing it first.*"

Tirak looked around. Even many of his own troops looked uncertain—and Uhura's defiance of Mure seemed to be getting stronger. Now the Kisaja warden was sweating.

Finally, the aging Linnik sighed. "Mure, release her. All of you, stand down." Kirk doubted that Tirak had truly been convinced—but he was enough of a politician to see that he could not win, and that his best bet was to reorient his message. It would do.

But that would not satisfy Nisu. "Protectors. Place Triumvir Tirak and Warden Mure under arrest." Several of the protectors who'd just been following those two's orders hesitated. "Unless you want to join them!" Nisu barked, her eyes flashing at them. They hastened to comply.

Kirk jogged over to his communication officer. Crouching before her, he clasped her shoulders. "Uhura! Are you all right?"

She was breathing hard, but she managed to muster a faint smile. "I thought of . . . music. Focused on . . . songs. It let me hold on. Blocked him."

He grinned. "Lieutenant, I think I've been underestimating you."

"Thank you, sir. Still . . . if Mister Spock could spell me . . . I could use a rest."

"Of course." Kirk helped Uhura to her feet while Spock slipped into her seat and took over the process of stabilizing the Web. "Spock, can you take care of things from here?"

After a moment's evaluation of the console readings, Spock said, "The work of automating the stabilization process is almost complete. I should be able to finish compiling the program . . . provided there are no further disruptions."

Kirk turned to the triumvirs. "Then I recommend you contact War Leader Vraq . . . and tell him you're ready to talk."

———

Grun awoke in an unfamiliar bed in a gray-walled room. He heard a repetitive thumping tone from overhead, the pace of which quickened as he twisted his head to look around him. On the wall behind his head was a black display screen with moving indicators and a red light that blinked in time with the thumping tone. "Wha . . . what is this? Where am I?" He struggled against the restraints that held him to the bed.

A craggy-featured human in a blue tunic approached. "Calm down, Grun. You're all right. There's nothing to be afraid of."

Grun struggled harder. "I fear nothing!"

The human's voice sharpened. "Then why don't you start acting like it?" Startled by the sting of that verbal cuff, Grun took a breath and stilled himself. "That's better," the man continued. "I'm Doctor McCoy. You're in my sickbay aboard the *Enterprise*. And you're lucky you have such a strong constitution, or you'd be in the morgue instead. Even I can only do so much."

"You . . . you healed me? Why? I am your enemy."

"No," the doctor replied. "You're my patient."

"There are no enemies here anymore," came a new voice. It was that traitor Rhuld, coming into the room with the accursed Kirk at his heels. Rhuld towered over the humans and was unrestrained; he could easily have torn them to shreds. Yet they stood alongside him without concern.

Kirk elaborated on Rhuld's words. "War Leader Vraq has declared a formal cease-fire, in exchange for which the Council of the First has released its records of the genetic change imposed on the Dassik people. The First Federation's scientists are already hard at work on devising a permanent cure, with the assistance of my own science officer."

"No! Rhuld, you fool! It is another of their deceptions. They will lead us to our doom!"

"We were already heading there ourselves," Rhuld countered. "Not just due to the mutation, but due to closed and hateful minds like yours. Your blind rage almost brought about the extinction of our civilization along with theirs."

"Better to die as proud hunters than become like them! Indecisive . . . cowardly . . ."

"Thinkers. Scholars. Capable of more than primitive bloodlust. That is the gift the Linnik gave us—the time to grow into more than we were. You would regress us back. You would condemn us to death . . . and make us deserving of it." There was no gloating in his eyes or his voice—only the weight of an unwelcome obligation.

Kirk spoke up. "The revelation of what the Linnik's ancestors did to ensure the First Federation's survival has been . . . sobering to its people. It's making them reassess a lot of their old assumptions about themselves and about you. Every society has shameful things in its past. It's harder to be judgmental toward others once you recognize that within yourself."

"And yet they will judge me now," Grun countered. "Punish me for the crime of fighting for my people."

Rhuld leaned closer. "You fought for your own pride,

Grun. You were a fool and a bully. You tormented and killed your own crew. I would love to see you executed." He steadied himself with a breath. "But the First have a higher claim to you. And so you will rot in their prison instead. Perhaps that is a crueler fate after all."

"I wouldn't be so sure," said Kirk. "I have it on good authority that their penal system is about to undergo some major reforms. I'm certain you'll be treated well, Grun. Who knows? You may even learn to like it on Cherela. It's a truly beautiful place."

Kirk's optimism disgusted Grun. He could not imagine a more terrible fate than to spend the rest of his life trapped within that sickly blue-white planet, staring at him from all around like his father's ruined eye, forever judging him.

Later on, though, as he lay alone in that bed with the pulsing thump keeping him awake, he could not elude the thought that stalked him through the shadows of his mind: that the only part of Grun's father that had come to Cherela had been what Grun himself had brought here. If anyone was keeping that cruelty and hatred alive . . . perhaps it was him.

Yet he retreated from the thought. It was easier, more comfortable, to cling to his hatred of Vraq, of Rhuld, of Kirk, of the betrayers who would now have him at their mercy. All of them were against him. The whole universe conspired to hold Grun down and humiliate him at every turn. But he would not give in. He would never stop fighting his countless foes, never stop hating them.

For Grun feared nothing.

Epilogue

"I can't believe it," Aranow said. "I'm looking at Cherela. From the outside!"

Kirk stood beside her, grinning at the childlike awe in her face and body language as she gazed down on her home from the *Enterprise*'s forward observation lounge. She barely seemed aware of the *tranya* glass in her hand, though she hadn't dropped it yet. "Seeing your planet from space for the first time has that effect on most people."

"But it's more than that," she said. "Most of us . . . we never thought we would."

"More like we were afraid to," Lekur Zan said from where he stood on her other side. He hovered near Aranow like a protective father, making Kirk wary of getting too close to her. "We thought it was safer on the other side of the clouds. Turns out we were wrong about that."

"And you are seeing it as it has never appeared before," said Spock. "The cloud patterns are already changing— beginning to reflect the presence of the Web beneath."

"So all the galaxy can see what a unique and beautiful world you've created," added Uhura, standing next to the Vulcan.

"It *is* beautiful," Balok breathed from beyond Lekur's bulk. "I have always thought so. So bright and blue, against the endless black beyond. A fragile thing that must be nurtured and respected."

"And it will be," Lekur affirmed. "Now." He cast his gaze out at the nearest of Cherela's large moons. "But maybe it won't be alone. If we're not going to hide anymore, then maybe it's time we reclaimed one of our old lunar bases, refitted it as a support base for visiting ships. The systems will be fried, but the vacuum will have preserved them well." He let out a low, growling sigh. "Who knows? After what happened here . . . maybe some people won't want to stay in the Web anymore. We can make it safe again, but for some, the memories . . ." He paused in remembrance of the many who had died. "It might help to have an alternative. Maybe we could return to our old homeworlds, have a try at making them habitable again. After all, we've gotten pretty good with biospheres."

"To see this space blossom with life again," Kirk said, "would be inspiring. Our Federation would be glad to help."

"Well, don't get ahead of yourself. It would be the work of centuries. And it's our responsibility." Lekur snuffled. "We keep insisting this is our space . . . it's time we did something more than just keep out intruders."

Balok laughed. "Now, that will be a relief. I can't tell you how tedious border patrols could be."

"Oh, I think we have some idea," Kirk replied.

The Linnik sighed. "Still, I will miss the *Fesarius*. Now, that is a beautiful orb."

Dave Bailey smiled down at him. "Linar and the rest will take good care of her, Balok. Sorry—*Triumvir* Balok!"

The newly appointed triumvir shook his head, now bared of its command headdress. "Oh-h, don't remind me. I don't look forward to cleaning up the mess Tirak left."

"But there will be rewards, Triumvir," Spock said. "Such as the challenge of negotiating the peace between the First Federation and the Dassik."

Balok stared up at him. "You have a strange definition of 'rewards,' my friend." Then he laughed. "No—you are right, of course. If I can play a part in healing that ancient wound . . . in reconciling our Jekyll with their Hyde . . . then that will be a fine legacy to leave."

"It will be a worthy challenge!" Kirk turned at the declaration from Koust, who raised his glass in tribute. He was staggering a bit, though he insisted that no mere Linnik drink could overcome him. "Luckily, you will have me here to assist you."

"Are you sure this is what you want, Koust?" Kirk asked. "To become a diplomat instead of a fighter?"

The Dassik sobered as best he could. "I am the one Dassik who has earned the trust of the First. I must be the true face of my people, to replace the false faces in their nightmares. Only then can I begin to bring us together." He gave a fierce grin. "Cherela will be a boon to the Dassik. The cure is only the start. There are many untamed lands within the Web, wilderness modules where we can hunt and sate our nature without the need to strike at Starfleet or Betelgeusians or others. And even the well-populated worlds of the Web are less tame now than they were. They will need rescuers and builders for a long time to come. In time, we could even join in Lekur's project to reclaim the worlds our ancestors devastated. I have learned that it takes far more strength and courage to build than to destroy. The Dassik will find plenty of opportunities to test ourselves—by serving life instead of death."

Kirk shook his hand. "I'm proud to know you, Koust."

The Dassik laughed. "As well you should be!" He slapped Kirk painfully hard on the back, then went back to the bar for a refill.

Aranow moved closer to Kirk's side, ignoring Lekur's glare. "He'll sure keep things interesting," she said.

"Better you than me," Kirk said, rubbing his shoulder. "I can only take so much Dassik enthusiasm." She laughed, and he looked at her. "I was really hoping you might decide to come with us, you know. Let me show you the galaxy."

She stroked his cheek. "I'd love that. But I still have to finish my term. As a triumvir. Duty, you know. And like Zan said—rebuilding our worlds could take centuries. Might be a while before any of us get out there. You know. Into the rest of the galaxy. Where you all are." Kirk nodded. "Well, except Nisu. Good to have at least one emissary. Isn't that right, Nisu?"

The graceful Kisaja strode toward them, finally out of her security garb and adorned in something more aesthetic, as befitted a diplomatic envoy. "I will certainly try my best, Triumvir. It is . . . unnerving . . . to leave the home I have always seen as a constant. But I have learned . . ." She turned to meet Spock's eyes. "I had let my isolation become a trap. It made me too vulnerable. Too limited in my options. I need . . . to get away from that. I welcome the opportunity to expand beyond my limits."

"Maybe I'll join you someday," Aranow replied. "Once my term is over. Then, maybe, if I'm not too busy rebuilding things, I'll come out into space. Deeper space. Visit the Federation. Yours, I mean. The United one." She pulled Jim closer. "And I'll find you. However far you travel—I'll catch up."

After the kiss that followed, Kirk felt as intoxicated as Koust. Though he sobered instantly when he realized there was a huge Bogosrin looming over him with arms crossed.

"Captain," Lekur Zan said, "I'd like a word with you . . ."

———

At an opportune moment, Spock and Nisu slipped away from the reception for a private conversation. "I have much to thank you for, Spock," the newly minted ambassador said. "When we met, I thought you were the one in need of rescue. But you have done so much, not only for my world, but for me. You have opened my eyes."

"We have assisted each other," Spock assured her. "You owe me no debt."

"Still . . ." Her gaze moved toward his. "I wonder if you have given more thought to what your future might hold."

"I believe it is more important to concentrate on the present for now, Nisu. As you helped me to realize, I have been influenced by drives of which I was not consciously aware. I must refocus on understanding and mastering myself before I can properly assess the best path for my future, whether professionally or personally."

"That is wise," Nisu replied. Some moments later, she added, "Spock . . . I would be glad to aid you in . . . further exploring your inner self. We shall have much time together on the trip to your starbase."

Though Spock had found her assistance invaluable, he hesitated at the subtext he sensed from her. "Nisu . . . one thing I can say for sure is that I am not currently seeking a new bondmate. That, too, is a decision I should not make until I have gained greater understanding of myself and my needs. Now that I understand the impulse within myself, I should be able to contain it.

"Nor would it be appropriate to seek any commitment from you at this time. You have just become aware of a new range of opportunities in your own life, and you should be free to explore all the options available to you."

She absorbed his words in contemplative silence. "You're quite right," Nisu finally said. "We should both be open to all the possibilities the universe has to offer. If we come together again in the future, let it happen because we deemed it the best of all the available options."

"A logical approach."

"Most logical." They paused, having reached Spock's quarters. "Still," Nisu pointed out, "we do have the next few days."

"Indeed," he replied. "I am sure there is still much we can learn from each other."

He opened the door and escorted Nisu into his quarters. The panel slid shut behind them, and her eyes rose and locked with his.

Captain's Log, supplemental.

With no Dassik raids reported for more than a week, Ambassador Nisu well on her way to Earth aboard the Ulysses, *and Commissioner Gopal's belated approval of David Bailey's official status as diplomatic liaison between the First Federation and the Dassik, I believe we can now put the Dassik crisis behind us at last. As for the* Enterprise, *Mister Scott's teams and the repair crews of Starbase 8 have nearly completed the new upgrades to the bridge and main engineering, and the starbase engineers have been eager to study the gift provided to us by the First Federation, a holographic environment simulator for our recreation deck. While Lekur Zan assured us the technology was safe so long as it was properly used, the Starfleet Corps of Engineers is wary when it comes to untried alien technologies and will observe the* Enterprise *as a test bed before deciding whether it is safe to distribute the technology to other starships.*

Now, with our upgrades and crew rotations completed, the Enterprise *is ready to resume our mission of exploration. Unfortunately, we will soon be losing Ensign Chekov, who has requested a temporary ground transfer to undergo Starfleet security training and will be departing the ship at our next rendezvous. But his replacement, Lieutenant Arex Na Eth, comes highly recommended, and I am confident that he will fill the navigator's seat ably until Chekov's return.*

"Stellar cartography reports the latest star maps are uploaded and integrated, Captain," Chekov announced, tapping a few last adjustments into the astrogator display. "Setting course for intercept point with the *Arcadia*. Estimated time to rendezvous is ninety-one hours."

"Try not to sound so eager to leave us, Ensign," Kirk teased him.

"I am not, sir! There are things I am eager to do . . . but I wish I did not have to leave to do them."

"It's fine, Mister Chekov. I'm sure we'll find a way to muddle through without you somehow."

"Starbase 8 has granted clearance to depart, Captain," said Uhura, one hand against the receiver in her ear. Her newest trainee, a bronze-maned Caitian female named M'Ress, watched over her shoulder as she worked.

"All moorings cleared," Sulu reported, looking back over his right shoulder. "We're ready to go fill in the gaps in those star maps." Kirk was still getting used to the sight of the secondary exit that had been installed to the port side, beside the main viewscreen.

"Engines ready and rarin' to go, sir," Scotty added with a huge grin.

After a moment, McCoy tapped the captain's shoulder. "Jim?"

"I heard, Bones," Kirk said. "I was just thinking. About the Web of Worlds . . . about what it would be like not to have this opportunity to see the stars."

"An opportunity that will now be available to them all," Spock added, coming down from his station to stand behind the captain's chair in a position that mirrored McCoy's. "So there is no longer any need to dwell on its absence."

McCoy frowned. "I wonder, Jim. Are they really better off now?"

Spock riposted with a lift of his eyebrow. "Without our intervention, Doctor, they would have ceased to exist within two decades."

"I know that, Spock. But what they had before . . . peace, security . . . hundreds of worlds and cultures to explore without needing to expose themselves to the dangers of the galaxy . . . it was their own Shangri-La. A kind of paradise."

"Cherela posed its own dangers, Doctor, as you remarked at great length during our stay there. And the cultures of the Web had their own internal dissent and conflicts—even aside from the price their extended isolation would have inflicted upon the Dassik. Paradise is an illusion and invariably an impermanent one. There is no value in living an illusion."

"Oh, I don't know," McCoy said. "Some illusions can be pretty useful. Like scarecrows. And corbomite." He threw Spock a sidelong look. "Or the supposed absence of emotion, hm? Isn't that just as much a false front as Cherela's clouds?"

"What illusions would you prefer, Doctor? The illusion of fear? Of hate? The false fronts that leaders like Tirak and Grun employ to entrap their followers by catering to their baser emotions? Logic provides the one thing Cherela did not, Doctor: clarity."

The doctor studied him. "Mister Spock, I'll grant you that fear is one of the worst emotions to live your life by. But when the *right* emotion hits you—like love, or awe, or even grief at times—it can bring you greater clarity than anything else in this universe. And I pray that one day, you will experience that for yourself, Mister Spock."

"And on that day, you shall weep, Doctor," Spock said. "For you shall have no more worlds to conquer."

McCoy stared, dumbstruck. Kirk chuckled along with the rest of the bridge crew, then said: "Alexander, Spock? I think that for today, at least, I prefer Tennyson. 'Come, my friends, 'Tis not too late to seek a newer world.'" He leaned forward in his chair. "Mister Sulu, 'my purpose holds to sail beyond the sunset.' Ahead, warp factor two."

Acknowledgments

The main acknowledgment here must go to Jerry Sohl, writer of "The Corbomite Maneuver," which was the first *Star Trek* episode I ever saw. I was five and a half years old, and I was intrigued by the promo I'd seen for a show called *Star Trek*, which as far as I could tell was about a funny-looking airplane that only flew at night. So my parents let me stay up to watch it with them when it came on, and it was "The Corbomite Maneuver," and I was utterly hooked. Seeing that episode was my introduction to *Star Trek*, to space, to science, and to science fiction, and it therefore set the course of my entire life. So naturally this episode has always been a particular favorite of mine, and I've long wanted to do the definitive novel about the First Federation. I first developed such a proposal for editor Marco Palmieri in 2008, but various circumstances led to the project being indefinitely postponed. I'm grateful to my current editor Margaret Clark for allowing me to do it at last.

Aspects of my portrayal of the First Federation are influenced by the novel *Star Trek: The Next Generation—Gulliver's Fugitives* by Keith Sharee, which is the only previous prose work, as far as I know, to depict members of Balok's species other than Balok himself. The designation "Fesarian" for that species was established in *Star Trek: Seekers #1—Second Nature* by David Mack. I estimate that novel takes place less than two months after this one, soon enough that knowledge of the species's true name might not have fully propagated across the Federation. My descriptions of the *Enterprise* bridge were assisted by the *U.S.S. Enterprise Revised Bridge Blueprints* by Michael McMaster, published in 1978 by Pan Galactic Press.

Lieutenant Rahda (Naomi Pollack) was introduced by John Meredyth Lucas in the *Star Trek: The Original Series* episode "That Which Survives." Her first name of Manjula was coined by Steve Mollmann and Michael Schuster in *Star Trek: A Choice of Catastrophes*, although "Rahda" is apparently a Germanic surname (the Hindi one is spelled "Radha").

Anne Nored and Gabler were created by James Schmerer in the *Star Trek: The Animated Series* episode "The Survivor." Gabler's first name of Frank comes from Alan Dean Foster's TAS novelizations. Ensign Lou Prescott of security is meant to be the same character as the Lieutenant Prescott who briefly appears in *Troublesome Minds* by Dave Galanter; presumably he got a promotion in the intervening year. The full name I gave him is a nod to *Star Trek: The Animated Series* producers Lou Scheimer and Norm Prescott. The holographic recreation deck is a nod to the proto-holodeck introduced by writer Chuck Menville in the *Animated Series* episode "The Practical Joker"; I would assume that its malfunction in that episode turned Starfleet off of holographic recreation centers for the next century. Chekov's departure and Arex's arrival are depicted in James Swallow's novel *The Latter Fire*, which presumably takes place immediately after this novel.

About the Author

Christopher L. Bennett is a lifelong resident of Cincinnati, Ohio, with bachelor's degrees in physics and history from the University of Cincinnati. He has written such critically acclaimed *Star Trek* novels as *Ex Machina* and *The Buried Age*; the *Star Trek: Titan* novels *Orion's Hounds* and *Over a Torrent Sea*; the two *Department of Temporal Investigations* novels *Watching the Clock* and *Forgotten History*; and the *Star Trek: Enterprise—Rise of the Federation* series. His shorter works include stories in the anniversary anthologies *Constellations*, *The Sky's the Limit*, *Prophecy and Change*, and *Distant Shores*, as well as the DTI novellas *The Collectors* and *Time Lock*. Beyond *Star Trek*, he has penned the novels *X-Men: Watchers on the Walls* and *Spider-Man: Drowned in Thunder*. His original work includes the hard science fiction superhero novel *Only Superhuman* and several novelettes in *Analog* and other science fiction magazines, several of which have been compiled in the e-book collection *Hub Space: Tales from the Greater Galaxy*. More information, annotations, and the author's blog can be found at christopherlbennett.wordpress.com.